GUILTY

MARTINA COLE
AND JACQUI ROSE
GUILTY

H

HEADLINE

First published in 2024 by
HEADLINE PUBLISHING GROUP

1

Cataloguing in Publication Data is available from the British Library

Hardback ISBN 978 1 4722 4950 0
Trade paperback ISBN 978 1 4722 4951 7

Typeset in 12/16pt ITC Galliard Std by Jouve (UK), Milton Keynes

Printed and bound in Great Britain by Clays Ltd, Elcograf S.p.A.

MIX
Paper | Supporting
responsible forestry
FSC
www.fsc.org   FSC® C104740

Headline's policy is to use papers that are natural, renewable and recyclable
products and made from wood grown in well-managed forests and other controlled
sources. The logging and manufacturing processes are expected to conform to the
environmental regulations of the country of origin.

HEADLINE PUBLISHING GROUP
An Hachette UK Company
Carmelite House
50 Victoria Embankment
London EC4Y 0DZ

www.headline.co.uk
www.hachette.co.uk

I would like to dedicate this book to my friend
Jacqui Rose to say thank you for all your
hard work and help.

Prologue

Kent

1987
February

Vengeance is in my heart, death in my hand, blood and revenge are hammering in my head.

William Shakespeare, *Titus Andronicus*

Steph Barker stared at her hands. She stood in her small lounge, unable to move as her gaze took in the scene in front of her. There was blood everywhere. Bloody fingerprints smeared the floral wallpaper and her new yellow cushions were stained a dark red. Her blouse was soaked in the stuff, and the coppery smell of death filled her nose.

She closed her eyes, swallowing down the urge to vomit. Her chest felt tight and it was all she could do to breathe. *What the fuck had just happened?*

Somewhere in the distance, she could hear music playing. Only a few days ago she'd been dancing around the kitchen table to some song on the radio, and now . . . *Fuck*, she needed to get out of here, but where could she go?

Steph forced herself to open her eyes. She'd hoped the darkness would hide it, but the glow of the fairy lights hanging from her mantelpiece lit up the body that lay motionless on the floor.

Almost in a trance, Steph turned and staggered out of the room on unsteady legs, closing the door behind her. But there was no escaping the blood. There were red splatters on the walls and a trail of smeared blood led from the hallway to the kitchen. Gripping the hallway table for support, Steph felt her stomach cramp and she began to vomit.

Still retching, she wiped her mouth, grabbed her car keys and raced out the back door. Her only thought was to pick up her daughter from her mate's house and get as far away from here as possible.

But at the thought of what would happen to Stacey if the Old Bill caught up with them, she stopped in her tracks.

What the fuck was she thinking? Every copper in the country would be looking for her, and if she got sent down, her daughter would be taken into care. Steph had first-hand experience of children's homes and foster parents. She couldn't put Stacey through that.

So for the next half hour, Steph scrubbed floors and washed walls, filling bowl after bowl with hot water and sluicing every surface, even the blood-splattered path by the back door. Then she went to the sink and held her hands under the flow of scalding water, scraping all the blood from her nails and scrubbing until her skin was raw.

Finally, she took the stairs two at a time and ran into her bedroom. The flames on the gas fire reflected off the silver tinsel she'd wound around her bedframe for a bit of glamour, giving off a weird glow as she rolled up the large rug beneath the window and dragged it downstairs.

At the lounge door she paused to steady herself before turning the handle. As the door opened, her gaze immediately went to the body. When she stepped gingerly towards it, she sensed movement and glanced up to be confronted with her own reflection, caught in the mirror above the sofa. Her face was drawn, her green eyes wide with panic and circled with dark shadows. She rubbed at the blood smeared across her cheek. The cut was deeper and angrier than she'd realised.

Fighting off another wave of nausea, she wiped away her tears and unrolled the rug next to the body. Then she wrapped her hands around the handle of the knife embedded in the torso. She was trembling so hard, the body began to shake beneath her. *Come on, come on*, she told herself. *You can do this.* Squeezing her eyes shut, she began to pull. As she did, a noise came from behind her. Startled, she let go of the knife and spun round, her heart dropping as the front-room door opened . . .

Book One

Kent

1986
December

Hell is other people.

Jean-Paul Sartre, *No Exit*

Chapter One

Steph Barker took a sip of her strong sweet tea and sighed with contentment. She'd bought the old council house a couple of months ago, but the novelty of owning her own home had yet to wear off. She kept the place spotless. Having everything spick and span was important to her. The smell of beef casserole wafted from the oven, filling the room. The dishes had been washed and put away, the tea towel lay folded neatly on the side and the polished pine cupboards sparkled with silver and gold tinsel.

She loved Christmas with a passion, from the carol singers, to the brandy butter she got half price from Safeways in Chatham, to the six-foot tree that only just managed to fit into her tiny lounge. When it came to decorations, the tackier the better in her view. Even when it wasn't Christmas, Steph always kept a few sparkly bits and bobs on display.

Not everyone was so cheerful about it, mind. Only yesterday her neighbours had complained about the giant inflatable Father Christmas she'd got her mate to put on her roof. Not that she gave two fucks what they or anyone else thought. Steph had long since stopped worrying what people thought of her. She was who she was, take it or leave it.

Finishing off her tea, she gave the cup a quick rinse and put it on the draining board. She grabbed her packet of Benson and Hedges off the side, lit one and stared out into her front garden, admiring the life-size plastic reindeer and sledge. It was going to cost her a bloody arm and a leg on the electric, but she'd been putting a bit of money away every week, so she wasn't overly concerned.

It was a far cry from how things used to be. She was sober, for a start. Apart from that dark time five and a half years ago when she'd fallen off the wagon big time, she hadn't touched a drop since she'd found out she was pregnant – and her daughter was thirteen now.

Steph smiled. She always did when she thought of Stacey. From the moment she'd first held that tiny baby in her arms, she'd loved the bones of her. When things had been tough, it was the thought of Stacey that kept her from falling back into her old ways.

A face suddenly appeared at the window and Steph jumped, stifling a scream. 'Fucking hell, Pete, what the hell are you trying to do, give me a flipping heart attack?' Stubbing out her cigarette, Steph scowled at her ex-partner. 'What do you want?' she demanded, making no move to let him in.

'Oh, that's a fucking nice welcome, ain't it?'

'I'm not here to give you the red-carpet treatment – just tell me what you want.'

Pete Brown's face twisted into a sneer. 'Just let us fucking in, Steph. I haven't got all day.' Conscious of his lack of height, he made up for it with bad attitude.

She folded her arms. Already he was getting on her nerves. 'That's not going to happen.'

'I want to see Stacey,' he yelled.

'She's not here. You know very well she has swimming every Monday.'

When Pete disappeared from the window without a word, it took Steph just a beat to realise what he was about to do. She grabbed the key off the hook and rushed to lock the back door.

Too late.

She threw all her weight against the door, but Pete planted his foot in the doorway making it impossible for her to close it, then began ramming the door with his shoulder. It was a routine they'd been through hundreds of times before. Whenever Pete broke up with a girlfriend or things didn't go his way, he'd be straight round to make sure Steph had a shit time of it too.

'Just leave it, Pete.'

'Steph, come on, stop pissing around,' he huffed. His nasal whine made him sound like he had a permanent cold.

Not for the first time, she wondered what she'd ever seen in him. She'd known from the start he was a wrong 'un, but the estate she'd grown up on was full of wrong 'uns – including her own father. Her earliest memory was of dear old dad battering her mum to a bloody pulp. She spent her childhood in and out of care while her mum's boyfriends came and went, leaving their mark in more ways than one – on her as well as her mother. So she'd known enough bad men to recognise the type, but she'd told herself Pete was different. It was only when he shifted from piling on the charm to piling on the punches that she realised what a vicious bastard he was.

She'd put up with him until Stacey was born. Determined to give her little girl a better life, she'd done a runner, trading Bethnal

Green for Gillingham in Kent, where she had a mate. After a few peaceful years, Pete tracked her down. He hadn't been happy that she was thriving without him, especially when he'd found out that she was with someone else. But by that time she no longer feared him. She saw him for what he was: a pathetic waste of space she could do without. Despite relentless pressure, she refused to take him back.

Even when Pete set up home half a mile away, she stayed put. She wasn't about to spend the rest of her days running away from him. Besides, she'd made a life for herself here. She had good mates and a job, and Stacey was happy in school.

Surprisingly, Pete turned out to be a decent enough dad – when he wasn't in prison, that was. Though she suspected him of using Stacey as an excuse to hang around, Steph never tried to deny him access. She didn't want her daughter to end up blaming her for keeping them apart, or imagining the father she'd never met to be some sort of hero. Steph had no doubt that regular contact would allow Stace to see for herself what a wanker Pete was.

'Pete, I'm busy. Standing here playing bleedin' tug of war with my door is not my idea of fun.'

Pete seesawed between hating her and being unable to live without her. When he'd found out that she was shacked up with someone else, it had messed with his head. For a while he'd hung around, spying on her, unable to let go. Soon as he realised the other bloke was off the scene, he'd celebrated with a couple of grams of coke, convinced that now she'd welcome him with open arms. Instead, she'd shut the door in his face. And here she was, doing it again.

'Pete, don't you ever get tired of this?'

She was using that weary tone of voice again, as though she

was too good for him. It made him laugh how respectable she tried to be these days: her tits were put away now, her arse was no longer hanging out of her skirt and her face was scrubbed clean of make-up, unlike when they'd been together and she was on the game. Christ, she'd trowelled it on then.

Steph sighed. 'Well, let me put it another way, then: can you just piss right off, Pete.'

Pete's temper flared. 'Who the fuck d'you think you're talking to?' He was tempted to give her a good hiding like he used to do. But there was something in her eyes these days that told him she wouldn't put up with it.

He jabbed his finger at her. 'Just because you don't spread your legs any more, doesn't mean you ain't still a whore, so you can stop with this high and mighty act. We both know you'll come crawling back to me eventually.'

Steph rolled her eyes. There was a time she'd have taken the bait, but she was tired of fighting with him. They'd been at it for years and it got them nowhere. She wasn't sure if it was his bruised ego or if he genuinely thought he could wear her down to the point she'd take him back. Either way, she wished he'd bugger off and leave her alone.

'Anybody would be too good for you, Pete. All you're doing now is reminding me why I shouldn't go near you with a fucking bargepole. Either you leave now or I'm calling the Old Bill.'

He snarled. 'And say what?'

'That I've got a fucking Christmas elf on my doorstep that needs locking up.'

'One day, Steph, you're going to push me to the fucking limit, and then you'll really regret it, darlin' . . .'

She jammed the door further on his foot making him wince and stumble backwards. 'Not unless you push me to the limit first, Pete, and you're the one who'll be feeding the fish at the bottom of the Thames. Now piss off.' She slammed the door.

The letter box immediately flicked open.

He peered through it. 'Steph—'

She kicked it shut, nearly trapping his fingers in the metal flap. 'I said, *piss off*, Pete! Oh, and don't forget it's parents' evening tomorrow at Stacey's school.'

Taking a deep breath, she reached for the ashtray and re-lit her cigarette. Although she wasn't scared of him, he still had a knack for winding her up. Taking a calming draw on her fag, she glanced across to the photo on the fridge and smiled. It had been taken seven years ago, when she was pregnant with Andy. She'd been so happy then.

Jerking away from that thought, she stubbed out her cigarette, got to her feet and grabbed her black plastic mac off the back of the chair. No way was she going to let that miserable fucker spoil her first Christmas in her new home. Right now she had more important things to do, like visiting her son . . .

Chapter Two

Hennie Matthews had seen enough dicks to write an encyclo-
paedia on them. Short ones, fat ones, crooked ones, skinny ones,
shrivelled ones – she'd seen them all. She had no particular pref-
erence. A dick was a dick, and as long as the owner of said dick
paid up, she didn't care.

She'd been on the game since she'd given her first blow job on
her thirteenth birthday. There'd been a time she could remember that day vividly, but years of heavy boozing had blurred her
memories.

As far as she could remember, her mum had taken her for a
drink in a working-man's club near the docks in Chatham. It
had been rough as fuck and the punters came in their droves.
It was where her mum went most evenings.

She was clear on only one thing: when one of mum's punters –
a stinking old pervert with a beer belly and a saggy ball sac – had
offered extra for the mother and daughter duo to give him head,
they'd been so drunk they'd agreed.

It had all been over quickly. Afterwards, she'd used her share
of the money to buy a quarter of sherbet lemons from the dusty
sweetshop in Gillingham High Street. Hennie found it strange
that she remembered the sweets but not the way she'd felt. Then

again, she'd been told that a whore's feelings didn't matter. She supposed her feelings died along with her childhood.

Forty years and nine STDs later, she'd been in the business long enough that she knew how to take care of herself. She'd abandoned her old patch in King's Cross for the relative safety of an abandoned car park down near the Thames and Medway canal. Most of her punters were regulars and, with the news full of the AIDS epidemic, she never agreed to unprotected sex – except when she was pissed, high or desperate for cash.

'Jesus Christ, be a bit gentler, will you?' Detective Sergeant Fred Walker growled, shifting uncomfortably. His sweaty arse was stuck to the pages of the *Sun* which he'd spread across the front seat to protect his brand-new Toyota. The bright-blue motor was his pride and joy, and he didn't want stains on his velvet upholstery even though his bitch of a wife wasn't around any more to mouth off about it.

'Oh, sorry, love.' Hennie smiled up at him, and went that little bit harder, pulling down the foreskin of his flaccid dick with a tug. She'd been working all day, and her shoulder was aching from the number of bastards she'd jerked off. None of them wanted to pay for the full works and were happy for her to get cramp all for a measly three quid.

'Fucking hell, what are you trying to do, circumcise me, you stupid cunt?' Fred's lip curled in disgust; the ugly bitch was far too old to be flashing her enormous tits. Only reason he used her was because she was cheaper than the younger girls his colleagues went to for a bit of light relief between shifts.

Hennie opened her mouth to say something else, showing off her last remaining stained teeth, and Fred caught a glimpse of a smirk.

'You think it's fucking funny?' He wiped the condensation from the window and cranked it open.

Hennie shook her head. 'Oh, wind your neck in, darlin', stop the bleating – it's not my fault if you can't take a bit of rough.'

'You want some rough?' He raised his eyebrows mockingly. 'I'll show you fucking rough!' He reached over and shoved his hand hard between Hennie's legs, trying to rip off her panties, twisting his fingers to grab her pubic hair.

She let out a high-pitch yelp and leaned over to bite his arm, sinking her teeth in.

Caught off guard, Fred bellowed, 'You fucking cunt!'

The slap he gave her broke the top layer of skin on her cheek-bone and Hennie could taste her salty blood trickling into her mouth. She went to claw at his face, but he ducked out of the way and reached across her again, this time grappling for the door handle. He pulled it open and kicked her out of the car, sending her face-first into the wet gravel. 'Now fuck off, you old hag.'

'Oi, where's my money? Where's my *fucking* money.'

'I should be charging you,' Fred screamed out of the open passenger door. Then he pulled it shut and drove off, spraying gravel over her.

Hennie watched the car's headlights disappearing into the night. She got up slowly, muttering to herself. 'Fucking bastard! Think you can treat me like shit? Well, think again, darlin'.'

She stuck two fingers up, brushed the gravel from her legs and pulled down her white skirt, not realising her hand was dripping blood.

Fuck, that skirt had cost her a tenner and now it was ruined.

She let out a sigh and wrapped her fake-fur jacket tighter around her. Fur coat and no knickers. That was her. She chuckled to herself. She'd always wanted one just like Elizabeth Taylor wore. Though she reckoned Liz didn't have to give a year's worth of blow jobs to afford hers. She laughed again. One thing Hennie Matthews didn't do was take herself seriously.

'Hennie . . . Hennie.'

Hennie looked up and smiled as she saw Joseph Potter rushing towards her.

'Hennie – my God, are you all right? I saw what happened.' Joseph glanced in the direction of the car. 'What a bloody animal.'

'Par for the course.' Hennie shrugged. 'Fucking Old Bill are the worst.'

Joseph towered over her. He wasn't an attractive man; the thick-rimmed glasses did him no favours and, judging by the ginger roots, that mane of jet-black hair was a dye job, the beard too. But he was tall and well built, with weathered skin like a fisherman's that made his steely grey eyes stand out all the more. Right now, they were full of concern. 'I know I'm wasting my breath, Hennie, but you should report this.'

That was the other thing about Jo: he was far too naive for his own good.

'Report it to who? He's a copper – half the force is down here most days. You think they give a shit about women like me? Forget it, sweetheart. It ain't gonna happen.'

Joseph's jaw clenched, but then he forced a smile and said, 'At least let me give you a lift home.' He gestured towards the white Citroën van he used for his Meals on Wheels deliveries. 'Your carriage awaits.' He winked at her. 'It might not be a limousine, but there's a flask of tea if you fancy some.'

'Listen, if it's got four fucking wheels and will get me home in one piece, I don't give a shit what it looks like! What brings you out this way, anyhow?'

He rolled his eyes. 'Nothing exciting . . . One of the other drivers is off, so they extended my route. I thought this would be a good short cut to get home.' He paused, looking slightly embarrassed. 'And now I'm glad I did.'

'Me too.'

They both stood there looking awkward until Jo nodded at Hennie's knee, which was trickling blood. 'That cut looks nasty. Come on, I've got some tissues in the van.'

Hennie was touched by his kindness. 'Thanks, Jo.' She stood on her tiptoes and kissed him on his cheek.

When he flushed bright red, she cackled. 'Fucking hell, Jo, you need to relax a bit. If that's what a little peck on the cheek does, fuck knows what a blow job would do to you. You need to tell your missus to give . . .' Hennie slammed her hand across her mouth. She'd forgotten his wife was dead; some sort of terminal illness, according to Steph. It was obvious, whenever it cropped up in conversation, that he was struggling to deal with the loss, especially with two teenagers to bring up single-handed. 'Sorry – I didn't mean that. Ignore me, doll.'

Joseph put his head down. 'It's fine . . . it's fine.'

She shook her head. 'It's not fine. I've got a big fucking mouth, and I don't think before I speak . . . I'm sorry, Jo.'

Instead of responding, he just stood there, fiddling with the zipper of his grey anorak. He looked so uncomfortable Hennie was afraid he'd change his mind about giving her a lift. She gave an inward sigh of relief when he said, 'There's no need to apologise. Come on, let's get you home, eh?'

'Yeah.' Hennie grinned again. 'And I'll have that cup of tea if it's still on offer.' She linked arms with him, and they began to walk towards his van.

'HENNIE!'

Hennie didn't have to turn round to know who was shouting her name. She quickly removed her arm from Jo's and pushed him away. 'You need to go—'

'But—'

'Go, just *go*,' she hissed. 'Unless you want to spend your Christmas in hospital, get in your van and get the fuck out of here *now*!'

Before he could say another word, Hennie turned and trotted towards the man who'd called her.

No one ignored Artie Rogers, not if they valued their life.

Chapter Three

Artie Rogers was tall and powerfully built, his skin covered in tattoos – most of them acquired while he was high on coke. He had a reputation as a ruthless bastard – a reputation he'd spent years building, establishing himself a nice little empire in the process.

He'd started out running a few girls, Hennie being one of them. Then he'd got into money-lending – 'with menaces', as the judges like to say. Not that he had to worry about being brought before a judge. Much as local residents and respectable businesses hated the way he was flooding the area with whores and drugs, not to mention the loan-sharking, it was well known he had the Old Bill in his pocket. After all, they were his toms' best clients, and he kept them sweet with gifts of nice cars and holidays for services rendered. Any pricks who went up against him could count on a one-way trip to hospital, or everything they owned burning down around their ears. And the only action the Old Bill would take was to look the other way.

The last fucker to take him on was Danny Denton, one-time king of the Medway, currently serving an eight-year stretch for armed robbery. He'd taken issue with the way Artie ran his girls, and declared his turf a no-go area for loan sharks. With him out of the way, the Medway had a new king and there was fuck all anyone could do about it.

The only person Artie cared about apart from himself was his older brother, Rob, who he idolised. A hit-and-run five years ago had left Rob in a vegetative state. Despite Artie's best efforts, the culprit had never been found. So the only thing Artie could do for him now was to see that he got the best care available, which meant paying extortionate fees to a private hospital in Dartford. Anything that messed with Artie's cashflow therefore equated to messing with Rob. And that was something Artie would not tolerate.

He glared at Hennie as she rushed up to him, breathless with fear.

'Guess who I've just seen,' he snarled.

'Father Christmas?' Hennie giggled, clearly hoping chirpiness would win Artie over. The narrowing of his eyes told her she'd got it wrong.

Artie clumped her hard around the head, then rapped his knuckles into her eye. Immediately, she felt it begin to swell up.

'Shut the fuck up, you stupid cow . . . I've just seen Fred. He pulled over and told me what happened. And if I say he was fucking steaming that's an understatement.'

He clipped her around the head again.

'Who cares what Fred says,' she huffed, determined not to let on how much it hurt. 'He's a tight bastard anyway. They all are. Just cos they're Old Bill doesn't mean they shouldn't pay the going rate.'

'*Who cares?*' Artie echoed in disbelief, poking her hard in her chest. 'Are you having a bubble? *I* fucking care, that's who. He's a client – a good one – so you treat him with respect, right?'

Artie grabbed Hennie's bag, tugging it so hard the strap

broke. He rummaged through the contents, pulled out a wad of cash and shoved it in his pocket.

'That's my fucking money!' Hennie whined. She'd been hoping to skim some of the money off before giving Artie his cut, so she could buy Christmas presents.

Artie tilted his head. 'Whose money? Whose money?' He threw down her bag and shouted into her face. 'I said, *whose money?*'

He kicked her hard in her thigh.

Hennie gasped from the pain. 'Your money, Artie.'

'*Exactly*. You work for me, so anything you earn is mine.'

Hennie nodded. She knew better than to argue with him. Last thing she wanted was to end up in hospital.

'You can piss off now, and think yourself lucky you got off lightly.' Artie pushed his face into hers, wrinkling his nose with disgust. 'Look at you, you're nothing but a drunken slag. You're supposed to be turning tricks – not frightening them off.' He grabbed the back of her hair, accidentally pulling off her wig to reveal thin greying wisps. Life hadn't treated Hennie Matthews well. She looked much older than her fifty-three years.

Artie threw the wig in her face. 'The state of you! You're well past it – too old to spread your legs, and a fucking liability besides. I don't want to see you around here again.'

Hennie's eyes filled with tears. 'Artie, please, I need this job.'

'Go home, grandma,' he hissed.

'Artie, don't do this to me. I swear I won't mess up again . . . This is my life. I haven't got anywhere else to go . . . I'm begging you.'

Artie continued to stare into Hennie's face. Her packed-on foundation was caked into the creases of her wrinkles. The thick blue eyeliner she wore was smudged, and sat in the bags of her eyes. She looked more like a ghoul from a horror show than a good-time girl. Seething with rage that she didn't have the good sense to leave when told to, he slipped his hand round her throat. 'Stop fucking whining! You're doing my head in – haven't I just told you to fuck off?' He shoved her hard and Hennie lost her balance, toppling to the ground. Artie pulled out his penis and began to urinate into the gutter inches from her face.

On her hands and knees now, Hennie quickly scrambled away.

'You make me sick; you know that?' He dipped his knees quickly as he tucked his penis back in.

'Go on then, clear off!' he roared, the steroids and coke surging through his veins, making him feel like a god. 'And don't let me see you around here again.'

A freezing gust of wind blew across the car park, sending used condoms skidding across the gravel. It never ceased to amaze Artie that punters would risk freezing their bollocks off in an abandoned car park just so they could get a quick hand job – not that he was complaining, long as they paid. But only the ones with a pensioner fetish would pay for Hennie's services, and that was a specialised gig – one he wasn't into. It was definitely time for her to go.

Time for him to go too. He needed to have a word with Fletch about the number of clients falling behind with their payments. It was the same every December: people thinking they could stiff him and spend the money on Christmas presents. What they needed was a visit from Fletch to remind them of their obligations.

With that thought, he shoved his hands in his pockets and stalked off to his car.

*

Hennie stayed in the gutter until he was gone, then she picked up her bag and got to her feet. Feeling a bit wobbly, she closed her eyes and took a deep breath, letting the icy rain fall on her face. Look on the bright side, she told herself, at least he didn't get piss on your fur jacket. Chuckling to herself, she set off across the car park. Hopefully, by tomorrow Artie would have calmed down. It wasn't the first time she'd been given her marching orders. He'd done it to all the toms he ran; she shared a house with seven of them – she'd heard the stories. She just needed to lay low for a couple of days, earn some money for him, then he'd let her back.

As she walked, her thoughts wandered to Joseph. She'd always fallen for men like Artie: hard, nasty, handsome fuckers, but maybe there was something to be said for the Joseph Potters of the world. What did looks matter so long as he was kind? At least she wouldn't have to worry about him raping her and battering her black and blue.

She let out a sigh. Thanks to that bastard Artie taking her money, her daughter and grandkid would have to do without the pressies she'd planned to buy them. After not having been in touch for a while, Carol had sent her a Christmas card inviting her to come and stay with them in London. She'd sent a card in return – her mate Julie had a big box of them and let her pick out a nice snow scene – accepting the invite. She hadn't been the best mum, what with the boozing and the gear, but she planned to make up for it by being a good nan to little Bobby. He was eighteen months old now and it had been over a year since she'd seen him, or Carol. All that lost time she needed to make up for . . .

She pulled a packet of fags from her pocket, along with her lighter, and lit up. 'You'll get there,' she told herself. Already she'd managed to wean herself off the gear, with Steph's help. If it hadn't been for her, Hennie didn't know where she'd be, probably in the cemetery by now. But with Steph's support she believed she'd be able to stay off it permanently. Carol deserved to have a better mum than she'd been, and Hennie was going to make her proud.

Smiling, she pulled out the photo-booth pic of Carol and Bobby she always carried in her bag. Giving it a quick kiss, she slotted it back into the inside zipper pocket before it got wet.

The canal path was muddy and treacherous underfoot, especially in her four-inch heels. The street lamps that were supposed to light the way had either been smashed or were so overgrown with ivy that they gave out a dim glow at best. Further along, the lights disappeared completely.

Though the rain was coming down heavier now, Hennie was feeling better. Fucking bastards the lot of them. Well, she was sick of being treated like she was nothing. 'Bastards, *all of you*!' she yelled, and laughed, careful not to lose her footing on the uneven path.

Hearing something behind her, she stopped and looked over her shoulder into the twilight. It had sounded like someone approaching. She paused to listened, then set off again, walking faster now.

She couldn't shake off the sense that someone was watching her. One of the girls who turned tricks by the canal had been attacked here a few weeks ago. The other women reckoned it was an attempted mugging, probably some of the lads who occasionally hung around here, thinking they'd be on to some easy money. Whoever it was clearly didn't realise what would happen if Artie caught up with them.

The girl, a junkie, had been too out of it to remember what had happened. She hadn't seen who it was who'd bashed her over the head; she'd been too intent on getting away. It had shaken up the rest of the toms; a lot of them had cleared off elsewhere, not wanting to work by the canal after dark. It was only the ones like Hennie who still risked it. Much as the place creeped her out, work was work and she needed the money.

Hurrying up the steps to the bridge, Hennie felt a sense of relief when she caught sight of Steph up ahead. Whatever the weather, she made a point of checking on the working girls, making sure they were all right.

'Steph? *Steph* . . .' Hennie hurried across the street to join her. Immediately, she saw that Steph had been crying.

'You okay, hun?' Hennie smiled and wiped away Steph's tears with the back of her hand.

'Not really. But I will be – you know me.'

Hennie knew there was only one reason why Steph would be upset like this. As much as the woman loved Christmas and all that came with it, it was also a difficult time of year for her. 'Have you been to see your boy?' she asked.

Steph nodded and opened the transparent dome umbrella she was carrying, holding it above their heads. 'I keep telling myself that it will get easier, but it never does.'

'I know, and I'm sorry.' Hennie couldn't imagine what it felt like to lose a child, and Steph's Andy was only a toddler when he'd died. 'You fancy some company? I could do with some myself – I've just had a run-in with Artie.'

Steph studied Hennie's face. 'Did he do that to you?'

'This was DS Walker' – she pointed to her cheekbone – 'but, yeah, the shiner's from Artie . . . Come on, how about we go to yours and you can show me that tacky fucking Santa you've put on your roof.'

As they set off, arm in arm beneath Steph's umbrella, Hennie listened to her friend's usual pep talk about finding a different line of work and someone who valued her, and wondered whether Joseph Potter might be that someone . . .

Chapter Four

Joseph was at home with his two children. He'd hurried back to change out of his work clothes before heading off again. 'Make sure you fold your uniform properly, Bel, and put it away neatly.'

Thirteen-year-old Bel stood in her bra and pants, hands behind her back, against the far wall beside her single bed. Her dad insisted on inspecting her bedroom every day to make sure she was keeping it clean and tidy. Aside from the bed, there was only a wooden chair and a large wardrobe. The only light came from a bare bulb that flickered on and off. The windows had been covered with sheets of cardboard.

When he was in a relaxed mood, he'd take the cardboard down so Bel could see out to the large garden. But such moments were rare. Usually he'd leave her locked in her room for hours, unable to tell whether it was day or night. It was the same for her brother, Zack.

One time, that hot summer when they'd first moved in, condensation had made the cardboard so damp a tiny gap had opened, letting in a chink of light. Peering out, Bel had seen a postman delivering letters. She'd been so thirsty that day it was all she could do not to shout out or bang on the window for his attention. But her dad had taught her and Zack never to call for help, so she hadn't. By the time her dad came home the following day, she was so dehydrated that she'd fainted.

'We don't want your clothes getting dirty, do we?'

'No, Dad.' Bel shook her head. Her auburn hair fell over her eyes.

Joseph crossed the room and swept her hair back with his hand. He stared into her eyes and gave her a long, hard hug, while she tried to hide her revulsion. Finally, he let her go, and asked, 'Have you been a good girl, Bel?'

'Yes, Dad.'

'You haven't had any bad thoughts, have you?'

It was the same thing he always asked; Bel had no idea why. 'No, Dad.'

He looked her up and down. 'You haven't been thinking about doing things with boys, have you?' He stroked her face.

'No, Dad . . . *Never.*'

Joseph smiled. 'I'm pleased to hear it. I don't want you ending up like those tarts. You wouldn't want that, would you?'

Bel shook her head again. 'No, Dad.'

'You really are my angel, Bel.' He sighed and ruffled her hair. 'I'll be back later . . . Goodnight, darlin'.' Then he walked towards the door, reaching into his pocket for the padlock key to lock her in.

'Can I have some water, please, Dad?' Bel spoke quickly. She'd thought she'd have time for a drink before he locked them in their rooms for the night, but today he'd been in a hurry and sent them up early. And they never knew how long he'd be gone for – sometimes a couple of days would go by before he released them.

He frowned. 'I don't think that's a good idea. You don't want to wet the bed, Bel.'

She chewed on her lip. 'Maybe . . . maybe you could leave the door unlocked tonight, then I can go to the toilet if I need to?'

Joseph's face darkened. 'I lock you in to keep you safe,' he replied through gritted teeth. 'What would happen if I let you and Zack roam around the house and you fell and hurt yourself while I was out? It's easy to have an accident in the dark.' Bel lowered her eyes, unable to meet his intense stare. 'I thought you'd know that.'

'Sorry, Dad.'

'Do you think I lock you in because I want to?'

'No, Dad.' Bel clenched her fists into balls, wishing her dad would go and never come back.

Joseph nodded in approval. 'That's right . . . I do it because I love you and your brother.' He smiled again and began to pull the heavy wooden door closed, but stopped halfway. 'Maybe later, when I get home, we could have another cuddle, and I'll show you how much I love you. You'd like that, wouldn't you . . .'

Chapter Five

Cheryl Brown slowly opened her eyes. She must have dozed off after smoking that bit of heroin. She'd been planning to save it till later, but after seeing Artie lay into Hennie, Cheryl had headed for the toilet block to lie low for a while. He never took kindly to seeing her, or any other toms who didn't work for him turning tricks, down by the canal. She'd once made the mistake of telling him he didn't own the car park, and he'd given her a kicking that left her with a fractured cheekbone and a couple of broken teeth. When he was in one of his moods, the only thing to do was get out of his way.

To think she used to fancy the bastard! There was a time when he'd rely on charm and his good looks to get what he wanted, but that was before some·fucker ran over his brother and left him brain-damaged, his little boy dead in the road beside him. Artie had torn up the manor trying to find the bastard responsible, but no one knew who it was. Now it was as if Artie hated everyone. These days, he was almost as unpredictable as his business partner, Fletch. Now there was a proper psycho. Everyone was terrified of him.

Cheryl knocked back the remains of the can of Diamond White and glanced at the cheap Casio watch she'd nicked from one of her punters. She was late as usual, but it couldn't be helped.

Standing up, she straightened her leather miniskirt and checked herself in the broken mirror over the handbasin. She was still an attractive woman, despite eight years working the streets. Big blue eyes, clear skin and a figure that hadn't changed much since she was a teenager. If it wasn't for her addictions, Cheryl might have landed a bit of catalogue modelling. As it was, giving blow jobs and spreading her legs seemed her only option.

She'd promised Steph that she would call in at the refuge, but she couldn't face it. Right now, what she really wanted was to head for the Bell and Anchor so she could get completely off her nut on booze – some of her regulars hung out there and could be relied on to buy her a drink or two. But that would have to wait. First, she needed to get to the STD clinic in Chatham to sort out her latest herpes flair-up. The blisters had burst and every time she went for a pee it was like someone had set a fire between her legs. If she didn't catch the seven o'clock bus, she'd miss her appointment, and she couldn't put up with another day of agony.

Wrapping her coat around her, she set off along the short cut through the woods that would take her to the bus stop. The path underfoot was slick with mud, and she cursed as her white stilettos sank in, slowing her down.

'Hello.'

Cheryl jumped at the sound of a male voice behind her. The near darkness made it impossible to see who it was.

'Over here.'

She took a few steps towards the voice, then stopped, not recognising who it was.

'How are you?' he asked.

Cheryl looked him up and down, but the effect of the drugs

and booze made it hard to focus. Was he one of her clients? Most of the time she didn't bother looking at their faces – it was their dicks she was interested in. But even through the heroin haze there was something about the way he was staring at her – all the while keeping his hand out of sight behind his back – that made Cheryl uneasy.

She started to back away, then turned and set off down the path as fast as she could. She just had to make it through the trees to the concrete steps that led up to the bus stop, then she'd be safe.

But he was closing in on her.

'Where are you going? There's nowhere to hide,' he taunted. 'It's pointless trying to get away . . . Don't you want to know what I've got for you?'

Terrified, Cheryl broke into a run. He was so close now she could feel the heat of his breath against the back of her neck. Her heart pounded as her legs began to give way. Next thing she knew, she was on her knees.

She screamed as the first blow landed on the back of her head. The ground came racing towards her as she fell face first, then he brought the claw hammer down on her head a second time, and a third . . .

He stared down at her in disgust. There was a temptation to go on pounding the hammer further and deeper, enjoying the crunch of her skull with each blow, crushing her brain into a bloody grey pulp. Instead, he stood there and studied her lifeless body as his breath formed a hazy mist in the cold night air.

Soon the flow of blood from her wounds would cease. Then the rain would wash it away.

He turned her over.

Guilty

Her expression was frozen, twisted in agony. He felt himself getting aroused, his erection growing until the sticky warmth exploded into his pants. He let out a groan, savouring the image of her lying there. Then as the rain began to fall harder, he scooped his hands underneath her armpits, dragging her body through the undergrowth towards his van. He was quite certain no one would miss her. After all, she was just a filthy whore.

Chapter Six

Seven o'clock in the morning and already Bill Lacy was out of his mind with worry. Yet again, Janey hadn't come home.

He'd let her know he was fucked off about it, but she didn't seem to care, not since she'd started hanging around with that arsehole Artie Rogers. The guy was taking advantage of her, but she just couldn't see it. If Bill got his hands on him, he'd wring the bastard's neck.

Not wanting to wind himself up by thinking about Artie, Bill focused on pushing the Silver Cross pram that he and his mates had nicked from Mothercare in Oxford Street. After screaming her head off most of the night, his six-month-old daughter Holly was out for the count and would probably stay that way for the next few hours. Dealing with her – and his prick of a neighbour who'd come round to complain about the noise – had left Bill knackered too. But there was no point trying to sleep it off, because the speed he'd taken had left him so wired he now had the shakes. He didn't know if it was the crap Janey was putting him through or the speed 'comedown', which he knew could last for days, but he felt so weighed down by sadness it was an effort to put one foot in front of the other.

'Cory – hold up, mate,' Bill called out to his three-year-old son as they hurried past a dilapidated block of flats on the east side of Melville Court, Chatham. 'Cory, be careful.' He broke into a jog as his son started to clamber up the wall that ran around the sorry excuse for a playground.

Catching up with him, Bill pushed the pram with one hand, and used the other to help Cory keep his balance.

'Where's Mummy?' Cory wriggled free of his dad's hand, stretched his arms out to the side, and walked gingerly along the wall.

Bill glanced at his son.

It was the same question Cory asked most mornings, and as usual Bill didn't know the answer.

'Is she coming home today?' The poor kid had suffered so many knock-backs in his short life Bill's heart broke for him.

He knew only too well what it was to have a shitty childhood. His alcoholic parents had dragged him up until the age of ten, when he'd gone to live with his aunt – who was only marginally better. He'd been determined that it was going to be different for his kids, but here he was, making almost as big a mess as his parents had. The only difference was he loved his kids more than anything in the world.

Bill lifted Cory off the wall and swung him round, which set off a fit of giggles.

'Fancy going to see Auntie Sarah?' he asked.

'Can I show her the picture I did for Mummy?'

'You bet you can, mate.' Bill grinned and started to push the pram again, but the moment his son turned away, the smile faded.

Five minutes' walk was all it took to get to Sarah's flat on Queen's Estate. The place had only been built a couple of years ago, but it had already been forgotten by the council. None of the flats had been completely finished, and the residents had all but given up enquiring when they would be. The only thing it had going for it was that, unlike the estate where Bill lived, it wasn't overrun with smackheads.

Bill knocked softly on Sarah's graffiti-sprayed plywood door, not wanting to wake Holly and set her off screaming again.

There was no answer so he knocked again, louder this time. After several minutes, during which he could feel his toes going numb in the cheap trainers he'd got from Woolies, the door was eventually answered.

Sarah's thin, boyish figure was draped in a long-faded T-shirt. There was sleep in her eyes and her long brown hair hung lank and greasy from a pink scrunchie. Although she was Janey's cousin, she'd missed out in the looks department. Bill had always got on with her – the three of them were the same age and had hung out together as kids – but she looked way older than her thirty years.

'Fucking hell, Bill! It's not even seven thirty. What you doing here?' She broke off scowling to crouch down and smile at Cory. 'You all right, hun?'

'Look.' Cory thrust the picture he'd drawn into her hand. 'It's for Mummy.'

Sarah glanced up at Bill, who shrugged.

'It's great, Cor. Let's hope she gets to see it, eh.' With a shake of her head, Sarah turned and walked back into her flat.

Bill followed, pushing the pram into the hallway.

'Have you seen her?' he asked. 'She ain't been home for a couple of days.'

'What's new?' Sarah didn't bother turning round as she mooched into the kitchen. She filled the kettle, switched it on, then tossed a packet of malted milk biscuits to Bill. 'Fancy a brew?' she muttered, taking a half-smoked joint from the silver ashtray.

'Yeah, go on, then.' Stepping into Sarah's flat was a welcome relief. Even though she was on benefits – topped up with a bit of shoplifting – she managed to make her place a home, unlike his gaff. It was always warm and tidy, and smelled of Haze lavender air freshener.

Bill didn't know how she did it. He tried to keep his maisonette tidy, but the housework grew like a fucking fungus. There was no keeping up with the laundry, the dirty dishes, the piles of toys and baby bottles. It made him feel like a fucking loser, living in squalor, but it all felt too much for him to manage.

Sarah handed him the joint, which he took gratefully. She flicked the radio on and Billy Ocean crooned out.

'You look fucked, mate.'

'Cheers for that.'

He gave her a lopsided grin, and his blond good looks and baby-blue eyes had their usual effect on Sarah. In her opinion, he was wasted on her cousin. Janey was a selfish bitch who didn't deserve him. Somehow, Bill was the only one who couldn't see that.

'Did Holly keep you up?'

'Yeah. Me and the whole estate. Geezer from next door came round moaning. I'm telling you, Sarah, he was lucky he didn't get a fucking slap.' He took a deep drag on the joint, hoping to kill the buzz of the speed.

Over the next few minutes they sat in silence as Bill smoked the joint down to the point where it was burning his nicotine-stained fingers. 'Are you sure you haven't seen her, Sar? I'm worried something's happened to her.'

Sarah pulled a face. 'No, I told you I haven't seen her. I wouldn't lie to you – you know that.' She frowned. 'Right now it would suit me if I never saw her again. That money she nicked from me—'

'I said I'd sort it, didn't I?' Bill interrupted. 'I've already paid you back half of it.'

'That's not the point. Who wants a fucking thief in their house?'

Bill bristled, but said nothing. He watched Sarah open the cupboard, grabbing the loaf of Mother's Pride she'd bought yesterday from the corner shop, along with a jar of strawberry jam. 'Has Cory had breakfast?'

'Nah, I was going to get him a butty from the caff.'

'He needs to eat, Bill. I know you're worried about Janey, but she's a grown fucking woman, she can look after herself, whereas Cory and Holly can't. They need you to put them first, not be running around at the crack of dawn looking for Janey. She might be my cousin, but I've got no time for her any more. I'm sorry to say it, Bill, but she's a sneaky little bitch and she proper mugged me off.'

Trying to keep his temper, Bill shook his head. 'I don't want to fall out with you, doll, but don't call her that, all right?'

Sarah dropped a teabag into his cup, poured in the boiling water, sloshed in some milk and stirred angrily.

'Janey has always taken the piss, and she'll keep on doing it so long as you're chasing after her. You need to sort yourself out.' She slammed the tea in front of him, then set about buttering a couple of slices of bread and jam for Cory. She then left Bill to drink his tea while she carried the food to the lounge, where Cory was watching TV.

'You know what your problem is, Bill.' Sarah stomped back into the room, snatched up a Charles and Diana royal wedding tea towel, and started drying off last night's plates.

'No, but I'm sure you can't wait to fucking tell me.'

'You can't see what's right in front of your face. Actually, no, you can, but you refuse to believe it. You're wasting your time with Janey. Take my advice and move on, if not for yourself then for the kids' sake.'

Bill stood. He didn't need to hear this shit. He knew that Sarah meant well, but he was sick of unsolicited advice – he got enough of that from his mates. No one seemed to understand. Then again, how could they when he didn't understand himself?

'Look, I get how you feel.' Bill's voice was tight. He rubbed his face, feeling the rasp of stubble. He badly needed a shave.

'I'm here for you, Bill – we all are. But Janey—'

'Can you keep an eye on the kids for me?' he cut in.

'No, Bill, I can't.'

'Come on, Sar, don't be like that, please. I need to go and find her.'

'I would if I could, but I'm up in court for nicking that joint of meat, remember? Fucking joke – I mean, who the frig makes an example of someone over a leg of poxy lamb? Although, I'm not going to lie, it was proper tasty.'

As he headed for the lounge to collect Cory, Sarah grabbed his arm. 'Listen to me, Bill. Do yourself a favour and go home. You and I both know Janey's probably hanging out at Artie's place. If you show up there, him and Fletch won't be too pleased to see you.'

'I'm not going to let them get away with this.'

'There's nothing you can do, Bill.'

He shook his head. 'That's where you're wrong. I've sat about long enough watching Artie walk around like he owns the fucking place. He destroys people's lives, and I'm going to make sure he's stopped.'

41

'Christ, Bill, he'll have you for dinner! You need to stay well away from him and Fletch. *Please*. Your kids need a dad, and if you're not careful we'll be going to your funeral before Janey's.'

But the only response was the slam of the door behind him.

Chapter Seven

Liza Harper forced herself out of bed and went to open the curtains. Stifling a yawn, she watched a man pushing a pram across the estate, his little boy running alongside, trying to keep up. Shivering, she turned away from the window and reached for her quilted nylon dressing gown and sheepskin slippers. The bloody flat was so cold it was a wonder she didn't wake up with icicles hanging from her nose.

Not that it seemed to bother her husband. Jack was still snoring away, not even stirring when their six-year-old, Jessica, came bustling through the door. Her impish little face creased in a frown.

'Mummy, Mandy's taken my blanket, and she won't bloody give it me back.'

'Young lady, what have I told you about swearing?'

'Not to do it.' Jessie twirled a strand of her mousy brown hair round her finger. 'But, Mum, it's bloody freezing in our room.'

She was a skinny little thing, so it was no wonder she felt the cold. Liza put it down to her being premature; she was so tiny at birth the priest had been hovering to give her the last rites, but she'd pulled through. It was Liza who'd struggled. She'd longed to be a mum, but after Jessica came along, swiftly followed by Bonny and Mandy, she'd been overwhelmed by such sadness it was even worse than what she'd had to cope with after her dad died. Jack had done his best, but it just got worse until it felt like she was losing her mind. Some days she just lay in bed, too numb with grief even to cry. She couldn't stand to have her daughters anywhere near her. The midwife, a dour Scot, had merely tutted when she'd tried to raise the subject of post-natal depression, so Liza hadn't mentioned it again. Even when she'd climbed on a ledge of the bridge across the Medway and an old man had to talk her out of jumping, she hadn't spoken of it. All she'd done was climb down and make her way home to fix the girl's supper, put them to bed and watch a bit of *Play Your Cards Right* on the telly until it was time for bed.

It was her secret. One that Liza battled every day to hide, along with her shame.

Still waiting for an answer, Jessie stamped her foot in frustration. 'Mu-um!'

'All right, why don't you go and tell Mandy to give it you back. Tell her Mummy says so.'

'You tell her, cos when I tried she hit me. Please, Mummy.'

Mandy, though only four, was the toughest of her daughters, so Liza had every sympathy for her eldest child.

'All right,' she sighed. 'I'll come in a minute.'

'And can you put the heating on?'

'Later. For now, go and put some clothes on. You need to get ready for school . . . And, Jess, I love you.'

'Love you too,' Jessie called over her shoulder.

Liza would have loved to turn the heating on full blast, but they couldn't afford to. Money was tight and it was a constant struggle to make ends meet. Another thing Liza blamed herself for. She'd tried to help out by applying for a part-time job at Radio Rentals in Rainham, where she used to work before the girls came along. The old Liza liked nothing better than a giggle with the customers, but new Liza found it such an ordeal to face them that she couldn't even last the day.

Sometimes, she wondered if Jack and the girls wouldn't be better off without her.

'You too busy to give me a kiss?' Sitting up in bed, Jack interrupted her thoughts.

Liza painted on her smile. 'Unless you're going to get the kids ready for school, cook their breakfast and make sure they've got their homework packed, then, yes, I'm too busy.' She did love him though, and she held on to that thought as if it was a life raft.

'How about I pull a sicky and then we can stay in bed? Let the girls stay home too – what do you say?' The last thing he wanted was to go to work on a day like this. Scaffolding in winter was a shit job.

Liza busied herself picking up the clothes he'd tossed on the floor last night. 'And who's going to pay the bills? You should see the price of food.' Since Chatham Dockyard had closed, Jack was forced to take any work he could get, often lining up in the early hours to pick up the odd labouring job.

He gave her a tight smile, wishing she wouldn't worry so much. He missed the carefree woman he'd fallen in love with. 'No worries.'

'Sorry, love, but if it wasn't for that bit of overtime you managed to get, I don't know how we'd cope, especially with Christmas coming up.'

Jack looked away sheepishly. He hated lying to Liza, but he wasn't about to tell her that the 'overtime' money had actually been a loan from Artie and Fletch.

He'd thought it would be a temporary thing, to tide them over until he got a job. But there were no jobs to be had, just the odd bit of cash-in-hand labour like this week's gig, freezing up a scaffold for a boss who liked to cut corners when it came to health-and-safety regulations. And at the end of the day there would be barely enough money for Liza to do a shop in Tesco's, let alone pay off what he owed.

So each time someone knocked at the door, he was shit-scared to answer it. The stress of it was affecting his entire life. He couldn't even take comfort in having sex with his wife because he couldn't get an erection – and she thought that was her fault, that he was turned off by the weight she'd put on in pregnancy and never lost.

He would have given anything to confide in her, but what good would that do? She'd probably end up taking to her bed again, like she did after the girls were born, crying all day and just adding to his stress.

No, some things were best left unsaid.

Chapter Eight

Fletch was blissfully unaware of how many people were thinking of him. Not that it would have bothered him in the least. He enjoyed seeing his victim's fear almost as much as he enjoyed dishing out violence.

The large portion of pie and mash he'd just finished off had given him a bad case of indigestion, and he made a mental note to have a *word* with Mike, the chef. He was taking the fucking piss. He'd wanted a meal, not something that would have him reaching for a packet of Rennie.

He took a sip of his whisky. The Bell and Anchor's grub might be shite, but the booze made up for it. That was one advantage of conducting business in the back room of a pub. The landlord was too scared of him to cause ructions. The Old Bill knew better than to come sniffing around; the bent ones he paid off, and the rest didn't want to risk their loved ones being harmed.

Belching loudly, he studied the tatty scraps of paper in front of him, each one covered with his scrawled lists of names and figures. Fletch loved money. Even as a kid, he'd been obsessed with it, forcing the younger kids to hand over their pocket money. At fifteen, he'd left school to join his old man down Billingsgate market. Before the week was up he'd been fired for stealing; his old man kicked the crap out of him and threw him out. He'd wound up in Soho, and soon worked his way up from collecting beer glasses to ejecting troublemakers.

It was there that young Sean Fletcher met Leonard Turner. Turner was a hard bastard who'd made a name for himself as a loan shark. He'd taken an instant shine to Fletch after watching him glass a punter in a nightclub off Berwick Street. When asked why he'd sliced open the man's cheek, Fletch had said: 'I didn't like the way he looked at me.' Over the next couple of years, Fletch earned Leonard's trust and became his right-hand man in the loan-shark business. Then Fletch battered Leonard to death in a car park off the Old Kent Road. He hadn't liked the way Leonard had looked at him. That same night he'd returned to his childhood home in Gillingham. The minute his old man opened the front door, Fletch kicked the shit out of him. Ten minutes later, his dad had packed his bags and gone. Fletch had lived there ever since.

'Thought I'd find you here,' said Artie, breezing in. 'Sorry I couldn't catch up with you last night, I had a lot of shit to deal with – fucking whores, sometimes I think they're more grief than they're worth. How's things with you?'

'Could be better.' Fletch winced and put a hand to his belly. 'I've just been looking at the books. There's too much money outstanding for my liking. We've been too fucking soft.' He pushed up his sleeve, showing the faded grey lion tattoo on his muscular forearm.

Artie raised his eyebrows. It amused him that Fletch called his scraps of illegible scrawl 'the books'. But his system seemed to work, and they were always in profit, so he let him get on with it.

'Bring us a whisky, Shaz!' Artie opened the frosted door he'd just come through and shouted to the barmaid.

Sharon, a petite blonde with shrewd green eyes and a badly fitted push-up bra that was straining under the weight of her enormous breasts, stubbed out the Embassy Regal she'd been smoking and reached for a tumbler.

'I'll bring it through, darlin',' she called back. 'On the house, of course.'

Artie knew only too well there was no chance of either him or Fletch being asked to pay for their drinks. It was an unwritten rule. The alternative would be to watch the pub burn down.

Artie yawned, shut the door again, and went to join Fletch in front of the fire. He was still fuming over the run-in with Hennie last night; it galled him that a tom would have the nerve to give him lip. Though he'd given Hennie her marching orders, he knew she'd come crawling back – they always did.

'I reckon it's time I went round and paid our clients a visit,' said Fletch. 'They need reminding that I'm running a fucking business not a charity.'

Artie leaned back on the wooden chair. 'Yeah well, this is the time to do it, when they're feeling a bit flush before Christmas. Make sure you get on it.'

Fletch lit a cigar and took in a lungful of smoke. 'It'll be my pleasure. I'm going to start off with that fucking toerag, Craig Arthur. Smarmy cunt needs bringing down a peg or two. I reckon it's time he had a visit from the dentist.' Fletch took out a stained pair of pliers and mimed removing a tooth.

'You're a sick fuck – you know that, mate?' laughed Artie.

Fletch shrugged. 'If it gets the job done.'

Artie reached for the small wrap that Fletch had left on the table. He tipped out a line of white powder then produced a small razor blade from the side of his boot. As he began chopping the coke, Sharon appeared with his whisky.

'Not in here, lads, eh.' The minute Sharon said the words, she regretted it, but it was too late.

'Who do you think you're talking to, you stupid bitch?' Artie lunged for her, sending his chair flying across the floor.

'I'm sorry, Artie. Ignore me. I didn't mean anything by it. Me and my big mouth – half the time I don't even realise what I'm saying. No hard feelings, eh?' Her words spilled out as she backed away.

Artie was having none of it. He grabbed her, pushing her down on the table. She screamed as her weight broke one of Fletch's empty whisky tumblers and the glass pierced her skin. 'Get off me, please. Get off me!' She wriggled and squirmed, earning herself a punch to the side of the head.

As Sharon lay slightly dazed, Artie grappled with his trouser belt, pulling out his penis and forcing Sharon's legs apart.

'No, no, don't. I'm sorry . . . Please, don't.' Tears ran down her cheeks. 'Artie, I'm *sorry.*'

He grabbed her face, forcing it closer to his. She could smell the alcohol and nicotine on his breath.

'Then maybe next time, darlin', you should do yourself a favour and keep your nose out of other people's business.'

She felt Artie tug her knickers down to her knees, then he laughed as he thrust his penis into her.

'That's it, mate – go on, son!' Fletch cheered, rubbing coke on his gums as he watched.

'*Oi, Artie, where the fuck is she?*' The door flew open as Bill barged into the room, pulling the pram in after him with Cory hanging on to his jacket.

Immediately, Artie shoved Sharon off the table. 'Well fuck

me, if it ain't Mary-fucking-Poppins.' He tucked his penis back into his trousers as Sharon staggered to her feet, pulling up her knickers as the blood trickled down her back from where the glass had cut her.

Artie walked over to Bill. 'Shouldn't you be changing nappies or something?'

'Where's Janey?'

Artie looked across to Fletch, who was busy snorting up a line of prime-grade coke. 'Have you heard this cunt, Fletch? Thinks he can march in here like he's the dog's bollocks, giving it the big I-am.' He cricked his thick neck, a whole nineteen inches of muscle built up by steroids. 'You've got some fucking front, I'll give you that, mate.'

'Just tell me where she is.' As Bill stepped forward, bringing him inches away from Artie, Holly began to cry in her pram while Cory tugged on the back of his dad's jacket for all he was worth.

Artie grinned. 'You want to know where she is right now, pal?' He glanced at his chunky gold Rolex. 'I'd say she's probably got someone's cock down her throat as we speak.'

Bill lunged at him, but the noise of Fletch's switchblade stopped him in his tracks.

'I'd get out of here if I were you.' Artie jabbed Bill hard in his chest. 'And if you *ever* come in here again, I'll slice your fucking face off.' He turned his gaze on the kids. 'Theirs too.'

Roaring with laughter, he watched as Bill gathered up his terrified son and wheeled the pram out of the room.

Chapter Nine

Craig Arthur heard someone banging on the front door but he didn't even manage to finish his mouthful of baked beans before it smashed wide open.

'What the fuck?' Wide-eyed, Craig jumped up from his chair.

Fletch strode into the kitchen and wasted no time in clumping Craig hard in the mouth. Beans and blood spurted over the table as Craig was knocked off his feet.

'Where's my fucking money?' Fletch growled. For him, this was the best part of lending money. This was worth all the grief. 'I said, where's my dough?' He swept the baseball bat the length of the kitchen counter, sending crockery shattering on the floor.

Craig, who until this moment had thought he could take care of himself and often boasted about his boxing days, staggered to his feet, hands raised in surrender. 'Fletch, mate.'

Fletch prodded the baseball bat under Craig's chin. 'I ain't your mate. Now cough up.'

Dizzy from the thump Fletch had given him, Craig pleaded, 'I told you, I don't get paid until next week.'

'Listen.' Fletch stepped forward, getting in his face. 'We had an arrangement. You were supposed to bring the money to the pub. It really fucks me off when I have to chase after my dough.

I should fucking charge you for a new pair of shoes, the amount of pavement I've been treading looking for you.'

Craig leaned on the table for support. 'Fletch, you know I'm good for it. I'm just a bit short right now.'

'I don't give a flying fuck what you are.' Fletch glanced at the plate of beans on toast. 'Hasn't stopped you fucking buying food though, has it?'

'Come on, Fletch. I've got to eat.'

'Nah, what you've got to do is pay me my money.'

'It's only fifty quid, mate.'

Fletch shook his head. 'Then if it's only fucking fifty quid, you cunt, pay me.'

Done with chat, Fletch dragged Craig across the kitchen floor by his hair.

'Fletch . . . *Fletch*, please . . . Not in front of the kids,' Craig whined.

'Why not? I reckon they need to see what a fucking loser their dad is, don't you?' Fletch laughed nastily, then drove his sovereign-ringed knuckles into Craig's face. There was a sound of cartilage crunching as his nose split open, but it was drowned out by Craig and his children's terrified screams.

'Stop it . . . *stop it*!' Craig's son was in floods of tears. 'Leave my dad alone,' he yelled, running forward.

Fletch raised his hand and slammed it across the child's head. The boy shrieked and fell against the cupboard, holding his ear.

'I'd stay out of it, mate, if I was you,' Fletch snarled. 'Wait until you've got hair on your bollocks.'

'Don't touch him!' Craig's pathetic appeal was barely audible.

'Or what?' Fletch brought back his foot and booted him hard into his ribs, then he rammed his knee on Craig's throat, causing him to gasp for air. He followed it up by going into his pocket and dragging out a pair of stained pliers. He rammed them into Craig's mouth, clattering them against his teeth.

Petrified, Craig squirmed underneath Fletch's weight as the big man clamped the pliers around his back tooth, twisting and tearing it out of his gum.

'For every fucking week I have to wait for my money, Craig, I'll keep coming back until you ain't got a fucking tooth in your head.'

Fletch stood up then.

He slicked his Brylcreemed hair back into position while Craig lay barely conscious, making gurgling sounds as blood filled his mouth. Irritated by what he saw as weakness, he booted Craig in his side, cracking one of his ribs.

Finally he turned to the little boy, huddled in a corner sobbing, and threw Craig's tooth at him. 'Here you are, mate. Put that under your pillow tonight – you never know, the tooth fairy might visit you.'

And with those words he left the house as quickly as he'd entered. He had a busy day ahead. There were a lot of people who owed him and Artie money, and they would all be getting a friendly reminder of just who they were dealing with.

Chapter Ten

Sharon sat shaking as she recounted her ordeal. 'I'm telling you, Steph, I'd have been done for if Bill hadn't come in the pub when he did. Artie and Fletch need to be put in their place, pair of fucking psychos . . .' Drawing hard on her cigarette, she leaned back against the tatty brown sofa Steph had found in a skip behind Woolworths. All the furniture she'd used to kit out the drop-in centre had been discarded or donated, and the women had helped her clean and repair each item.

She'd secured the house in Forge Lane for a peppercorn rent of ten quid a year, thanks to a council official who didn't want his wife finding out he was one of Hennie's regulars. The council had even agreed to pay her to run it as a refuge for women, and given her a fucking name badge to show she was legit. Not that she wouldn't have done it for free – she knew from personal experience how badly abused women and sex workers needed a safe haven. Some, like Sharon, just needed temporary respite, a place where they could pour out their troubles to someone who'd been in their situation, who wouldn't judge them. Others wanted to make a permanent break, to start a new life, but were so beaten down they had no self-belief and no idea what resources were available to them.

'What do you want me to do, darlin'?' Steph asked, reaching

for the jar of instant coffee. Parents' evening at Stacey's school was tonight, and she didn't want to be late. She'd only come into work because Cheryl had told her she'd be popping in, and she wanted to see how she was after her appointment at the STD clinic.

'Have a word with him, Steph. Tell him he's out of order.'

Over the four years she'd been running the refuge, Steph had learned how to deal with the angry husbands or pimps who came barging in shouting the odds. It went with the territory; even if it earned you a clump, you had to stand up to them, show the other women it could be done. There was little point calling in the Old Bill; the majority of them could barely hide their disgust for the refuge clients, while others were on Artie's payroll. They would come in demanding free sex or money, and if the women refused they'd be threatened with arrest for soliciting.

Steph finished making the coffees and set them on the table next to Sharon. Then she sat down beside her and took her hands. 'Artie's not going to listen to me. Rob was the only one he'd listen to, and now—'

'He might do. Couldn't you at least try to talk to him. *Please.*' Sharon was close to tears. 'How can I carry on working in the pub when I'm frightened to death of those two? And I really need that job.'

Steph knew Artie wouldn't take kindly to her digging him out, but she gave a reluctant nod. 'Okay, I'll try – but don't hold out much hope, hun.'

'If you can't talk him down, Bill will put a stop to him. He phoned me earlier and he was fucking fuming. He's planning something.'

'You and I both know that won't end well, Shaz.'

Sharon shrugged. 'At least he's going to try, which is more than anyone else is doing.'

Bill Lacy was a decent bloke. The thought of him trying to take on Fletch and Artie filled Steph with dread. 'Look, if you see Bill, tell him not to do anything yet. Not until I see him and not until I can speak to Artie . . . I know Bill's pissed off, and I get it, but he's no match for Artie or Fletch, and he'd be taking on the pair of them . . . Did he tell you what he's going to do?'

Sharon shook her head. 'No, but I know he won't let it go this time.'

'*Hello?*'

Both Sharon and Steph stopped their conversation and turned towards the door at the sound of a man's voice.

'Sorry, I didn't mean to disturb you . . . Shall I come back later? I don't mind.' Joseph Potter stood in the doorway carrying a large tray piled high with meals covered in foil. 'These were going spare, and I thought some of the women might like them. It's cottage pie today.'

'That's great, Jo,' said Steph, adjusting her red miniskirt and coming over to help him.

As always, her voice went right through him. Carrying on like she was the queen bee, like her cunt tasted of honey, when he knew it would stink of filth. She was a common cow, with her cheap clothes and her cheap perfume, but he liked to watch her. He liked to watch them all.

'Smells delicious, everyone will appreciate this, hun.' Steph's voice broke into his thoughts. Turning to Sharon, she went on: 'Jo's the only man the women will let in here – ain't that right, darlin'?' She laughed. 'He always brings something tasty.'

Wondering where Hennie was, Joseph shrugged. 'I'd hardly

call Medway council's cottage pie tasty. Anyway, it's nothing – the leftover meals would be thrown away if I didn't bring them here.'

Steph regarded him. 'It ain't nothing, Jo. What you do is more than most people do. And Hennie told me what a hero you were yesterday.' She winked at him as she picked a piece of tinsel out of her fishnet tights.

Joseph placed the tray down on the draining board in the corner. 'Hardly. I scarpered when Artie showed up. Bit pathetic really.' Automatically, he grabbed the large bag of dirty towels that he always took to the laundrette each week.

'I'd say it was sensible, darlin', otherwise we might have been visiting you in hospital today. Anyway, Hen says you were a god-send, and that's good enough for me.' She reached for the kettle. 'You going to stay for a cuppa, Jo?'

'No, I've got the kids in the van.' Knowing she would invite them in, he hurried to cut her off. 'It would've been their mum's birthday today, so I kept them off school . . . I'm taking them to see Nora – she's expecting us, so I can't hang about.'

Steph walked across to the door with him. 'I was thinking, maybe it would be nice for Bel to come over this week and spend some time with Stacey. And Zack, of course, if he wants to.'

For a while now, Steph had been nagging him to take his children over to her house. That was never going to happen. Ever. As if he'd let her put filth into their minds. The hatred he felt for Steph whirled in him, and he clenched his fists, letting his fingernails dig into his palms. 'Bel's still on that course of antibiotics for her tonsils,' he said. 'Perhaps another time, yeah?'

'I thought you told me it was for her tooth abscess?'

Joseph buttoned up his coat. God, she was a nosy bitch! He forced a smile. 'Sorry, that's my fault. I didn't explain properly.

She's got tonsillitis – or did have – and it's infected her tooth as well. So with that and missing her mum she's not feeling great. And Zack's too shy to go anywhere without Bel.'

'Another time then.'

'Yeah, of course . . . Anyway, must dash.'

'No worries – and thanks again for the food . . . Oh, are you going to parents' evening?'

'Yeah, so perhaps I'll see you later.'

Steph watched him go, her thoughts already returning to Artie. It was true what Sharon said: he was out of control. The problem was there was no stopping him – or Fletch. Sooner or later, some-one was going to get killed, the only question was who.

Chapter Eleven

Nancy Miller had a lot on her mind, but it wasn't the kind of stuff she could share with the seven other toms she shared a house with. Like her, they all worked for Artie, which was how they'd ended up living in this dump on Maidstone Road. She needed someone who could be relied on not to go running to Artie, someone whose advice could be trusted. In other words, Steph.

There was a time she could have gone to her mum and dad for help; they would have stood by her no matter what. Then again, if they were still alive, she'd never have got into this mess in the first place. Her mum had gone first – cancer. Nancy had been seventeen at the time, working in the Wag Club in London's West End, but when her mum had become sick she'd given it up to stay at home and nurse her. Two weeks after they'd buried her mum, her dad had been taken ill. The next thing she knew, he was being rushed to the stroke unit in Maidstone.

Four months later, the doctors diagnosed dementia. Nancy had gone to view the care home they'd suggested: it was a fucking dump she wouldn't even put a rat in. So she stayed at home to nurse him, but after a year or so their savings ran out. An old mate from the Wag Club was working as an escort, and it seemed the perfect way to earn money at night when her dad was asleep.

Until she came home one morning to be met by the police: they'd found Dad wandering the streets in his pyjamas. So she gave up the escort gig to become a full-time tom, servicing her punters in the front lounge. Her mum would've turned in her grave if she'd seen her giving blow jobs by the marble fireplace, but all Nancy cared about was keeping her dad safe and cared for. As she'd done for her mum, she nursed him every day until he took his last breath.

She'd lost count of how many blow jobs and hand jobs and rusty trombones she'd had to perform to afford his funeral, but she'd been determined to give him the funeral he'd always wanted: a glass carriage pulled by six black Friesian horses, with black feather plumes.

A few weeks later, she'd met Artie. That was five years ago and he could be charming back then – until the *seasoning* began: the mental and emotional manipulation, building to threats and intimidation, then beatings and rape, which had left her too terrified to leave. She belonged to him now. He owned her, and unless she wanted to risk having her legs broken – or worse – she wasn't going anywhere.

Nancy sighed and checked her watch. She and Hennie were booked in at new beauty parlour on the high street for a manicure later. Even though Hennie was older than her, they'd clicked straight away, and within weeks they'd become the best of mates. She yawned. Well, seeing Hennie was running late, she'd go for a nice hot bubble bath.

She touched her stomach gently and smiled. Artie would go fucking mad when he found out she was pregnant. She was already around four months gone, but thank God she wasn't showing yet.

It was crazy, she knew it was, and all her instincts told her it was utterly insane to want to keep it. But she did. All Artie would care about was the money he'd lose when she was heavily pregnant. But it was *her* baby and she desperately wanted it. Family was important to her, and Nancy longed to have that sense of belonging that she used to when her mum and dad were still alive. And, unlike a lot of the women who regularly had sex without a condom for extra money, Nancy didn't, so she knew precisely who the father was.

But she needed to weigh up her options quickly before it was too late. That's why she needed Steph's advice. Maybe she could even get her to have a word with Artie on her behalf, although the thought of that terrified her. But if anyone knew what to do, it would be Steph. After all Steph had done it, hadn't she? She'd moved to Kent with her baby daughter, running away not only from her arsehole of an ex but her pimp too. The way Steph told it, he'd sounded even worse than Artie.

Perhaps, if Steph could do it, so could she.

In the meantime, Nancy was going to keep her mouth shut. She certainly wouldn't be telling any of the other women about her pregnancy – not even Hennie, who she usually told everything to. And definitely not Janey. She was a nasty, snide bitch who would run straight to Artie with the news. None of the women trusted Janey. Whenever anything went missing or was nicked in the house, she was usually the one who'd done it.

Nancy knew that if she stayed with Artie for much longer, the way he was now, bang on coke and steroids, there was every likelihood of her or one of the other women ending up dead. A pimp was supposed to offer some protection, but Artie didn't care if the punters stank or were covered in sores, or if they fucked her so hard she could barely walk.

Her train of thought was broken by a loud hammering on the

front door. Since none of the others seemed to be in a hurry to let the visitor in, she went downstairs, hoping it wouldn't be Fletch or Artie.

Instead, she found Bill standing on the doorstep.

'Hi, Bill, how's it going?' She wrapped her thin dressing gown around herself and smiled fondly at him.

'Is Janey here?'

Nancy didn't answer him.

'Come on, Nance, I'm going out of my head. I've been looking for her everywhere. I've got a mate watching the kids, so I've only got an hour. Please, if she's here, let me in.'

Nancy nodded slowly. 'Yeah, fine, she's here . . .' Like most people who knew him, Nancy felt sorry for Bill. 'But the question is, should you be here, doll? If Artie finds you . . .' Nancy trailed off. Janey just wasn't worth it.

'I don't give a fuck about Artie.' Bill shrugged.

'You will when he's got a baseball bat to your fucking head. Why don't you see her later, eh? I'll get her to come round to you.'

Bill shook his head. Sleet was beginning to fall and he was getting wet. Through gritted teeth he demanded, 'Just fucking let me in, Nancy.'

'Bill, please, this is stupid. You're on a death wish. I heard what happened in the pub. You need to leave it. Turn round and go home.'

'I'm not going anywhere until I've spoken to Janey. And let me tell you something, sweetheart: I don't care what any of you think. Sooner rather than later, I'm going to make sure Artie and Fletch pay for what they've done to her. I spoke to Sharon earlier on the blower, and she's well up for me doing something about them.'

'Sharon's out of order to encourage you, cos it's not her who'll end up buried.' She sighed. 'Bill, if you know what's good for you, go home.'

'I already told you, I'm not going anywhere until I've seen her.'

'Fine, she's upstairs in her room – but don't say I didn't warn you.'

Chapter Twelve

Bill stood tapping on the door to Janey's room. It took a while until she responded with a sullen, 'Yeah, what?'

He squeezed his eyes closed. Fuck. The relief of hearing her voice washed over him. Every time she did her disappearing act, he lived in fear she'd turn up dead. He hated what this lifestyle was doing to her, how weak and slurred her voice sounded.

Artie and Fletch were the scum of the earth. Yeah, Janey had always liked to party, but it was only when Artie got his claws into her that she wound up hooked on the brown.

'Who is it?' Janey called. 'If that's you, Nance, you can piss off. I told you already, I never took your fucking bubble bath.'

'It's not Nance, it's me, Janey. Open up. I've been looking everywhere for you. I was worried about you. The kids miss you, darlin' . . . I miss you. Can you open the door, please?'

At first, he thought Janey would tell him to piss off too, but then the door was opened by a small, skinny woman whose blue eyes were as flat as the tone of her voice.

'All right, Bill, what are you doing here?' Janey made no attempt to hide her irritation. No matter how many times she told him to leave her alone, he showed up like her fucking shadow.

Bill glanced down the hallway. Even though the women could

come and go, Artie ran the place like a fucking prison. 'I was worried about you. I needed to see you – that's all. See how things are with you.' He was doing his best to keep it casual, but there was a tremble in his voice, not because he was afraid Artie might show up but because he couldn't get over the state she was in.

Janey had been the love of his life since the day he met her. She'd been so fucking beautiful. Even now, to him she was still beautiful, though her once thick strawberry-blond hair was a greasy mess of matted knots; her skin, once flawless, was dotted with angry red spots and sores; and her blue eyes seemed devoid of life.

Bill still couldn't get his head round the way everything had spiralled out of control. Loads of his mates had used drugs; they still did, including himself, but none of them had been hooked the way Janey had. Then again, they didn't have Artie feeding their habit. He was a fucking vulture, grabbing all the money she earned in return for this dingy room and a steady supply of drugs.

'I suppose you better come in then.' Janey sighed.

Her room was a mess. The curtains were drawn and the only light came from a few candles.

'Fucking hell, you're living like a vampire. This ain't going to make you feel better, is it?'

Janey turned her back on him and flopped on to the dirty mattress.

'Thanks a fucking lot. If you're only going to dig me out, Bill, why did you bother coming?'

'I'm sorry. I was only joking.' Bill knelt down, joining her on the mattress and bringing her in for a hug. 'I missed you.'

He felt her stiffen. She'd told him she hated it when he got all loved up with her. It wasn't that she was past caring – it just felt like a lot of pressure that she didn't need.

'It's not the same at home without you there.' He leaned over to kiss her on the forehead and then on the lips, gently yet full of passion. Fuck, it was doing his head in. For the sake of his kids, he knew he should drop her, get himself a new girlfriend who would spend proper time with him: meals, drinks in the pub, day trips to Margate, all the kind of shit that normal people did. The problem was he was as hooked on her as she was on the smack.

Pushing him gently away, Janey lay down on the bed. 'I've got a client coming in later and I need to get some kip.'

Bill clenched his fist and smashed it against the wall. 'What the fuck, Janey. You're going to fucking kill me.' He buried his head in his hands. '*Fuck.*'

'Bill . . . *Bill*, look at me,' she said wearily.

'I can't fucking look at you . . . *Fuck.*'

'Bill, you know what I do, and why.'

'It doesn't mean I have to fucking like it.' He lowered his hands and looked at her, swiping away his tears. 'And you don't have to stick it in my face.'

'I'm not.' Reluctantly, she added, 'I'm sorry, okay.'

Bill snapped. 'You ain't fucking sorry, because you know how I feel and you know I fucking love you, but that doesn't seem to be enough for you, does it, Janey?'

Janey touched Bill's face, keeping her hand there. 'I love you too.' She didn't sound convincing.

'But you love that shit more, right.' He stared at her. 'You know most blokes would just walk away from you.'

Janey snapped back. 'No one's asking you to fucking stay . . . You know what, just go . . . Go on, get out. GET OUT.'

Bill got up then, but he stopped, and rested his forehead on the door. 'I can't.' He turned back round. 'I can't.' He shook his head. 'I love ya, and if I walk away, then they'll have won.'

'What you on about?'

He walked back across to the bed and sat down next to her again. 'Maybe if you'd fallen in love with another geezer, I could walk out that fucking door and not look back. But the gear and Artie – they mean nothing, not really, and if I go they'll have won. And I'm not going to let them win. I'll wait however long it takes to get the old Janey back.'

Janey didn't say anything. She needed a fix, and having Bill get all soppy on her was only making the craving worse. Leaning across to the small cream bedside table, she grabbed her drugs paraphernalia.

Bill watched as she tied a piece of thin rubber tubing round her upper arm and then used a lighter to heat the heroin on the dirty dessert spoon. It immediately started to bubble and hiss. Quickly, she drew the liquid up with the syringe, then fiddled to pull the tubing even tighter which caused a vein in her arm to bulge out.

She plunged the needle into her arm, avoiding the scarred track marks that were already there.

The drugs took effect immediately. Her body went limp as she let out a small grunt and closed her eyes. Bill hated seeing her like this, but for several minutes he sat and watched the mother of his kids, the only woman he'd ever loved, fall into a drug-induced sleep.

He had to go; it was time to pick up the kids. He delved into his pocket, pulling out a picture that Cory had drawn for her on a scrap of paper. He laid the picture and a fiver on the bedside table. It wasn't much, but it was all he had. He only hoped she'd spend the money on food rather than another fix.

He lit a cigarette and, letting it hang at the side of his mouth, he paused for one last look at her.

Something wasn't right.

'Janey?' He dropped to his knees and repeated her name, louder this time. 'Janey . . . *oh fuck.*' He shook her by the shoulders as he watched her lips turn from pink to a bluish tinge. The pupils of her eyes went pin small as they started to roll back into her head. 'Janey, *Janey* . . . can you hear me?' Her face was turning pale and clammy, and Bill noticed her chest wasn't moving up and down. Panicked, he shook her harder this time, causing her head to flop back and forth like a rag doll. 'No . . . no, no fucking way, you don't do this to me. You don't fucking die on me.'

Bill slapped her face, but she showed no reaction. Then, battling his desire to scream, he scooped her up in his arms and raced for the door . . .

Chapter Thirteen

While Bill was still upstairs with Janey, Nancy was downstairs in a panic. Having gone to get a drink from the kitchen with Hennie – who'd returned a short while ago – she'd run into a very agitated Artie.

'What are you doing here?' Nancy was rattled. Not only was she worried about Bill being upstairs, but Artie would know that she was the one who let him in, which wouldn't go down well. She didn't want him battering her so hard that she miscarried, especially as she was now thinking of keeping it.

Artie glared at her. '*What am I doing here?* Are you taking the fucking piss? I own this place, you stupid cunt.' He continued walking towards the stairs, but she blocked his way. She spoke loudly, hoping that if Bill was on his way out, he'd hear them talking and dive back into Janey's room. 'Some of the girls told me that Steph was looking for you earlier.'

He scowled at her. She was beginning to get right on his wick. 'So? What the fuck do you want me to do about it?'

'I'm just saying, apparently she said it was urgent.'

Hennie was saying nothing. She'd told Nancy she was going to keep out of Artie's way until he'd calmed down; she wasn't about to risk winding him up.

Artie rolled his eyes. 'Oh, do me a fucking favour and shut

the fuck up. I don't need some hysterical tart getting in my face.'

'I'm only the messenger.' Nancy shrugged. 'Maybe she's in trouble.' She could see how pissed off he was, but she was hoping he'd turn on his heel and storm out – anything rather than go upstairs.

'What did I just say to you?' Artie scowled.

'Well, excuse me for caring,' Nancy muttered sarcastically.

Without warning, Artie grabbed Nancy by her chin, pushing her against the hallway wall. She felt the dado rail poke into her back as Artie snarled at her. 'What the fuck did you just say to me?'

The hairs on the back of Nancy's neck stood up. This wasn't how it was meant to go. 'Artie, you're hurting me.' It was difficult to get the words out he was squeezing her face so hard.

'Hurting you? You should know me by now, sweetheart. This doesn't even come close to hurting you. I'll cut your fucking tits off if I have to . . . But right now, I want to know, where do you get off talking back to *me*?'

'I was only trying to tell you about Steph – that's all.' Nancy's voice trembled.

'Too much fucking chatting, Nance, that's your problem.' He grabbed her hand, bending it backwards and dislocating three of her fingers. The pain and shock soared through Nancy as she screamed, holding her hand between her legs.

'Yell as much as you like, bitch – it won't make a difference to me,' Artie roared, and buried his fist into her face.

The blow filled her mouth with blood, and she slid down the wall as Hennie screamed and tried to pull him off as his fist came back to hit Nancy again, but he was far too strong for her.

'Nance! *Nance* . . .' Bill's voice was heard before he was seen.

He appeared at the top of the stairs carrying Janey. 'I think she's overdosed – you need to call an ambulance. NOW!'

The mixture of surprise and anger at seeing Bill showed clearly on Artie's face. He stared up at him as Nancy struggled to her feet.

'No one's calling a fucking ambulance,' Artie yelled.

'She's going to die if she doesn't get to hospital.' Bill glared at him.

'And how's that my fucking problem?'

'It's because of the shit you've been giving her that she's OD'd.' Bill glanced towards Hennie and Nancy. 'Call an ambulance, quick.'

'We ain't got a phone here.' Nancy tasted the blood in her mouth as she spoke. She felt dizzy from the pain in her fingers – she was only thankful that he hadn't punched her in the stomach. 'I'll have to go to the phone box up the road.'

Artie grabbed her. 'Don't you fucking dare.'

Nancy's eyes widened. 'You heard what he said – Janey's OD'd.' For all Nancy disliked Janey, there was no way she was going to let her die.

'And you heard what I said. *No ambulance.*'

Placing Janey on her side at the top of the stairs, Bill charged down and lunged at Artie.

'Get out of my fucking way. She's needs to go to hospital,' he yelled.

It took Artie by surprise, but he was much stronger than Bill, and soon recovered. Scrambling up, he raised his foot and kicked Bill's kneecap square on.

'*Fuck.*' Bill yelled in agony and collapsed. His kneecap felt as if it was going to pop out of the joint. Artie seized the opportunity and began pommelling his fists into Bill's face.

'Get off him.' Nancy rushed forward, but she was met by a hard backhand.

'Fucking *cunt!*' Artie screamed.

'Nance . . . run, *run*. Go call an ambulance.' Bill was desperate, unable to get to his feet and go himself.

Nancy did as she was told.

Incensed, Artie went after her, running outside to catch her. He grabbed her hair to stop her, dragging her into the gutter. He kicked her in her sides, pushing her and rolling her with his boot into a dirty puddle. Instinctively, she protected her stomach.

'Just get back to fucking work, you hear me, you stupid bitch? And you best hope that you bring enough money back tonight to make me forget what just happened. And as for you' – he turned in time to see Hennie heading off up the street – 'where the fuck are you going? *Oi, you stupid cunt, I'm talking to you!*'

'I can't let her die, Artie,' Hennie shouted over her shoulder as she hitched up her skirt and ran as fast as she could along the road. 'She needs help, Art. We just can't leave her.'

'Then this time you *really* can FUCK OFF . . . There won't be any second chances this time – do you *hear me*? And if I see you again I'll slice you up and put you in the fucking ground.'

Artie was bursting a blood vessel. He charged back into the house to finish what he'd started with Bill, who was attempting to stand up.

Instantly, Bill felt Artie's fist smash down into his face again. Through the blood running into his eyes, he saw Artie pull his knife out of his pocket. He tried to move away, but the knife slashed open his cheek.

Like he had with Nancy, Artie dragged Bill outside into the road and slammed his head against the kerb. 'I fucking warned you this morning, didn't I? You're lucky I'm in the Christmas mood, otherwise you'd be pushing up daisies.' Then, with one final kick to Bill's head, Artie stormed down the road, pissed off that he'd got blood on his new white trainers.

For the next half hour, Bill fell in and out of consciousness. As the blue lights came speeding down the road, it was clear to Bill that he hadn't a hope of stopping Artie or Fletch on his own. There was only one person he knew who could take them on.

It was high time Bill paid Danny Denton a visit.

With that thought, Bill passed out.

Chapter Fourteen

Nora Turner's house on Victoria Street was one of Joseph's regular stops on his meals on wheels round. Letting himself in, he strode through to the front lounge and announced in his cheeriest voice, 'Only me, Nora! Are you all right, love?'

The chintzy pink wallpaper and matching draped curtains had seen better days, and the Axminster carpet was threadbare in places, but the heating was turned up high. Nora was sitting in her chair with a large ball of yellow wool and knitting needles tucked by her side, and a wide smile on her face. She was thin, frail and her face heavily wrinkled. Despite her monthly blue rinse, set and curl at Reenie's in Gillingham, her hair was thin and lifeless. But the delight in Nora's eyes was clear to see as she sat looking up him.

'Sorry I'm a bit late – I was over at the women's refuge.' The words conjured an image of Steph in her miniskirt and fishnets. The more he thought about it, the more he was convinced she was trying to come on to him. Always telling him how wonderful he was. His mother had warned him about women like Steph, and she'd been so right. Just thinking about that bitch made him sick.

'You're here now.' Nora smiled again.

'How are you?'

Nora brushed the cake crumbs from her tartan skirt and tried to get up to greet him, but immediately she fell back into her chair. 'I know I shouldn't complain, Jo . . .'

Joseph stifled a snort of derision. All she ever did was moan and complain. She was just like his wife in that respect.

'. . . but my bloody back is playing up again,' Nora continued. 'Not to mention I can't get rid of this nasty cough. It keeps me awake all night. I reckon I'll have to go back to the doctor to get some more of those sleeping pills.'

'Let me know when, and I'll take you, if you like.'

She held out her crinkly hand. 'What would I do without you?'

Joseph gave her hand a squeeze and laughed warmly, though his thoughts didn't match his benign expression. 'I'm sure you'd manage . . . Anyway, I've brought you round some soup. None of that meals on wheels rubbish for you today.' He winked at Nora, and held up a brown flask. 'Bel made it.' He abruptly called over his shoulder. '*Bel* . . . *Zack*, come through . . . Come on.'

His children, who'd been waiting for their cue, shuffled awkwardly in.

He smiled at them, then looked back at Nora. 'This is Bel and Zack who I'm always telling you about.' He gently pushed Bel forward. 'Go and say hello, sweetheart.'

Bel walked towards Nora with Zack by her side.

'Hello. Nice to meet you.' Bel hid behind her long auburn hair, peering out timidly with her big green eyes to give Nora a small smile.

'Your dad's told me a lot about you both. You're all he ever talks about.' She stared at Zack.

Zack turned crimson. He was an awkward teenager, almost as tall as Joseph. Skinny with a large head that looked far too big for his body. His auburn hair was long and scraggly. His face was covered in marks and blemishes where he'd squeezed his spots.

'Would you like something to eat? I think I've got a packet of Wagon Wheels in the cupboard.'

'They're fine, Nora. We're not here to eat you out of house and home, are we, kids?'

Bel shook her head. 'No, Dad.'

There was a long silence.

'Well, it's lovely to see you,' said Nora eventually. She leaned back into the large velvet wing chair, rested her head on the crocheted doily and reached over for the glass that held her dentures. Having popped them in, she asked, 'Are you sure I can't get you anything, love? It's no trouble. My niece is in the kitchen making a cup of tea for me. I feel awful that I can't persuade you to have anything.' Nora smiled warmly at Bel and then Zack, who was standing self-consciously next his sister.

'It's okay . . . really,' Bel stammered. She hadn't wanted to come. Not that she could tell her dad that, of course. Neither she nor Zack would dream of disobeying him. Bel only hoped that they didn't have to stay too long.

Nora glanced from Zack to Bel and then to Joseph. 'What lovely manners you've got, but it doesn't surprise me.'

Joseph shrugged. 'That's all down to my late wife, not me. She was a stickler for manners.' He thought again about his wife, Suzi, and how much she'd disgusted him. Even now, the very thought of her turned his stomach.

Nora frowned then and continued to fuss. 'Why don't you come and sit down, make yourself comfortable. You look a bit tired, love.'

'She is.' Joseph beamed again at his children. 'It's been tough recently. Christmas is always a hard time for us without their mother . . . Thankfully it's the holidays soon, so less running around for them.'

Before Nora had a chance to reply, the kitchen door opened and Liza came in, carrying a tray.

'Joseph, you know my niece Liza, don't you?'

Undoing his anorak, he nodded to her. 'We've met before . . . Good to see you again.'

Liza greeted him warmly. 'Hello. I've got so much to thank you for. Nora doesn't stop rabbiting on about the things you do for her.'

Joseph grinned. 'All good, I hope.'

Liza rolled her eyes. 'If she could, she'd make you into a frigging saint.'

The phone began to ring then, and Liza automatically handed the tray of tea and cups to Bel, who was standing nearest to her. 'Hold this for me, will you, sweetheart.'

Bel winced, then quickly lowered her head.

'Are you all right, doll?' Liza stopped and looked at Bel's hands. 'What did you do to your fingers?'

'She burned them.' Unperturbed, Joseph walked up to his daughter and took the tray from her. 'She was making me a drink, weren't you?'

Bel nodded. 'I did it with the kettle.'

Liza gave a quick sympathetic smile. 'Sorry, I better get that for Nora.' She rushed to the phone and answered.

A moment later, Liza's face dropped, all thoughts of how odd Joseph's children seemed disappearing from her mind as she listened to the person on the other end. Eventually, she put the phone down and turned to face them. She was deathly white. 'That was Ricky, Jack's mate – there's been an accident. Jack's been taken to hospital.'

Chapter Fifteen

Steph was sitting next to Pete in the cold, airy school hall of Stacey's secondary school. This was one of the first parents' evenings he'd bothered to attend since Stacey was in primary school. Although he'd promised to come in the past, he invariably ended up down the pub instead.

She'd almost missed tonight's session herself, after wasting time looking for Artie and leaving message for him at his usual haunts, the Bell and Anchor, and the bookies on the high street. She wanted to deliver on her promise and have a word with him, though she doubted he'd listen. And after several nights spent lying awake thinking about Andy – Christmas and birthdays always made her feel the loss of her little boy more deeply – she felt too sad and exhausted to face Artie.

She was also starting to get hassle from Fred. He'd driven past the refuge in his police car a couple of times and had tried to question some of the women about Rachel. No doubt he'd stepped up his campaign because she hadn't gone running back to him like a dutiful wife should, so he was piling on the pressure. It was a pattern Steph had seen many times before. Christ knows, she was an expert on that one, with Pete still trying to do it to her.

'*What the fuck do you mean? What are you on about?*'

Snapped out of her thoughts by Pete raising his voice at the teacher, she prodded him hard under the table.

'Sorry about him,' Steph apologised to Mrs Edwards. The science teacher was a heavy woman with a tight perm and a sour expression. Steph believed they discriminated against Stacey, judging her not on her performance but on the fact her mother used to be a prostitute. And now here was Pete, making matters worse.

Pete snarled and Steph got a whiff of the alcohol on his breath. If he wasn't complaining about something, he was boozing.

'No, don't apologise for me, Steph, not when she's saying that Stace needs to start concentrating a bit more. I mean, what the fuck are we supposed to do? Maybe if her lessons weren't so fucking boring, Stacey might pay more attention, I mean . . .'

Steph sat back and sighed. Across the hall she could see Joseph. Bel and Zack had only joined the school nine months ago; before that they'd been at a school in Rainham, although Joseph had been helping in the refuge for a lot longer than that. She wondered whether his parents' evening was going any better than hers . . .

'. . . We're obviously seriously concerned about their attendance, Mr Potter. This last week they haven't been in at all.'

Joseph sat bunched up next to Bel and Zack on the uncomfortable wooden chairs provided. 'They haven't been well, and it would've been their mother's birthday today.' Joseph repeated what he'd told Steph earlier. Though for the life of him he couldn't remember when her birthday had actually been.

Mr Riley, the headmaster, smiled sympathetically. 'We do understand how difficult things must be for you, Mr Potter. Not many fathers do what you're doing. But the good news is, when they are in school, all the teachers are very pleased with their progress. Everyone says how polite they are. They're always turned out so nicely as well. They're a credit to you, Mr Potter.'

It was so cold Joseph's breath formed a cloud in front of his face as he spoke. 'Thank you, I appreciate you saying that.' He stood and shook the headmaster's hand before nodding and smiling at Bel and Zack. Then they headed for the exit, passing Pete, who was mid-rant at some unfortunate teacher, en route. Joseph wondered where his slut of a wife had got to.

They found Steph leaning on the playground wall, smoking a cigarette. She appeared lost in her thoughts, gazing at the stars, but on hearing them approach she glanced in their direction.

'All right, Zack? Hello, Bel. How are you doing?'

'I'm fine thanks.' As usual Bel put her head down as she spoke.

Taking one more drag of the cigarette, Steph smiled at Joseph, then back at Bel. 'I was saying to your dad here, maybe we can arrange for you to come over and spend some time with Stacey.'

Joseph seethed inwardly at Steph's nerve, trying again to get his children to go over to her house, but he didn't say anything.

'I know this week isn't good for you, but maybe in the holidays. And you're welcome too, Zack . . .' She leaned closer, studying the boy's face, then frowned. With her Benson and Hedges in one hand, she reached out with the other and gently touched Zack's face. 'That's a nasty bruise, doll.'

Joseph sighed. 'Tell her what you did, Zack.'

Zack, like Bel, was chronically shy, and he looked down as he mumbled a reply, which was almost inaudible. 'I was chasing after Bel, and I tripped.'

'What was that?' Steph couldn't hear him.

'They were messing about on the stairs, which I always tell them not to do,' Joseph told her. 'They're always getting into scrapes. Sometimes I worry I'm not doing a good enough job, especially the older they get . . . When their mum was alive, she made it look so easy.'

'You're doing great, Jo, and even more reason to drop them off at mine then . . . It's a madhouse sometimes, but it'll give you a break – we all need one from time to time.' Steph looked again at Bel. 'Honest, you're more than welcome.'

Joseph came to stand behind his daughter and rested his hands on her shoulders. 'That's really kind, Steph.' He spoke warmly but the anger of her continuing to interfere seethed within him. 'Perhaps in the new year would be better. I think right now it's nice for us all to be together at home.'

Steph shrugged. 'Fair enough. Whatever works for you – just let me know.' She turned to Zack. 'And you need to get some ice on that, mate. Believe me, I've seen a fair few bruises in my time, and that's the quickest way to get it down – Oh, sorry, I'll be back in a minute. I need to catch someone.' And with that Steph rushed away, leaving the Potters standing in the playground.

Steph clattered across the car park as fast as she could in her high-heeled patent boots, yelling as she ran.

'Artie . . . Artie. *Wait up!*'

Artie turned towards the sound and immediately wished he'd kept on walking. Before she could get a word in, he cut her off.

'Listen, Steph, I don't need any more fucking grief right now. I've had a shitload today, and—'

'No, we need to talk *now*.' She did up the top button of her coat to stop the sleet trickling down her neck.

'Catch me another time, all right.'

He began to walk off, but Steph ran in front of him.

'I already told you, darlin', I don't want any more shit tonight.' Whenever he saw Steph, his thoughts immediately turned to Rob. It was times like this that he especially missed his brother. Things had never felt so out of control. Rob had always been the calm one, and always seemed to know what to say and have the answer to everything.

'I don't care what you fucking want, Artie, because I want a word with you . . . Sharon came to see me.'

He stopped and shrugged. His handsome face grew dark and aggressive. 'And?'

'What do you mean, *and*.'

Artie glared at her. 'I mean exactly that. *And*, what about it?'

Steph held his glare. 'You raped her, Artie.'

Shaking his head and looking round at nothing in particular, he let out a loud, embittered laugh. '*Rape!* Are you being fucking serious, sweetheart?' He went to move again, but once more Steph blocked his way.

'Yeah, I am, Artie. I couldn't believe it when she told me . . . Actually, no, I could. The way you're behaving right now, you're out of control.'

'Fucking hell, what is it with you women? Sharon's a cheap little tart who's happy to give it out . . . Just like you were.'

The slap to Artie's face was quick and hard.

He bit down on his lip and clenched his fists. He looked away again, breathing heavily before turning back to Steph. Holding his temper in check, Artie hissed at her through gritted teeth. 'If you were *anyone* else, I would cut you up and fucking bury you, but let me tell you something, Steph, if you ever do that again, you won't make it to Christmas cos I'll fucking kill you.'

Book Two

Beware; for I am fearless, and therefore powerful.

Mary Wollstonecraft Shelley

Chapter Sixteen

'Get him a cup of tea, Nancy, will you?' It was Wednesday morning, the day after Janey's overdose and Steph was fussing over Bill. He'd arrived at the refuge in a state, and was now sitting in the same chair where Sharon had sat the day before.

Most of the women weren't keen on blokes coming into the refuge, but everyone knew and liked Bill and, in the same way they accepted Joseph, they recognised that Bill posed no threat to their safety.

'Haven't you got anything stronger? My face is fucking killing me.' The cut on Bill's cheek, which had been stitched up at the hospital, was covered in a bandage that took up most of his face.

'Didn't they give you painkillers for that in the hospital?' Steph asked.

'A couple of fucking tramadol that haven't even touched the sides,' he seethed. 'And an injection in my frigging arse.'

Steph gave him a small smile. It did look nasty, and she was in no doubt how much it must have hurt at the time, let alone now. She was also in no doubt how angry Bill was about it.

'How is Janey?'

'Here you go, darlin'. I put a couple of sugars in it. Shame I ain't got any whisky. You look like you could do with some.'

Nancy interrupted Steph to hand Bill a steaming mug of tea, then she perched herself on the torn leather couch alongside Hennie, who wasn't feeling too clever herself. None of them were.

The run-in with Artie had shaken everyone, especially Hennie. She'd gone against him, and by doing so she'd messed up any hope of him allowing her back. By calling the ambulance she'd crossed the line. She was well and truly fucked.

Nevertheless, she tried to put a positive spin on it. After all these years, she was finally free. But she'd been under Artie's control so long, being free to make her own decisions felt scary.

Steph was still waiting for an answer. She looked at Bill, who was absentmindedly rubbing his finger over the chip on the rim of the mug.

'She discharged herself this morning.' He shrugged. 'If it wasn't for Hennie calling an ambulance, she'd be dead.'

Steph gave a quick sidewards glance to Hennie and Nancy. Hennie had told her what had happened when she turned up on Steph's doorstep last night, cold and frightened with nowhere else to go. Steph had put Hennie up in the box room and offered to let her stay for longer, but Hennie had suggested she stay at the refuge tonight, and perhaps for the next couple of days, until she came up with a plan.

Steph didn't have a problem with that. Over the years they'd taken in a number of frightened women who'd needed a place to hide out from one bloke or another. The facilities at the refuge were basic, but it was better than living rough. 'Where is she now then?' Steph lit a cigarette and took a deep draw on it.

'She's gone back to Artie's.' Bill's handsome face was pained. 'When I was having me stitches done, Artie came to pick her up. She must have called him.'

'What? You're fucking joking!'

Nancy shook her head in disgust. The bruises on her cheek were angry and swollen. One of her eyes was partly closed and bloodshot from the shiner Artie had given her, and after realigning her three dislocated fingers the doctor had put them in a splint; how was she supposed to give hand jobs when she couldn't use her hand?

'She's taking the piss, Bill. We put our fucking necks on the line for Janey – Hennie's been kicked out because of it, and for what? For Janey to rock up again at Artie's like nothing happened. This is fucking typical of her. Well, you can tell her from me, if she ODs again, she can call the pissing ambulance herself!'

The others sat in silence as Nancy stormed to the other side of the room, throwing herself into an armchair by the window and picking up a magazine.

Hennie turned to Bill.

'She's got a point. Janey is bang out of order. Hard truth, hun, is that Janey cares about no one but herself. Why would anyone bother to look out for her after this?'

Bill didn't like to admit it, but deep down he knew Hennie was talking sense. He felt the same way himself, but he just couldn't let Janey go. 'Sorry, Hen.' He attempted a smile, but his face was killing him.

'It ain't you who should be sorry though, it's her.' Hennie was fuming. She'd never liked Janey. She was a shady bitch who'd rob her own kids if she thought she could get a bit of money from them. 'I don't ever want to see her face again.'

'Come on now,' said Steph. 'We all know it's not really Janey's fault. Loads of us have been in that situation, where the only thing we can think about is the gear – or the booze, in my case.'

Hennie raised her eyebrows. 'Or both in mine.' She let out a self-deprecating laugh.

'She needs help,' Steph continued. 'But she has to accept that she needs help, and obviously Janey's not at that point yet.' She took another pull on her cigarette. It was one habit she wasn't about to give up.

Bill blew on the tea that Nancy had made for him. It was too hot to drink. 'So what the fuck am I meant to do? Sit around waiting for her to come to her senses?'

'Yeah. Basically that's all you can do, Bill. Just be there for her.' Steph paused. 'But don't allow her to drag you under too. An addict will let you drown with them. You've got those kids to think about, so you need to make sure you look after yourself.' She glanced towards Cory and Holly, who were both fast asleep; Cory on the couch, Holly in her pram.

Bill began to feel agitated. 'That's the problem, Steph. I can't sit around and wait for her to die. And, let's be honest, that's what's going to fucking happen if this isn't sorted. None of this would be happening if it wasn't for Artie.'

Steph wasn't sure that was true. She'd known Janey a few years, and she was inclined to agree with the other women: Janey would've been on the gear with or without Artie – although he certainly hadn't helped.

'If he isn't stopped, Artie's only going to get worse. Look at what he did to Sharon, and Nancy—'

'And he threatened to bury me,' Hennie chipped in, giving a lopsided grin. 'But I guess that's nothing new.' She reached over, took the lit cigarette from between Steph's fingers, and began to smoke it.

'Anyway, I've made up my mind. I'm going to see Danny,' Bill announced.

'Danny Denton? You can't, Bill,' she whispered. There was real fear in her voice. 'You know what will happen, it'll only blow up in your face. Look, I'll have another word with Artie.'

Bill waved his arm dismissively and stood up. He needed to get the kids over to Sarah's. She'd agreed to have them for the rest of the day so he could get some kip. He was knackered. 'Talking isn't going to cut it, Steph. Their time's up.'

'I'll try again,' Steph pleaded. 'Don't do anything yet, *please*.'

Bill narrowed his eyes. 'You can't want him to carry on the way he is, surely?'

It sounded like an accusation.

Steph bristled. 'Of course I bloody well don't. I care about what happens to Janey, like I care about all the women round here . . . I care about you as well. I want Artie stopped as much as anyone.'

Bill stared at her. 'Do you? Do you really?'

Steph raised her eyebrows. 'What's that supposed to mean?'

He brought down his voice and jabbed a finger at her. 'When it comes to Artie, everyone knows you've got divided loyalties.'

'You're out of order, Bill,' Hennie chipped in.

Bill threw her a glare. 'Hen, I know you and Steph are mates, but come on, darlin', what I'm saying isn't bullshit, and you know it.'

'Steph's always been there for us,' Hennie insisted.

'I'm not saying she hasn't, but can you honestly look me in the eye and tell me she hasn't got a tie to Artie that can't be broken?'

'That's not true, and you know it.' It was Steph who jumped in this time.

'But I don't believe you. If it came down to it, I think you'd choose Artie over any of us.'

Steph swallowed down her anger and took a deep breath.
'That's not fair, Bill, and it's not true. Look, I can see you're
upset—'

'Upset? I'm more than fucking upset. He nearly killed Janey,
and not for the first time. I want Artie to pay, and whether you
like it or not, Steph, that's exactly what's going to happen.'

He stormed across to the pram, flicking off the brakes. He
took hold of Cory and headed for the door, but before making
his way out, he turned to Steph. 'And you know what Danny's
like: if anyone gets in his way when it comes to Artie, he'll blast
them down too. So if I was you, Steph, I'd make up your mind
whose side you're on.'

Chapter Seventeen

Bill's words had upset Steph more than she wanted to admit. Perhaps it was silly to be hurt, but she was.

Trying to put a brave face on it, she waved to Rachel as she sauntered in. When Rachel Walker had first turned up at the refuge with a broken eye socket and three cracked ribs, she was still making excuses for her husband. Steph couldn't say she was shocked to find out that her old man was Detective Sergeant Fred Walker, but she understood why Rachel felt she had nowhere else to go, and no one to turn to, given that Fred was Old Bill.

Steph didn't know if in the long-term Rachel would go back to her husband, but each day away from him gave Rachel time to recover mentally as well as physically. It was another reason Fred and his police mates had no time for Steph and the refuge. They saw her as an interfering bitch; it was as if, deep down, they felt threatened by the idea of women empowering themselves and breaking away from pimps and violent abusers like Fred.

Like many of his colleagues, Fred was a regular client of the toms in the area. He had a reputation as a rough, nasty piece of work and most of the women would have turned him away, given the chance, but Artie wouldn't allow it. It was natural that they'd sympathise with Rachel, and over the time she'd been visiting the refuge they'd got to know her. For her sake, they didn't let on that Fred was a punter.

Music suddenly blared out of the hi-fi system Hennie had got from a punter called Eddie who worked in Rumbelows electrical store – in return for the full works and a couple of blow jobs. Steph grinned at the sight of Hennie trying to drag Nancy out of her chair for a dance, obviously trying to cheer her up.

'Thanks for coming in, Rach – I owe you.' Steph raised her voice to be heard above the music. Rachel volunteered twice a week; today wasn't one of her days, but she'd agreed to cover so that Steph could attend a meeting at the town hall and then head over to Dartford.

'No worries, I'm happy to help out any time.' Rachel smiled. 'By the way, have you heard from Cheryl? She said she'd help me make decorations for the women to take home to their kids.'

'No, sorry, I haven't. I was hoping to catch up with her myself.'

Rachel pulled a face. 'Last time I spoke to her, it sounded as if she'd been on a bit of a bender. I got the feeling she was going to stop coming here.'

'I know it's hard, hun, but sometimes women drop out from coming to the refuge for all sorts of reasons.' Steph gave Rachel an encouraging smile. 'Either they're not ready or other stuff is going on in their lives, or they might be getting grief from their pimp, or sometimes they end up going back to their husbands . . .' Steph didn't add that she hoped Rachel wouldn't do that. 'This place isn't for everybody, and it has to be their choice. All we can do is hope she comes back, and be here for her when she does.' Steph pulled on her blue mac and picked up her handbag. 'Listen, I better go or I'll be late.'

*

Steph was making her way down the rickety wooden stairs when someone called out, 'Steph, can I have a word?'

She turned round to see Nancy hurrying towards her. 'Course you can, darlin'. You didn't fancy having a dance with Hennie then?'

Nancy rolled her eyes, but not unkindly. 'You're not in a hurry, are you?'

Steph was, but she wasn't about to admit it. The women came first. 'No, it's fine . . . What's up, doll?'

Nancy gestured with her head for Steph to follow as she walked out of the house into the cold day. Rather than have the conversation in the front garden, she carried on through the gate and stepped into the street. She didn't want to risk any of the others overhearing.

'I'm pregnant.' Nancy blurted it out.

'Oh fuck . . . Are you okay? What are you going to do about it?'

Nancy shoved her hands deep into her coat pockets. Her fingers were killing her, on top of which she could do with a cigarette, but she'd read somewhere that it wasn't good for the baby, so she was trying to quit. 'I dunno. One minute I'm happy, the next it's terrifying the shit out of me.'

Steph nodded. She blew out her cheeks. She'd been exactly the same when she'd found out she was pregnant with Stacey. 'How far gone are you?'

Nancy chewed on her lip. 'Around four months. Thank fuck, I'm not showing yet but . . . I'm worried about telling Artie, and what he'll say. That's why I don't want anyone else knowing until I've decided what I'm going to do – but I can't leave it too long.'

Steph let Nancy's words sink in. 'Yeah, because right now if Artie finds out—'

'He'll kill me.' Nancy shrugged. 'But if I stay with him any longer, that's what's going to happen anyway, unless Danny can put a stop to him.'

Steph felt sick at the thought.

'Do you reckon I'm stupid to even think about keeping it?' Nancy's eyes filled with tears. 'I don't even know if I'd be a good mum, but the thing is' – she drew in a deep breath – 'I miss having a family and waking up around people who care about me. I miss that, Steph. I never wanted any of this . . . Being a hooker isn't all I am.'

'I know, sweetheart.' Steph touched Nancy's battered face. Then she wiped her tears away with a clean tissue. 'Of course I don't think you're stupid. Far from it, darlin'. It's only that . . .' It was Steph who now felt like crying, but she fought back her own tears. It was no good getting emotional. That wasn't what the women needed. They needed her to be strong; and even if she wasn't feeling strong, she wanted them to think she was. But she found it hard to watch their struggle and see how many of the girls were trapped like she'd once been.

Pulling herself together, Steph continued: 'I think it's dangerous for you. The way Artie is right now, it's really risky. I wouldn't want to see you get hurt.'

'But you did it. You got away.'

Steph nodded. 'I did, but Pete still found me.'

'But Pete wasn't your pimp, was he?'

Steph shook her head.

Nancy spoke quickly. 'So that's what I mean: if you can get away, why can't I? And look at Scottish Bridget – she pissed off too, didn't she? Just fucked off one night and never came back. I could do that as easily as she did.' She sounded desperate.

Like Nancy, Bridget had come to Steph for advice about

getting away from Artie. She'd seemed so uncertain about where she could go and how she'd manage for money that her sudden departure had come as a surprise. Then again, Steph knew that was the safest way of doing it. When she had run away from Pete and Big Tony, her pimp, she'd left everything behind except Stacey and the clothes she was wearing.

So, when it came down to it, Steph couldn't have been happier for Bridget. Any woman who managed to get away from Artie had her full support. 'Nance, you can get away, but you have to do it properly. You have to keep yourself safe . . . I've never regretted it. It was the best thing I ever did, but it wasn't easy.'

Nancy sighed. 'I haven't decided if I'm definitely going to go through with it, but if I don't decide soon it'll be too late to go to the clinic. I want it to be *my* decision. I don't want it to be because I'm too fucking scared of Artie.'

Steph looked at the mess Artie had made of Nancy's face. She was so angry with him. 'I know. And if you're determined to have the baby, then you won't be able to stay here – you do know that, don't you? You'll have to get out of the area, and that's not easy. Going to a new place where you won't know anyone, and having a kid on your own – it's tough.'

Nancy was crestfallen.

'I'm not trying to put you off,' Steph went on quickly. 'Or tell you what to do. I'll support you no matter what.'

Nancy cheered up then. 'Well, I know who the father is, so I could always go to him.'

Steph was surprised to hear this. A lot of the women rarely used condoms because punters would pay extra for unprotected, even though she was always telling them that their health was more important than an extra few quid, especially when it would only end up in Artie's pocket.

'Who is he? I mean, you don't have to tell me if you don't want to, doll, but you know you can trust me. You can tell me anything and it won't go any further.'

Nancy smiled and nodded. 'I know. I wanted to tell Hennie, but she's got a mouth on her like a fucking foghorn, and I can't risk that fucking bitch Janey hearing about it and running straight to Artie.' She pulled down the hem of her low-cut satin dress.

'So go on, who is it?' Steph had to admit she was intrigued.

Nancy blushed. 'All I'll say for now is that you know him, and I think you'd be surprised. But I reckon he could be my way out of this, Steph, if I can get some money from him.'

Steph frowned. There was no way Nancy would let any of her punters get her pregnant, surely. They were only interested in her for sex, nothing else. She thought some more, and all of a sudden she became animated. 'Oh fuck, don't tell me it's Fletch's baby.'

The previous New Year's Eve, Nancy had confessed that she fancied him. Looks wise, Steph could see why some women might find him attractive, but who'd want to get mixed up with a nutter like him?

'Nance, he's Artie's best mate! You're playing with fire there, doll . . . If he is the father, you'll have to think really fucking long and hard about what you're going to do. You can't possibly expect Fletch to help you escape from Artie. He'd drag you right back to Artie – that's where his loyalties lie. And take it from someone who's known him for years: if it's money you're after, Fletch makes Scrooge look generous. You'd have to prise his dead hands open for him to give you a penny.'

Nancy was able to laugh then. 'Do I look that stupid? I ain't got a death wish. Besides, he hasn't got a caring bone in his body – he makes Artie look like Prince Charming. Just because I fancy him, doesn't mean I'd let him anywhere near me.'

Relieved to hear it, Steph decided to back off and let Nancy tell her in her own time.

A car horn behind her made Steph glance into the road. It was Fred in his new motor. He pulled up by the kerb and rolled down his window.

'Loitering with intent, Stephanie?' Fred sneered at her.

'Piss off.'

'That's not very nice, is it?'

She scowled at him. She'd never been keen on the Old Bill, but Fred was worse than most. 'What do you want? Are you here to have another go at Hennie? I saw what you did to her.'

'Have you got any evidence of that?' He laughed. 'Thought not.' His piggy eyes narrowed. 'Where's my wife? Is she in there?' He nodded towards the refuge. 'I want a word with her.'

'You mean the wife that left you because of the way you treated her? That one?'

Fred turned scarlet. 'I'd be careful what you say if I were you.'

'Yeah well, I don't get scared easily. If Rach wants to talk to you, she knows where you are, doesn't she?'

Steph folded her arms and stared at him until he put his foot down on the accelerator and sped off, and sticking two fingers up as he went.

Steph sighed and turned back to Nancy.

'What a prick!' She patted Nancy's arm. 'We will sort this out, Nance, and remember, you're not on your own. But whatever else happens, darlin', please don't do anything to put yourself in danger. Keep it between us for now, because there's no telling what Artie will do to you if he finds out.'

As she walked away from Nancy, Steph blinked away the unexpected sting of tears. She thought about Artie and Fletch, and the fear they were creating in the area. Tension was building to the point where it could blow any minute. And there was nothing she could do to stop it.

Chapter Eighteen

Fletch had always liked to make an entrance, and after polishing off a full English breakfast at the greasy spoon on the high street, he raised his foot and kicked down the front door of Liza's council house.

'Where's Jack? I need a word with that fucking cunt,' he yelled as the door swung open on its one remaining hinge.

Liza screamed as Fletch stormed into the kitchen. His face was red, and he was extra pumped up this morning from injecting steroids and snorting quality coke. There were too many people taking the piss and he planned to teach them all a lesson – and he was loving every fucking minute of it.

Terrified, Liza reached for the carving knife on the draining board. She pointed it at him. 'Who the hell are you? *Get out! Get out of my house.*'

Fletch laughed. 'What are you going to do, love, stab me? Come on then, darlin', though I don't fancy your chances.' He opened his arms wide, roaring, 'Hurry up then, you've got a clean shot. Come in for the bullseye, I dare you.'

Liza began to back away. The bloke was built like a brick shithouse, and it was obvious he was on some kind of drug. She wasn't about to let him rampage through her house though. 'I don't care who you are. You can't just come in here.'

Fletch shrugged. 'It looks like that's exactly what I'm doing.' He glanced at the kettle. 'I don't mind if I do. Two sugars and make it milky.' He sat down on one of the orange plastic kitchen chairs and kicked the table to the other side up of the room, letting out a loud belch. 'Come on then, love, I ain't got all day. I've got other people on my list.'

Liza shook her head, then took off running, hoping to reach the phone in the lounge. Next thing she knew, he had her by the hair and was yanking her back to the kitchen.

'Turn it in, darlin,' he warned when she squealed and tried to prise his hands off. 'Otherwise it ain't going to end well. You see, I'm all for women's lib and all that shit, and I reckon I'm Thatcher's number-one supporter, so when she talks about female equality I'm with her all the way. Which means, you stupid cunt, I'm just as happy to smash your fucking face in as I am your old man's.'

Liza's eyes darted across this man's face. 'What do you want?' Her voice was barely a whisper.

'Like I said, first off I'd like a nice cup of tea, and then we can talk about your old man and what he owes me.'

'He's in hospital.' Liza burst into tears then; it was all too much for her. The last twenty-four hours had been a nightmare. Her nerves were shredded. Yesterday when Ricky had called to tell her that Jack had fallen off the scaffolding she didn't know what she would have done if Joseph Potter hadn't offered to drive her to the hospital.

She hadn't been able to see Jack though: he was in surgery. She'd waited for hours, but even when they'd taken him to the recovery room she wasn't allowed in. As a result, she'd spent a sleepless night, not knowing the extent of his injuries. This morning, she'd had to take a couple of Valium to calm her nerves.

'Mummy?' Four-year-old Mandy appeared in the doorway. She'd kept the girls off school today, not being in any fit state to take them.

Liza turned her head. 'Go upstairs, sweetheart.'

'Who's that man?' Mandy pointed.

'I'm a friend of your daddy's.' Fletch winked at her.

'Mandy.' Liza's voice was firm. 'Upstairs. *Now.*'

Mandy suddenly appeared frightened. She turned and ran upstairs, leaving Liza alone with Fletch. 'I want you out of here,' she said.

Fletch casually picked up a pile of letters and started flicking through them before throwing them on the floor. 'I will, if you pay me what's mine.'

'Pay you?' Liza was confused. 'What are you talking about?'

Fletch shook his head and switched on the radio that was sitting on the windowsill. Chris Rea's 'Driving Home for Christmas' blared out. Humming along, Fletch pulled out a cigar from his jacket pocket.

Keeping his eyes on Liza, he lit it with his gold lighter, sucking in the smoke to savour the taste. He cleared his throat. 'So he hasn't told you.'

Liza rubbed her chest. It felt like she couldn't breathe. 'Told me what?' Her eyes filled with tears, and she was annoyed with herself that she was showing this man how frightened she was.

Fletch got up and moved towards her, wiping her tears with his leather jacket sleeve. She hit his hand away. He sneered. 'Your old man owes me a grand, a whole fucking grand, darlin', and I want it back, and I want it back *today.*'

Liza blinked. 'He can't— I . . . I don't believe you.'

'You think that I'm here to play fucking games?' Fletch pulled out the scrap of paper on which he'd listed names and money owed. He grabbed Liza's head, slapping the paper against her face.

She yelped in pain.

'Here you go. How about you take a good hard look at this, sweetheart?' He squinted as the cigar smoke drifted into his eyes. 'Your old man took out a loan, a fucking big one, and he needs to pay it back, understand?'

Fletch scrunched the paper up and slipped it back in his pocket. He walked towards the door, but stopped to look back at Liza. 'Give Jack a message from me. Tell him Fletch wants his money.' He smiled at her and tilted his head. 'Your daughter's a sweet little thing, by the way. It really would be a shame if something very bad were to happen to her . . .'

Chapter Nineteen

'Jack Harper, please tell me you didn't get money from a bloody loan shark. Please tell me it's all some horrible mistake.' Dressed in a beige woollen coat and matching bobble hat, Liza had rushed to Jack's bedside in the men's ward on the third floor of the hospital. She was in a right old state. She'd been in floods of tears since Fletch's visit. She'd wanted to come and see Jack straight away, but the visiting rules were strict, and, besides, she'd needed to take the kids over to Elaine's house first.

By the time she made it to the hospital the Valium she'd taken that morning had worn off and her stress levels were through the roof.

'Can you keep your voice down, please?' a stern, painfully thin nurse snapped at Liza.

Shaking, Liza shook her head. 'No, I bleeding well can't, unless *you* want to tell my husband what a bloody idiot he's been, borrowing from loan sharks.'

'Mrs Harper, your husband's had major surgery. He needs peace and quiet, as do all the other patients. And if you can't keep your voice down I'll have to ask you to leave.'

Liza felt like throttling the stupid bitch. As for her husband, right now she was in no mood for feeding him grapes or mopping his fevered brow. She just wanted answers.

Jack lifted his head and stared at his wife. 'What's going on?' He was deathly pale underneath his bruised and swollen face.

'That's exactly what I want to know.' Liza marched around his hospital bed. 'What the hell were you thinking? Loan sharks? Jack, please tell me you haven't.'

Jack found it hard to look at his wife. 'I was hoping you wouldn't find out.'

Ignoring the tubes and machines he was attached to, she leaned over him and hissed through her teeth, not wanting to be thrown out of the ward before she'd had time to speak her mind. 'Not find out? You're a joke, Jack, only I'm not laughing. How the hell were you going to keep it a secret?'

He wiped his face with his hand and Liza could smell the iodine they'd used to disinfect his skin.

'Well, I have been.'

She frowned. 'What's that supposed to mean?'

'I've been borrowing money for the past year, and you didn't know.'

Liza gasped. She couldn't believe what she was hearing. 'A year? You've been lying to me for a whole bloody year?'

Jack was distressed. He was not only in pain from the operation, but he hated to see Liza in such a state, especially when he knew it was his fault. 'I wasn't lying.'

'Then what were you doing?'

'I just didn't tell you.' Jack knew it sounded pathetic. 'When I told Ricky—'

'So Ricky knows?' Liza interrupted. 'But you didn't think to tell me?'

She rolled her eyes in exasperation and caught the middle-aged man in the bed opposite watching them, fascinated.

'This isn't the bloody afternoon matinee you know!' she snapped, and drew the curtains closed round Jack's bed.

'Liza, listen to me. I didn't tell you because I didn't want you to worry.'

'Well, I can make up for it now then, can't I, especially as our child has just been threatened.'

'What do you mean?' Jack felt his heart racing.

'Yeah, that's right. That fucking shark forced his way into our house this morning and threatened to harm Mandy!' Her anger turned to tears. 'Why did you do it, Jack? Of all the stupid, bloody things you could've done.'

'What was I supposed to do? We had bills coming out of our bloody ears and then the girls needed school uniforms . . . It just went on and on and on.'

'We could've done without some of those things.'

'I was trying to make you happy, Liza. I was trying to make you smile again.'

She raised her voice. 'Are you stupid, Jack Harper, are you FUCKING STUPID?'

Jack turned his head away. It was too painful. Not only had he failed to provide for his family, he'd gone and put them in danger.

'What are we going to do, Jack?' Liza's voice broke.

'I dunno.'

'You don't know? Is that the best you can do? Ain't you been listening to me? Someone *threatened* Mandy.'

'What do you want me to say? I fucked up.'

Liza shook her head. 'I want you to fix it. I want you to say, *It's going to be all right*, and that it's all a fucking mistake.'

Jack battled his emotions. 'I can't. I owe him over a grand and every day it's becoming more.'

107

Liza covered her mouth. 'Oh my God. How are we going to pay that back? What's going to happen when they find out we haven't got the money?'

'We could sell something.'

Liza's eyes widened. 'We've got nothing worth selling, Jack. The furniture is falling apart, the television is on the blink and my wedding ring won't be worth more than twenty quid at the pawnbroker's. I doubt I could even get anyone to take most of our stuff away for free, let alone sell it.'

'What about Nora?' Jack suddenly thought about Liza's aunt. 'Can't you ask her for money?'

Liza felt sick. 'She hasn't got that kind of money, Jack. She lives off the small pension she gets each week – you know that . . . You never should've borrowed from them.'

'I wouldn't have had to if you'd gone back to work like most bloody women,' he snapped. The moment he said the words, he regretted it, but it was too late. The look on Liza's face said it all. 'Liza, I'm sorry. I never meant to . . .'

'Yes, you did.' She grabbed a tissue off the locker to blow her nose. Her breath was short and shallow. 'Yes, you bloody well did.' She was shaking now.

'Listen to me, Liza – it isn't true.' Jack winced in pain as he tried to turn over to look at her. 'This is my fault, not yours. I thought I'd be able to keep it under control, but the interest Fletch charges just keeps on building.'

Liza took a deep breath. 'How are we going to sort this, Jack? Because that man's deadly serious, and he's coming back.' She sounded as desperate as she felt.

'I'll think of something.'

'*Thinking* won't pay him back, will it.' Liza was terrified.

She raised her voice again. 'They're predators, the whole lot of them.'

The nurse suddenly appeared through the curtains. 'I'm sorry. I'm going to have to ask you to leave.'

Liza turned to her. 'Fine, fine, I'm going.' She glanced at her husband. 'But this mess needs to be sorted, Jack. Maybe I can talk to him. Maybe he'll wait for his money until you're back on your feet again . . . Oh God, I can't do this.' She turned and ran out as Jack shouted after her.

'Wait . . . Liza wait, I need to tell you something . . . Liza.'

Liza hurried out of the unit and made her way into the corridor. She didn't want to hear anything Jack had to say, not when he'd landed them in a nightmare situation there was no way out of. 'Take me home, Joseph.'

Joseph, who'd been entertaining himself by flicking through a discarded copy of *Woman's Weekly*, jumped up. 'Are you sure you don't want to stay longer? I don't mind waiting.'

Liza began to march towards the lift. 'I've said all I need to say . . . but thanks, Jo.'

Joseph seemed bemused. 'For what?'

She gave him a sidewards glance. 'For driving me. I was in such a state earlier I doubt I'd have been able to get the bus. It was Nora's idea to call you, so you can blame her for lumbering you with me.'

He pressed the lift button, and wrapped his red scarf tightly round his neck. 'I don't mind – I'm always happy to help. Look, I'm not sure what's going on, and I'm not asking, but if you ever need to talk . . .' Joseph trailed off with a shrug.

'I appreciate that.'

'How is Jack, by the way?'

'I don't know – I didn't even ask. And you know something, right now I couldn't care less.'

Jack squeezed his eyes shut. There was no knowing when he was going to be back on his feet. The doctors had told him his road to recovery would be a long, slow one. He wouldn't be able to work, and as a result his ability to pay Fletch was non-existent. He really couldn't see a way out of this mess, which meant he and Liza were well and truly fucked.

Chapter Twenty

After dropping Liza off, Joseph returned to his large, detached home. The house was a stone's throw from the Riverside Country Park, rural and remote, and it creaked with age as the wind howled round it. The place always seemed cold, which was why he was sitting in his kitchen wearing a thick burgundy cable sweater and thermal long johns under his corduroy trousers.

In front of him was a small black bible, along with a plate on which sat an under-cooked poached egg and a buttered slice of Mother's Pride. The kitchen cupboards were a putrid green avocado with contrasting white panels, floral tiles covered the walls and the mustard lino was curling up at the edges. A large starburst clock hung loosely on one screw above the brown stove, the hands permanently on midnight. There were no Christmas decorations here or in any other part of the house.

Joseph raised his eyes to look at Bel and Zack, who sat silently waiting for their father to speak. 'Shall we say grace?' he prompted. Immediately, they brought their hands into a praying position with their heads bowed. He watched them close their eyes and thought about Steph's concern for his children. The tiniest of smirks appeared on his lips. 'For what we are about to receive may the Lord make us truly thankful . . . *Amen.*'

Both Bel and Zack muttered Amen at the same time, then they opened their eyes and picked up their knives and forks.

Zack tucked into his evening meal straight away, but Bel put her cutlery down and sat staring at the slimy egg. Under the table, she squeezed her hands into tight balls, willing herself not to show revulsion at her father's cooking. Not to think about the food Mum used to prepare for them. The things that had happened to her . . . the things her dad had done. Every time she thought about her mum, even the tiniest of thoughts, it was hard not to get upset.

'Is there a problem, Bel?' Joseph's deep voice broke through the silence.

Bel jumped. She unclenched her hands and fiddled with her fingers. She shook her head. 'No, Dad.'

'Then why aren't you eating like your brother?' He gestured with his knife towards Zack.

Bel continued to look at the egg, which had a thick membrane of slime hanging from it, and a large fleck of blood in the centre. It made her feel sick. 'I'm not very hungry.'

Holding his knife and fork, Joseph nodded. He gave Bel a tight smile. 'You're not very hungry?'

'No, Dad.'

Joseph slammed both his fists on the table. 'EAT IT!'

Bel's eyes brimmed with tears. Trembling, she scooped up a piece of runny egg on her fork, feeling the thick slime hit the inside of her mouth. Fighting the urge to vomit, she swallowed and it slithered down her throat. Almost immediately, Bel could feel it threatening to come back up.

Joseph gave Bel another of his tight smiles, then passed his napkin over to her so she could wipe her eyes.

'How was your day at school today?' He spoke quietly now and bit into a slice of the white bread.

'It was fine, thank you,' Bel answered as she continued to struggle with her food.

'Good.' He took the napkin back from his daughter, and dabbed his mouth gently, all the while holding her in his stare. 'I was very proud of what they said about you at school . . . both of you.' He glanced quickly at Zack, who kept his eyes down.

Joseph paused and turned his gaze towards the window that looked out across the vast garden. He spoke as he stared at the gnarled oak tree by the broken fence. 'You aren't encouraging Steph's daughter, Stacey, to keep inviting you to their house, are you, Bel?' He turned slowly back to her. 'You know that we like to keep ourselves to ourselves, don't you?'

Bel nodded. 'Yes, Dad.'

He got up and moved towards her, pulling out the chair next to hers.

Bel didn't turn her head to look at him.

'I just want to make sure you're concentrating on your lessons, Bel, and not getting distracted. I want the best for you and your brother, and I'm not sure if Stacey's the kind of girl you should be friends with.' Joseph reached up then and carefully took hold of a strand of Bel's hair between his fingers. 'It looks like it's time to go to the hairdresser's. It's getting long.'

'Yes, Dad.' Bel allowed her gaze to fall on Zack, who gave his sister the briefest glance in return.

'It's always important to keep yourself neat and tidy,' Joseph continued. 'Appearances matter, Bel.'

Bel squeezed her hands together again under the table. 'Yes, Dad.'

Joseph noticed, and he pulled Bel's hands back up and set them on the table. He looked at them, examining the burns on her fingertips. 'Does it still hurt?'

Bel gave the tiniest of nods.

'Well, let's hope it doesn't happen again. You need to be more careful next time.'

That's when Joseph kissed the end of Bel's fingers. 'Kiss them better, shall I?'

Bel stiffened.

He stroked her face. 'Did you like that Bel? Would you like me to kiss them again?'

Bel's heart raced. She knew her dad. If she said no, which she wanted to, he'd get angry and punish her, and if she said yes, it might lead to other things like all those times before, stuff she didn't want to do. 'I . . . I . . .' She swallowed hard.

Joseph laughed. He whispered into her ear. 'You're a good girl, Bel . . . so innocent. My little girl.' He kissed her fingers once more then he turned to Zack, who was watching closely, but Zack quickly looked away.

'And you, Zack, you could do with a trim too. Maybe we should go into town at the weekend, treat you and your sister to a tidy-up. You've both done so well this term – you deserve a treat.'

Joseph went to sit down again. He sighed and opened the bible. His thoughts returned to Steph and for the second time the tiniest smirk appeared on his lips.

Chapter Twenty-One

As soon as her meeting with the suits at the council was over, Steph had made a dash for the bus that would take her to the private hospital in Dartford. She was sick with worry. Everything that had happened in the last couple of days was bothering her. There'd been trouble before, of course, but not like this. If Bill made good on his threat to involve Danny, things could only get worse.

God, she felt exhausted, and it was only 6 p.m.

Still, it was good to be here. Unlike the NHS hospital in Gillingham, it was an oasis of calm. In fact, this was one of the few places she could get some *real* peace. She just wished the circumstances were different. As usual she'd made an effort with her appearance, dressed to the nines in a new black leather miniskirt and a white satin blouse, unbuttoned enough to show off the fake pearl necklace. She enjoyed looking smart, though her four-inch stilettos were murder to walk in.

Rob's room had a large window overlooking the manicured gardens. Sleet was battering the glass as Steph sat by his bed and finished off the Penguin biscuit she'd swiped from Stacey that morning. She rummaged in her shopping bag and pulled out a packet of Blu-tack and a handful of Christmas cards.

'I'll put these up here, shall I?' she said, sticking them to the corkboard above the bedside cabinet. 'A few of them are from the girls – Hennie and Nancy and Mary. I forgot to bring them last time. And remember Julie? All boobs and backcombed red hair? Well, she popped this one through the letter box last night. It's the exact same card she sent us last year and the year before that. I reckon she must've nicked a fucking truckload of them.'

Steph attached the card to the grey metal bedframe. 'Here you go, darlin', have a bit of Santa coming down the chimney!' She forced a laugh, then sat down again, taking Rob's hand in hers.

Until some bastard hit-and-run driver put him in here, she'd been all set to marry Rob. Five years he'd been lying in this room; some days it felt like a lifetime, but right now it was like it had all happened yesterday.

She'd loved Rob with every fibre of her being, and she still did. She missed him, felt lonely without him, yet it was hard to visit him. It hurt too much, seeing him lying in a hospital bed, hooked up to the machines that kept him alive in the persistent vegetive state he'd been in since the accident.

For the first few weeks after he was admitted to hospital, his eyes had been closed. When they'd opened, it had given her hope that he could see her, that she could reach him and by some miracle he'd recover. But the doctors at the Medway Hospital said his facial movements were involuntary and there was no hope for him. Artie had raged at them, blaming NHS inefficiency. That was when he'd had his brother moved to the private hospital. He'd been here ever since.

'So anyway,' Steph continued, trying to come up with some cheerful banter and failing. If Rob *could* hear, she didn't want him to hear her crying or telling him all her troubles, but with all that was going on the strain was too much for her. 'I saw

Artie the other day, Fucking hell, I sound like everyone's echo, but he's totally out of control, and so's your mate Fletch . . .' She decided not to mention Bill wanting to get Danny involved – that was another level altogether. 'Oh, and guess what, Nancy's pregnant. Fucking hell, what a shitshow, eh?'

Steph fidgeted with her hands, which were trembling now.

'I'm sorry I'm offloading, but I wish you could sort out your brother. You're the only one he ever listened to. One word from you, and that was it . . . but then, I know he misses you too . . . I don't want to make excuses for him, but that's part of the problem, I think.' She squeezed Rob's hand as her tears ran silently down her cheek. 'I know I say this all the time, but none of us are the same without you. None of us.'

It was true. Artie had always been a bit wild, but without Rob to keep him in check he'd turned into a total bastard. It was as if he wanted make the whole world pay for what had happened to his brother. She could understand how he felt; it had fucked her up too. Even though she hadn't seen the accident, she'd had recurring nightmares where she was right there, watching helplessly as the car ploughed into him . . .

Her doctor had prescribed antidepressants, and for a while she'd taken them – and everything else she could get her hands on that might dull the pain. But the prospect of social services taking Stacey away from her had got her back on the wagon. Setting up the refuge and having women who relied on her had given her another reason to keep going.

She closed her eyes, listening to the music which was always playing in the background. It was one of the cassettes Artie had compiled of Bruce Springsteen, REM, David Bowie – all the stuff Rob liked. Someone had told Artie about a guy who'd been brought out of his coma by hearing his favourite song, so he'd given the staff strict instructions to leave it playing night and day. Whether or not it would make a difference, Steph didn't know, but Artie certainly paid enough for Rob's care to demand whatever he wanted.

She opened her eyes and glanced across to the small Christmas tree she'd brought in, making a mental note to ask the nurses to keep it watered. 'I went to the cemetery to see Andy.' Her voice was flat. 'I bought him a little blue teddy bear . . . I told him you love him, of course, and I wrote a little Christmas card from you. I just put, *To Andy, love Dad.*'

Steph reached for a tissue to wipe her eyes. The guilt she felt as the only one out of the three of them still alive, messed with her head. She knew it was a guilt that would never leave her.

She'd been tired that evening; Andy had been teething and keeping her up all night. Rob had wanted to treat her, so he'd packed eight-year-old Stacey off for a sleepover at her mate's and they'd gone to a nice country pub to save her having to cook dinner.

He'd treated her like a queen. They'd had steak with all the trimmings, and Andy had slept in the pram throughout the entire evening. When they got home, they'd sat by the open fire enjoying a nightcap, until Andy started crying. To settle him down, Rob had taken him out for a little walk in his pram while Steph stayed warm by the fire.

They never came back.

After a while, she'd gone out looking for them, and that's when she'd seen their bodies by the roadside, lying in a pool of blood.

Steph rested her head on the bed and placed Rob's hand on her hair as he lay motionless and unresponsive. 'Please, please, please, please, wake up, Rob, *please.* Or just show me a sign, anything, to let me know you can hear me, darlin' . . . I need you, now more than ever. It feels such a long time without you, and I don't—'

The door suddenly opened, stopping Steph finishing what she was about to say. She raised her head and saw Artie standing in the doorway.

She hurried to get up.

'You don't have to go on my account, Steph.' Artie's voice was warm.

She stared at him. 'Yeah, I do.' She grabbed her bag and gently leaned over Rob, giving him a kiss on his lips. 'Your little brother's here, so I'll see you soon . . . I love you.'

Without looking at Artie, she made to pass him, but he grabbed her arm. 'Are you all right?'

'I'm fine,' she snapped.

'Look, why don't you stay. I can come back later. I've got a bit of business to deal with, anyway . . . And I'm sorry what I said yesterday. I was fucked off.'

Her temper flared then.

'You think you can go around doing what you like to people because you've had a bad day? Well, I'm sorry, that's not how life works. We're all fucked off, but we don't go around beating the living crap out of people. I'm ashamed of you, Artie, and Rob would be too.'

His face flushed. 'Leave it out, Steph.'

She shook her head. 'The way you're running things, it has to stop.'

'What did we agree?' His eyes flashed with anger. 'What did we always say? When we're with Rob, we don't talk business. Being here is about family, nothing else, and I expect a bit of loyalty from you.'

'Oh, don't play the family card with me – we're only family when it suits you.'

'That's not true . . . We might have our differences, but we'll *always* be family, Steph. Remember that, darlin'. Nothing comes before that. You watch my back, and I'll watch yours.'

As she walked away, a cold feeling of dread washed over Steph. Artie's words had made her more uneasy than ever.

Chapter Twenty-Two

Nancy was lying on her back with her legs wide open, chewing gum and pondering what to do with her life. Confiding in Steph about her pregnancy had lifted some of the weight from her shoulders, but she was no nearer to making the big decision.

She yawned while the punter on top of her pumped away with his pasty spotty arse bobbing up and down. 'God, you're a dirty bitch, Nance. Daddy likes it though, ooooh. Does it feel good for you?' he panted breathlessly.

Nancy rolled her eyes. 'Yeah, darlin', you're the best.'

Dave was one of her regulars; a big man, in every way, his body rubbed uncomfortably against hers as he lay on her. He was her twelfth client that morning and she was sore and exhausted. It was always the same when she had to work indoors instead of down by the canal.

Last year, Artie had bought the house next door and turned it into a knocking shop. There weren't enough rooms for all the girls, so they were on a rota, alternating between the house and the canal car park. This week, she was in the knocking shop. The only good thing about it was it saved her freezing her tits off outdoors. That aside, it was the short straw. With Artie keeping a close eye on them, there were no breaks between clients, no opportunities to bunk off and have a laugh with the other girls – and that was the only thing that made this life bearable.

Some of the girls had got used to it. They were the ones who used booze or gear to block it out. Nancy felt and saw everything she did – and she fucking hated it.

Perhaps it was because she was pregnant and her head was all over the place, but she felt like shit. Back when she was working out of her own living room, she'd taken several baths a day to get clean – not that she ever felt any cleaner. Working for Artie, baths weren't an option, but since she'd found out she was pregnant she'd started to clean herself obsessively again.

And then there was the violence. The slaps, kicks, punches, rapes . . . Jesus, she'd been through it all. The Old Bill didn't give a shit what happened to whores, no point running to them for help.. And Artie couldn't give a rat's arse either; moaning about a punter would just earn them another beating. He'd got Janey out of hospital and put her back to work the following morning. Not that she cared about Janey – stupid cow deserved everything she got.

Bill said he'd talk to Danny, get him to put a stop to Artie once and for all. From what she'd heard, if anyone could deal with Artie and Fletch, he could. But that would take time, and Nancy didn't have time. She wanted out now.

Suddenly, Dave withdrew and let out a loud fart. 'I can't seem to come, Nance. Will you finish me off, sweetheart?' He shuffled over on to his back on the twin massage table that doubled as a bed.

Nancy's heart sank when she saw his semi-erect penis drooped over to one side. 'Sure, darlin'.'

She'd give it till New Year's, then she was out. What did it matter if Artie killed her? So long as she stayed here, she was good as dead.

With her right hand still in a splint, she had to wrap her left round Dave's sticky dick. He resumed his groaning and panting at the exact same time Hennie popped her head around the door and mouthed *see you later*. Nancy blew her a kiss and grinned.

Hennie ducked back out of the room. She'd have to say goodbye to Nancy later; once she was in London she could phone the refuge and they'd have a proper chat. She daren't hang around here any longer; she'd waited until Artie set off for lunch at the Bell and Anchor before nipping in to grab her bits and pieces from her room and she needed to be gone before he came back.

Having retrieved her massage bag from the back room of the knocking shop, she was ready to go. The bag held a collection of sex toys that had cost her a bloody fortune. There was no way she was going to leave them behind. Besides, they were the tools of her trade and she didn't know when she might need them again.

After all these years, she was finally leaving. She'd imagined this moment for so long, but now she was actually walking out the door it was scary to think of life without Nancy and the others. But she wouldn't be alone, she reminded herself; she'd have Carol. Her daughter had invited her to stay at her place in London, so she would get to spend some time with her and little Bobby.

Hennie was almost out the door when she stopped and glanced back at the kitchen. She checked no one was watching, then tiptoed over to the far cupboard.

Taking a deep breath to steady herself, she opened it.

The tall glass jar inside was where the girls stashed their earnings each day. But this wasn't their money; this was *Artie's* money. Listening to make sure no one was coming, Hennie stared at the jar full of notes, thinking about all the years she'd worked for him, all the batterings she'd taken, all the abuse, all the insults, and all for bloody what?

And as Dave finally came to a noisy climax in the next room, Hennie emptied the jar, knowing full well that Artie would slice her up into little bits if he ever found her. If she had to get out of the game, then she was going to do it in style. Fuck Artie. Fuck the lot of them.

Chapter Twenty-Three

It was eight fifteen and Hennie should have been in Finsbury Park by now with Carol, but she'd only made it as far as Gillingham. After leaving the knocking shop, she'd caught a bus to the refuge, wanting to say goodbye to Steph. She'd hung around as long as she could, waiting for her to get back from some meeting with social services, but in the end she had to leave without seeing her. And she couldn't risk asking one of the other women to pass on a message; now that she'd nicked his money, Artie would be putting the screws on everyone, trying to find out where she'd gone. The fewer people who knew she was with her daughter in London, the better. She didn't want him within a mile of Carol or her grandson.

When she got off the bus at Gillingham station, the place was packed with frustrated travellers. A signal failure had brought trains to a halt, and no one knew when they would get moving again. She hung around for a couple of hours before deciding to take the Invictaway coach instead, but that meant a long walk to the bus depot.

Stumbling along in her stilettos, Hennie jumped as she heard a car horn just behind her. Terrified, she clutched her bags and started to run, her feet slipping on the icy ground. The headlights grew brighter as the driver closed in on her.

Her heart thumped as the horn blared again. The fear of what Artie was going to do to her rushed through her veins.

'Hennie! Wait! *It's me!*'

Hennie stopped abruptly. She turned, and burst into tears.

Joseph leapt out of his van and ran up to her. 'Hennie, are you all right?'

Hennie could only stand there, shaking uncontrollably. The sleet was coming down hard now, her coat was soaked through and her heavy make-up was running down her face.

'What's happened?' He hunched over her, shielding her from the rain.

She swiped the tears from her eyes, smudging her eyeshadow even more. 'I . . . I thought you were someone else.'

'Not someone you wanted to see, clearly.'

'That's a fucking understatement, Jo.'

'Can I offer you a lift?'

Hennie smiled at him. Here was her knight in shining armour. It was stupid, but she was overjoyed to see him. Getting a lift with Jo suited her just fine.

She licked her lips. 'Depends where you're going.'

'Well, where do you need to be?' Joseph's eyes twinkled. He hadn't seen Hennie in a couple of days and the timing was perfect.

'I'm actually trying to get to London.'

'Hop in then.' He reached for her bag, which she handed over gratefully before hurrying round to the passenger seat.

Joseph got in and put the van into gear. 'Turn the heater on if you want.' He waited a beat, then asked, 'So who did you think I was?'

Hennie pulled a face. 'I'll give you one guess.'

'I have no idea . . . a punter?' Joseph glanced at her then looked back at the road.

'Nope – Artie. I did something that maybe I shouldn't have done . . .' She trailed off, not wanting to go into it. 'And he was already pissed off with me before that – I dare say you've heard.'

Joseph shook his head, focusing on the road as he steered round a large puddle. 'No, I'm all ears though.'

'Well, he went off on one and threw me out for good this time. I'm surprised Steph didn't tell you. She offered to let me stay at the refuge, but I think it's better if I get away completely, especially after what I've done . . . Once Artie finds out, he'll kill me.' She shrugged as if it was nothing, though she was genuinely terrified.

'I'm sorry, Hennie. Is there anything I can do?' he offered.

'You're doing enough already.'

'Hardly.'

She smiled again. 'So what brings you to Gillingham?'

Joseph sighed. 'It's been a crazy day. I've been looking after the kids and doing my meals on wheels deliveries, and then one of my old ladies has a niece whose husband is in the hospital. She asked me if I could run the poor woman home. She's not coping very well.'

Hennie put her hand on Joseph's leg. She felt him tense, and she had to work hard not to giggle. 'You're a good 'un, mate.' She took her hand away and looked out the window into the darkness. Physically, there wasn't anything about Joseph that appealed to her. He was tall and strong, but that was about it. She'd even go so far as to say he was an ugly fucker, and yet she was attracted to him.

Sex was nothing to her. Most of the time it was brutal and

violent, and she took no pleasure from it. If it weren't her only means of earning cash, she'd quite happily do without it. But the thought of having sex with Joseph made her catch her breath. 'Can I ask you something?' She shuffled round in her seat to look at him.

'Of course.'

'Do I put you off?'

'Put me off?' Joseph sounded surprised. 'I don't understand.'

'Who I am, what I do, does it put you off me? I mean, you and me, could you . . . well, could you . . .'

'Look at someone like you?' This time Joseph slowed the van in the empty lane and turned to her. 'Is that what you were going to say?'

It was another first for Hennie: she felt herself blush.

'Of course I could.' Joseph smiled at her and turned back to face the road.

Joseph felt like gagging. The woman disgusted him, how could she even think that he would see her as anything other than scum? Filthy, stinking scum. That cheap perfume she doused herself in couldn't hide the smell. And her voice – it was almost as bad as Steph's.

After a couple of minutes' driving in silence through the heavy sleet, Joseph spoke again. 'You look cold – want some tea?' He nodded his head towards the flask on the dashboard.

'You ain't got anything stronger?' Hennie pulled off one of her false lashes, which had partially peeled away from her eyelid.

'I'm afraid not,' he laughed. 'Two tea bags in the flask is as strong as it gets for me.'

Grabbing the flask and unscrewing the lid, which doubled as a cup, Hennie poured herself some tea. As she did, she glanced at the cross hanging next to the air freshener on the driver's mirror. 'You religious then?'

Joseph indicated left at the junction, driving carefully so Hennie wouldn't spill the tea. 'I'm a believer, if that's what you mean. It helps guide me to do the right thing.' He touched the cross. 'What about you?'

'Me?' Hennie cackled. 'Fuck that! The only time I get on my knees is when I'm giving someone a blow job.' She took a sip of tea, relaxing in Jo's presence. 'Mind if I put the radio on?' Without waiting for an answer she turned it on. The van filled with the sound of Jennifer Rush belting out 'The Power of Love'.

'So what are you going to do about Artie?'

'I'm off to stay with some mates.' As much as she trusted him, Hennie still thought it was best not to mention Carol's name.

'Won't you miss your friends here?'

It was warm in the car and Hennie was feeling sleepy . . . and happy now. 'Some of them . . . That's the thing about being on the game, you're tight with the other girls because you have to be, watching each other's backs, but women come and go. Look at Bridget – remember her? Scottish girl. We'd all been mates with her, then one day she just took off, never seen or heard from her since. But that's how it goes. Before you know it, another woman with another life story comes along and fills her place . . . But I'll miss Steph for sure.'

He glanced at her, trying to keep his breathing even. 'So you've made up your mind?'

'Yeah, or rather Artie made up my mind for me. I can't stay here.' She thought about the money she'd stolen. 'Like I say, if he catches me, I'm in big fucking trouble.'

'Well then I better make the most of your company while I can.'

'We can always stay in touch. I mean, once I've sorted myself out.' Hennie gave him a coy glance. God, what was she like – she was a fucking hooker, yet here she was blushing like a school girl.

Joseph nodded. 'I'd like that. I think we could have fun.'

'Really?'

Joseph clenched the steering wheel. He hated breathing the same air as her. 'Really.'

Hennie smiled. Maybe leaving Artie really was the best thing that could have happened. But she was tired now, and her eyes were becoming heavy. 'Mind if I have a little kip, Jo?'

'Not at all.' Joseph glanced at her as she laid her head against the window, dropping off into a deep sleep.

'Sweet dreams, Hennie . . .'

Chapter Twenty-Four

The hangover from hell pounding in his head, Bill sat in the cold visitor's room of Maidstone Prison. The walls were painted a dull pale green. The barred windows were too high up to offer a view, and the glass was so thick with dirt you couldn't see through them anyway. There was a constant hum of background noise, and the stench of sweat mingled with disinfectant made him gag.

Chewing on the piece of gum he'd had in his mouth since he dropped the kids off at Sarah's, he glanced over his shoulder at the screws. Big, beefy fuckers, and no doubt happy to dole out a clump if you got in their way. They were almost as bad as the Old Bill. Almost. Giving them a dirty look, he turned away.

His injuries from the beating still hurt, though not as much, thanks to the benzo pills Micky from the next block had sold him. He'd seen Artie a couple of times since, striding across the estate like he owned the place. Bill had steered well clear. Sharon had told him that Archie and Fletch had been acting the show-men in the Bell and Anchor, laughing and joking like they didn't have a care in the world.

Every time he thought about it, it made him sick. Even Janey was pissing him off at the moment. She'd popped round over the weekend. They'd started arguing the minute she walked in the door and hadn't let up until the early hours of the morning when she'd stormed off, no doubt to shoot up somewhere.

For once he hadn't run after her. Partly because it would've meant leaving the kids on their own, but mostly because he was fed up with begging her to stay.

Janey's overdose and Artie battering the shit out of him had opened his eyes. Though it made him feel guilty to admit it, as a wife and, worse still, as a mother, Janey was a fucking mess.

He needed her to be there for Cory and Holly; he needed her to be there for him. And the only way that was going to happen was if somebody took Artie out of the picture.

The metal door separating the visitors' room from the prison corridor opened with a bang. Bill looked up and there, striding in like he owned the place, was Danny Denton.

Even in regulation prison shirt and trousers, Danny was strikingly handsome. From the look of him, he must be working out in the prison gym morning, noon and night. Even the hardest men found it tough, being banged up on a long stretch, but his old mate seemed unfazed.

He sauntered across to the small, rickety table Bill was sitting at, scraped back the chair opposite and sat down.

'Fuck me, what happened to you?' he asked.

Bill shrugged. Almost a week after the beating, his face was still a mass of purple and yellow bruises, and both his eyes were a swollen mess. When Cory had seen him, he'd cried, and it had taken Bill a while to convince the boy he was his dad and not a fucking monster.

'Come on, what's this all about, then?' said Danny.

It had been three years since he'd visited his old mate. At first it was because he'd been too worried to leave Cory – who'd just been born – with Janey. Even back then, all she wanted was to go out and score. And he couldn't ask Sarah to help out because she was banged up in Holloway for shoplifting. With all that to contend with, visiting Danny in Maidstone hadn't been an option.

Seeing one of the prison officers looking across, Bill kept his voice low. 'I need your help, mate.'

Danny gave a wry smile. His cool blue eyes were soft though. 'You've got some front, ain't you? How many years has it been since you paid me a visit?'

'Three.' Bill wasn't going to give excuses. 'And yeah . . .' Bill had the decency to look down. 'I'm sorry.'

Danny could see that Bill meant it. He'd heard what a fucking disaster Janey was, and how Bill had his hands full trying to get her off the gear. But then as far back as Danny could remember, Janey had always been trouble. Every single geezer on the estate had rinsed her. She'd open her legs for anyone – including him.

Not his proudest hour, but Janey had handed it on a plate to anyone. Offer her a spliff or a bag of powder and she was yours. Bill had no idea most of his mates had fucked her, and Danny wouldn't dream of telling him. Much as he'd been a cunt himself for going there, Danny didn't want to upset Bill. 'So go on then, spill.' Danny leaned back in his chair.

'It's Artie, he's out of fucking control. I hear you're getting out after Christmas, and I could really use your help.'

'I'm all ears, mate.'

Danny listened intently to Bill's story, only interrupting to ask about Janey and how she saw it all. After Bill had finished, Danny sat rubbing the stubble on his chin as he mulled it over. 'I'm going to be out on licence, so I need to be careful. Don't want to end up back in here serving the rest of the sentence.' He paused. 'And what about Steph? What does she have to say about it?'

'I've told her it's time she made up her mind whose side she's on.'

'How did she take it?' Danny raised his eyebrows.

'Who knows with Steph. She keeps her cards close to her chest.'

Danny thought some more. It was a risk, no doubt about it. Most of the blokes who used to work for him had either been banged up themselves and were still doing bird, or they'd fucked off after Artie and Fletch put the frighteners on them. The thing was, if he wanted to move back to the Medway on his release – and he did – Artie and Fletch would have something to say about it. He'd end up in a worse state than Bill if they got their hands on him, so his only option was to bring the pair of them down.

'Okay, mate, I'll help. If it means bringing that cunt to his fucking knees, then I'm in.'

Bill breathed a sigh of relief. Even though he and Danny went back a long way, he hadn't actually known until this moment that he'd agree. 'I owe you, mate.'

Danny shook his head. 'Don't owe me yet. I'll need to get everything in place first, make a proper plan, otherwise we'll all be fucked.'

Bill was curious now.

'Problem is, my money' – Danny leaned forward, lowering his voice so no one but Bill could hear – 'and a few other items I'll be needing, is all stashed away under the floorboards at my mum's house.'

'How's that a problem?'

'Remember when I was first sent down, me and Mum had that falling out.'

'Yeah.'

Danny glanced over to where a kid was playing noisily in the visitors' room toy box. 'Well, she proper disowned me, mate.' Danny shrugged. He'd never had a great relationship with her, and things had got worse after his father had died. She'd blamed him for not being at home when his old man had a heart attack, said it was the stress of Danny getting sent down that brought it on. Grief did strange things to people, but he'd never thought she'd cut him out the way she had.

'But you'll talk her round once you're out.'

Danny shook his head. 'She died over a year ago.'

Bill looked at him in surprise. 'Fuck, I had no idea. I must have been too caught up in my own shit. I'm sorry, mate.'

'Don't be. She well and truly did a fucking number on me.' Danny shook his head again. 'I thought she'd leave me the house, you know, being her only child and that.' There was real bitterness in his voice. 'And get this, when the governor gave me permission to attend the funeral, there was no one there apart from me and the screws. He couldn't even be bothered to go to the fucking funeral.'

Bill frowned. 'Who couldn't?'

'The bloke she left the fucking house to.' Danny folded his arms, his muscles straining at the seams of his shirt. 'Can you fucking believe it? And it wasn't as if it was some fancy man she'd taken up with. He was just some geezer that popped in to deliver her meals on wheels. Bloke called Potter . . . *Joseph fucking Potter.*'

Chapter Twenty-Five

'Time to get yourself ready for bed, hun!' Steph called up the stairs to her daughter.

'Okay, Mum. I've already started – just got to brush my teeth.'

Steph smiled. Stace was a good kid who'd never given her an ounce of grief. Not that she would have minded; that was all part of growing up, wasn't it? Maybe it was the memory of how Steph had lost it when Andy died. Even though she was only eight at the time, Stace had been her rock, so brave and caring; she couldn't have got through that awful time without her. It might just be the two of them now, but Steph was going to make sure they had the best Christmas possible.

She'd tried to do the same for the women at the refuge. This time of year was tough for a lot of them, especially the ones whose kids had been taken into care by social services, or whose family wanted nothing to do with them.

Cheryl had been one of those women. Her parents had kicked her out when she was a teenager, and ever since she'd struggled to get off the smack and booze. Steph had done what she could, making her appointments at the STD clinic, trying to get her to look after herself. She'd been gutted when Cheryl stopped coming to the refuge. She could only hope that, having got away from Artie, she'd made a better life for herself somewhere else.

Yawning, Steph made her way through to the kitchen. Soon as she'd had a cup of tea, she'd be heading up to bed herself. An early night would do her good. She flicked on the kettle, lit herself a cigarette and gazed out at the sleet coming down. If only it would snow, so they could have a white Christmas. She tried to work out when was the last time they'd had one, then it hit her: 1981. That first awful Christmas without Andy and Rob.

To distract herself from the wave of sadness sweeping over her, she stubbed out her cigarette and set about her chores. The kitchen bin was full, so she emptied it, tied up the bin liner and went outside to put it with the rest the rubbish, ready for the bin men in the morning.

By the gate, a noise to the side of her made her freeze. She glanced into the darkness. Her heart began to beat faster. Bloody hell, there was someone there. She saw a silhouette by the row of garages. Whoever it was, was watching her.

Trying not to panic, and hoping it wasn't some angry husband or pimp, Steph started to back towards the house.

'You could've come and visited me.'

Steph's stomach felt like it had somersaulted about twenty times in a second. There was no mistaking that voice.

'Danny? What the fuck are you doing here?'

He stepped from the shadows and walked towards her, taking the rubbish bag out of her hand. He placed it in the metal bin by the gate. 'Or at least a letter. Anything would've been better than silence.' He strolled up to her, coming to a halt inches away. His cool blue eyes stared intently at her. 'It made the time harder, darlin'.'

Steph had to look away then. This was what she had been dreading.

'So, how have you been?' Danny's voice was gravelly.

She gave a small nod. 'Good, thanks. You?'

He laughed then. 'After four years banged up, I'd say I was feeling pretty fucking fantastic to be out, and I feel all the better for seeing you, doll.'

Steph ignored that comment. 'When did they release you?'

He looked at his watch, and gave her a lopsided grin. 'Three hours and twenty minutes ago, give or take.' He shrugged. 'I thought I'd be in for Christmas, so it was a touch getting out a week early.'

Steph once again felt uncomfortable with what Danny was saying, and again she tried to keep it matter of fact. 'I thought you'd have gone to see your mum.'

'She's dead, darlin'.'

'Oh God, I had no idea . . . I'm sorry, Danny.'

'It's fine. Shit happens . . .' He didn't want to get into that right now. The whole situation had left a bitter taste. And the fact that another man was now living in his old home made matters worse. Not wanting to think of Joseph Potter or what he might do to him, Danny focused on why he was here. 'I've missed you.'

'Danny, please . . . *Don't.*'

He tilted his head. 'I'm a bit confused, Steph. Any geezer would be, wouldn't they?'

'I don't know what you mean.'

He put his fingers under her chin and gently lifted her head towards him. His eyes met hers. 'Yeah you do . . . What is this, Steph?' He frowned. 'Has this got something to do with Artie? You worried he'll find out I'm here?'

'No, of course not,' she snapped, too quickly.

'I'm out now, so if you're worried about him, you don't have to be . . . You know I'll protect you. I'd never let him hurt you.'

'I told you, it's not that, and I don't need protecting.'

'Then what? Before I was sent down, you and me—'

'That was a mistake. I was going through a difficult time.' Steph hated sounding like a bitch, but she needed to nip this in the bud.

'That's not quite how I remember it.'

She tried to sound casual, but she felt far from it. 'Things change, people change.'

Danny nodded. At six foot three he towered over her. 'I don't believe that's all there is to it.'

'Think what you like, Dan. I'm sorry, but that's how it is.' She could see the hurt in his eyes, but more than anything she needed to convince Danny to move on. What had happened with him . . . Well, she'd been in a dark place. She'd been lonely and scared, and in so much pain after losing Andy and Rob.

She'd fallen off the wagon with an almighty crash. Overnight she'd gone from teetotal to necking vodka by the bottle, taking pills and snorting powder. She'd been a wreck. Artie had been too intent on finding the bastard responsible to help her. Danny had been the one who wiped up her vomit, cooked meals for her and Stacey, and kept Pete – who'd been circling like a vulture – well away from her.

It would have been so easy for him to take advantage of her, but he didn't. Only once she'd straightened herself out did anything happen between them. For a while, she'd imagined she liked him, really liked him. But when he got sent down, it was like cold water had been thrown over her. That was when the guilt hit her: how could she do that to Rob? Not to mention the fear of what Artie would do to her if he ever found out.

'Steph, you need to give yourself a break. What happened

between us wasn't wrong.' Danny spoke as if he was reading her mind.

In the distance a party was getting underway; someone had turned up the music. She felt him squeeze her hand, wanting her to say something.

'Danny, don't, *please*.'

He let go. A frown appeared on his face. 'You can't put your life on hold.'

Steph bristled. 'I'm not.'

The warmth in his eyes made it hard for Steph to hold his stare. 'That's exactly what you're doing.'

'And I told you, I'm not . . . Rob isn't dead. I made a mistake back then, with you. That's all it was.'

'Okay, okay.' He put his hands up in surrender. 'But don't think this conversation is over. Whether you want to admit it or not, I know we had something.' Danny leaned down and gently kissed her on the forehead, then he began to move away, walking backwards as he held her gaze. 'But maybe it would be best if you didn't tell Artie you've seen me.'

'Then you shouldn't have come, should you?'

'And miss out on seeing you?' He smiled, that old cheeky smile. 'No chance, darlin'.'

Then he turned, pulled up his collar and walked into the rainy night.

Steph watched him go. She didn't move. She felt sick with guilt.

'*Steph! Steph!*'

Jolted out of her daze, she spun round and groaned when she saw Pete staggering towards her, a can of lager in his hand.

'What the fuck do you think you're doing?'

Steph's heart leapt into her mouth. 'What . . . what are you talking about?'

'Don't come the fucking innocent with me. I saw you talking to that cunt.'

He was swaying on his feet. Steph prayed he was in no state to recognise who she'd been talking to, or to remember it in the morning.

'You're drunk, Pete, and you don't know what you're talking about.'

He sneered at her. '*Slut* . . . I knew eventually the mask would slip. It may have taken a few years, but the true you is shining through.' He took a swig of lager, gulping it down noisily. 'You can take the whore out of the city, but you can't take the whore out of their cunt.' His words were slurred, and a dribble of saliva ran out of the corner of his mouth and down his chin.

'You need to fuck off out of here, Pete. I'm in no mood for your crap.'

'When did you become queen of fucking Kent? It's a free country, and I'll go where I pissing well want.' He jabbed his finger angrily in the air.

Steph rolled her eyes. He'd been making a nuisance of himself ever since Cath, his latest girlfriend, had kicked him out.

'What would Artie say if he could see you now?' he sneered. 'I've a good mind to go round and tell him.'

'Go on then, tell him,' she jeered. 'He knows what a prick you are – he won't believe a word you say.'

Pete suspected she was right; even if he did believe him, Artie was liable to shoot the messenger for delivering bad news. But this had given him much-needed leverage, and he wasn't going to waste it.

'Come off it, Steph. You're bricking it right now, aren't you?' He took a pull on his lager. 'Tell you what, though, if you do me a favour, I promise not to tell him.'

'A favour?' Steph laughed. 'You are joking!'

'I need you to give me an alibi. If the Old Bill come knocking, I want you to tell them—'

'You can stop right there,' she cut in. 'Whatever it is, I ain't giving you a fucking alibi.'

'So you'd rather the father of your kid be sent down?'

'In a word, yes. The only time I get peace from you, Pete, is when you're shacked up or banged up. What are they after you for this time?'

'Cath is saying I nicked her jewellery. Stupid cow.'

'In other words, you did. You're pathetic, Pete.' Steph shook her head. Then she turned her back on him and walked towards the house. 'You need to get a fucking life and stop robbing people. Now do us all a favour and go sober up.'

Suddenly Steph was yanked backwards. He'd grabbed her by the hair and used it to drag her towards him. 'You think your shit doesn't stink, you fucking tart?'

'Get off me!' Steph yelled, scrambling to keep her balance as she reached for his crotch and squeezed his balls as hard as she could.

'*FUCK!*' Pete screamed, letting go of Steph's hair and dropping to his knees. 'You *cunt.*'

Breathing heavily, Steph brushed off her clothes and looked down at him in disgust. 'Your days of raising your hand to me are well and truly over, darlin'. If you ever touch me again, you'll be sorry.'

'Not as sorry as you,' he groaned.

'And I hope the Old Bill do fucking bang you up,' she shouted as she hurried inside, slamming the door behind her.

Chapter Twenty-Six

Pete was still fuming an hour later. He'd bought himself a four-pack of Kestrel lager and a bacon butty, which was stone-cold by the time he sat down to eat it, giving him another reason to feel pissed off.

Vindictive bitch! Who the fuck did she think she was? He cracked open a lager and took a swig. Her refusing to give him an alibi would put him right in the shit. It would serve her right if he did go to Artie. He might have had a few, but he knew what he'd seen. There'd definitely been something going on between her and that bloke. That was probably why she kept knocking him back.

It hadn't been so bad when he'd been seeing Cath. Okay, she was well past it, fifty if she was a day, and after pushing out six kids her cunt was as wide as the Blackwall Tunnel, but it was a nice cushy number for him while it lasted. She'd done all his cooking and laundry, given him some beer money out of her wages from the funeral parlour and would have been happy to keep on doing it if it hadn't been for her son. Fucker had the nerve to accuse him of poncing off her!

After breaking young Eric's nose with a spanner, Pete had given her an ultimatum, telling her it was either him or Eric. To his surprise, Cath had chosen Eric. Ungrateful bitch should've

143

been grateful to him for servicing her – after all, what bloke in his right mind would put his dick within six feet of her flabby cunt. To teach her a lesson, he'd helped himself to a few items from the jewellery box she kept hidden away at the back of her wardrobe. Not the whole lot, just a couple of rings, a necklace and a few bracelets. How was he supposed to know she'd clock that they were missing! And now he had the Old Bill breathing down his fucking neck.

It was all Steph's fault. He should be putting his feet up in her lounge while she waited on him hand and foot, like in the old days. Back then, all he had to do was raise his hand and she'd be cowering in fear. She'd turned extra tricks so she could pay the bills and give him his pint money. He'd been a kept man, until she did a runner, taking his daughter with her.

That had been over a decade ago, but his life had been on the skids ever since. By the time he'd caught up with her, Steph had grown a pair of fucking bollocks. Now he was living in a shitty bedsit while she owned her own house.

He let out a long burp and shoved his hand down his trousers to scratch his balls, wincing when he discovered they were still sore where she'd grabbed him. If Artie wasn't such an unpredictable psycho, he'd be round there now, spilling the beans about Steph's new bloke. But maybe there was a better way of making her suffer. He'd been toying with an idea for a while, something to pay her back for the grief she'd caused him.

The time had come to turn Steph's world upside down.

Chapter Twenty-Seven

At first Hennie thought it was heavy rain falling on her. She'd woken to find her head and body racked with pain. She was weak from loss of blood, and something was blocking her nose, making it hard to breathe. And when she tried to open her eyes, it felt as if something wet and heavy was weighing on her eyelids.

Sheer panic took over as Hennie smelled the damp earth that was depriving her of oxygen, making her chest feel as if it was being compressed with a steel bar. She tried to raise her hands, to kick out, but the rope binding her cut into her flesh.

She was being buried alive and there was nothing she could do to save herself.

Barely conscious, choking on her own vomit, it came as a relief when death claimed her.

Joseph Potter threw aside the spade, wiped his hands on his trousers, and looked down at Hennie's shallow grave. Aroused, he savoured the sensations rushing through his body.

He'd rid the world of yet another filthy whore.

Book Three

Christmas

Be careful who you trust; Satan was once an angel.

Anon

Chapter Twenty-Eight

Christmas morning had finally arrived. Steph was standing in her lounge, admiring the presents under the tree. She'd already opened the bottle of Avon perfume from the women at the refuge and sprayed herself liberally. Her hair and make-up were immaculate. Steph liked to look her best on Christmas Day.

She'd woken up at 6 a.m., determined to push all the upset of the last few weeks out of her mind. Easier said than done. Danny's visit the other night had thrown her, and Pete's threat to tell Artie had left her uneasy. Fuck knew what Artie would do if he found out.

If there was one thing that was guaranteed to take her mind off her troubles, it was watching Stacey open all the presents she'd been buying and hiding away over the past year. So she'd gone into Stacey's bedroom, waking her with a rousing chorus of 'Merry Christmas'. But Stacey was having none of it. Instead of rushing downstairs, she'd groaned and turned over, then gone back to sleep for another couple of hours.

Now that Stacey had finally come downstairs and was sitting bleary-eyed on the sofa, Christmas songs playing in the background, it was time to tackle the pile of presents, some of which were stacked up behind the sofa because there wasn't enough room under the tree. It wasn't about spending a fortune on her daughter, more about making her feel special and loved, giving her happy memories to look back on.

Steph had precious few of those from her own childhood. Her parents wouldn't get out of bed until it was time for the pubs to open, and she wouldn't see them again until closing time, assuming she was still awake. Things weren't much better when she was in foster care. Those were memories she did her best to forget.

She'd had only one Christmas with Andy. He was just a baby, too young to take it in. He was gone before they'd had time to make memories, and the few she had of him were fading.

Losing him had made it even more important that she give Stacey as many good memories as she could. You never knew when the ones you loved were going to be snatched away.

'Go on then, Stace, open them. Then I'll cook us a nice fry-up.'

To get things going, she crouched by the Christmas tree and passed her daughter a large squishy silver present, wrapped with a red bow. As usual, Steph had gone all out. 'Let's see what Father Christmas has got you, eh.'

Stacey laughed. 'Father Christmas? Are you being serious?'

'Too bloody right I am.' Steph took a drag on her cigarette.

'Mum, you do know how old I am, don't you?'

'Yeah.' Steph giggled, causing the smoke to puff out of the side of her mouth.

'I stopped believing in him a long time ago.'

With her cigarette clenched between her teeth, Steph jumped on the sofa next to Stacey and began to tickle her. 'You're never too old to believe in him.'

'Mum, *stop!*' Stacey's laughter rang out. '*Mum!*'

'Not unless you say you believe in him.'

'Okay, okay . . .' Stacey pleaded, breathless with laughter. 'I believe in him! I believe in Father Christmas.'

Steph stopped then. Placing her cigarette in the ashtray, she gazed at her daughter and gently stroked her face. 'You know how much I love you, don't you?'

Stacey adored her mum, and was used to her being gushy. She nodded happily and began to unwrap the first of many presents.

While Stacey was ripping through the wrapping paper, Steph glanced at the presents with her name on the tag. The one in the snowman paper was from Hennie; she'd given it to her at the start of December to make sure it would be the first one under the tree – it had become a bit of a tradition. Steph was going to miss her; Hennie was a real character, and always made her laugh. But it was for the best; she'd be better off in London with her daughter.

The blue one she was sure was from Nancy, the reindeer one from Rach. She frowned then. She couldn't remember who'd given her the gift wrapped in shiny green paper. In fact, she had no recollection of putting it under the tree.

Steph reached for it. 'Is this one from you, Stace?'

Stacey shook her head. 'My one's over there.' She pointed to a rectangular box wrapped in kitchen foil. Her mate's mum had brought back some duty-free fags from her holiday in the Costa del Sol, and Stacey had bought a box from her. She'd had to tap her dad for the money, which he'd reluctantly handed over after calling her mum all sorts of names.

'Well, clearly Father Christmas has brought me a surprise then.' Smiling, Steph began to tear open the green paper. She peeked inside.

Instantly, her hands began to shake.

'Mum, are you okay? *Mum?*' Stacey noticed her mum's face had turned ashen.

'Yeah . . . yeah, I'm fine.' Steph found it hard to speak. 'I'm . . . I'm just going to grab a piece of toast. I feel a bit dizzy.'

Stacey nodded and continued to examine the box of Elizabeth Duke make-up she'd just unwrapped.

Using the arm of the sofa for support, Steph got to her feet. Not trusting her legs to hold her, she paused for a moment before staggering to the lounge door. A wave of nausea clutched her stomach and she had to clamp a hand over her mouth to keep from splattering the tinsel-taped cupboards with vomit.

'*Only me, darlin'.*' The back door opened and Artie walked in, holding an armful of gifts. The minute he saw the look on Steph's face, he stopped. 'Are you all right?' He stared at her hand, covered in sick. 'Fucking hell, you been out on the lash?' He was joking, but a frown settled on his face.

Trembling, Steph wiped her mouth. 'I'm fine . . . I ate something dodgy last night, that's all.' She attempted a smile.

'What you got there?'

He nodded to the partly unwrapped present in her hand. 'Oh . . . it's . . . it's a present from . . . from Nancy,' she lied, not wanting to deal with Artie's reaction when he found out what was in it.

Artie rolled his eyes but said nothing as Steph placed the present on the draining board and washed her hands at the sink.

'Well, I brought these for Stace, and there's a couple for you.' He put the beautifully wrapped presents on the kitchen table. 'Are you sure you're okay? If there's a problem, you know I'll sort it. Like I say, we're family.' His voice was unusually gentle, and she was tempted to tell him, but there was no question he'd completely lose it. And she didn't want to deal with Artie's temper on top of everything else.

'Everything's fine, Artie.' Steph struggled to speak. 'I just feel a bit rough.'

'Okay, if you're sure you're all right, I better get off. Tell Stace I'll catch up with her later. I'm heading over to see Rob this morning, but I'll be back this afternoon.' He made it to the door, then paused. 'I know it's a tough time for you at Christmas – I ain't forgotten that.'

Steph could barely nod in reply.

As soon as he was gone, she tore away the green wrapping paper and stood by the draining board taking long, deep breaths. The babygrow was covered in what looked like dried blood. It was almost identical to the one Andy had been wearing the day he'd been killed.

She retched again and slid down the wall, sitting next to the pool of her own vomit.

She was crying now. Rocking back and forth, desperately trying not to make a sound in case Stacey heard. What kind of sick fucking bastard would do such a thing?

But what Steph really couldn't understand was how anyone would know what Andy had been wearing that day.

Not wanting to look at it any more, Steph scrunched it up. As she did, a card dropped out of it.

Merry Christmas Mummy

This time she couldn't help herself. She let out a scream and hurled the card across the room.

Chapter Twenty-Nine

In the Harper household, Liza wasn't having a great time of it either. She was distracted by her own thoughts when usually she loved watching her girls open their presents on Christmas morning.

She'd been a bag of nerves, even more than usual. All she could think of was Fletch. When she'd asked a friend on the estate if she'd ever heard of someone by that name, the woman had reeled off the names of people he'd harmed and warned her to under no circumstances borrow money from him. Apparently he carried a pair of pliers that he used to rip people's teeth out. She didn't know if it was true of not – she only hoped to God it wasn't.

Two days ago she'd called in at the job centre, hoping to apply for sickness benefit for Jack, or at least pick up the forms. They'd taken down all the information, then led her into a stuffy room where she'd waited over an hour until a snotty-faced cow came in carrying an armful of files. It seemed Jack wasn't entitled to sickness benefit because he'd been working cash in hand. Worse, they were now going to open an investigation. Instead of an emergency payout to tide them over, she'd come away with more shit to worry about.

It was hardly surprising she wasn't sleeping. This morning

she'd had to slap on a heavy layer of foundation to cover the dark circles under her eyes.

Her appetite was shot to pieces too. She felt too nauseous to think about eating. As for Jack, she couldn't face him, so she hadn't been back to visit since that bossy nurse asked her to leave.

He'd sent Rick and Elaine round to let her know the doctors said he could come home soon after Christmas. They seemed to think she'd be happy at the news, but apart from still being angry with him, she now had to worry about one more mouth to feed.

This would be her first Christmas without Jack since they'd been together, and part of her missed him, but another part of her wouldn't care less if she never set eyes on him again.

Liza sighed heavily. She didn't even have money to buy Christmas dinner. A bit of back bacon and a can of beans on toast was all she could afford. Nora had invited them for dinner, but she wasn't sure she could face it. All she wanted to do was hide away. Thank fuck for the Valium. If it wasn't for her pills – which she'd stepped up the dose of – she didn't know how she'd get by.

'Mummy, look . . . Look what Father Christmas has got me!' Mandy squealed with delight at the second-hand Barbie Liza had picked up from the charity shop.

'It's beautiful, darlin',' Liza said, knowing full well it wasn't. The doll's face was partly scraped off, and its pink ballet dress was threadbare. Still, Mandy seemed to love it.

The smile on Liza's face changed to an expression of fear as a loud bang came from the front door.

'Ho, ho, ho!' Fletch strolled in. He was off his nut. 'Season greetings, darlin'.' He winked. 'I told you I'd be back.'

'Get out.' Liza stood, trying to put herself between him and the girls.

Ignoring her, Fletch sniffed, tasting the remnants of the coke he'd just snorted. He crouched down where the girls were opening their few presents, which were mainly from other people.

'What have you got there, darlin?' Fletch aimed his question at Mandy.

'It's Barbie.'

Liza's heart pounded. 'Girls, come here . . . come here *now*.' Her voice was verging on the hysterical.

Fletch turned to her. 'Wind your neck in – you'll frighten them.'

'Don't tell me what to do with my own children.'

Liza opened her arms to them, and her daughters, picking up on their mum's tone, gave Fletch a nervous glance before running to her. But before Liza could stop him, Fletch reached out and grabbed Mandy.

'Put her down . . . put her *fucking down!*' Liza cried as he scooped her up in his arms.

Mandy started to cry. '*Mummy . . . Mummy . . . Mummy . . .*' Her eyes were wide with fear, mirroring her mother's.

Fletch raised his voice at Liza. 'I told you that you'd frighten them, and now look what you've done. Stupid bitch,' he sneered.

'Please, put her down . . . I'm *begging* you.'

Still holding Mandy, who was now in floods of tears, Fletch bent towards Liza. 'Have you got my fucking money?'

Liza's face was drawn in terror. Breathing heavily, she gave a tiny shake of her head. 'Not yet.'

Fletch's stare narrowed, and Liza had a clear view of the large black cross tattooed across the ridges of muscle on his neck.

'Not yet? You knew I was coming back, and you haven't bothered to get it?'

'It wasn't like that.'

'I don't fucking care what it was like. The long and short of it is, you haven't got it. So I reckon she's a fair exchange, don't you?' He strode towards the door and Liza let out a scream. She charged in front of him to try to block his way.

Fletch roared with laughter and placed Mandy down gently. 'Turn it in, darlin', I was only having a laugh. Fuck me, whatever happened to Christmas cheer?'

'YOU FUCKING BASTARD!' She charged at Fletch, pounding her fists against his chest. 'You think that was funny?'

Fletch batted her away easily. She fell backwards into Mandy, who tumbled to the floor with a shriek.

'Can't you shut her up? She's starting to do my head in,' Fletch grumbled as he wandered into the kitchen. He strolled around, opening and closing the fridge, then the empty oven. 'Where's the turkey?'

Liza didn't bother answering. She stood there, shaking, while Fletch continued to prowl around her kitchen. She felt violated. How dare he come in here, acting like he owned the place. She glanced across to the kettle, which she'd just used to make a mug of tea. She wondered if there was any boiling water left in there to throw at him. That thought soon passed, replaced by anger towards Jack.

This was all his doing. Why hadn't he told her there was no overtime to be had, that he couldn't make enough to cover the bills?

Deep down, though, she knew he'd kept it from her because he was worried how she'd cope. And, God, that made her feel guilty.

157

While Liza watched him, Fletch grabbed her handbag from the back of one of the kitchen chairs. He tipped the contents on to the kitchen table, snatched up her battered purse and unzipped it.

He pulled out a five-pound note.

'It's the only bit of cash I've got left,' Liza pleaded.

Smirking, Fletch tucked it into his jeans pocket. Artie had told him to double his efforts on collecting debts, along with the interest of course. Every little helped.

'So how is your old man?'

'I don't know.' Liza was telling the truth. 'He's still in hospital.'

Fletch pulled one of the chairs out and sat down. His muscular body filled the whole room, making it feel small. He rapped his fingers on the table as he contemplated what to do. 'This all sounds like it's going to be a bit of a problem. No dough, your old man laid up . . .' He leaned back in the chair and scanned the room for anything worth taking.

'Maybe . . .' Liza shrugged. 'I dunno, maybe you could wait until Jack has got back on his feet?'

'I ain't a charity, darlin', but I tell you what I'll do. Instead of insisting on the whole amount now, I'll let you pay it off in instalments. A little bit each week. How does that sound?'

Liza nodded eagerly. 'That would be good . . . thank you.' Her eyes sprang with tears of relief.

Fletch wiped his tongue over his teeth. 'So how about we say a hundred notes a week?'

'I . . . I can't afford that,' Liza gasped. 'I haven't got that sort of money . . .' She hated that she was trembling in front of this thug. 'And that's not a small amount.'

He laughed. A hollow sound. 'It is if you owe me a couple of grand.'

'A couple?' Liza wasn't sure if she'd heard him correctly.

'Why the surprise?'

She felt ill, and she found she needed to support herself with the kitchen worktop. 'You told me a grand – and that's what Jack said it was too. A bit over a grand.'

Fletch wagged his finger at her, the gold sovereign ring flashing in the light. 'That's right, but when you choose to pay in instalments, the interest goes up.' He shrugged. 'I can't be expected to be out of pocket.'

Liza did the maths.

'That's one hundred per cent interest. You can't do that.'

'Firstly, sweetheart, I can do what I want. Secondly, if you don't like it, you should've gone to TSB.' Fletch glanced through to where the few presents sat under the dog-eared artificial tree.

He strode through to the front room, which was furnished with an old burgundy three-piece suite and very little else, apart from some books and toys belonging to the girls, and a tall ugly wooden lamp in the corner.

'What's he doing, Mummy?' Mandy asked as she watched Fletch collect up the presents. 'Mummy, where's he taking them?'

Liza didn't reply.

Fletch smiled at Mandy, who sat cross-legged on the yellow-and-green carpet, staring up at him. 'Let's just say it's part of this week's instalment from your mummy.' He snatched the doll from her hands.

With all the girls now crying, Fletch crowed, 'Happy Christmas!' Balancing the presents in his arms, he headed for the door.

It was all Liza could do not to fly at him. She'd never hated anyone as much as this bastard.

Fletch turned to look at her. 'As I'm feeling generous, I'll give you exactly one week to come up with the next payment. So this time next week I'll expect my money – or that joke I made about taking your daughter will become a reality.'

Chapter Thirty

Joseph put down the phone, having managed to catch only half of what Liza had been saying between sobs. He'd got the gist of it, though, and had offered to go over straight away. Liza wasn't like the rest of them. She didn't tease him like the others did. Like Hennie had. Like Cheryl had.

Turning round, Joseph stared at his children, who were both on their hands and knees scrubbing the bloodstains out of the vinyl floor. He booted the bucket of soapy water. 'Make sure you get it all out.'

'Yes,' Bel muttered.

Joseph grabbed hold of her hair, tugging her head back. His steely eyes flashed with anger. 'You're forgetting something, aren't you?'

Bel knew better than to cry. 'I'm sorry . . . I mean, yes, Dad.'

Joseph smiled then, letting go of her hair. He stroked her head. 'There, that wasn't so hard, was it?'

'No, Dad.'

He crouched down next to her and began to twirl her hair in his fingers 'You're a good girl, Bel. Not like some of them. Not like your friend Stacey. You do know she'll end up a whore, just like her mother, don't you? You're not going to end up a dirty little bitch like your mother, are you, Bel?' Joseph's voice was smooth and quiet.

'No, Dad.' Bel kept on scrubbing. She tried not to shiver at his touch. She wished he wouldn't speak about her friend like that, or her mum. Her stomach suddenly tightened as a flash of her mum's bloodied face came into Bel's mind. She tried so hard not to think about things, but the memories would rush into her head, and she couldn't stop them, no matter how hard she tried. She remembered so clearly how her dad used to lock her mum up, tying her hands and wrists to the radiator so they'd blister and burn.

'Bel!'

Her dad's voice made her jump and the door shut on the memory.

'I hope you weren't thinking bad things?'

It was the same question he asked her all the time.

'No, Dad.'

Feeling his knees twinge, Joseph stood. Children were pure and he had to protect them and keep the streets clean from filth. 'What would I do without my precious children, eh, Zack?' He turned to his son, who, like Bel, was scrubbing the stains out of the floor. He had his head bowed low. There were things he'd seen that made him terrified of his father and made it difficult for Zack to even look at him.

'I'll be going out later, but I thought you'd like these.' He went into the top cupboard and pulled out some money. He handed two five-pound notes to each of them, then he reached back into the cupboard, grabbing a red hairbrush and a grey Parker pen. The brush went to Bel and the pen to Zack. 'Happy Christmas.' He smiled at them both.

'Thank you, Dad,' Zack mumbled.

'Thank you.' Bel turned the brush round in her hand. Usually her dad didn't even bother with Christmas for them. At the most he'd bring some sweets home, but that hadn't happened for a couple of years.

Joseph nodded. He'd found the items, along with a wad of money, in Hennie's bag. Most of her stuff had disgusted him – the tools of a whore – but the brush and pen had seemed perfect.

'Behave yourself, both of you. Finish washing the floor, then go straight to your room. Do I make myself clear?'

Bel and Zack nodded at the same time.

Satisfied, Joseph headed out of the kitchen, but at the door, he looked back at the floor, visions of Hennie coming into his mind. He entered his bedroom, shutting the door and unzipping his trousers. He pulled out his penis, beginning to caress it. Hennie. The stupid bitch had really thought that when he'd brought her back to the house, he was interested in her. How could she possibly think that someone like him would be interested in scum like her?

Joseph groaned as he thought of Hennie begging him not to hurt her. The look of terror and surprise on her face as he'd smashed his fist into her ugly face. Her high-pitched scream had almost deafened him when he'd brought down his foot and booted her hard in her stomach. That's when he'd pulled her dress up, taking the knife and slashing her tarty clothes off to expose her wrinkled tits and mound of pubic hair.

He moaned again. His breathing became heavier as he rubbed at himself harder and faster, while he remembered tracing the claw hammer down her naked body. He'd wanted to prolong her fear, so he'd only hit her once with the hammer. The memory of it penetrating her skull before he'd thrown her into the shallow grave made Joseph begin to climax.

Half an hour later, Joseph had changed, grabbed his keys off the hallway table and walked out of the house. Satisfied with how purposeful his life felt – picking off one by one the plague of whores that polluted the air, and cleaning up the streets – he hummed as he got into the car, smiling as he started up the engine.

What Joseph didn't see, though, was Danny watching him.

Chapter Thirty-One

The last thing Steph wanted was to spoil Stacey's Christmas, but it was a strain keeping up the pretence that all was well and she could see her daughter wasn't convinced. For once it was a relief when Pete showed up, giving her the excuse to nip out for a walk while he gave Stace her present.

Seeing the babygrow had completely thrown her. What at first appeared to be dried blood turned out to be red paint, but that didn't make it any easier to stomach. What kind of sick bastard would do a thing like that?

She picked up her pace, oblivious to her surroundings as she thought back to the other night when she'd collected the big bag of presents that the women had left there for her. She'd grabbed the bag without really taking much notice of what was in it. When they'd got home, Stacey had put them all under the tree.

It must have been left at the refuge by some pissed-off pimp or boyfriend; there was no way any of the women would have pulled a stunt like that. She made a mental note to ask Rachel if anyone unusual had come in.

But the mystery of how the parcel had got under her tree wasn't as worrying as the fact the sender had known what Andy was wearing on the day he'd died.

'Looking for business?'

Steph glanced in the direction of the voice and saw DS Walker driving alongside her, calling out of his car window. She would have liked to slap that smirk off his face. Even though they came from completely different walks of life, he reminded her of Pete. Two grown men acting like kids. No, worse than kids.

'You do know I could have you arrested for soliciting,' Fred chuckled.

Steph stopped walking and turned to face him. 'Haven't you got anything better to do on Christmas Day?'

'Oh, I could think of something.' He looked down towards his crotch.

'No wonder Rachel left you. Fucking arsehole.'

His face darkened then, and he pointed at her. 'I've warned you before – you need to be careful how you talk to me.'

'What is it about the men I'm surrounded by right now that they think they can behave how they want and not be pulled up about it?'

'What?' Fred frowned.

Steph's temper flared. 'Blokes like you, Fred, pathetic idiots getting off on trying to make people's lives a nightmare.'

'What do you expect?' Fred snarled. 'Mouthy women like you are just asking for trouble.'

'Like Rachel, you mean? Is that why you battered her – because she stood up to you?'

A horn blasted behind them, cutting Fred off before he could respond. Steph glanced over her shoulder and saw Joseph's van. He waved to her and slowed down to a stop. When he wound down the window, Steph noticed a woman sitting in the passenger seat beside him.

Guilty

As she crossed the road to speak to him, Fred sped off. What an idiot. Thank God for blokes like Joseph.

'Hello, Jo, you all right? How are the kids? Did Santa visit?' She gave a quick smile to the woman.

'Oh yeah, Father Christmas came all right.' Joseph laughed at some secret joke. 'This is Liza, by the way. She's had a bit of an upset.'

Steph glanced at Liza. 'I'm sorry to hear that, doll.'

Joseph turned off the engine. 'I'm pleased I saw you, actually. I was trying to tell Liza that maybe it wouldn't be the wisest of ideas for her to go to the police.'

Steph rolled her eyes. 'I wouldn't bother going to them for anything, if I were you. Let's just say I'm not their biggest fan.' She smiled again at Liza. 'What's it to do with anyway?'

'It's more a case of *who* it's to do with,' Joseph said.

Steph shivered. She hadn't bothered putting her coat on and now she was really feeling the cold. 'I'm still not following you.'

'Fletch has been up to his usual tricks.'

'Fletch?' She looked from Joseph to the woman. 'Big fucker? Fingers full of sovereign rings, and a massive black cross tattooed on his neck?'

Liza glanced at Joseph and then back at Steph. 'Yeah, that's him. That's who I'm talking about.'

Steph raised her pencilled-in eyebrows. She reached into her pocket for the packet of cigarettes and offered one to Liza and then to Joseph, both of whom shook their heads. Bending down to peer through the open window at Liza, she said, 'Jo's right. You really don't want to put in a report about Fletch –' she paused to light her cigarette, drawing the smoke into her – 'unless of course you've got a death wish.'

Liza frowned.

'If Fletch finds out you've gone to the Old Bill – and he will – he'll kill you. I don't know what he's done to you, darlin', and I'm not asking you to tell me, but, whatever it is, you going to the police will make things a hundred times worse.'

Liza burst into tears. 'What am I supposed to do? Just let him break into my house and threaten my daughters whenever he wants?' She covered her face with her hands.

Steph walked round to the passenger side, opened the door and crouched beside Liza, taking her by the hand.

'He's a loan shark, but he's also a nasty fucking bastard.' Steph shrugged. 'He's not scared of the police – he won't care what they say to him – but he *will* care that you've reported him. And it won't stop him getting what he wants.'

Liza began to shake. She knew what Steph was saying was true, but it didn't make it any easier to take. She was trapped in a nightmare. It wasn't as if she could just run away with her girls, tempting as it was. With nowhere else to go, she couldn't leave her home. But she couldn't face Fletch terrorising them. 'I've got three little girls and they've got no presents and no Christmas dinner.' Liza could hardly speak now. She felt so ashamed. How could she call herself a mother when she couldn't even provide for her children?

'Where are they now?' Steph asked.

'With my neighbour. I'll have to get back soon. I only left them so Jo could drive me to the police station, even though he advised against it.' She turned and gave Joseph a small smile.

Steph had an idea. 'I tell you what, why don't you go back and get them, and then Joseph can drop you off at a drop-in centre I run. We always do a big Christmas dinner and there'll be more than enough to go round.' She looked at Joseph. 'You okay to drop them off?'

'Er . . . No problem at all.'

'Good. That's settled then.' Steph stood up. 'There'll be loads of us there and loads of kids. It's mayhem, but it's fun. Music, games – it'll be a laugh. I know it's not going to solve your problems, but those can wait until tomorrow – believe me, I know . . . And if you're up for it we can find a quiet corner and have a chat. What do you say? Will you come along?'

It was the first time since the whole mess started that Liza had felt some relief. 'If you're sure, I'd love that. I know the girls would too. It's been a shit Christmas so far for them . . . *Thank you.*'

Steph winked at Liza. 'Come on, wipe those tears, and go and get your girls.' She smiled again.

'Can I give you a lift anywhere?' Joseph asked. He smiled at her warmly.

'No, it's fine, Jo. I like a bit of fresh air. I'll see you later.'

Steph watched them drive off and took a deep breath, then she began to stride towards home. After all it was Christmas, and she wasn't going to let any fucker spoil that.

Chapter Thirty-Two

'Who the fuck has he brought?'

Nancy was staring at Joseph in disbelief. He was done up like a kipper in a brown suit, white shirt and yellow paisley tie. In Nancy's opinion, the woman he was with didn't look that much better. She reminded Nancy of one of the conservative MPs on those flyers that were always being put through the letter box.

'Her name's Liza.' Steph lowered her voice. 'Be nice, Nance. She's going through a hard time.'

Nancy rolled her eyes and tutted. 'Ain't we fucking all?' And with that, she stomped off to get another sausage roll.

'Liza, I'm so glad you came.' Steph gave her a warm hug as she greeted her. 'And I'm guessing these are your lovely girls.' She knelt down so she was eye-level with them. 'And what's your name?'

The little girl looked shyly at Liza, who nodded encouragement. 'I'm Mandy, and I'm four.'

Steph grinned. 'Well, I'm Steph and it's lovely to meet you, Mandy. And are these your sisters?'

'Yeah.' She twirled her hair in her fingers. 'She's Jess and she's Bonny.' Mandy pointed.

'Well, all three of you look beautiful in your pretty dresses.

I tell you what, why don't you go and get some food from over there, where the other kids are,' Steph suggested.

They nodded and skipped off towards where a group of youngsters were dancing away, playing musical statues to a Slade cassette that Rachel had brought in.

'I can't tell you how grateful we are.' Liza sounded emotional. 'The place looks great.'

Steph smiled. It did look lovely. Last night, she'd dragged Stacey along to help her put up yet more decorations, and one of the market traders had given them a couple of Christmas trees, which they'd covered in fake snow so the place looked like a winter wonderland. All the women had dropped in on their regular punters who worked in shops, asking for donations; the men, none too pleased to have them show up at their place of work, had supplied them with food just to get rid of them. Margaret, the mother of one of Stacey's mates, had done most of the cooking.

The end result was an almighty feast, and enough presents for all the kids. It was something Steph did every Christmas. God knows, they all needed it more than ever this year.

Steph smiled at Liza. 'It's a pleasure, love. Christmas dinner should be arriving in an hour or so. In the meantime, how about I introduce you to some of the others . . .'

'Thanks for bringing her, Jo. Hopefully it'll take her mind off things.'

Joseph smiled at Steph, taking in her pink satin skirt and black satin blouse. She looked like the scrubby little whore she was. An old slut dressed up like a spring chick, but it amused him that she believed she looked smart.

'It wasn't any bother . . . You look lovely, by the way.'

He glanced around at all the whores. His mother had warned him about women like that, trying to contaminate him with their filth. He took a deep breath. His head was full of chatter, making it hard to concentrate on what Steph was saying.

'Are you going to go and pick up Bel and Zack now?' she asked, grabbing a cheese-and-pineapple stick and stuffing it into her mouth.

'No. They didn't want to come. They wanted to stay at home with all their presents.'

Steph nodded. 'That's like Stacey. I left her plastering her new make-up on her face.'

Joseph averted his gaze. He'd been right when he'd thought that Stacey was the same as her mother. 'Kids, eh.'

'So are you heading off now?'

'No, I thought I'd hang around a bit. Bel and Zack seemed quite happy without me.' He laughed. 'I can go though, if you'd rather a man-free zone?'

'You're fine, and Bill's over there anyway. But if you are staying, you've got to wear this.' Steph grabbed one of the party hats and shoved it on his head. 'You're king of the castle . . . Thanks for everything, Jo.' She gave him a quick peck on the cheek.

He reached up to adjust the party hat and saw her eyes dart to the scratches on his hand.

'Stupidly, I thought it would be fun to get Zack and Bel a kitten for Christmas.' He shrugged and grinned. 'I had to hide it for a week, and the bloody thing kept scratching me.'

Steph laughed too.

'Still, it was worth it to see their faces this morning,' Joseph continued. 'It cheered them up, I think. They always miss their mum even more around this time of year.'

Steph's eyes shone. 'I'm sure they loved it, Jo. No wonder they didn't want to come with you if they've got a new kitten. Listen, I'm going to mingle a bit. Go grab yourself some food from the buffet. Margaret's made enough to feed the five fucking thousand!'

'You've got some fucking cheek, coming here!'

The sight of Janey brought Nancy storming across the room in a rage. She still hadn't forgiven her for forcing Hennie to do a runner. There was no one for her to have a laugh with now. Hennie could always be relied on to make her feel better, no matter how shitty life got. Christmas just didn't feel the same without her.

'It's because of you that Hennie had to piss off. She stuck her neck out for you, but then you've always been a selfish bitch, ain't you. No one wants you around, so why don't you just fuck off.'

Janey might look fragile, but she could give it out when she wanted to. 'Who the fuck d'you think you're talking to?'

'I'm talking to you, because you're the only shady bitch in here.'

Janey stood up from the couch. She ripped off her party hat. 'Shady bitch, am I? Are you fucking having a laugh?'

Bill stepped between them. 'You're out of order, Nancy.'

'Oh, fuck off and keep out of it, unless you want a mouthful as well. In case you've forgotten, it was me who helped you out with Artie. I should've let him bury you.'

Steph hurried over. 'Bill, do as Nancy says and keep out of it.'

Bill glared. 'That's my missus she's talking about.'

People were starting to look over now.

'Is that before or after she's sucked half the dicks in Gillingham?' Nancy hissed at him before Steph could stop her.

'You fucking cow!' Janey pushed Nancy in the chest. 'You can't talk like that in front of my kids.'

'I wouldn't worry about that, sweetheart. They probably don't even know you're their fucking mum, the amount of time you spend with them.'

That was it.

Janey flew at Nancy, knocking her backwards into a tray of sausages on sticks, which flew across the room and clattered to the floor with a bang. Then Nancy, regaining her balance, grabbed Janey by the hair.

Janey screamed, twisting her body in an effort to free herself. She tried to bite Nancy's arm, but Nancy struck out with her elbow.

'Stop, for fuck's sake!' Steph shouted as some of the other women began to cheer on the fight while several kids started to cry.

'Get off her!' Bill grabbed Nancy's arm, and for his troubles he got Nancy's other elbow in his ribs. Janey took the opportunity to pull Nancy into a headlock and drag her to the floor, slapping her hard in the face.

'I said, *stop!* Stop being such selfish cows, both of you!'

Steph's words made no difference. The women ignored her and carried on rolling on the floor, fingernails clawing at each other. Steph was trying to pull them apart, but she didn't wanted to hurt either one of them.

'*Get off her, Nancy! I'm warning you!*' Bill bellowed.

Steph had to let go of the women to hold him back. She could not stand by and let a bloke raise his hand in here.

'Janey, that's enough . . . Nancy, no!' Steph yelled. She was furious with them both.

It looked as though Janey was starting to get the upper

hand, but as she moved to straddle her opponent Nancy screamed, 'Get the fuck off my stomach – I'm pregnant!'

Janey stopped.

She rolled off Nancy and stared at her wide-eyed. Apart from some kids crying and Cliff Richard crooning from the hi-fi, there was silence. All the women who worked for Artie knew what being pregnant meant.

'Oh fuck.' Nancy's eyes filled with tears. She hadn't meant to blurt it out.

Steph pulled Nancy up and caught sight of Joseph standing in the corner. She gave him an apologetic smile. She doubted he was used to the sight of women fighting.

Just as she was working out what to do next, the door opened.

A woman Steph had never seen before walked in and glanced around her at the chaos.

'Can I help you, love?' Steph asked.

'I'm Carol, and I'm looking for my mum. Her name's Hennie . . . She was meant to be coming to stay with me, but she never showed up. I was hoping that I might find her here.'

Chapter Thirty-Three

'I know she said she was going to come and see you at Christmas, but Hennie has never been the best at keeping to dates and times.' Steph was being tactful. It was an understatement.

'But she wrote it in the Christmas card she sent me. Look.' Carol pulled it from her jean pocket. Steph hid her smile. Hennie had obviously bought it from Julie. It was the same card design as she'd given her and Rob for the past few years.

'She said she was looking forward to spending Christmas with me, but we also spoke on the phone about it. I was expecting her last weekend.' Carol was clearly upset. She'd left her son, Bobby, with her mate. He had a nasty cold and hadn't slept properly for a week even though she'd given him Calpol. She wasn't feeling great herself. She was tired out, but when her next-door neighbour had said that he was driving down to Kent today to see his nan, she'd paid him a couple of quid towards the petrol, and hitched a lift.

Being a single parent was bloody hard, but it was better than living with her prick of a boyfriend, Brian. She'd thrown him out after he beat her up and stole her milk tokens, and there was no way she'd ever take him back. But she envied the other women at the toddler group who could always turn to their mums for support. That was why she'd been so happy to hear from Hennie, especially when she'd said she'd kicked the drug habit and was determined to stay clean.

Although her childhood had been pretty crappy, and she'd left home as soon as she could, Carol still loved her mum and wanted to have her about. She'd never judged her for being on the game, only for not being there when she needed her.

'This Christmas was supposed to be special,' Carol sniffed. 'I was looking forward to it – we both were.' London felt such a lonely city at times, but she knew if her mum was about everything would feel different. They could've taken Bobby to the zoo, had a laugh, done the weekly shopping at Tesco's together, and she could have finally given her mum the presents she'd bought her for her last three birthdays and Christmases on the trot, all of which were still sitting back at home in Finsbury Park.

Steph gave her a sympathetic smile. 'Look, I'm sure she's just met up with a friend or something.'

'No, she promised she'd come last weekend,' Carol insisted. 'Something must have happened.'

Joseph spoke up. 'Sorry, I don't mean to stick my nose in, but that fits with what Hennie told me.'

This was news to Steph. 'What are you talking about, Jo? And why are you only mentioning it now?'

'I had no idea there was a problem.' He looked at Carol. 'I saw Hennie last Saturday. She was in a bit of a state. She said she was on her way to see you and she had to get out of the area as soon as she could. I offered to give her a lift, but she didn't want one.' His tone was flat. 'I'm sorry. I wish I'd insisted. I did think at the time that she seemed scared.'

'What do you mean, scared?' Carol asked, and Steph could hear the concern in her voice.

'She talked about Artie. She was terrified he was going to kill her,' Joseph added.

'Oh my God.' Carol's eyes were wide open. She looked at them all.

'What else did she say?' Steph turned back to Joseph.

'Well, I was trying to persuade her to let me drive her to London. I wouldn't have minded, seeing how upset she was. She mentioned going over to the bus depot in Dartford. I think . . .' Joseph hesitated

'Go on, Jo. Spit it out,' Steph urged him.

'I got the impression she wanted to earn a bit of money. She didn't say as much, but . . .' He glanced at Carol. 'I don't mean to offend.'

'No, it's fine. I know what my mum does. I just want to make sure she's all right.'

'She didn't want Artie to know where she was going,' Joseph continued. 'I don't know why.'

Steph did. Artie had been gunning for Hennie since he'd found out she was the one who'd stolen his money. Come to think of it, wasn't that last Saturday? She only hoped that Artie hadn't caught up with her and done something stupid.

'Why don't I have a drive around later, Steph? Maybe you could tell me her old haunts?' Joseph asked.

'Sure, and thanks, Joseph.'

He nodded. 'And if we don't find her today, I'll have a scout around tomorrow.' He smiled at Carol.

'Thanks, but maybe I should go and speak to this Artie,' Carol suggested.

'*No*,' Steph answered quickly.

She looked up and saw that Nancy was heading for the door

'Nance . . . Nance, are you leaving?' Steph called. 'Sorry, give me a minute, will you?'

Leaving Carol and Joseph, she ran to catch Nancy before she left. 'Nance, why don't you stay for a bit of turkey. It should be ready soon.'

'I've lost my appetite. Janey's a fucking skanky bitch. I hate her.'

'Well, why don't you come and speak to Carol instead? She's worried about her mum.'

Nancy shrugged. She looked miserable. 'You know as well as I do what Hennie's like. She'll turn up. She probably went on a bender on Artie's money . . . Besides, I've got my own bloody problems to think about now I've opened my big fucking mouth.'

'What are you going to do?'

'I haven't much choice, have I? I'm going to get the fuck out of here. I'm not staying around for Artie to hear the news from Janey. I'm going to get my stuff together and then, later, I'm going to pay a visit to this baby's dad.'

She placed her hand on her stomach and gazed around the room. 'It's time he took some responsibility for what's happened.'

'Nance, please don't go off like this,' Steph pleaded.

'I've made up my mind.'

'Then at least promise me you'll stay in touch, let me know you're all right, won't you?'

Nancy welled up. 'Of course I will.'

'I love you.' Steph gave her a hug.

'I love you too.'

'Promise you'll call me later, or tomorrow. I need to know you're okay.'

'I will – I swear.'

As Nancy walked out, from the other side of the room, Janey watched her go. 'Good fucking riddance to that BITCH!' she shouted. 'She thinks she's better than everyone else. Just wait till Artie finds out that she's PREGNANT,' she yelled after her again.

Liza, who was sitting next to Janey, started to move away.

'Don't mind me.' Janey glanced at her and smiled. 'Me and Nancy are always arguing. We don't mean nothing by it most of the time.'

Liza's expression suggested she didn't think the fight had looked like nothing, but she made no comment.

'What's your story, anyway?' Janey enquired as she nibbled on a twiglet.

'Nothing much.' Liza didn't feel comfortable telling this woman who had the look of a drug addict.

'Oh, come on, you wouldn't be sitting here on Christmas Day in a fucking women's refuge if there wasn't something up.' Janey frowned at her. 'What is it, your old man beat you up?'

Liza shook her head.

'He's been touching the kids?'

'No, of course, not. He's a great dad.'

Janey tilted her head. 'Has he got a habit?'

Liza felt under pressure. 'No, no he hasn't. He's a good man and he works hard.' Sadness overwhelmed her because it was true. Jack was a good man. He'd always protected her, always loved her and the girls, but he'd made a stupid mistake and now she was punishing him for it. Once more, Liza was overwhelmed with her own shame.

'Then what?' Janey wouldn't let it go.

'We owe money. A lot of money.'

Janey looked disappointed. 'Is that it?'

'We owe money to a loan shark, and we can't pay it off.'

Janey had started to lose interest now. 'So what's the big fucking deal? Pay it off and stop moaning about it. There are people here with real problems,' she snarled.

Liza watched her girls on the other side of the room playing with some of the other kids. They were having a great time. 'That's what I'm saying – we can't. My husband's in hospital and I haven't got a job.'

Janey shrugged. 'Like I say, I can't see what the fucking drama's about. Use what's between your legs – that's what we all do, one way or another. Trust me – it'll solve all your problems . . .'

Chapter Thirty-Four

Bel was creeping along the gloomy hallway. Zack had gone to his room as soon as they'd finished washing up the blood, and wouldn't risk coming out in case Dad came home and found them. But it was so rare that he left without locking them in that she wasn't going to waste the opportunity.

They'd moved in around three years ago. Before that, they'd moved from rented house to rented house, always in the Medway area, but far enough apart that they had to change schools each time. It was the first time they'd had a home of their own and the longest they'd stayed in one place. The old lady who'd owned the house before them had been one of Dad's meals on wheels clients. She'd left it in a right state – not that it was much better now, especially this side of the house, which she wasn't supposed to be in. The beige wallpaper was peeling off, there were large damp spots dotted with mould and in the corner a big pile of rubbish bags filled with the old lady's belongings.

The first time she'd come in here, she'd found a dead rat covered in flies and maggots. She'd known what the smell was before she saw it; that wasn't the first time she'd smelled a dead body . . . Memories of her mum flashed through her mind: the way she'd plead with Dad when he yelled at her, calling her names, the same sort of names he called Steph. The times he'd tie her to a chair and gag her so she couldn't answer back. Bel couldn't actually remember a time when her mum had ever left the house, although her dad always accused her of sneaking out to meet men whenever his back was turned.

She remembered the times she'd helped her mum get into a bath of salt water to try to heal the wounds; the times her mum would ask her to put Sudocrem on her back, the feel of the cuts and weals under her small fingers as she traced the wounds her dad had inflicted.

Bel gulped down her tears as she battled to force the memories from her mind. Instead she thought of the old tabby cat she'd hidden away upstairs, and after a minute or two she'd calmed down enough to climb the staircase.

The cat was the reason she'd risked sneaking over to this side of the house. Dad would never let them have pets – he didn't allow *any* animals in the house – but when Bel first spotted the cat in the garden a couple of weeks ago, it was so thin it could barely stand. It felt wrong to leave it out there in the cold, so she'd brought it indoors and hidden it in an attic bedroom that was never used.

The room was in an even worse state than the rest of the place. The floorboards were broken, the plaster was falling off the walls, and the floor was strewn with rubbish: empty medicine bottles, rusty tins, an old kettle, even a car exhaust pipe. In the far corner was a stained mattress and a broken leather chair with the springs sticking out of it.

Bel wandered over to the cardboard box she'd turned into a bed for the cat. She slammed her hand over her mouth. Tears pricked her eyes . . . Oh no, *no*. She dropped to her knees. The cat wasn't moving.

Bel put her head close to it to see if it was breathing . . . It wasn't. Her heart sank . . . She supposed it *had* been very old, and at least it had spent the last couple of weeks of its life indoors. That was something.

She was going to miss looking after it, even though it had meant disobeying her dad by leaving her room and creeping up here. Breaking the rules had consequences that terrified Bel, but it was worth it to have something to ease the crushing loneliness she felt. Of course she loved her brother, and was protective of him, but he'd withdrawn into himself and it was all she could do to reach him.

As she picked up the box with the cat in, she thought she heard something moving on the floor below her. She set the box down and listened. There was creak of stairs.

Footsteps.

She knew it wasn't Zack – he was too afraid to come to this side of the house.

Her heart thumping, she spun round, looking for somewhere to hide. The only option was the leather chair. She darted behind it and kept as still as she could. The footsteps were coming closer. All Bel could do now was wait, and hope that whoever it was didn't see her . . .

Chapter Thirty-Five

Danny had been watching as Joseph Potter left the house, booted and suited, looking like a proper mug. He'd climbed in his van and driven off; presumably someone had invited him to Christmas dinner. Danny was hoping he wouldn't be back any time soon.

The first time he'd set eyes on the guy swanning out of his mum's old house like lord of the fucking manor, he'd been tempted to march straight up to the cunt and sort him out. The only thing that stopped him was the thought of being banged up in Maidstone again so soon – giving Potter a clump would be a one-way ticket. Sorting Potter out would have to wait until he'd dealt with Artie and Fletch.

Danny had given it twenty minutes or so before letting himself into the house. His mum's key had been on his keyring when he'd been nicked four years ago, so it had been returned to him on his release, along with the rest of his clobber.

It was always strange to be out after a stretch, but stranger to be back in his mum's house. It was fucked up. He'd had a good nosey around downstairs: everywhere looked the same – almost. Weird thing was most of the doors had large bolts so they could be padlocked from outside. Even the fridge had a padlock on it. Fuck knows why. But, apart from that, nothing had changed. It was still a cold, miserable place.

A couple of rooms were padlocked, but now wasn't the time to break in and see what he was keeping in there. He thought he'd heard someone moving about in one of the bedrooms, but he couldn't be sure. Perhaps Potter kept a dog in there; he wasn't stupid enough to go and find out. Right now, the only thing he needed to focus on was Artie, although that was easier said than done when he couldn't stop thinking about Steph.

Had he really been so fucking naive as to think they could pick up from where they'd left off? He knew in his gut what she'd said about there being nothing between them was bull-shit. He'd fucked enough women to know that what they had was more than just sex. Even now, he reckoned they had a future. Once Artie was out of the picture.

The stench that greeted him when he reached the top of the stairs brought him right back to the here and now. Christ, it stank! This side of the house had always been a shit hole. It was even worse than he'd remembered. His mum had struggled to keep such a big house clean and had closed this section off a long time ago. Which was why it had been the perfect place to hide his stuff.

Danny walked into the attic room and glanced around. There was rubbish everywhere. Frowning, he picked up one of the empty prescription bottles. The label had been torn off. The rest of them were the same. Danny threw it down and walked further into the room.

Fucking hell! There was a dead cat in a cardboard box – no wonder the place smelled so bad. Eager to do what he'd come for and then get out of there, he crossed to the far side of the room and knelt down by the skirting board. The nails were rusty, which allowed him to lever a couple of floorboards up without the bother of using the crowbar he'd brought with him.

Jamming his hand inside the floor space, Danny rummaged around . . . *Fucking bingo!* He smiled as he dragged out the holdall he'd hidden here a year or so before he'd been banged up. He opened it and pulled out the sawn-off shotgun, along with a handgun. He shoved his hand in again and dragged out a sealed bag.

It was just like he'd left it. Five grand and half a kilo of coke. It wasn't a king's ransom – far from it – but it would be enough to set him up for a short while, giving him a chance to work out the best way to bring down Artie and Fletch.

Tossing everything back into the holdall, he got to his feet and muttered, 'Let the fucking games begin.'

A sound from the other side of the room caught his attention. Danny reached for the gun and rushed to where the noise was. Without taking the time to look, he reached behind the chair grabbed whoever it was by their hair, keeping the gun aimed at their head as he dragged them out.

'*What the fuck are you doing?*'

'I'm sorry, I'm sorry . . . I'm sorry.'

Only then did Danny realise it was a young girl. A terrified one at that.

'Who are you?' he growled, releasing his grip. Scaring the fuck out of kids wasn't his thing. She couldn't have been more than thirteen. Still, he didn't know who she was and what she'd seen.

'I . . . I'm . . . I'm Bel.' She struggled to get the words out.

'What the fuck are you doing up here, spying on me?' Danny glared at her, but seeing how terrified she was he lowered the gun.

'I . . . I wasn't. I promise . . . I live here.'

Danny frowned. 'Here?'

Bel nodded.

He'd presumed that she was some tearaway, breaking in to people's houses when they were out, like he and his mates used to do when they were teenagers. He had no idea anyone apart from Joseph lived here. When he'd walked through the house, there'd been no Christmas decorations, nothing to suggest there was a kid living here. Still, that was none of his fucking business, was it? What people did or didn't celebrate was down to them.

'What did you see?' Danny snapped. 'What did you see me doing?'

'I didn't see anything.' She looked as if she might throw up.

'Are you sure?'

'Yeah . . . I had my eyes shut.'

Danny stared at Bel as she looked up at him from underneath her fringe. He wasn't sure whether to believe her.

'If I find out you *did* see something' – Danny wasn't happy about having to threaten her, but he couldn't risk her talking – 'and you open your mouth about it, 'I'll come back here and use this gun on you.' He felt like a cunt, seeing how she shrank away from him.

Bel nodded again, unable to speak.

'Okay, I'm glad we understand each other.' He picked up his holdall and made for the door.

'*Wait!*'

Danny slowly turned round. To say he was surprised that she was brave enough to call him back was an understatement. He tilted his head. 'What?'

Trying to stop herself from shaking, Bel clenched her hands into a ball. 'You . . .' She stopped then.

Danny shrugged. He was curious now. 'Go on.'

'You . . . you won' t tell my dad you saw me up here, will you?'

Of all the things that Danny thought she was going to say, this wasn't on the list. 'I don't know your dad,' he answered matter-of-factly. 'Besides, I ain't a grass.'

Bel didn't say anything else.

Danny reached into his pocket and pulled out a Fry's Peppermint Cream bar he'd bought earlier. 'Take it – go on.'

Bel didn't move.

'Go on.'

She held his stare, then with her hand shaking she reached for it.

Danny gave her a crooked smile, his handsome face full of warmth. 'Now remember what I said: keep your mouth shut.'

Again, Bel didn't answer. She pocketed the chocolate to share with Zack later – it was bound to cheer him up.

As Danny headed out of the room and back down the stairs, an unsettling thought crossed his mind. Why did he get the impression that the girl seemed more scared of her dad finding out she was in that room than she was of him pointing his gun at her?

Chapter Thirty-Six

Steph was on a mission. She'd left Hennie's daughter at her house watching a James Bond film and eating a box of Quality Street with Stacey. Now, as she picked up her pace, eager to reach her destination and get out of the rain, her thoughts turned to Liza. She wished she'd been able to have a proper chat with the poor cow, but they'd only managed to have a quick word. Still, she'd got her number and she'd give her a call tomorrow to see how she was getting on.

Pausing at the door to shake the rain off her brolly, she barged into the pub.

The place was heaving, which was to be expected on Christmas night.

Even though Steph was a smoker herself, she felt her eyes start to burn from the smoke haze hanging over the room. The music was banging out: Kenny Loggins on the hi-fi, struggling to be heard over the drunken voices.

Steph weaved her way through the crowd, giving a wave to Sharon behind the bar. She looked back at her, red-faced and frazzled. She was dressed in a tight pink miniskirt and a cream blouse, which was unbuttoned to show off her lacy black bra.

'All right, darlin'? Happy Christmas!' Steph leaned over the sticky wooden bar and gave Sharon a kiss on her cheek. 'How's it going?'

Sharon shrugged and glanced around. 'It's been like this since we opened – fucking madhouse! I haven't even had time to take a piss. You all right?'

Steph nodded and shouted over the din. 'Yeah, good, thanks . . . Are they here?'

'*Come on, love! I'm dying of thirst here.*' A punter was banging his empty pint glass on the bar, demanding service.

Ignoring him, Sharon rolled her eyes and focused on Steph. 'If you're talking about Pinky and fucking Perky, they're in the back.'

Steph left Sharon to deal with the irate punter and pushed her way through the throng to the double glass doors. In the dim hallway beyond, the sound was muted. She carried on past the fire exit until she reached the private room where Artie and Fletch were.

She barged in without knocking.

Artie was hunched over a fat line of coke, and one of his toms was butt naked and on her knees with Fletch's dick in her mouth.

Steph looked at the woman. 'Trish, can you give us a moment, darlin'?'

Tricia raised her eyes past Fletch's dark mound of pubic hair. He nodded and pushed her off.

Grabbing her things, she tottered past Steph looking relieved and mouthing a silent *thank you* as she made her exit.

'Fancy finishing me off, Steph?' Fletch nodded to his erect penis.

'Wind your neck in, Fletch – that's fucking out of order.' Artie threw a dark stare at him. Steph was with Rob – no one else. And that's the way it was going to stay. Just because Rob was laid up didn't mean it was all right for Fletch – no matter how off his nut he was – to be disrespectful. He'd have a word with him later.

Fletch zipped himself up, glared at Steph, then turned his attention to pouring himself a line of coke and chopping it up. 'What the fuck do you want anyway?'

'First off, I want a word with him.' Steph pointed at Artie. 'Guess who I've just seen, Art?'

Artie sighed. She was spoiling his buzz. 'How the fuck should I know?' He shrugged. 'Goldilocks and three fucking bears.'

Steph walked up to where he was sitting. She kicked one of the chairs out of the way. Then stared down at him, suddenly feeling overwhelmed by the entire situation. 'This isn't a joke, Art. I saw Carol. Hennie's daughter. She's looking for her mum.'

'What the fuck has that got to do with me?'

'What have you done with her?' Steph hadn't wanted Carol to worry any more than she already was, but when Joseph had implied that Artie had something to do with Hennie's disappearance, it had started alarm bells ringing in her head. 'I swear to God, Artie, you better not have done anything to her.'

Artie jabbed his finger in the air. 'Where the fuck do you get off giving it the big 'un? What I do or don't do with my whores is my business, especially when they're thieving bitches.'

'Well, I'm making it my business too. Hennie's my mate, and her daughter showed up this afternoon saying she'd been expecting her for Christmas and she never turned up.'

'Why are you getting your tits in a twist over it? She's a fucking whore!'

The shock of finding that Babygro under her Christmas tree had left Steph's emotions in turmoil. Her usual tactic with a coke-fuelled Artie would be to tread carefully, but her temper had been simmering all day and she was in no mood for his bull-shit. 'You've done something to her, haven't you? Where is she?'

Artie slammed his fist down on the table, sending up a cloud of coke. 'I don't know – and if I did she'd be a fucking goner.'

Steph saw the smirk on Fletch's face. She turned on him. 'Do you know something?'

Laughing, Fletch raised his hands in the air. 'Don't start shooting me down. You crack on with Artie – leave me out of it.'

'Really?' Steph was on a roll. 'You think your shit doesn't smell? From what I hear, your shit smells worse than anyone's.'

Fletch squeezed the bridge of his nose. 'Do me a fucking favour' – he glanced at Artie – 'sort her out, will you? This bitch doing my nut in.'

Steph wasn't about to back down. 'You know, I met a woman today: she's in bits. She's got three kids and she's terrified. One of her daughters said to me, "Mummy's scared of the bad man coming back." She was talking about you, Fletch.' Steph shook her head in disgust. 'You can't get much more lowlife than that, can you? Rob would be ashamed of you – both of you.'

'Don't you fucking bring him into it!' The anger in Fletch's eyes changed to pain. Rob had been his best mate; in his fucked-up way, he was as devastated by the loss as Artie.

'Why not?' Steph shrugged. 'It's true. I don't even fucking recognise who you are any more.'

Fletch got up. 'Fuck this, I'm going for a piss. I can't deal with this shit.' He marched across the room, stopping in front of Steph to snarl at her: 'You should be careful, Saint Steph – one day, someone's gonna knock off your fucking halo.' Then he stormed out, leaving her and Artie alone.

It wasn't lost on Steph that a lot of blokes weren't happy to have her around. Still, after years of being on the game, she was used to men hating on her.

'Can't you do something about it? He's got this woman – Liza, her name is – fucking petrified. Get him to back off with the interest or something. You're his business partner, so you have a say in it as well.'

Artie picked up the five-pound note he'd rolled up earlier, and snorted another line. He held his nostrils, breathing it in and making sure none of the coke spilled back down his nose.

He brought his stare slowly back to Steph. 'You want me to ask him to back off?'

Feeling the heat from the fire, Steph nodded.

'What do you think will happen then, eh? If we let this woman and everyone who's got a sob story off, how the fuck do you think I'm going to pay Rob's hospital fees? Don't get me wrong, I'll spend however much it fucking costs to keep him alive . . .'

He paused to take another line of coke, and it was a moment before he spoke again.

'. . . But to do that, Steph, I've got to make sure those women earn as much as they can, and people who borrow money from me pay it back when they say they will. They know what they're signing up for. They know the name of the game.'

Artie closed his eyes for a beat, then opened them and glared at Steph. 'So before you come around here, shouting the fucking odds like *your* shit don't smell, remember: we both want the same thing. And that costs.'

Steph shook her head. 'You're not being fair, Artie.'

He laughed nastily. 'Since when is life fucking fair?'

Chapter Thirty-Seven

It was dark and the car-park lights gave off a dim glow, just enough for Danny to see Steph hurrying away from the pub. She looked upset, and he wanted to go to her, but he stopped himself, knowing that if he did, it could ruin his plans.

Pushing Steph out of his mind, he turned to Bill. 'You all right, mate?'

'Could be better.' Bill stood in the shadows. He felt out of his depth, but he could hardly refuse Danny, given he was the one who'd invited him to get involved in the first place.

Danny winked. 'Just keep your mouth shut, and you'll be fine. No one will know it's you.'

Bill nodded and pulled down his balaclava. Danny glanced around, making sure no one was about. He checked his watch, and gave a quick hand signal to Bill, then he knocked and waited.

It took a minute for the double doors to be opened.

Sharon's face appeared. 'All right?' She checked over her shoulder, and Danny could see how nervous she was. 'Coast is all clear. Come on through.'

'Thanks for this. I won't forget it.' Danny gave her a quick kiss on the cheek as he and Bill followed her in.

'I'll keep this door unlocked for you.'

Without another word, she hurried off across the cold beer

cellar and up the chipped concrete stairs. Once they were in the darkened corridor, she lowered her voice. 'It's down there. That door.' She pointed.

Danny could hear the noise of the pub and the sound of the drunken punters.

'When I go back through to the bar,' she continued, 'I'll put the bolt on, so no one can come in or out of this area. But you've only got five minutes – that's all I can give you.'

'That's all I need, love. Trust me.'

Sharon turned away, but Danny gripped her arm gently. 'I'm going to sort this, all right? Believe me, this is only the start of it.'

He let her go then, and turned to Bill. 'Remember what I said: keep your fucking balaclava on and, whatever you do, keep your mouth shut. Otherwise they'll recognise your voice.'

'What about you?' Like Sharon, Bill kept his voice low.

'Oh, I'm fine, mate. I'm looking forward to this.' And with those words Danny raised his sawn-off shotgun and marched down the corridor. Seconds later, he booted the door open with Bill close behind him.

'Long time no fucking see, eh?' Danny snarled at Artie and Fletch as he pointed the gun at them. 'Surprised to see me, gents?'

The two men spun round at the same moment. They were shocked, but their reactions were dulled by the coke and booze. When Danny kicked the table, Fletch tried to stand up but struggled to keep his balance. The hatred on his face was clear enough though.

'You've got a fucking death wish,' Fletch growled, his words slurred.

Danny laughed and leapt forward to slam the butt of his

shotgun into Artie's head. The skin tore open, spurting blood all over his face.

'*You fucking cunt!*' Artie roared as he fell to the ground, too dazed by the clump to do anything about it.

Danny grabbed him by the hair and dragged his head back. He pressed the shotgun to Artie's temple. Bill was keeping the handgun pointed at Fletch.

'I could blow you away right now,' Danny hissed.

'*Fuck you!*'

Danny expertly twisted the gun in his hand to bring the butt of it down on Artie's face a second time. There was a crunch as it struck his nose.

Despite all the booze and gear in his system, Artie yelled in agony.

'This is a little courtesy call, gents.' Danny let Artie's head go, then stepped back and launched a kick that connected with Artie's ribs. Then he nodded to Bill and began to back out of the door. 'Your days are fucking numbered round here. This is my patch, and I'm taking it back . . . You've been warned.'

With Bill close behind him, Danny hurried along the corridor and down into the cellar. He hadn't wanted Artie and Fletch to hear through the grapevine that he was out. He'd needed to show them that he still was a player. If they'd known it was only Bill behind the balaclava, it would have ruined the effect. Danny had been in this game long enough to know that it was like playing poker. Even if you had a bad hand, you never let your opponent know that. And right now Danny knew he'd left the cunts worried and that was all that mattered for the time being.

Danny and Bill had disappeared into the night by the time Artie and Fletch made it to the car park.

'FUCK!' Artie roared. His face was covered in blood, and his nose was broken. He'd been caught completely off guard. He'd had no idea that Danny was out.

Seething, he glanced at Fletch. 'That cunt is going to wish he was back inside by the time I've finished with him.'

Fletch was too angry to speak. Like Artie, he hadn't known Danny was out. It made him feel like a mug. And no one made a mug out of Fletch.

'Artie . . . *Artie.*'

Artie turned towards the voice coming from behind the wheelie bins.

'What the fuck are you doing here? Fuck off and go back to work.'

Janey pulled a face. 'Fine, have it your way.'

Artie brought back his fist and smashed her in her face. She tumbled to the wet ground. 'I've had my fill of fucking cunts today. You know what's good for you, you'll get back to work, you stupid cow.'

Janey licked away the blood pouring from her split lip. It hurt, but not as much as it hurt to go cold turkey. Bill had nagged her to stay in with the kids, but she'd waited for him to go out, then slipped out herself. She didn't see the big deal: they were asleep in their cots, and if they woke up, all they'd do was cry themselves back to sleep. Not that she thought they would – she'd dipped their dummies in a tiny amount of the methadone left over from when Bill tried to wean her off the gear.

What choice did she have? She needed a fix, so looking after the kids wasn't her first priority. Problem was, Christmas night was always quiet, and she hadn't been able to pick up any punters. She'd come to the pub hoping Artie would feel in the Christmas spirit and slip her a bag. Not that he ever let her have it for free; he added it to her tab. The way she was going, she'd owe him for life.

'Go on, piss off before I give you something to cry about,' Artie growled, wishing she'd get her miserable fucking face out of his sight.

'I need a fix,' she whined. She could feel the cold sweat creeping over her, and cramps in her stomach.

'Then open your cunt and get someone to fuck it. Earn your keep.'

Janey sidled up to him, her beady eyes darting over his face. 'I've got some information for you.'

'What information?'

'I know something about tonight. About Danny.' She licked her lips. 'And I reckon what I've got to tell you is worth a fix.'

Artie looked at Fletch then back at Janey. He grabbed her arm and roughly pulled her inside.

'Then you better start talking . . .'

Chapter Thirty-Eight

While Artie and Fletch were listening to what Janey had to say, Liza was on the phone. She'd only picked it up because she'd thought it might be Steph and she was hoping she'd made good on her promise to have a word with Fletch. Not that Liza was holding out much hope he'd give them extra time to pay. He didn't seem the type to take pity on anyone.

But the voice on the other end of the phone had been Jack's. And he'd had more bad news for her.

'Liza, *Liza*, are you there?'

She cupped the mouthpiece of the receiver. She couldn't speak.

'Liza, please, for fuck's sake say something.'

The phone still pressed to her ear, she stared out of the kitchen window. The girls were fast asleep. By the time they'd got home, they'd been exhausted, almost too tired for the bubble bath she'd run for them. The minute their heads hit the pillow, they'd been out like a light.

As Christmas days went, it had been a success, especially with the girls. They'd stuffed themselves with a lovely turkey dinner and trifle. They'd even won a couple of games of pass the parcel, though Liza suspected that Rachel had deliberately waited until one of her three was holding it to stop the music. Most of the women had been lovely, the only exception being Janey. All she'd done was bitch about the others and ignore her two kids.

After the shitty start their day had got off to, the trip to the refuge had been just what they needed. And now here was Jack with news she could do without.

'Liza . . . Liza . . . *Please*, darlin', say something.'

'What do you expect me to say?' Her voice came out as a whisper as she sat in the dark.

'Anything: shout at me, tell me I'm an arsehole, say anything, but don't give me the silent treatment.'

Tears filled Liza's eyes, but she hurriedly wiped them away. She reached for the bottle of Valium, unscrewed the top and tipped one out, and a couple extra. She just couldn't cope right now. 'It's . . . it's a shock, Jack. I thought when you came out of hospital you'd be back on your feet in no time.'

'The doctors aren't sure how long it will be. It's because of where the nerve damage is. It might be only a couple of months or so.'

'A couple of months? And you're going to tell Fletch that, are you?'

'I can get around a bit. Maybe in a few weeks I'll be able to drive, and Ricky said he'll ask around, see if anyone's looking for a delivery driver. In the meantime, maybe I can get myself a desk job.'

Liza didn't know whether to laugh or cry. Only a few hours ago, she'd been feeling guilty for giving Jack a hard time. This phone call had brought the anger flooding back.

'A desk job? The only time you've picked up a pen in the last ten years is to write a name of a horse down at the frigging bookies.' She felt more alone than ever before. 'So what now, hey? Are we supposed to give Fletch a sick note?'

'Liza, listen—'

'I'm done with fucking listening to you. You're the one who dumped us in this shit.' She slammed down the phone, then with a surge of anger grabbed it and threw it across the room before sinking into a heap on the floor.

It took her a while to calm her breathing and stand up. She needed a drink. Not tea – this called for something stronger. Maybe a bit of vodka mixed with her Valium would do the trick. She didn't want to spend another night staring at the clock, knowing that each minute that went by was another minute closer to Fletch's next visit, terrified of what he'd do when she told him there was no money.

Shaking, she went to the cupboard and took out the bottle of Smirnoff. Then she grabbed her *World's Best Mum* mug and poured herself a large drink.

It hit the spot, and straight away Liza closed her eyes.

She thought about calling Joseph. Then she changed her mind. She'd leaned on him enough already. She couldn't tear him away from his family twice in the same day.

Her thoughts drifted back to the women at the shelter, but especially Janey. She might be a druggie and a bitch, but maybe she'd been right when she said, *Use what's between your legs . . . It'll solve all your problems.*

Liza took another gulp of vodka. She could feel herself getting drunker by the minute as she stood in front of the mirror and stared at herself. Putting down her mug, she shook her hair out of the scrunchie, letting it tumble down to her shoulders. She turned to one side, then the other; she'd put on quite a bit of weight over the years, but there was still a figure there. Her boobs weren't down to her waist, and her bum was still as big and round as it had always been. She sighed and turned away.

By the time Liza went next door to ask the neighbour to watch the kids for her, she was completely off her face . . .

Chapter Thirty-Nine

Liza was in a drunken haze from her vodka-Valium cocktail. She'd been walking for what seemed ages, oblivious to the rain. She had a vague recollection of seeing Steph hurrying along the road at some point, and ducking behind a row of cars to avoid being seen. She had no idea where she was now or what time it was – everything was so fuzzy, except for her fear of Fletch.

She found herself in a lane that was lit only by a couple of dim streetlights. The rain seemed to have stopped. There were women hanging around, smoking and laughing amongst themselves. Despite the cold, they were hardly wearing any clothes. Passing cars were slowing down as they kerb-crawled past the women, who paraded up and down on their six-inch heels, rolling their hips from side to side.

A Ford Escort came to a stop and a tall blonde bent down to speak to the driver. A moment later the woman got into the car and it drove off, the lights disappearing into the distance.

Liza pulled up her collar and made her way past the women.

'Who the fuck are you?'

Liza turned to find the women standing behind her, hands on hips.

She opened her mouth, but she wasn't sure what to stay so she just stood peering at them in the dim light.

'Cat got your fucking tongue?' sneered a dark-skinned woman in thigh-high patent boots, a skirt that showed her red knickers, and a crop top stretched to the limit by her boobs.

'Sorry . . . sorry, I shouldn't be here.' The words came out slurred. Liza had sobered up enough for panic to set in. What the hell had she been thinking?

'Too fucking right you shouldn't be here, darlin'.' The woman blocked her way, folding her arms. 'What business you got coming here?'

Liza said the first thing that came into her head. 'I . . . I thought Janey might be here.'

'I don't know who the fuck Janey is. Do you, girls?'

The other women shook their heads.

'Never heard of her,' said one.

The dark-skinned woman turned back to Liza. 'Looks like you're a lying bitch then, don't it?'

'You reckon she's Old Bill, Jean?' This from another of the women.

Jean looked Liza up and down. 'Nah, she ain't Old Bill. More likely she thinks she can come here and work on our patch.'

Liza shook her head. 'That's not what I'm doing, I swear. I thought I'd come and speak to Janey some more, that's all. I saw her earlier at—'

'Saying her name again won't make me know her, love. You think I don't know your game? This is our area, and there's no way we're gonna let some snotty cow like you come here and steal our punters.'

'I swear I wasn't—'

Jean spat at her, then she nodded to the others, who immediately piled in. One grabbed a handful of hair, and Liza screamed as a fist hit her face. It left her dazed, but somehow she managed to stay on her feet. Her lip was bleeding, but before she could lift her hand to check the damage someone gave her a slap that made her ears ring. Next thing she knew, Jean had rammed her against the tree.

'I'm going to batter the living daylights out of you, teach you a fucking lesson,' Jean snarled as she clumped Liza round the head. Liza's shriek was cut short by the sound of a flick blade being opened.

'Reckon I should cut her, Jean?' one of the other women yelled.

Before Jean could answer, Liza caught her off guard with a shove that sent her sprawling. Then she took off down the lane, their taunts echoing behind her.

'If we see you back here again, we'll kill you, you hear!'

By the time she made it home, Liza was sober, shivering with cold and feeling more miserable than ever. As she let herself into the house, she heard the sound of the TV. She hurried into the front room, expecting to find the neighbour who was keeping an eye on the kids.

'Amy, I'm so sorry . . .'

Her voice trailed off when she realised it was Jack sitting in front of the telly.

'Rick and Elaine brought me home. You sounded upset on the phone, so I discharged myself . . . I thought it would be a surprise. I wanted to spend Christmas night with you, but it looks like you had other plans.' He looked her up and down. 'Now I'm the one who's got the surprise, ain't I?' He glanced at his watch. It was gone one in the morning. 'So how about you tell me where the fuck you've been . . .'

Chapter Forty

It was the early hours of the morning and Nancy was a bag of nerves. She'd packed up the few belongings she wanted to keep and thrown the rest in bin bags, then she'd gone to say her goodbyes to the other girls. Leaving behind everyone she knew had turned out to be more difficult than she'd thought. But it hadn't been as difficult as building up the courage to come here.

Standing on the front doorstep, Nancy rummaged in her bag and pulled out the miniature bottle of whisky. She took a deep breath. She wanted to be a good mum – not like that cow, Janey, who couldn't stand being around her kids. She wanted to be like Steph, always putting her kid first, but she couldn't do that if she worked for Artie. She had to get out, and she needed money to do that.

She sighed and watched her breath turn to mist.

She took another sip of the whisky. Not too much, because of the baby. Just enough to give her a bit of Dutch courage. Then she raised her hand and knocked on the front door.

After a minute, she heard footsteps inside the house and the door swung open.

'All right?' Even though Nancy was nervous, she put on a brave face. Years of being on the game had taught her how.

'What are you doing here?'

'We need to talk.' She took a deep breath. 'I'm pregnant, and I reckon it's yours.'

Joseph Potter stared at her in disbelief.

'How did you find out where I live?' There was a note of suspicion in his voice.

Nancy didn't want to admit that she'd asked one of her regular punters to follow him in exchange for a blow job. She'd been surprised to find out Jo lived out here off the Lower Rainham Road. She might be wrong, but she had a feeling Danny's mum used to live around here somewhere.

'I asked around.' Nancy shrugged and, without being invited in, she entered the hallway. She wasn't sure what she thought Joseph's house was going to be like, but the way he'd always talked about his home, she didn't think it would be so bloody gloomy. There weren't even any Christmas decorations up. It felt like a funeral parlour. She supposed with his wife having died, he might not feel like celebrating Christmas.

She followed him through to the kitchen, thinking how little she knew about him. They'd only had sex once. A couple of the other girls had bet her a fiver she couldn't get him to go all the way. Nancy reckoned she was on to a loser. She doubted Jo would even let her give him a hand job, he was so bloody uptight. It came as a surprise when he let her into the back of his van and went at it like a sex-starved rabbit. She'd put it down to the fact that he probably hadn't had a shag since his missus died. The minute they stepped out of the van, her mates had appeared from behind the trees, laughing their heads off as they handed over her winnings. Maybe that was why he'd been a bit odd with her ever since. He probably felt humiliated.

The next day when she saw him at the refuge, she let him know she felt bad about it and told him she'd sworn her mates to secrecy. In truth, she'd done that for Hennie's sake. She knew her friend had a soft spot for him.

'Take a seat.' Joseph nodded.

Nancy sniffed. There was a strange smell in the air, although the kitchen was clean and tidy.

'Are your kids asleep?'

Ignoring Nancy's question, Joseph got straight to the point: 'What do you want, Nancy?'

She pulled out a chair and sat down. 'I'm going to make this quick . . . I want enough money so I can fuck off out of here. I ain't going to work for Artie any more. I'm pregnant – over four months gone – and leaving is the only way I can keep this baby . . .'

Joseph nodded. It surprised him that she'd turned up at his house. He'd heard her shout out that she was pregnant when she was going into that fight at the refuge, but it had never crossed his mind that it was his.

He could only imagine what his mother would say if she was still alive. A child of his, in the womb of a dirty, filthy whore like Nancy. Shame crept over him. He recalled the way she'd flirted with him that day, flaunting her tits the minute he let her into the van. She kept thrusting her erect nipples in his face until he became aroused, then she'd laughed as she stripped off her knickers, rubbing her cunt against his leg.

As a rule, he tried to resist sex. He knew it was dirty and his mother wouldn't approve, but sometimes the urge was so great inside him he'd go up to Soho or across to Bromley where there were plenty of whores. But Nancy had caught him off guard. If her stupid friends hadn't suddenly appeared, laughing like hyenas, he would have taken her somewhere no one would hear her scream and made her pay for what she'd done.

Joseph's breathing became heavier. In his mind he could see himself smashing her face in with a brick while he let the blood run into her mouth until it choked her. Anything to shut her up. His penis started to harden, but thankfully it was well hidden under the baggy wool sweater he was wearing.

He sat down, just in case the bulge started to show. 'How do I know it's mine, Nancy?'

'Cheeky cunt!'

Joseph bristled. She had a filthy mouth as well as a filthy hole.

'I don't usually go round having sex with geezers without a condom, you know, so count yourself lucky. You didn't even have to pay for it.'

'I am now though, aren't I, Nancy?' He gave her a tight smile, and there was something about the way he said it that took away a little of her cockiness.

'So what are we going to do then, Jo?' she asked, brazening it out. 'Because I don't think you'd want everyone knowing about it, would you? I know I promised I wouldn't tell, but I've got the baby to think about now . . . I mean, imagine what Steph would say. I think she'd look at you a bit differently, don't you, if she knew you weren't the saint she thinks you are?'

Under the table, Joseph clenched his fists. 'I'm not sure she'd believe you.'

She'd obviously thought he was going to be a pushover. It hadn't occurred to her that he would be completely unruffled by her demands.

'I think she would.' Nancy sounded defensive. 'She knows what blokes are like.'

'So I've heard.' He looked down and absent-mindedly traced the patterns on the tablecloth with his finger. 'So, did you tell anyone you were coming here?'

He looked up at her and watched her shake her head. He wanted to bite her so hard she would scream with pain, to inhale the stench of her when she begged him to stop. Bitch!

'I need to fuck off as soon as I can, and I don't want Artie chasing me down. I need some money then I need to be long gone, especially now that cow Janey knows I'm pregnant.' She tutted. 'Some fucking Christmas this has turned out to be.'

Joseph brought his hands up on the table. He rubbed the scratches on them. That cat had put up quite a fight.

'How did you get here?' he asked.

'Hitched a ride to Rainham, then walked the last bit.'

'So you haven't got a mate outside waiting to give you a lift?'

Nancy shook her head. 'This is our secret. I haven't told a soul – and I won't tell, as long as you help me out with a bit of cash.'

He leaned across the table and grabbed her hands in his. 'You did the right thing.'

Nancy couldn't work him out. He seemed calm, and he hadn't raised his voice to her, but he had a weird expression on his face and the way he was staring at her was giving her the creeps.

Glancing behind her, she suddenly caught sight of something. Over by the back door, a rubbish bag had toppled over and something yellow was spilling out. She pulled her hands away from Joseph and went for a closer look.

'Is this Hennie's?'

She held up a yellow leopard-print scarf, identical to the one Hennie always wore. 'Why the fuck have you got it?' She peered into the bin bag and saw what looked like Hennie's blouse, but there was a massive red stain on it – and that was Hennie's wig! 'What the fuck is going on?' Nancy could hear the panic in her own voice.

Joseph said nothing. He just continued to stare at her.

'Jo, I'm talking to you . . . Why the fuck have you got these things? What's happened to Hennie?'

Still he said nothing, but a smile appeared on his lips and quickly spread across his face. Then he began to laugh. He'd kept them for a few days while her stench lingered on them, savouring the memory of what he'd done to her. The smell was fading now, so they were fit for nothing but the garden incinerator. But seeing Nancy handling them was giving him an erection.

'You're being so fucking weird, that's it, I'm going.' Nancy reached for the door.

Joseph watched her rattle the handle, trying to open it, but it was locked.

'*Nancy!*'

Like a well-trained dog, she turned at her master's command.

Joseph smashed her in her face with one of the pans from the draining board. He watched her drop to the ground, falling into a semi-conscious heap and groaning in pain.

He used his foot to pull up her skirt. She wasn't wearing any knickers. Filthy bitch. Ready to give herself to any man. Never satisfied. Greedy bitches, always wanting more. Well, he would show her – he would teach them all – what happened to greedy bitches.

He began to rip off her clothes, pressing her face into the kitchen floor as she struggled for breath. But suddenly he stopped.

He wasn't a monster.

He didn't go around killing children, especially his own. They were the innocent ones. Why should they suffer because of the sins of their mother?

He placed his hand on Nancy's stomach, and bent his head

down and kissed it. Another Potter was to be brought into the world.

Then Joseph stood and, while his children stayed locked in their rooms listening to the screams they'd lived with all their lives, he grabbed a clump of Nancy's hair and dragged her down the darkened hallway . . .

Book Four

Boxing Day

And after all, what is a lie? 'Tis but the truth in a masquerade.

Lord Byron

Chapter Forty-One

Sharon was woken by the noise of her front door opening and closing. She sighed to herself. She had hoped to get a few more hours' kip. Boxing Day was one of the few lie-ins she was allowed. She wasn't working until tomorrow, so she'd planned to treat herself to a lazy day in bed. She might even cook herself a fry-up, and later she'd pop over to see Steph.

She rolled over on her side to glance at the radio alarm clock her cousin had given her for Christmas. It was only seven thirty.

'*Hello, darlin.*'

Sharon screamed in terror. Dressed in only a T-shirt and knickers, she scrambled out of bed.

'What are you doing here?' she asked, her face drained of colour.

Fletch strolled into her bedroom, his fingers toying with the knuckleduster on his right hand. 'A little birdie tells me that you've been really silly, darlin'. So I thought we should have a little chat.' He wandered around her room, picking up and dropping her belongings as he went.

Sharon had never felt terror like it. 'I . . . I don't know what you're talking about.'

Fletch nodded and wandered over to the white chest of drawers in the corner. He grabbed her perfume, sprayed some into the air and sniffed. 'You need to change that – smells a bit cheap, if you ask me . . . Still, I don't suppose you need to be worried about that now.' He turned to face her. 'So come on, Shaz, tell me what you did.'

Sharon was shaking now. Fletch was so tall and solidly built that he seemed to take up all the space in her room.

'I don't know what you mean.'

Fletch laughed. Then he launched a kick at the dressing table, knocking it over and sending her make-up and jewellery flying. His eyes flashed. 'Don't mug me off – you know exactly what I'm fucking talking about. So I'll ask you again, shall I? What the fuck did you do?'

'I didn't do anything.' She swallowed hard.

'So you're telling me that you didn't let Danny into the pub last night.'

Sharon felt like she was going to wet herself she was so frightened.

She shook her head. 'I didn't.'

Fletch sighed. 'Oh, I think you did, darlin'. I think you were more than happy to fuck me and Artie over.'

'I didn't, I swear. I would never—'

'You keep saying that, Shaz, but you and I both know that you let them in. Not only that, you told them where we were. Did you really think we weren't going to find out?'

That's exactly what Sharon had thought. She had no idea how they'd found out it was her. Danny had promised no one would get wind of it.

'The thing is, love,' Fletch continued, 'someone needs to pay for what happened last night. You should see the state of Artie's face. That cunt proper went to town. He's bust Artie's nose, left him looking like he's gone a few rounds with fucking Marvin

218

Hagler, and I don't reckon Danny should get away with that, do you? I *also* don't think the person who helped him should get away with that.'

Sharon glanced down at Fletch's knuckleduster. She felt sick.

'If you act like you've got a pair of bollocks, Shaz, I'm going to treat you like you have and teach you the sort of lesson I'd teach any bloke who had the fucking front to go up against us.'

That was when Sharon made a dash for it.

She made it as far as the landing before Fletch caught up with her.

He slammed his elbow into her face. As she staggered into the wall, he gripped hold of her hair, pulling it so hard that it felt as if her scalp was on fire.

'You're a fucking piece of shit, you know that?' he snarled, then he slammed her head, once, twice, three times against the picture hanging on the wall, breaking the glass into tiny fragments. Then he threw her to the floor and kicked her again and again.

She screamed as her ribs cracked. When she attempted to crawl away, he kicked her up the arse, sending her sprawling. Then he laid into her with his fists.

He kept at it for five minutes. Then, wiping his sweat and Sharon's blood from his face, he stepped over her motionless body and headed down the stairs.

All he had to do now was find Danny Denton, and any other cunt that thought they could get away with being a fucking snake . . .

Chapter Forty-Two

'I just can't get my head around what you're telling me.' Jack's voice was a mixture of anger and pain. He and Liza had spent the whole night arguing and they were still at it on Boxing Day morning.

Liza stood in the lounge in her dressing gown. She had a hangover. She'd puked on her clothes last night, but she'd felt too ill to have a shower and change properly. She'd just made herself a mug of hot, sweet tea, but now it came to drinking it she couldn't face it. She swallowed a couple of paracetamol and some more Valium. It was the only way she could cope.

'We've been round and round this, Jack.'

'Then we'll go over it *again* until you come to your fucking senses!' he raged.

She didn't know how long she could take Jack having a go at her. He should be supporting her, not yelling at her. 'I haven't decided anything yet.'

'WHAT THE FUCK DO YOU MEAN? THERE ISN'T ANYTHING TO FUCKING DECIDE!' Jack picked up the glass ashtray from the coffee table and threw it against the wall.

Liza flinched as it shattered into pieces.

'For God's sake, Jack, stop! How is this going to help?' Her eyes pricked with tears. 'The girls have been through enough without you coming home and being a prick. Why don't you stop feeling sorry for yourself, for one moment, and listen to me.'

'Are you serious? Feeling sorry for myself?' He dropped his hands to stare at her. 'I'm in agony, hobbling around on two sticks like some fucking old man, and I've no idea when or if I'll be back on my feet again, which means I can't provide for my family. And if that's not FUCKING bad enough, you're telling me that you want to earn money down the lane! I should give you a fucking slap.'

'Oh shut the fuck up, Jack.' Liza had had it. 'Stop being so selfish.' The emotion caught at the back of her throat. 'Do you think I WANT to do that?'

'Who knows?' Jack muttered.

'You bastard! You fucking bastard! Right now, that's the only thing I can come up with to get us out of this mess. Fletch is a psycho. All he cares about is getting his money. There's no telling what he'll do if we can't pay him.'

'He's not going to hurt a woman,' Jack insisted.

'Oh, you know that for certain, do you?' She shook her head in disgust. 'Anyway, it's not me I'm worried about. It's the girls. You weren't here when he threatened to take Mandy. Do you really want to wake up one morning and find her gone? Can't you get it into your head? Me working on the lane is our only hope.' Liza's voice trembled.

'There must be another fucking way out.' Jack couldn't bear to look at her. What she was suggesting made him sick to his stomach. 'You know what amazes me? You're contemplating opening your legs for another bloke, but you couldn't hold down a job in Radio Rentals!'

'How fucking dare you! This is your shit, Jack, which I'm trying to clean up.'

Jack suddenly had a thought. 'Is this because we haven't been having sex? Is this why you want to do this?'

Liza didn't know whether to laugh or cry. 'What is wrong with you?' She shook her head. 'Jack, do you really think that I want some stranger touching me, mauling me . . . *fucking* me? Because if you do, then you don't know me at all.'

He slapped her then. It was the first time he'd ever raised his hand to her. 'You were quick enough to try to whip your knickers off last night.'

She slapped him back. Not from anger but from humiliation and hurt. She needed his support not his judgement. She was desperate, but she was also terrified. 'I went to *see*, that's all, Jack. And what I found were a bunch of women who didn't choose that life – that life chose them.'

'What if someone saw you? What if someone from the girls' school saw you? What then? Jesus Christ! What would they think of you, and what would they think of me, letting my missus out on the game?'

'Is that all you care about, Jack, what people will think of *you*?'

'I'm not going to let you do this, Liza, I *can't*. I don't want you to do it.'

'What you want doesn't come into it,' she snapped. 'This is about making sure the girls are safe. Instead of thinking about yourself, you should be worrying about them.'

'Hello? It's only me.' Steph's voice called out cheerily as she walked in wearing her favourite fishnets and heels. She took in the scene. Liza's eyes were swollen from crying. Steph wasn't sure who the bloke was, but he didn't look too clever either. In fact, he looked like he'd been bawling his eyes out too.

'Sorry, the door was ajar and I heard raised voices, and I thought—'

'You thought you'd just walk into someone else's gaff?'

'*Jack!*' Liza turned on him. 'Sorry,' she said to Steph. 'I can't have closed it properly when I went outside for a cigarette.'

Steph was surprised to learn that this was Liza's husband; she hadn't mentioned that he was out of hospital. She wouldn't have come round if she'd known. When she heard raised voices, she'd barged in thinking it was Fletch giving Liza a hard time.

'I can come back. I tried to phone you, but there was no reply . . . I only wanted to check how you were, I'll catch you later, yeah? Nice to meet you, Jack.' She turned to go.

'Steph, no wait,' Liza called after her.

'Oh, so this is Steph.' Jack's voice dripped with bitterness. 'The infamous fucking Steph, eh?'

Surprised, Steph turned to face him. She'd only met Liza yesterday, so she wondered what he was talking about.

'You've got a fucking nerve, coming around here,' Jack snarled. 'Was this your idea?' he added aggressively.

'Was what my idea? I'm sorry, I don't know what you mean.' Steph knew the only way to deal with domestic was to keep calm. Shouting would only make things worse.

'Really?' Jack laughed bitterly. 'I know the sort of tramp—'

'Jack, *stop it*!'

'It's fine.' Steph smiled at Liza. She could see the woman was embarrassed. Years of dealing with Pete had left her immune, but she still remembered how it felt to be publicly humiliated by him, and her heart went out to Liza. 'He can say what he wants.'

'Too fucking right I can – this is my home!'

'I should go,' Steph said gently.

'Yeah, you fucking should!' Jack hissed. 'I don't want whores in my house or near my kids, you understand me?'

Steph looked at him with no malice. She nodded. 'I hear you.'

She walked away and this time she *did* leave. She'd speak to Liza later.

Liza immediately turned on Jack. 'Who do you think you are, treating my friend like that?'

This was too much for Jack. 'FRIEND! SHE'S A FUCK-ING WHORE!'

'She's not. And, even if she was, better that than a nasty, unsupportive *cunt* like you!'

Then she ran out of the door after Steph.

'Liza . . . Liza, wait . . . wait . . . Liza, for fuck's sake!' Jack called after her. 'Get back here now . . .'

Chapter Forty-Three

Liza charged across the estate, desperate to catch up with Steph, shouting at the top of her voice, 'Steph . . . Steph . . . *Wait!*'

Steph, who was just unlocking her car, did exactly that.

'I'm so sorry about Jack,' Liza blurted. 'He's talking shit.'

'Listen, you don't need to apologise for your old man. As blokes go, he was pretty polite actually.' She grinned but her smile fell as she noticed Liza's swollen mouth.

'He's not usually like that . . .' Liza fiddled with the sleeve of her dressing gown. 'He's usually loving and kind.' She shrugged. 'It's a lot for him – that's all.'

'I'm sure it is. The accident must have given him quite a shock.'

Liza shook her head. 'I didn't mean that – although the doctor says he might not get back on his feet for a while.'

'I'm sorry.' Steph reached into her pocket and pulled out her packet of cigarettes. She offered one to Liza, and this time she took one. 'Did Jack do that to you?' she asked as she lit their cigarettes.

Liza touched her mouth. She shook her head. 'No, no, that was Jean.'

Steph frowned. 'Jean?'

Liza looked around. 'Have you got a minute – you don't have to rush off, do you?'

'No, I'm fine. How about we sit in my car and have a chat?'

Steph listened in silence to Liza's sorry tale about what had happened last night.

'. . . So that's it really. I didn't get in until gone almost two in the morning.' Liza shrugged. 'I don't suppose you've had a chance to ask Fletch about giving us longer to pay, or at least dropping the interest?'

Steph gave Liza a tight smile. 'I spoke to Artie, but, you know, he just wasn't listening.'

'Yeah, yeah, I get it.' Liza battled her tears. 'Thanks for trying.'

Steph didn't want to be thanked. She'd gone to bed thinking about what Artie had said, and she'd woken up thinking about it. The guilt was weighing on her like a lead fucking balloon. She knew Artie spent the money on Rob, so maybe he was right and that somehow made her part of it. If that was so, when it came down to it, she was no better than Artie or Fletch.

As Liza opened the passenger door to go home, Steph put a hand on her arm. 'Call me later. You've got my number, and the refuge is always open during the day and early evening.'

'I'm going to do it.'

'Sorry?' Steph was missing something. 'Do what?'

Liza took a deep breath. 'Work on the lane.'

'What? No, Liza, no . . . I . . .' Steph was truly shocked. Yes, Liza had just finished telling her how she'd wound up down the lane yesterday, but she hadn't made it clear what her intentions were.

'I've got no choice.'

'Oh fuck . . . *Shit.*' Steph slapped the dashboard. She was angry. With herself, with Fletch. With Artie. With the whole situation. 'Liza, I don't think you know how hard it is out there on the streets. It's brutal.' She couldn't stand to think about Liza having to sell herself. 'It can be dangerous.'

'I'll be fine.'

Steph doubted it. 'Listen, please think about this.'

'I have. I just need your help.'

'Oh Jesus.' Steph closed her eyes, and it was a long minute before she could open them again.

'So will you? Will you help me?' Liza pleaded. 'You won't change my mind. I'll do it with you or without you.'

Steph nodded reluctantly. 'Okay. Of course I will. I'll make it as safe as I can for you. I'll show you the dos and don'ts.' Her voice was a whisper. 'But promise me you'll give it a bit more thought.'

Liza nodded but she knew this was the only way out. Fletch was coming back in a week and she needed to pay him. It was as simple as that.

'*Steph!*'

Steph and Liza looked up at the same time. It was Bill.

'I better go, Steph. I need to make sure Jack's all right.'

'Listen, about Jack – don't make excuses for him. He's not the victim here. He needs to support you, all right?'

Liza nodded.

Steph squeezed her hand. 'Take care of yourself . . . I'll see you soon.'

Liza walked away as Bill ran up to the car. She felt like driving off and leaving him there, but she waited to hear what he had to say.

'We've been looking for you,' Bill panted. 'Danny's over there in the car.'

'What is it? Is Janey all right?'

'Yeah, yeah, she's fine.' He didn't want to mention the row

he'd had with her last night when he'd come home and found she'd left the kids on their own. 'It's Sharon – she's in hospital. She's in a really bad way . . . We think Fletch did it.'

Liza, waiting for a break in traffic so she could cross the road, overheard every word. A cold terror passed through her and she set off running for home.

Chapter Forty-Four

Steph, Danny and Bill ran for the lift that would take them to the fifth floor of the hospital where Sharon was. She'd left her own car in Chatham, knowing Danny would get them here faster. On the way, they told her what had happened last night.

'I can't believe you got her involved!' Steph couldn't bear to look at the pair of them, so she focused on the indicator showing the changing floor numbers. It felt like it was taking a lifetime; she'd have been better off taking the stairs. 'What the fuck were you thinking?'

'She wanted to help,' insisted Bill. As usual, he was preoccupied with thoughts of Janey. She'd come home off her face last night, and it'd been hard to wake her up. There'd been a moment when he'd thought she had OD'd again, but then she'd let out a loud snore. This morning, he'd left the kids with Sarah, though she wasn't too happy about it.

Steph glared at Bill. 'Oh, do me a favour. This is Sharon we're talking about – of course she wants to help. She's scared shitless of them, she wants them gone, but that doesn't mean you should have let her get involved. And how the hell did Fletch find out that she was the one who let you into the pub?'

Bill shrugged. 'Someone must have seen her.'

'Who?'

'I don't know. You were there – you tell me.'

Steph narrowed her eyes. 'What's that supposed to mean?'

Bill turned on Steph. 'I'm just saying you need to make up your fucking mind who's side you're on. For all I know, you could've told him.'

Before Steph could answer, Danny cut in.

'Don't talk to her like that,' he growled. 'Watch your mouth. We're all fucking stressed about this. What we don't need is everyone turning on each other.'

There was an uncomfortable silence. It confused Steph, being so close to Danny . . . She kept her eyes focused on the indicator, but she could feel him looking at her. And she was relieved when the lift doors finally opened.

They hurried out, rushing down a corridor that reeked of bleach until they came to the Intensive Care Unit. According to the woman on reception, this was where they'd find Sharon.

At the glass door of the unit, Steph pressed on the bell. It was answered quickly.

'Hello, we've been told that Sharon Higgs is a patient here.'

The buzzer opened the door, and Steph made her way to the nurse on duty.

'Where is she?'

'She's down there, bed eight. But I must warn you, she hasn't regained consciousness yet.'

Steph immediately set off, followed by Danny and Bill. The minute she saw Sharon, Steph felt sick to her stomach. Sharon's eyes were closed, and an oxygen mask was covering her mouth. Her face was so swollen she was unrecognisable. A huge wad of gauze was taped to the side of her shaved head. There was a stain where blood had seeped through. A bag of blood hung on a metal pole, dripping into a tube attached to Sharon's arm.

'Fletch is going to pay for this,' Bill muttered.

Steph spun round to look at him. 'Ain't you done enough? I told you that getting Danny involved would only make things worse.'

'It couldn't get much fucking worse. Look what they've done to Janey.'

Steph raised her voice then. 'Oh my God, have you heard yourself?' She pointed at Sharon. 'This is so much worse. Janey's a junkie who brings it on herself; you've got to stop blaming everyone else for her behaviour.'

Bill leaned into Steph, his eyes blazing with anger. 'And you've got to stop making excuses for Artie.'

Danny pulled him off. 'I told you, wind your neck in. I ain't going to tell you again.'

'What's your problem?' Bill snapped at Danny. 'You know what I'm saying is true.'

Danny shook his head. 'No, I don't. And I don't want to hear that shit again, or you're on your own.'

Steph suddenly noticed that the gauze on Sharon's head was beginning to turn a brighter red. She raced out into the corridor and flagged down a nurse. 'It looks like the side of my mate's head is bleeding badly. Could you come and take a look?'

The nurse hurried through to Sharon and grabbed a bigger dressing off the metal tray by the bed. She held it firmly against Sharon's head, taping it over the dressing already in place.

'What's going on?' Danny asked. 'What do those numbers mean?'

'It's nothing to worry about,' the nurse answered but Steph thought she looked concerned as she studied the monitor Danny had indicated. 'It's just her blood pressure dipping a bit – her heart is speeding up to compensate.'

Suddenly an alarm went off and this time Steph saw a look of panic on the nurse's face. She raced to the doorway and called down the corridor to her colleagues: '*Can someone get the doctor? I need him in here NOW! She's in cardiac arrest.*'

A loud beep came from the monitor and Steph could see all the coloured lines on the screen had gone flat. A moment later, several doctors and nurses rushed in.

'*Start CPR,*' one of them shouted. Steph stood back, frightened for Sharon as she watched the doctors connect more wires and pads to her chest.

'Do you mind waiting outside?' said a young Jamaican nurse to Steph, ushering her out, along with Danny and Bill.

'Is this something to do with her head wound?' asked Steph.

'No, she's probably got internal bleeding and that's caused her to arrest.'

'Will she be all right though?' As Steph spoke, Sharon was wheeled out of the room on the bed, the doctors feverishly working on her as they rushed past.

'Where's she going?' Danny's voice was no longer calm.

'They're taking her to surgery . . . Maybe it's best if you come back later.'

Steph turned on Bill. 'Are you fucking happy now?' She had a mind to slap him. 'If anything happens to her, I'm blaming you . . . I'm blaming you both.'

'Me? You're fucking blaming me? This is Artie, this is Fletch, this ain't got anything to do with me,' Bill snarled. 'All I was trying to do was stop the fucking train wreck.'

Danny took Steph's hand, and he was surprised when she didn't pull it away.

'Why don't you go home, Steph? You look tired. I'll hang about here, and I'll let you know as soon as there's any news.'

'I'm not some delicate fucking flower, Danny. I'll be fine . . .' Steph blew out her cheeks, suddenly feeling ashamed of herself. 'Sorry, Dan. Everything's getting on top of me right now.' Yesterday had been a nightmare, and Boxing Day was turning out to be no better.

'That's why you need to go home. There's nothing you can do here. Do you need money for a cab to get back to your car?'

Steph shook her head. She couldn't think straight. She'd been planning to go from Liza's place to the storage unit in Rainham to pick up some heaters for the refuge. Right now, she couldn't face it. As badly as they needed those heaters, she couldn't face seeing anyone. Feeling that she was letting the women down, it occurred to her that perhaps Joseph would go and get the heaters for her; he was always so willing to help, so she was sure he wouldn't mind.

Waving away the notes Danny was proffering, she told him, 'Call me if there's any news.' Then she walked away without bothering to speak to Bill. Deep down, she knew it wasn't only because she was so fucking angry at him. She was scared. She knew that Sharon was only the start of it. Before this was over, a lot more blood would be spilled.

Chapter Forty-Five

While Bill went to pick up his kids, Danny wandered down to get a coffee from the hospital cafe. They'd taken Sharon to surgery an hour ago, and no one had told him anything. Under any other circumstances, he wouldn't be hanging about in the daylight while this shit with Artie and Fletch was going on, but Danny knew there was no way they'd show their faces here. They'd be lying low for a while.

Not bothering to get the lift, Danny sauntered down the flight of stairs. His footsteps echoed in the stairwell. It'd been a stressful couple of hours, but it had felt good seeing Steph, though the tension between her and Bill troubled him. He wasn't stupid, he could see what Bill was getting at, but he understood that the ties Steph had with Artie were complicated.

Steph was the glue that held things together – she always had been. What Bill wasn't seeing, was that Steph's connection with Artie enabled her to speak to him and *try* to calm him down when he was on a fucking rampage. The only reason the women, *including* Janey, were able to go to the refuge for a bit of time out was because of Steph. She fought their corner, never backing down even when Artie tried to intimidate her. Yes, with Artie being Rob's brother, there was a bit of loyalty there. She was the mother of Rob's kid – that made her family. But she was still treading a dangerous line, and he only hoped she was smart enough to know what she was doing. Bill was the one who needed to get a dose of reality.

'Oh, for fuck's sake,' Danny mumbled as he saw the *Canteen closed* sign. 'Oi, mate, where's the nearest coffee machine?' he called over to a porter who was smoking a spliff by the rear entrance.

'A & E – follow the blue signs.'

Danny took off down the long, cold corridor. He needed to work out what he was going to do next. He definitely needed to make some phone calls to find out who was in or out, but he decided his top priority once he was done here would be to off-load his stash of coke. He needed a bit of money behind him to pay anyone who agreed to come aboard. They weren't going to take on Artie and Fletch for free.

Arriving at the A & E waiting room, Danny made a beeline for the drinks machine but stopped in his tracks when he spotted a familiar face.

He lowered his voice. 'You kept your mouth shut then.'

It was the teenage girl from his mum's old house.

She looked up as if her heart was about to leap into her mouth. 'Yeah . . . of course . . .' She could hardly speak as she stared at Danny.

He hadn't meant to scare the kid. The fear on her face made him feel uncomfortable.

'It's okay . . . it's okay. Listen, I'm joking, it's all good. I'm sorry, all right. It was a bad fucking joke.'

He saw her eyes pricking with tears. She was shaking. Had he really scared her that much? Fuck. 'Look, I'll leave you to it. Pretend you never saw me, all right.' Danny paused then. 'You all right, darlin?' She was clutching her arm. 'What's happened . . .'

'She tripped and fell. Didn't you, Bel?'

Danny glanced up then.

It was Joseph Potter.

Close up, Danny saw that, while he might be a plank, he was a tall and well-built plank.

'Is there a reason why you're talking to my daughter?'

Bel lowered her head and fidgeted nervously with her fingers.

'Bel, who is this man?'

'How the fuck would she know?' Danny instinctively wanted to get the focus off Bel. 'It's you I wanted to talk to . . . I've been following you, mate,' he lied. There was no way he was dropping himself – or, more to the point, this kid – in the shit. He hadn't forgotten that even when he'd turned up the heat, holding a gun to her head, her biggest concern had been her dad finding out that she was in the attic room.

Joseph blinked at him, stunned.

'You see,' Danny continued, 'you've got something of mine, and I ain't happy about it.' He kept his voice low, but his face was inches away from Joseph's. And as Danny stared into those grey eyes, it struck him how dark they were, how devoid of any emotion. Most blokes he knew would have been intimidated; even when they were trying to pretend they weren't, it showed in their eyes. But with Joseph there was nothing. His eyes were dead.

'I think you must have the wrong person.' Joseph remained calm.

'No, I know exactly who you are. You're living in my mum's house and, one way or another, I'm going to get it back.'

'Ah, your mum is— sorry, *was* Paula.'

Danny got the sense the guy was amused.

'Yeah, and while I was banged up, somehow you got your grubby hands on my house.'

'I had no idea . . . No idea at all she had a son – she never said. Never mentioned you at all.' Joseph paused. 'Look, I can understand why this whole situation must appear strange to you. I mean, I only used to pop in to deliver her meals, so you can imagine how shocked I was when I found out she'd left the house to me.'

Danny poked Joseph hard in the chest. 'Why don't I fucking believe you?'

'I can't answer that.' Joseph held Danny's glare.

Danny shook his head. This was one smug cunt. 'I'm watching you, Potter. And, trust me, this isn't over.'

Danny turned and stomped away.

A smirk appeared on Joseph's face. He closed his eyes. A rush of excitement went through him as he remembered Paula Denton's last moments . . . *Crack went her skull.*

Chapter Forty-Six

After leaving the hospital, Steph had stood in the car park for a while, trying to decide what to do next. Seeing Sharon in that state had left her shattered, incapable of doing anything, so she stood smoking a cigarette, half listening to the Christmas songs blaring out from a shop across the street car.

Eventually, she'd hailed a cab to take her back to her car. She couldn't face going home. Stacey was round at her mate's, and would be staying the night there, so it would be just Steph and Carol. And she wasn't up to speaking to Carol about Hennie. It wasn't that she didn't care, just that she needed to take a bit of time out.

And then it came to her: she would go to the cemetery to see Andy. She wasn't going to allow some sick bastard make her too upset to think about her little boy. The only thing to do was to let her anger go and move on.

It was always tough, going to the cemetery, but there was also a kind of peace. It was the same when she went to see Rob.

She parked the car under a large oak tree just as the sun made a rare appearance. Stubbing out her cigarette, she twisted round in her seat and reached for the blue helium balloon she'd bought for Andy on Christmas Eve.

She'd been intending to visit yesterday, but finding the Baby-gro had wrecked her plans.

She leaned her head on the steering wheel and breathed deeply, trying to calm herself. Fuck. *Fuck*. Fuck. She hated feeling like this. Five years had gone by – wasn't time supposed to heal? But the pain was as sharp as ever. It still took her breath away.

Not a day, not an *hour* went by without her wishing she could hold Andy in her arms again. And if she couldn't have that, then she wished she could remember the good times – the day trips to the seaside, feeding the ducks, the way he'd giggle when Rob lifted him on to his shoulders – without picturing his little broken body on the side of the road, his hair stained red with blood . . .

Steph opened the car door, breathing in the cold air. She got out, the balloon bobbing in the air, and focused on putting one foot in front of the other on the pebbled path that would lead her to Andy.

It took a couple of minutes to get to the far end of the cemetery and the small plot by the cherry blossom tree where Andy was buried.

Steph suddenly stopped. The balloon slipped through her fingers as she stared at the grave.

'Oh my God!'

She dashed towards it. The entire headstone had been doused in red paint.

Dropping to her knees, Steph frantically tried to wipe it off, but her efforts only made it worse, smearing and covering the gold epitaph. With her hands covered in paint, Steph tugged her coat off, but the plastic mac was no use, so she pulled off her jumper, and used that to scrub at the headstone instead. She was crying hysterically as she tried to remove enough so the inscription would be legible.

Who was doing this to her? And *why?* Who would be sick enough to do this to Andy?

Sobbing, she sat back on her heels and watched the remains of the paint trickling down the sides of the grey marble stone. She had to get out of here. She was too angry. She hurried back to the car and got in, not caring that she was covering the seat with paint. She smashed her fist on the steering wheel.

As she turned in to Franklin Road, she spotted a police car behind her. Automatically, Steph slowed down. She didn't need a speeding ticket on top of everything else. But it was too late, they flashed her.

Sighing, she pulled up and immediately the police car came alongside her. It was DS Walker. He sneered at her, then sped off without saying anything.

Steph watched him go. A thought struck her.

Oh my God. That was it. The only way anyone would know what Andy was wearing on the day of the accident was if they'd been there, or at least seen the crime-scene photographs. And the only people who had access to those were the Old Bill. Fred. Only the other day, that bastard had been mouthing off to her, hadn't he? He was a sick enough to do this, and he was certainly pissed off enough about her helping Rachel. He blamed Steph. He'd said as much. He hated the fact that his wife had broken free and was getting support at the refuge. It all made sense.

'Oi, you catching flies there? There's a law about stopping in the middle of the road.'

Steph jumped as someone banged on the window. She turned to see who it was. Her heart sank. It was Pete. God, he was the last person she needed to see right now.

'Fancy giving me a lift?' He grinned through the window, showing off his stained, broken teeth.

'Not really.' She turned away and was ready to drive off again. 'Not after the way you behaved the other day. I'm so fucking sick of it, Pete.'

'I don't suppose you've thought any more about that alibi, have you?'

'I already said: *no*. Maybe you should bloody learn not to take things that don't belong to you.'

Pete sulked. 'Who's been rattling your cage?'

She shook her head. 'Go and pester someone else, Pete.'

'Don't be like that, Steph. I promised Stacey I'd come and pick her and her mate up and take them to the carnival in Rainham.'

Steph rolled down the window. 'And you're paying?'

'Ahhhh, well no – that's where you come in, darlin' . . . No, no, don't look at me like that. What was I supposed to say? She wanted to go, so I said I'd take her and Karen.'

'And you didn't think you might need some money to do that?'

He shrugged, and without waiting to be asked he jumped into the back seat. 'You don't mind, do you? I should be getting some wheels of my own soon. My mate Tel is being sent down – he's looking at a three stretch – so he said I could use his motor while he was away. So, you see, you won't need to be my chauffeur any more . . .' Pete stopped his rabbiting and frowned. He looked around the car. 'What the fuck have you been doing? You look like you've been in a fight with Dulux. Jesus!'

Steph held her emotions in check. She didn't want to have a row with Pete, but she was furious, and she knew her patience would be thin. 'Leave it. I don't want to talk about it.'

'Why? What's going on, darlin'?' Pete sounded genuinely concerned.

'Nothing . . . It's fine.' Steph took a deep breath, pulled herself together and began to drive; she just wanted to go home.

'It's clearly not nothing . . . You look well stressed.'

Steph bit on her lip. 'I said I'm fine, didn't I?'

They continued the short drive in silence until they reached Steph's house. She turned the engine off and put on the handbrake. Wearily, she headed for the house, with Pete following, and let herself in.

Pete hovered while she washed her hands, trying to scrub off the paint. 'How much do you need?' She glanced at him. 'I mean for the girls to go to the carnival – which doesn't include you having a few rounds.' She went to the cupboard and grabbed the tea caddy that always had a bit of money in it. She flicked open the lid and handed Pete a few notes. 'Make sure you spend it on Stacey and Karen, all right? And make sure you go straight to pick them up. I don't want Karen's mum saying you never showed.'

'What do you take me for?'

Steph didn't bother replying.

'Look, Steph.' Pete brought his voice down. 'I know we've had our ups and downs, and I know . . . well, sometimes I'm not the easiest geezer to get on with. But that doesn't mean I don't care . . . You're the mother of my kid, so I'll always care what happens.'

Maybe because she was so on edge, Steph started to open up. Something she'd never do with Pete ordinarily. 'It's Andy.'

'Andy? As in . . .' He stopped.

Steph nodded. 'His grave – it's been trashed. I'm fucking fuming.'

'What? When?' Pete stared at her. He looked at the paint that stained her clothes. 'It's probably those fuckers from the estate across from the cemetery.'

'No, it's more than that,' she told him. 'There was a present left for me, and when I opened it . . .' She drew in a deep breath to steady herself. 'It was a Babygro, almost identical to the one Andy was wearing on the day of the accident, and it had been covered in paint, to make it look like blood.'

'Fucking hell!'

Steph decided not to say who she thought was behind it. There was no way right now she could prove it was Fred.

'I'm sorry.' Pete gave her a small smile. 'You shouldn't have to go through this.'

He went in for the kiss then.

Shocked, Steph shoved him away hard. He clattered against the kitchen cabinets. 'What the fuck do you think you're doing?' Instinctively, she wiped her mouth with her sleeve.

'You looked upset.'

'Upset and angry, yes, but not fucking desperate! That's just typical of you, ain't it?'

'You know your problem,' Pete snarled. 'That job at the refuge is turning you into a fucking dyke.'

Steph was incredulous. 'Because I don't want to be kissed by you? Just get out, Pete.'

She snatched the money from his hand.

'What about the carnival?' he whined.

'I'll take her myself . . . now get OUT!'

Steph pushed him out of the back door, but as she did she rolled her eyes at the sight of Artie and Fletch getting out of a car. *This* she certainly didn't need.

243

Chapter Forty-Seven

'Did you know? Did you FUCKING know?' Artie had barged into Steph's kitchen with Fletch. They glared at her. 'Did you know that Danny was back?'

Steph dried her hands on the tea towel. She grabbed for one of the packets of cigarettes Stacey had given her for Christmas that she'd left on the windowsill. The kitchen was full of the smell of baking from the cakes Carol had cooked earlier as a way of saying thank you for letting her stay. 'Leave me alone, Artie. I've got nothing to say to either of you. Now I'd appreciate it if you went.'

Artie cricked his neck from side to side. 'That's not a fucking answer, Steph. I asked you a question.'

Steph shook her head. She watched Fletch prowl round her kitchen, opening and closing the cupboards. 'Who the hell do you think you are coming in here, demanding anything from me after what you did to Sharon? You make me sick, and I don't have to tell you *anything*.'

Artie slammed his fist on the table. He glared at her, and Steph could see the veins at the side of his head.

'Oh yeah you fucking do, darlin'. That's what families are about. We don't keep secrets from each other.'

Steph was having none of it. 'Families! Are you fucking joking? You're not my family. I don't want *anything* to do with you. I saw what you did to Sharon. They had to take her down to surgery. I don't even know if she's going to make it.' She glared at them. 'So you two can fuck off out of my house *and* my life . . . You're lucky I don't phone the Old Bill. The only reason I don't is because it wouldn't make any difference.' She felt nothing but disgust for Artie or Fletch. There wasn't even any remorse on their faces.

Fletch looked at her with contempt. 'Sharon was a snake – she got what was coming to her. Let that be a warning to anyone who thinks they can shit on us.'

Steph could see he was wired. 'You really have lost it, haven't you . . . Oh, and for your information, yeah, I did know Danny was back. And you know why I didn't say anything? It's because I knew it would bring nothing but trouble. I tell you something, though, I'm actually glad he's out. Somebody needs to stop you two.'

This time Artie smashed his fist into one of Steph's kitchen cupboards, leaving a dent in it. His eyes were wild. 'You've crossed the line this time.' Then he grabbed her face in his hand.

Steph's eyes were hard. She was sick to the back teeth of men who used their fists to get what they wanted. She'd seen enough of that to last her a lifetime. 'I'm not one of your women that you can intimidate. You don't scare me, Artie.'

'Artie . . . *This* is Artie?'

Artie let her go, and Steph turned round and inwardly groaned as she saw Carol standing at the kitchen door. Before Steph could say anything, Carol charged at Artie, screaming at him.

'What have you done with my mum? What have you done with her?' Never very good at keeping her temper when she was upset, Carol proceeded to claw at Artie's face. 'I know you've hurt her . . . I know you have.'

Artie grabbed her wrists and sent her flying across the room. As her body clattered against the fridge, Carol let out a yelp.

'Who is this crazy fucking bitch?'

Steph rushed over to help her up. 'This is Hennie's daughter, you fucking prick.'

Artie rolled his eyes. 'And I already told you, whatever's happened to Hennie is nothing to do with me.' He turned to face Carol. 'Your mum's a fucking thief, and if she knows what's best for her she'll stay well away.'

As Fletch looked on in silence, Carol glared at Artie and launched into a rant. 'Well, I'm going to go to the Old Bill – let's see what they have to say.'

Artie laughed. 'I can't imagine them saying anything. I don't think they're going to send out a search party for a missing whore, do you?'

'Piss off,' snapped Carol. 'Like I give a shit what you think.'

Fletch stepped forward. 'You will do.' He glanced at Steph. 'You need to explain to her how it works when some bitch starts mouthing off.'

Artie grinned. 'It must be something in the air, or perhaps it's a full fucking moon. Either way, the women round here seem to have gone batshit crazy. First Hennie, now I hear Nancy's up the fucking duff.' He shook his head again, and muttered to himself, 'Wait till I get my hands on that silly bitch.'

Artie and Fletch walked out then, leaving Steph and Carol in the kitchen.

'I don't care what they say – I know something isn't right,' Carol insisted.

Steph's stare followed the men as they walked down the path. Her stomach knotted. That felt like the understatement of the year.

Chapter Forty-Eight

It was Saturday and Steph wasn't feeling comfortable. She'd tried to persuade Carol not to go to the Old Bill until she'd had time to ask around. Someone must know something.

She'd known Artie and Fletch long enough to have a pretty good idea when they were lying. It seemed to her that they genuinely didn't have a clue where Hennie was. And that worried her.

Her head was spinning with all these bloody unanswered questions. She understood the need to disappear without trace. Back when she'd done a runner to get away from Pete and Big Tony, she hadn't told anyone – except the friend who'd offered her a place to stay in the Medway. And if she'd had to change her plans, she would have let her friend know. Why hadn't Hennie done that? Something must have happened to prevent her phoning Carol and telling her where she was.

Carol was of the same opinion, which was why she insisted on bringing the Old Bill in despite Steph's efforts to talk her out of it. Which meant Steph could either let Carol go on her own, which would be a complete bloody disaster, or go along with her and try to stop her saying anything that might get her in trouble. Fletch didn't make idle threats. What he did to Sharon was proof of that.

At least she'd talked her into visiting a station outside of the area, somewhere outside Artie's turf. They'd decided on Dartford.

'It's like no one else cares, apart from me . . . and Steph, of course. But I know something's happened to Mum.' Carol's eyes filled with tears as she sat in the interview room across the table from Detective Constable Natalia Whiteside.

DC Whiteside was a slim, attractive young woman with the bluest of eyes. She smiled warmly at the two women and seemed to empathise. Having assured them the police would take the case seriously, she said she would ask her sergeant to come down and talk to them.

'Can't you sort this out for us?' Steph asked. It was rare for the Old Bill to show her any respect, but DC Whiteside seemed genuinely kind.

'I'm afraid not, but don't worry. He'll be down shortly.' Then she paused and looked at Carol. 'You did the right thing, coming in . . . You both did.' Then she gathered up her notepad and left them.

Forty minutes later they were both watching the clock.

'Maybe we should go?' Steph suggested.

'You can, but I need to do this before I go back to London.'

Steph turned to her. 'You do know that you're welcome to stay longer if you like.'

'Thanks, Steph. You've been great and I appreciate it, but I've got to get home for the baby.'

'Okay, but if you want to come back, you can always bring Bobby to mine – it'll be nice to have a little one around.' Steph caught her breath as the image of a bloodstained Babygro flashed through her mind.

'Thanks, but I also think I should get back to the flat in case

Mum does show up. She'll be wondering where I am.' Carol stifled a yawn. She hadn't slept properly in a week, and this morning she'd caught a glance of herself in the mirror: with her hair scraped back tightly from her face, she looked drained, and years older than she was.

'Well, the offer's always there.' Steph knew what it was like having a young kid when you were on your own; she remembered how tough it had been with Stacey. It was completely different with Andy. Rob had done more than his share. Steph quickly shut down that thought, and she was grateful when the door opened. Until she saw who it was.

Steph groaned. *Fuck.*

'Hello, Steph, you're a bit far from your manor, aren't you? I didn't think I'd see you in here, not unless you were in handcuffs, that is.'

Steph hadn't realised that Fred Walker worked out of the station in Dartford. This was a nightmare. 'Yeah, well, it's strange to see you in here too. Usually when I see you, Fred, you've got your dick down some poor cow's throat.' She stared at him hard, trying to put her feelings about him to one side.

DS Walker laughed nastily, threw his pen and notepad down on the table, then spent the next few moments rubbing the egg stain off his navy tie. 'When I heard you were here, I was intrigued.' He winked at Steph. 'I wasn't looking forward to having to cover this station over the holidays, but you've made it worthwhile.' He plonked himself down in the chair. 'So my colleague said you were looking for a missing whore.'

'She never said that,' Steph snapped at him. 'I know she wouldn't have done.'

He smirked. 'Well, what would you call her then?'

'She's my mum.' Carol was upset.

Fred looked at her. 'You have my condolences, love.'

'You're such a fucking arsehole,' Steph muttered under her breath.

'Did you say something, Steph?' He glared at her.

Steph didn't reply.

'So, according to my colleague, your *mum* hasn't been gone that long. He leaned forward, breaking wind at the same time. 'We are talking about Hennie, aren't we?'

Carol nodded miserably. 'You know her?'

Fred leaned back in his chair then. 'I do . . . very well. I think the whole station does.' He chuckled.

This was one of the reasons why Steph hadn't wanted to bother with the Old Bill. No copper was going take them seriously, especially a prick like Fred.

'You see, I know Hennie has done this sort of thing before, hasn't she?' Fred was condescending. 'Disappearing on a whim, then turning up again when she feels like it.' He used his pen to scratch his shoulder blade.

Carol glanced at Steph. 'Yeah she has, but—'

'So there you go. Mystery solved.'

Carol was speechless for a moment. 'But she said she was coming to mine for Christmas. She promised.'

'And Hennie's never broken a promise before? I'd hardly call her reliable.' Fred raised his eyebrows. 'Come on, she works the streets.'

'What difference does that make?' Steph asked him.

'I think it makes a lot of difference. You need to face facts: if she was remotely interested in being a mother, she'd be at home right now, wouldn't she? She wouldn't be doing what she does for a living.'

'That's crap.' It angered Steph to hear Fred speak like this, but it didn't surprise her.

'Well, you would say that, wouldn't you,' sneered Fred. 'Look, she's probably enjoying herself more than we are. A bottle of whisky, a few pills . . .' He shrugged.

Steph shook her head. 'No, she was in a good place, booze and drugs-wise.'

'People relapse, Steph – you of all people know that.'

Steph had to count to three to hold her temper.

'Are you going to help me or not?' Carol's voice broke.

Fred frowned. 'I've already told you what I think: she got a better offer and she's gone off with some bloke. She'll crawl back when she's ready.' He looked square on at Steph. 'How about this . . . if you want me to help you, maybe you should tell my wife to come back home. Seems only fair. You scratch my back . . . or you can always scratch something else.' He winked at her suggestively.

Steph had to stop herself going for him. 'If Rachel has any sense, she'll never go back to you.'

Fred's expression turned nasty. 'Birds of a feather, the whole fucking lot of you.'

'It's attitudes like yours that allowed Sutcliffe to get away with his crimes for so bloody long.'

He rolled his eyes. 'Oh, do me a favour, Steph. For a start, there were dead bodies everywhere in that case. All that's happened here is Hennie doing what she does best: disappearing for a while. Secondly, like my mate who worked on that case said, what do you lot expect if you will go off in strangers' cars? Did no one tell you not to talk to strangers when you were growing up?' He roared with laughter, which turned into a coughing fit.

Eventually, red-faced, he wiped his mouth. 'But if it makes you happy I'll file this one for you . . . under *missing Hennie*.' He grinned and stood up then.

'And Nancy.' Steph's tone was urgent.

Fred frowned. 'Nancy. What about her?'

'I don't know where she is either.' Steph hadn't wanted to allow herself to be worried any more than she was. She knew it might sound hysterical, but Nancy had promised to call her, and she hadn't. Like a lot of the women who didn't have family, she turned to Steph for support, so she would've expected to hear from her.

'Since when?' There was a look of disdain on Fred's face.

'Since Christmas Day.'

'Christmas Day?' Fred laughed. 'What is this, Steph? You back on the tipple or something? You do know wasting police time comes under Section 5 of the 1967 Criminal Law Act. It carries up to six months in prison. So if I were you I'd think twice before you start spouting any more of your rubbish.'

Steph chewed on her lip. There were so many reasons to hate Fred. 'Something doesn't feel right. Nancy told me she was pregnant, and she was leaving, but she also said she'd call me, and she hasn't . . . and Hennie hasn't contacted Carol. It feels like there's something wrong.' She didn't want to upset Carol, but the more Steph thought about it, the more her gut was screaming at her. Something was off.

Fred leaned forward. 'I tell you what, Steph, how about we do this? How about you come back here when there's a body, eh?' He winked again.

Steph was so angry she was shaking.

'That can't be it – we drove all the way here for this?' Carol complained.

Without bothering to answer her, Fred headed for the door. He opened it, gesturing for them to leave.

'*Wait*, there's a bloke called Artie,' Carol blurted out. 'I think he did something to my mum.'

Steph shook her head. They'd discussed it in the car on the way over and she thought they'd reached an understanding that Carol would *not* bring Artie's name into it. 'We don't know that, Carol. We're just wanting to find Hennie, aren't we?' She hoped Carol would take the hint.

Carol's eyes were wide open. 'But everyone knows he threatened her.' She glanced back at Fred. 'So you better go and speak to him, as well as his mate Fletch.' Carol was firm.

'She's upset,' Steph pleaded, trying to defuse the situation. This was a disaster. 'She's worried about her mum – she doesn't mean anything by it.'

'I *do* mean it.' Carol turned on Steph. 'I do fucking mean every word of it.'

'Carol, come on – let's go.' Steph got up and gently pulled Carol off her chair, and towards the door. DS Walker was the worst person she could have said this to. By the time they got out of the station, he would've picked up the phone to Artie and Fletch.

'I think you should listen to her. You wouldn't want anyone finding out you were here, would you?' Holding his notebook, Fred threw a cold stare at Carol.

'But I want to report—'

'*Not here!*' Steph raised her voice, but quickly brought it down. Her intention wasn't to upset Carol, rather she needed to protect her from herself. '*Please,* let's go. It's not going to do any good . . . It's pointless.'

Steph gave Carol no choice, dragging her out as Fred stood in the doorway of the interview room and watched them go.

They hurried towards the main exit of the police station, but Steph stopped in her tracks. 'Wait here for me, Carol. I'll be back in a minute.'

She turned and rushed back, hurrying to catch DS Walker. 'Wait up . . . *Hold on.*'

He turned to look at her. 'What now?'

Steph kept her voice low. She pointed her perfectly manicured finger at him. 'I know what you did, you sick fucking bastard. I know it was you who sent me that present and destroyed Andy's grave. Did you really think that would break me? I know I can't prove it yet, but I swear to God one day I'll have you for it, Fred. Trust me, you won't get away with it.'

When she was done, Steph walked away with her head held high. *Prick.*

But one thing troubled her: Fred hadn't looked like he had any idea what she was talking about . . .

Chapter Forty-Nine

There was no word on Sharon yet. Danny had called the hospital three times. In the meantime, he shifted his focus to getting some of his old acquaintances on board. He had a feeling Artie and Fletch would be on the back foot right now, but that wouldn't last long. Problem was, everyone he'd reached out to so far had turned him down or decided that they had short fucking memories. How many blokes had he helped over the years, eh? And not one, not fucking one so far wanted to return the favour.

He slammed down the phone. '*Cunt.*'

'What's up?' Bill said as he skinned up a joint on his large, battered couch. He and Danny had decided that he'd stay here for the time being.

'I thought I could rely on Kev, but apparently he's out of the game. Which is fucking bullshit, because we both know that if I was offering him five grand to help me he'd be here faster than a streak of piss.'

Bill lit his joint and took a deep drag on it. 'Can't you just go in and finish what you started? Blow the cunts away?'

'Do I look like Pablo fucking Escobar?' Danny tried not to sound irritated, but this wasn't turning out how he'd thought it would. 'I'm not spending the rest of my life behind bars for

255

those two cunts. I have to be smarter than that. I want to do this properly – there can't be any fuck-ups. Artie and Fletch have well and truly got this whole manor stitched up.'

'Then what are we supposed to do?'

Danny had thought about this already. 'If we can't start at the top, we'll start at the bottom.'

Feeling stoned, Bill shrugged. 'What do you mean?'

'We can get some of the girls that work for him on our side. I know most of them.'

Bill raised his eyebrows. 'That's risky, ain't it?'

'Depends who we ask . . . I know Artie takes every single fucking penny they make. None of them are happy with that, so what I'm thinking is it won't take much to give them a better deal than they're getting from Artie and Fletch. They'll be begging to come work for us.'

It made sense to Bill, but he could see a problem. 'But they're terrified of him. Shit-scared. Even if they wanted to come and work for you, they wouldn't dare. The way Artie and Fletch treat them . . .' He took another drag on his spliff as he thought about it. 'It's like . . . it's like he's fucking brainwashed them through fear. Either that or he's got them bang on the gear.'

Danny sank into the chair by the fireplace.

It was taking some getting used to, being on the outside. Last night he'd struggled to sleep because he'd found it so quiet. He was used to lags yelling and banging on their cell door, making a fucking racket.

He sighed and glanced around the untidy lounge. There were opened packets of nappies and heaps of laundry that needed folding. Cory's toys were scattered over the floor, along with Holly's changing mat and a tin of SMA formula milk. Bill had told him that he'd put Holly on that the minute she was born due to all the gear in Janey's system. Not that Janey was remotely interested in being a mother, from what Danny had seen. She was a selfish cow, like she'd always been.

Thinking of bad parents, his thoughts returned to Potter. The plank had been on his mind since he saw him at the hospital. He wasn't sure what he was going to do – it would have to wait until he had Artie and Fletch sorted.

Suddenly it came to him. 'I know – we give them protection. We give them a place to work out of that Artie and Fletch won't know about. It's not perfect, but it would be a start.'

Bill looked sceptical.

'I'm not saying it'll be easy, Bill, but it's a way to do it. Apart from fear, the other thing Artie and Fletch have going for them is money. If we stop the flow of notes, then it'll make it harder for them to stay on top. Trust me, mate. Knock the bottom out, and the top comes tumbling down.'

Bill nodded. That made sense. 'I still like the idea of you blowing the cunts away.' He laughed.

Danny winked at him. 'Oh, believe me, that will come.'

'*All right?*' Janey put her head round the door. Her hair was matted, and she was sporting a black eye from where Nancy had clumped her one on Christmas Day. 'I thought I'd go for a walk, get some fresh air.'

Bill looked suspicious. 'I'll come with you.'

She scowled at him. 'I've got my own shadow – I don't need another one.'

Bill was hurt. He didn't know why Janey pushed him away all the time. He was also worried that she was going out to score. He didn't trust her to come back. He knew it was fucked up, but he enjoyed having her around and missed her when she wasn't here.

'The kids have been doing my head in,' she said, softening slightly, and Bill had to stop himself pointing out that they'd been with Sarah most of the morning. Soon as they got home, they'd both fallen asleep. And when Holly had woken up, *he'd* been the one to give her a bottle.

'Okay, why don't you take Holly then? She could do with some fresh air too.' Bill nodded towards the pram in the corner where their daughter was fast asleep.

Janey thought about refusing, but even that seemed too much effort. 'Fine.' She tutted and walked across to the pram.

Bill watched her. 'Love ya.'

'Yeah, whatever.' Janey rolled her eyes.

Danny watched her flick off the brakes and push the pram through the open doorway. Not for the first time he wished that Bill would get rid of her. She was nothing but trouble.

Janey pushed Holly down the corridor and out through the concrete hallways of the estate. She paused to grab the packet of Silk Cut cigarettes that was tucked under Holly's blanket, and quickly lit it.

Glancing over her shoulder to make sure Bill hadn't decided to follow her, she hurried through the empty children's park, crossing over the junction by the pub on the corner where she looked behind her once more. Being around Bill always made her feel claustrophobic. He just didn't seem to get that she couldn't be what he wanted her to be. And him crowding her and following her wasn't going to change that.

With the coast clear, she broke into a jog, pushing the pram down the street, turning into the disused car park and heading for the big metal bins.

'Where the fuck have you been?' Artie shouted as he got

out of his black Mercedes Benz, leaving Fletch in the passenger seat.

The conversation with Steph yesterday had fucked Artie off and he was still brewing about it, not to mention the shit with Danny.

He grabbed Janey by her face, bringing it within inches of his.

Janey squealed as Artie squeezed her cheeks hard. 'I should give you a right fucking clump. When I say you're to be here at a certain time, I mean it. Understand?'

Janey gave him the smallest nod.

He let her go. 'Well?'

Janey found herself glancing around again. It would be typical of Bill to follow her, so he could keep an eye on her and Holly, and she certainly didn't want him to see her here talking to Artie with Holly in tow. There'd be murders.

She'd only told Artie about Sharon – she'd kept Bill's name out of it. She didn't want Artie or Fletch putting *him* in hospital. If that happened, she'd be lumbered with the kids.

'He's there. Danny's staying with Bill.' Janey sounded breathless.

Artie swore. Danny was a brazen cunt, he'd give him that, and whatever he was up to he was determined to find out. He didn't want any more nasty surprises.

'So what was said?'

Janey shrugged.

Artie punched her hard in the side of her head and she fell back into Holly's pram. Immediately, Holly began to cry.

Ignoring the screaming baby, Artie snarled at Janey. 'Where do you get off shrugging at me?'

Janey scooped Holly up. Not because she was bothered about her wellbeing, but she hoped it might stop Artie giving her another whack if she had the baby in her arms. 'Sorry,' she muttered.

'I should think so too . . . Come on then, what was said?'

'I couldn't hear much. I swear. They only came back from the hospital a short while ago . . . But it was mainly that a lot of the blokes Danny had thought were going to help him don't want to know . . . They were talking too quietly for me to hear anything else.'

Artie gripped Janey's arm. 'You'd better not be lying to me.'

'I'm not.'

Artie let her go and he stalked back across to the car.

'Hold up, Artie . . . *Artie!*' Still carrying Holly, she hurried after him. 'You said if I'd told you, you'd sort me out . . . Art, you promised.' Wide-eyed, Janey whined at him.

Artie stared at her in disgust. She was like a rat, trying to sniff out something. She worked for him, and therefore if he said jump, she would fucking jump. 'You haven't told me anything though, have you?'

'I will. They're bound to talk in front of me. Bill won't suspect anything.'

Artie held her stare and moodily rummaged in his pocket, pulling out a small wrap of brown. She grabbed it greedily. 'If you want more, you need to get me actual info on what's happening. It's your job to play the doting girlfriend – can you manage that?'

She nodded. Bill would be made up that she was staying in the flat for a while instead of going back to Artie's. And Janey reckoned it would be the easiest bit of smack she'd ever earnt. 'Yeah, course I can.'

'Good, because then there'll be plenty more where this came from.'

Guilty

She nodded again, and hurried to put Holly back in the pram so she could go and shoot up in the public toilets round the corner.

As Janey ran off, Artie watched her. She might be a hopeless smackhead, but for now she was going to be very useful to him. She'd sell her baby for the next fix, so getting information from her about Danny would be piss easy.

He got back in his car, and turned the engine on. That was one problem solved. The other problem might be trickier: where the fuck did that whore Nancy get to?

Chapter Fifty

Joseph was standing in the dark basement of his house. A small battery light flickered over in the far corner. This was his private space. No one came down here apart from him. It was a place where he could live out his fantasies away from judgement, away from the noise that was so often in his head. Just being in here soothed it.

He stared at Nancy, inhaling her stench. He could smell the filth that poured from her. She disgusted him. And he tilted his head as he stared at the blood from her scalp, which had now dried down her face, making her look even more monstrous. Like the vile creature she was.

He smirked as he watched her shivering, curled up in fear. Naked. Exposing herself to him like she'd done on that day. Like she did to all men.

Her mouth and hands were bound with tape and the thin blindfold he'd put on her was tied tightly. Her helplessness, her fear was perfect. His silent laughter became manic as he imagined the terror she was feeling right now.

Amusing himself, he tapped his foot on the cold concrete. He had to bite down on his lip to stop himself chuckling out loud as she whipped her head towards the noise then shuffled further into the darkness.

Joseph closed his eyes and rotated his neck to release the tension. Opening his eyes, he crept as silently as possible, hoping to surprise her, but the way her body tensed, he realised she'd already heard him. She'd spoilt it.

Annoyed, he crouched and pulled down her blindfold. His face was inches away from hers and his breathing became heavy. 'Hello, Nancy. Did you have a nice sleep?'

Her eyes sprang wide open. She started to grunt and make muffled sounds. Tears trickled down her face, stuffing up her nose. Her breathing became laboured as the gaffer tape pulled on her mouth.

The knife Joseph held in his hand caught the light in the basement. He studied his reflection in the blade. With a smirk, he pointed the tip towards her. 'Don't scream, Nancy. Understand?'

She nodded and he ripped the tape from her mouth.

'He'll fucking kill you, Jo, when he finds out what you've done.' Nancy swallowed hard, it felt such an effort to get her words out. 'Artie will proper fuck you up for this.'

Joseph gave her a pitiful look. 'You said yourself that you didn't tell anyone. Artie has no idea you're here. And, anyway, do you *really* think that he'd miss someone like you? . . . Look at you. You stink. You pollute the air that I breathe. No one will care what happens to you.'

'You're wrong.' Nancy sobbed. 'Once they realise I'm missing, the Old Bill will come looking for me.'

'The police?' He laughed loudly. 'They'll be *pleased* the streets are being purged of women like you.' Joseph tilted his head again as he stared at her, and he brought his voice down to a whisper. 'No one will care . . . I'm all you've got.'

He trailed his finger down her cheek and leaned in to lick her tears away with his fat, sticky tongue while his beard scratched across her skin.

Nancy fought the urge to be sick. 'Steph will care. I know she will.'

The grin on Jospeh's face turned demonic, and his eyes were dark with a vacancy that Nancy had never seen before. 'That interfering bitch doesn't know that you're here . . . And believe me, Nancy, she doesn't care about you either. Steph only thinks about herself.'

Nancy shook her head. 'You have to let me go, Jo.'

'Oh, but I don't.' Delighted, he hugged himself. 'I don't.'

Nancy couldn't stop herself trembling. 'What . . . what are you going to do to me?'

He placed his hand on her naked stomach. A rush of excitement went through him.

She jolted back.

'I'm going to wait, Nancy . . . A child doesn't deserve a whore for a mother. They're precious. They're the innocent ones,' he whispered.

Nancy's heart was thumping hard.

His lip curled in disgust at her. 'But *you* . . . you're worth nothing to me. You do know that, Nancy, don't you?'

Her face was so close to his he could bite it off. The fear oozed from her, and Joseph found himself savouring her terror.

He stood up, his erection bulging.

Nancy watched as he paced back and forth, chattering to himself as if there was someone else here. All she'd wanted to do was escape from Artie and feel like she was human again. But that wasn't going to happen now. And the realisation of what Joseph would do to her once this baby came suddenly hit her.

Hearing a noise, Joseph looked up.

She was vomiting.

He stared at her in revulsion. But then, while she was here, he might as well use her . . . Bending down, he pulled her legs wide apart.

And as Joseph unzipped his trousers, upstairs in the hallway, Zack trembled in terror as he listened at the door. His dad had brought home another one.

Chapter Fifty-One

It was Sunday evening and Danny was checking over his shoulder as he hurried up the path. 'Steph! *Steph!*' He kept his voice low as he jogged up to her. He was freezing. He'd walked over to her place, constantly checking if anyone was watching. He'd thought about knocking, but there was a slim possibility Artie and Fletch might be there.

'What are you doing here?' Steph was surprised to see him. She was also nervous about Danny being here.

'I wanted to have a quick chat, if that's all right.'

Steph glanced at her watch. She'd taken a call from Liza a short while ago and promised to meet her. Not that she fancied going out this evening. She was shattered.

This morning, she'd bundled Carol on the train back to London. She'd wanted her gone before Artie and Fletch came looking for her; DS Walker was bound to have told them Carol had tried to make a report. Steph owed it to Hennie to look after her daughter, and there was no way she was going to allow anyone to harm her.

Ever since Carol had showed up, Steph had been hoping Hennie would phone and put them out of their misery, or even turn up in the dead of night like she'd done so many times in the past. But she hadn't, and Steph was afraid she never would.

'Yeah, sure, I've only got five minutes though.' The last few days had taken it out of Steph. She'd been hoping for a hot bath and an early night, but the phone call from Liza had changed all that. By the time she'd checked on Stace and her friend Tammy, who was staying over, she'd only had time to pull on a pair of clean jeans and a turtle-neck top.

'You know most people round here, don't you?' Danny said, and once again Steph found herself having to look away from his intense stare. 'So I wondered if you knew some bloke called Joseph Potter. He's got a daughter, Bel, about Stace's age.'

'Joseph?' Steph hadn't expected this. 'Yeah, yeah, I know him. I know him well, actually. He's a nice guy, helps out at the refuge. How do you know him? How do you know Bel?'

Danny didn't answer the questions directly. 'It's Potter I'm interested in.'

'Can I ask why?' Steph shuddered as it began to drizzle.

'He's living in my mum's house.'

Steph blinked several times, trying to process this information. 'Wait. What. Jo is living in Paula's house?'

Danny clenched and unclenched his fists. Just the thought of that cunt made him want to throttle the bastard. 'Yep, thieving bastard took it from right under my nose. I don't know how he managed to persuade her, but she changed her will and left the house to him.'

Steph raised her eyebrows. She wasn't sure what to say. She'd never asked Joseph where he lived, but then why would she? Likewise, he'd never asked where she lived either. Asking personal questions for no particular reason was something Steph didn't do as a rule. She'd learned from working on the streets and running the refuge that prying into people's business uninvited, *wasn't* the way to build trust.

267

Martina Cole

'I had no idea, Dan. Small world, eh.' Steph heard the bemuse-
ment in her own voice. 'The most he's ever mentioned is that he
lives somewhere outside Gillingham.'

'Just off the Lower Rainham Road, actually. It's fucked up,
that's what it is . . . You don't think it's weird he never said anything to you.'

Steph shrugged. 'Well, I guess he doesn't realise I know you,
so it wouldn't be a talking point. He's quite a private bloke
anyway.'

'He got his fucking feet well under the table.' Danny started
to wind himself up. 'Going round to Mum when I was banged
up, playing the good fucking Samaritan. That can't be right,
can it?'

'All I know is the old ladies seem to love him. He spends so
much of his time with them.'

Danny glowered. 'What sort of bloke does that? Spending
your days visiting old ladies – do me a favour!'

Steph hid her smile as she zipped up her leather jacket. 'I suppose when people are on their own and don't see anyone all day,
they value his visits. Paula was probably grateful to see Jo . . . It's
no different from a doctor going out and about on his rounds.'

'Yeah, Dr fucking Crippen.'

Steph did laugh then. 'Dan, he's a decent bloke.'

Danny wasn't laughing. 'Nah, I'm telling you, Steph, that
geezer is a wrong 'un. His daughter is terrified of him. That
doesn't say "decent bloke" to me.'

Steph's smile dropped then. 'Bel? What do you mean?'

'I saw her in the hospital when we went to see Sharon, and
the way the geezer looked at me . . . Steph, you don't live a life
like I have and not know when someone is pretending to be
something they ain't.'

268

Steph flicked a glance at her watch again. She had to go. She could understand why Danny would be pissed off that Paula had left her house to Jo, but clearly he had been there for her when Danny hadn't. She knew there had been tensions with his mum long before he was sent down. That was why she'd never been to Paula's house when she was seeing Danny.

'Listen, I'm sorry but I really have to dash.' Steph began to walk away. 'And I swear, Dan, you'd like Jo if you got to know him. He spends most of his time looking after his kids. His wife died, so he does it all. He's harmless.'

'I've been inside that place. I've looked around, and there's something not right . . . I'm telling you, darlin', that Joseph Potter isn't what he seems.'

Chapter Fifty-Two

Steph arrived late; thanks to roadworks, she'd had to take the long way round. The whole drive over, she'd thought about what Danny had said. She didn't want to know why he'd broken in to Joseph's house, and she couldn't think why he would say Bel was terrified of Jo. Maybe it was Danny she'd been terrified of; from what she'd seen of them, Joseph's children led a pretty sheltered life.

Perhaps everything was getting too much for Jo and he wasn't coping as well as he made out. Maybe there was something she could do? She wouldn't usually drop round unannounced to people's houses, but it sounded like Jo was someone who needed help only he didn't know how to ask for it.

Making her mind up to pop round when she had the time, Steph parked her car opposite the refuge. She got out, tucking her keys into her pocket, and strode across the road. Liza was standing outside waiting for her. Christ almighty, Artie and Fletch had a lot to answer for.

'All right, darlin', sorry if I've kept you waiting . . . You could've gone inside, you know.' Steph could see how tense Liza was. She could also smell booze on her breath.

'No, I didn't want to. I was fine out here.'

Steph smiled. 'How's Jack?'

'Not good.'

Steph nodded. It sounded like Jack was being a right pain. No matter how hard it was for him, he needed to be there for Liza. 'What did he say?'

Liza shivered in the biting wind. 'Nothing. I said I was going to Nora's. He's giving me too much grief.'

Steph thought Liza was going to say something else, but she didn't. Instead, she looked away, and for a moment they stood in silence before Liza looked back at Steph.

'I'm so angry, Steph.'

'I know.' Steph couldn't remember a Christmas where she'd been surrounded by so many people with problems, and most of them could be traced back to Artie and Fletch. The one good piece of news was that Sharon was in a stable condition, but after the beating she'd taken who knew what long-term damage she might have suffered.

'Look, hun, why don't we go inside,' Steph urged. 'Come on, what do you say? I can make you a nice cup of tea and we can have another chat.'

'No, I'm all right.' Liza was firm. 'Do you mind if we go now?'

'Sure . . . of course, come on.' Steph walked the short distance to where she'd parked her car. She opened the passenger seat and let Liza in, before hurrying round to the driver's side.

Steph reached for a cigarette and offered Liza one, but she shook her head.

'You been decorating?' Liza said flatly. She nodded to the paint stains that Steph hadn't been able to remove.

'Something like that.' Steph wasn't about to go into it. She switched on the radio and changed the subject. 'How can this be the Christmas number one? I'm not a fan myself – I prefer a bit of Slade.' She laughed, trying to make small talk, but it sounded hollow even to her.

'I quite like it.' Liza shrugged. She knew that Steph was only trying to be friendly, but she didn't want to talk. She turned her head and watched night fall over Gillingham as the car filled with Jackie Wilson singing 'Reet Petite'.

The journey only took fifteen minutes, but it was completely dark by the time they arrived. Steph turned off the engine. 'Ready, love?'

Liza didn't answer. They both got out and walked slowly along the lane, the dim streetlights illuminating their path. Even though Liza wasn't saying anything, Steph felt her tension.

'All right, darlin'? How was your Christmas? Mine was fucking shit!' Jean greeted Steph.

'Don't even ask!'

'That bad, eh . . . So what brings you here?'

'I'm here to introduce you to Liza . . . I think you've already met though. She's here to work the lane.'

Chapter Fifty-Three

'You're fucking kidding me! You hear that, girls?' Jean stood with her arms folded, glaring at Liza. The other six women, all regulars on the lane, gathered round to see what was going on.

'That's the bird from the other night.' Claudette, a small black woman with straightened relaxed hair, scowled. She wore a fluorescent-pink skin-tight dress under a cropped fur coat that she'd nicked from Selfridges.

'Skanky bitch,' lisped a woman so thin she looked on the verge of anorexia. There was a gap where her two front teeth had been knocked out by her boyfriend.

'Watch your mouth, Mary. There's no need for that.' Steph threw her a hard stare.

Mary didn't back down. 'That's exactly what she is. She never even asked permission from Jean. Some fucking front, if you ask me. You should've seen her, Steph, thought she was fucking Marilyn Monroe the way she was wiggling her arse about.'

Steph doubted that was true. Mary was always causing trouble and trying to wind the other women up.

Jean pulled a face. 'Yeah, and now she's gone running to you, Steph. Fucking grass.'

'That's not how it was. Come on, Jean, you know the score.' Steph, who was pleased she was dressed in warm clothes, spoke firmly. She'd known Jean for a good six or seven years. When she'd first met her, Jean had been running from her husband who doubled as her pimp. He was also father to her six kids, all of whom had been taken into care. Back then, Jean hadn't been sassy like she was now. She'd actually been terrified and had spent most of the first year looking over her shoulder.

'It looks like it to me.' Jean took a defiant puff on her spliff. The sleet had turned into a light drizzle, and it was freezing. 'Why should we let her work the lane?'

Steph rolled her eyes. She'd run into the same problem with Jean before. 'Can I remind you that, until this lane is named after you, it's not actually down to you who works it.'

Jean grinned at her. She respected Steph and had all the time in the world for her. 'It would sound pretty fucking good though if it was. Jean's Lane.'

Claudette cackled. 'Lain with her legs open, more like.'

The women all laughed, and the tension seemed to subside a bit.

'So, listen you lot, if Liza wants to work here, then I'm telling you she can.' Steph looked at them all. The lane was an area where the women who didn't have pimps worked. It was more dangerous for them in one way because there was no protection from punters, but in another way, not having a pimp like Artie gave them a certain freedom. 'Not only that,' Steph added, 'but the same way you lot look out for each other, I want you to look out for her. This is all new to her.'

'Fucking hell, we've got a virgin with us!' This from Becky, a heavy woman in her forties, who'd been on the game since her liking for booze had turned into an addiction.

Steph glanced at Liza. She could see this was difficult for her, and she reached for her hand and held it. 'Come on, girls, you

Guilty

remember what the first time was like. It's fucking tough – we all know that.'

'First bloke I went with I got fucking herpes from!'

'That's not helpful, Kate.' Steph raised her eyebrows at the petite blonde who looked to be in her forties though she was a decade younger.

'What? I'm only saying.'

Jean gave her a nudge. 'And who's fucking fault is that, Kate? What do we always tell you?'

'Use a fucking rubber!' the women all chorused.

'I can't even remember my first punter,' said Jean. 'I think it was sometime after my first kid.' She shrugged. 'One dick looks same as another to me.' She turned to Liza and saw that the poor cow looked terrified. Softening towards her, she confided, 'It's no different from fucking your fella. All you have to do is lie back and think of what you're going to have for tea tomorrow night.'

Claudette nodded. 'If they ask you how old you are, tell them you're twenty-one.'

Liza attempted a smile.

'And ask them for twenty quid – any more, you might put them off. She only charges a tenner.' Claudette nodded towards Kate. 'Mary sometimes only charges a fiver – but then her fanny is minging!' She winked at Mary, who grinned back at her. 'And if they ask you for something you don't like, you don't have to do it. If you're not comfortable with any of the blokes, follow your gut. Don't put yourself at risk. There are some right fucking weirdos out there, ain't there, Steph?'

Steph nodded, trying not to think about Hennie and Nancy.

'Don't look so scared,' Jean continued. 'Seeing as Steph asked so nicely, we'll look after you, won't we, girls?'

275

All the women nodded

'The thing is, doll' – Claudette pulled a face – 'you look more like a school teacher than a tom. Unless the punter is into discipline, you'll put the fucker right off.'

Liza looked down at the navy skirt and cream blouse she was wearing. It was the outfit she'd worn to her nan's funeral.

'I tell you what, love . . .' Claudette walked up to Liza and shoved her hand up Liza's blouse, rolling over the waistband of her skirt a few times to make it shorter before proceeding to tuck the bottom of her blouse under her bra to make a crop top. She stood back, admiring her handiwork. 'There you go, how's that? You'll have the punters drooling now.'

'You can see my stretch marks.' Liza's voice broke as she looked down at her exposed flesh.

'They won't care about that. As long as you've got a pussy, an arsehole, one hand that works properly and a mouth that opens, they couldn't care less.'

'I don't know.' Liza was panicking now. It was as if the Valium she'd taken had suddenly worn off and it all felt too real. But then she thought of her girls, and what Fletch had threatened to do if she didn't have the money, and that gave her strength.

'Listen, you don't have to do this.' Steph turned to her. 'We can go back to the refuge or come back to mine and have a nice cuppa, and we can try this again some other time, or not at all.'

'Go back home, darlin'.' Claudette smiled at her.

Everything in Liza wanted to do just that. To take the kids and run. 'I can't though. I have to do this.'

'Why?' Jean was curious.

'I owe money.'

Jean frowned. 'Who to?'

'A bloke called Fletch.'

Guilty

'Oh fuck.' Mary pulled a face. 'You better whip off your knickers right now then, girl.' She laughed and the others laughed too, lightening the atmosphere again.

'It'll only be for a short time.' Liza shrugged.

'That's what they all say.' Kate grinned at her. 'I was only going to do this for a month to pay for me kids, but look at me – ten years later and I'm still here. I reckon I'll be here until I take me last breath. I only hope I don't die with a cock in me mouth!'

Jean burst out laughing. 'Look, if you don't want to get into anyone's car, for now you can always use the hut behind them trees. I warn you though, a lot of punters don't like it in there cos it stinks of piss, so you might lose their business. But maybe for now, until you find your feet, take them in there.'

Liza glanced at Steph. 'You will hang around, won't you?' Her words rushed out.

'Of course. I'll be over there in the car.'

Liza nodded. Even though Steph was going to be close by, she had never felt so alone in her life.

Chapter Fifty-Four

'Do you think she's going to be all right?'

Jean had come over to join Steph as she sat in her car watching Liza, who was standing under one of the streetlights.

'I hope so, for her sake.' Steph sighed. 'But she's already a fucking wreck.'

'Reckon she's going to stick it out?' Jean sniffed and took a sip from her miniature bottle of vodka. It looked like it was going to be a slow night, which meant a long one, so she had to keep herself warm somehow.

'Who knows. She hasn't even told her old man . . . He's being a complete arsehole about it.'

'Which bloke isn't?'

Steph grinned. 'In one way, I wish she'd get back in the car so I can take her home. But she needs the money and, well, you know yourself, there are some things we would never do if we weren't desperate, and Liza's desperate.' Steph took a draw on her cigarette. 'You know what Fletch is like. He's proper put the fucking fear up her.'

'Can't you have a word?' Jean wondered.

Blowing smoke out of the window, Steph glanced at her. 'I've tried, but right now it's all a mess. Fucking bastards, both of them . . . You know they put Sharon in hospital?'

Guilty

'I heard . . . I also heard Danny's back.'

Steph took a deep breath. 'Yeah. It's going to blow up, I'm telling you, Jean.'

'Were you pleased to see him?'

Jean was one of the few people Steph had confided in. 'I wasn't,' she confessed. 'But now . . . I dunno. It's nice to see him, and it would be great if he could sort Fletch out without anyone else getting hurt – there's been too much of that already. Still, if I'm honest, it's messed with my head a bit. I still belong to Rob.'

Jean smiled. 'I know you do, but letting yourself have a bit of happiness won't change the way you feel about Rob. You can love two people . . . Look at me, I love several fellas every night.' She cackled. 'All I'm saying is, don't rule it out. You deserve to be happy. We all want to see that.'

'Are you going to tell Artie that, or shall I?' Steph grinned.

'Fuck him. He's another arsehole, but Danny will sort him out.' Jean laughed again. 'By the way, next time you see Nancy, tell her she owes me a fucking apology.'

Steph looked surprised. 'How come?'

'We were going to hook up on Christmas night. I saw her on the Maidstone Road, coming out of Artie's place. She said she was off to see someone, but she'd come to my gaff afterwards for a celebration drink.' Jean shrugged. 'She never showed though.'

'What was she celebrating?'

'She said she was about to come into a bit of money.'

'Her and Hennie' – Steph rolled her eyes – 'I tell you, Jean, between them, they've done my fucking head in this Christmas.' She let out a shaky sigh. 'To tell you the truth, I'm worried sick about them. Hennie was supposed to go up to London to stay with her daughter and she never showed. Now Nancy seems to have disappeared as well. She swore she'd call me, and she hasn't. Maybe it's something and nothing. Girls come and go, but . . .'

Jean grinned. 'You're like a mother hen, you know that? Maybe they've pissed off together to the Costa del Sol with all that money Hennie nicked. I wouldn't blame them.' She cackled. 'And Cheryl's probably with them.'

Steph frowned. 'Cheryl?'

'Yeah, no one's seen her in a while either. But you know what she's like. Love her, but she's a scatty cow. Worse than the whole lot of 'em put together.' She winked at Steph, but before she managed to say anything else, a driver slowed in the distance and flashed their hazard lights.

Jean immediately hitched up her boobs in her low-cut top. 'I'll see you in a bit, doll.'

'Hold up, Jean.' Steph tried to call her back. 'Wait, tell me a bit more about Cheryl. What exactly happened?'

'Sorry, got to go, hun – a girl's gotta do what a girl's gotta do. Catch you later.' Jean waved and shoved the vodka in her pocket, tottering off towards the car where it had parked halfway down the lane.

Steph squinted through the rain, watching Jean hurry away. She couldn't see properly, and as the lights faded into the gloomy night she suddenly sat up straight. A few feet away, she noticed a bloke walking up to Liza. It crossed her mind to get out of the car, but she waited when she realised they were walking towards where she was parked.

They wandered past and Steph could see the strain and fear on Liza's face. The bloke Liza was with was short and far too heavy for his height. He waddled along next to her. Thanks to his polyester trousers, she could actually hear his thighs rubbing together. Steph couldn't make out if it was beads of sweat sitting on his bald head or raindrops. She kept her an eye on Liza in the driver's mirror until they turned the corner, heading towards the hut . . .

Liza could feel Steph staring at her as she walked past her car. She hadn't looked. She hadn't dared to. Both the Valium and the quarter-bottle of gin she'd knocked back earlier had worn off. The reality of what she was doing made her feel sick, and she was struggling to breathe.

What should've been a quiet evening in front of the telly watching crap with the girls and Jack was now being spent with some bloke who hadn't even agreed to the twenty quid. The punter, who'd said his name was Brian, offered her fifteen and Liza had decided she wasn't in any fit state to bargain with him. So she'd agreed, and he'd followed her along the road to the hut at the far end of the waste ground behind the lane.

The women hadn't been kidding when they told her it stank of piss. A battery lamp hung from the ceiling. There was a wet, stained mattress that made Liza's skin crawl just to look at it. There was a pile of used condoms in the corner and a grubby tube of KY jelly on the dusty wooden shelf.

'Get your top off. Show us your tits,' Brian growled.

Liza found she couldn't move. She was frozen to the spot.

'I said, *show us your tits*.' Brian's tone became aggressive, and Liza closed her eyes and began to unbutton her blouse. Slowly she took it off until she was standing in her bra and skirt.

'And that . . . take that off too.'

Liza opened her eyes then to look at him.

'Your bra. Go on then, hurry up, before I explode.' He rubbed the bulge in his trousers.

Liza unhooked her bra at the back and dropped it to the floor.

Brian stared at her then and leaned forward to flick her nipples, leering at her before cupping her heavy breasts in his hands. To Liza it felt like there were insects crawling under her skin, and she had to swallow hard not to be sick.

Brian moved his hands away and quickly fumbled with his belt, unzipping his trousers and dropping them to his knees. His semen-stained Y-fronts swelled at the front and Liza could hear his breath getting heavier as his pudgy fingers popped out his penis from his pants.

He began to pull his foreskin back and forth, making himself groan, and in that moment, Liza didn't know if her legs would hold her or not. She reached out to lean her weight on the side of the hut for support.

With one hand on his penis, Brian's other hand fumbled up Liza's skirt, pulling her knickers to one side. He plunged his fingers hard inside her. It was like an electric bolt had run through her. She screamed and, pausing only to pick up her bra and blouse, she hurtled out of the hut, tearing through the car park and along the road.

Steph had been dozing off when she heard a scream. She immediately jumped out of the car and saw Liza, semi-naked, running towards her in the heavy rain.

'What's happened?' Steph rushed up to her. 'Did he hurt you? Because if he did, I'll fucking kill him.'

Liza could only shake her head and Steph took off her coat to wrap it around her. She led her to the car.

'Just take me home.' Liza was crying hard.

Steph opened the door and helped her in. The poor cow was really shaken up. She hurried round to the driver's side, wanting

Guilty

to get Liza out of here as soon as possible. She wasn't ready for this life, and Steph wondered if she'd ever be.

With Liza sobbing next to her, Steph turned the engine on. She glanced around the dark, rainy lane and her stomach knotted. She was suddenly overwhelmed with dread as she thought about the three women: Hennie, Nancy and now Cheryl. All missing.

Chapter Fifty-Five

'Well?' Joseph sat at the end of the table. He moved his gaze between Bel and Zack. 'Where did it come from?'

It was Monday morning and the room was so cold Bel could see her breath. The whole place was freezing. It was hard – not to mention expensive – to keep an old house warm, especially when none of the windows fitted properly and there was a constant draught under the doors.

On the table in front of them sat the Fry's Peppermint Cream wrapper. Bel had eaten half and given the rest to Zack. She hadn't told him where she'd got it, knowing he would only worry. He had promised to throw the wrapper away when he put the bins out, but clearly he'd forgotten.

Bel had thought a lot about the fella who gave it to her. When she'd seen him in the A & E the other day, she'd been terrified he was going to say something to her dad, but he hadn't. It was strange because, even though he'd been in the house *with a gun*, she hadn't been scared of him like she was of her dad. That night, she'd even imagined him coming back and putting a gun to her dad's head and taking him away forever.

Joseph stared at the wrapper he'd laid out in front of him on the table. He leaned forward, resting his arms on the table as the grandfather clock in the hall chimed. He slammed his fist on the table. 'Is no one going to tell me how it got into the house?'

Bel and Zack remained silent.

Joseph nodded, looking from one to the other, but they didn't meet his gaze. He scraped back his chair and went to fetch the cast-iron kettle from the stove, then he turned on the tap and filled it.

He glared at his children again before lighting the stove and placing the kettle on the burner. Then he turned round to face Bel and Zack, his arms folded.

No one spoke or moved.

The kettle began to boil, and Bel stared at the steam coming out of the spout. Her knees were trembling under the table. She gave a quick sidewards glance at Zack, and saw the colour drain from his face.

Bel wasn't sure what was wrong with her brother. The last few days, he'd been looking even more scared than usual. She'd tried to speak to him about it when Dad went out, but he'd gone up to his room without answering her.

Bel continued to watch the kettle as the steam twisted in the air.

'Is no one going to tell me?' Joseph's voice was harsh.

She heard Zack's breathing change, and from the corner of her eye, she saw him start to shake. He looked so much like their mum, especially when he was frightened. Zack had been so close to her. As soon as their dad went out, he'd do his best to care for her on those days she'd been too weak to get out of bed because of the things Dad had done to her. But all Zack could really do for their mum was hold her hand.

'It was me.' Bel spoke up. 'It was me, I brought it into the house. It was *nothing* to do with Zack. He didn't know anything about it.'

Joseph, who was wearing a green cable sweater Nora had bought him for Christmas, grabbed the chequered tea towel from the side. He used it to cover the handle of the kettle as he slid it off the burner and poured the water into his mug. Then he dropped in a teabag and placed the kettle on the table before opening one of the kitchen drawers.

Pulling out a small orange medicine bottle, Joseph popped off the top. He shook the pills on to his hand, then dropped them into the tea, stirring it with a teaspoon, making sure they'd properly dissolved. All the while he kept his eyes on his daughter.

He smiled at Bel. 'Go on.'

'I . . . I . . . I got it from Steph.' The minute Bel said it, she wished she hadn't, but she couldn't think of anything else to say.

'Steph?' Joseph narrowed his eyes at his daughter. 'Why would Steph give you a bar of chocolate? And *when* did she give it you?' The teaspoon rattled on the mug as his stirring became more violent. Brash, tarty bitch, poking her nose into other people's business..

'It . . . it was, er . . . I saw her after school, before term finished.'

'And she gave you the chocolate?'

'Yes, Dad.'

He lowered his voice. 'She's trying to make you like her, Bel. That's why she gave you that.' He nodded to the wrapper. 'She wants you to be just like her. A filthy little bitch.' He stared at her with his dark eyes. 'You need to remember that. You don't

286

want to end up like her, do you? You don't want to end up like your mother?'

These words terrified Bel. She wouldn't let her thoughts go back to that day. She watched her dad. She balled her hands into fists to stop herself from shaking. 'I'm sorry.'

Even if Steph had given her the chocolate, which she hadn't, Bel couldn't see why it was such a bad thing to be like Steph.

Joseph came to sit down next to Bel. He gently flicked back her hair from her shoulder. Keeping his eyes on his daughter, he spoke to Zack. 'Go to your room, Zack.'

Bel threw a troubled stare at her brother as he hurried, head down, from the kitchen.

Turning back to Bel, Joseph took her hands in his. His voice was quiet she had to strain to hear it. 'And you and I, Bel . . .' He stroked her face, then pushed the cup of tea he'd made towards her. 'Drink it.'

'No, Dad, *please*.' She shook her head. He had that dead, far-away gaze in his eyes. '*Daddy*, no.'

Joseph lunged forward and grabbed her hair. '*Drink it!*'

Bel's eyes filled with tears. She knew what was going to happen. Trembling and with no choice, she took the chipped mug and began to sip the tea.

'All of it, Bel.'

He didn't take his eyes off her until she'd finished it all, then he sat and watched her and waited . . .

Half an hour later, Joseph carried a sedated Bel down the hall-way towards his bedroom.

There was a loud knock on the door.

'*Jo, it's only me*,' Steph's voice called through the letter box. '*Jo?*'

Joseph froze.

'*Joseph, you there?*'

Still holding Bel in his arms, he crept towards the window, craning his neck round the curtain. He watched Steph looking up at the house and gazing around. As usual, she was dressed like a cheap tart. The anger rose up in him and he wondered how she'd found out where he lived.

The knocking became louder. '*Jo? It's Steph.*'

Shaking with hatred, he closed his eyes, steadying his breathing. He pictured his wife and remembered her screams. All the things that he'd done to her because she'd been a cheating whore. The pain he'd inflicted on her. The terror he'd forced into her. She'd deserved every single moment of it.

With that thought playing in his mind, Joseph smiled. A feeling of warmth flooded through him as he made his way to his bedroom carrying Bel.

Standing in the rain, Steph frowned. She could've sworn she'd heard someone moving inside. Never mind. Hopefully Joseph would be at the refuge later, and she could grab a quick word with him to make sure everything was all right. It seemed like everyone was having a tough time of it right now. The new year couldn't come round quickly enough for her liking.

As she moved away from the front door, she noticed the tyres on Joseph's van were covered in thick mud. Without giving it another thought, Steph got in her car and drove off.

Down in the basement, Nancy had heard Steph's voice. Her hands were taped behind her back and there was gaffer tape over her mouth, but she'd tried desperately to bang her feet against the wall to draw attention to herself. The walls were too thick though. All she'd managed to do was hurt the soles of her feet.

Convinced her one and only chance of escape had just passed her by, Nancy curled up in a ball, trying to keep herself warm.

She going to die down here. It was just a question of when.

Chapter Fifty-Six

Danny could just about see the entrance to Bill's block of flats from where he was sitting. He'd been parked in the alleyway for over an hour, watching the comings and goings. So far, no one apart from a group of teenagers and an old dear pushing her shopping trolley had come out of the block.

Turning the heat to full blast, he resisted the urge to light another cigarette.

The passenger door opened.

'Fucking hell, it's freezing.' Steph jumped in. Her face was red from the cold. 'Sorry I'm late, Dan. I popped over to see Joseph.'

'How did you get on? What did the cunt have to say?'

Steph shook her head. 'Nothing, I didn't see him . . . Anyway, what's this about?'

Danny had called the refuge this morning, asking to meet with her. She'd thought about refusing, but it'd sounded urgent. She needed to visit Rob – the hospital had just called telling her he'd picked up yet another chest infection – but she'd agreed to swing by and see Danny first. 'So go on, what's so important?'

Danny kept his eyes focused on the flats' entrance. He supposed he could've waited to speak to Steph, and maybe it was an excuse to be near her, but he'd wanted to run something past her. With tension between Bill and Steph at an all-time high, her coming to the flat wasn't an option, so he'd told Bill he was meeting up with an old mate.

'You're close to Artie's women, aren't you? They trust you.'

Steph nodded. 'I hope so. Most of them do, anyway. Why?'

'I want you to ask them if they'd consider working for me.'

'What?'

Danny shuffled round in his seat to look at her. 'Working for Artie and Fletch, they're like prisoners. They get fuck-all money, and they're treated like punchbags.'

'And you want me to ask them to risk their necks by jumping from one pimp to another? What do you take me for, Dan?'

'It wouldn't be like that.'

'That's exactly what it would be like. I want them to get out of the game, not do a sidestep. I can't be part of that, Danny.'

Perhaps he shouldn't be, but he was irritated now. 'So what, you'd prefer for them to get a hammering every time they don't bring back enough money?'

'That's bang out of order, Dan.'

'Is it?'

'Yeah, it fucking is. I'm here for the women, not you.'

He shrugged. 'Then you should see it makes sense for them to work for me. The ones who are with Artie already can trade out of a place I'm trying to sort, and the ones down the lane can come and work there too – it would be a lot safer.'

Her thoughts turning immediately to the three missing women, Steph felt a lump form in her throat. 'Maybe,' she said quietly.

'Eh, what's up?'

She looked at him. 'You know three women have gone missing? Hennie, Nancy and Cheryl. They've just vanished. I keep saying to myself it's just the way things are on the streets. Girls

Martina Cole

come and go, but deep down I know something's wrong. I know something's happened to them.'

'You think Artie's involved?'

She shook her head. 'No. I mean, I can't swear by it. If it was just Hennie, maybe, but Artie didn't have a problem with Nancy, not really. She was pregnant, so he was more likely to drag her down the clinic than anything else.'

Danny wasn't so sure. Artie and Fletch wouldn't think twice about getting rid of a tom who caused them grief.

'And they had no connection with Cheryl,' Steph continued. 'She didn't even work for them.' Steph clenched her fists. She didn't want to get over-emotional, but she couldn't keep kidding herself that all three women had just decided to move on without a word to anyone. 'I'm scared, Dan. I'm scared for them.'

Danny had never seen Steph like this, and he'd known her a long time. 'What are you going to do about it?'

'I don't know. What can I do? Apart from tell the women to be careful. The Old Bill ain't going to look into it until dead bodies start showing up.'

'Then get the women to work for me. I can keep them safe.'

'Are you joking? Have you heard yourself? I've just told you my mates are missing, and all you can think about is putting money in your pocket.' Steph started to get out of the car.

'Wait, Steph.' He reached over and held her hand.

It was like a jolt of electricity shot through her at his touch. She pulled away guiltily.

'I'm not saying this to take advantage of the situation. I wouldn't even take a big cut, hardly anything. The women can keep most of what they earn.'

'So you're trying to tell me you're doing it out of the goodness of your heart?' Steph's voice dripped with sarcasm.

292

'I'm doing it to destroy Artie and Fletch. Like I told Bill, the way to bring them down is to stop their flow of money. For a start, without money, they can't pay off the coppers, which means they won't be protected by them.'

Steph could see how it would be a much better deal for the women. Danny wasn't a bastard when it came to pimping, far from it. The women who'd worked for him before he'd been sent down had said he was the best. But, when it came down to it, a pimp was still a pimp.

'If you want to ask them, be my guest, but I'm not recruiting for you, Dan. I'm sorry – I can't.'

'Even if it means them being safe?'

There was a bang on the window. They both jumped.

'Hello, Dan. So it's true then?' Mary, one of the regulars on the lane, grinned at him. 'You're out.' She waved to Steph as Danny rolled down the window.

'Hello, darlin'. It's good to see you.' Danny spoke to her warmly. 'How are you?'

As Mary launched into the saga of her ingrowing toenail and Steph let herself out of the car, Danny caught sight of Janey hurrying out of the block. A car he recognized pulled up at the kerb in front of her. It was Artie's black Mercedes Benz. Danny watched her get in, and wondered what she was up to . . .

Chapter Fifty-Seven

'Do you want me to swing by and pick you up later?' Joseph asked as he pulled up outside Nora's.

Beside him in the passenger seat, Liza sat staring ahead of her. She had dark rings under her eyes, which were swollen from where she'd been crying. She'd sounded subdued when she'd rung him earlier, asking if he could give her a lift to her aunt's place, and she'd barely said a word since she got in the van. He wondered if she was coming down with something. Must've caught it at the refuge on Christmas Day. Those filthy sluts, spreading their germs as usual.

'No, I'm fine, Jo. Thank you.'

He could see she was far from fine. And, according to Nora, that husband of hers wasn't helping matters. Since he'd got out of the hospital he'd been knocking back booze and pain medication, leaving her to get on with everything.

'Soon as I get a bit of spare cash, I'll sort out some petrol money for you,' she said, clearly embarrassed. 'You've been driving me around like you're my personal bleedin' chauffeur lately.'

'Now you're being silly. It's no bother, really. I'm more than happy to help.' He smiled at her. 'Anyway, if you're sure I can't pick you up later, I'll see you soon.'

'I'd like that.' Liza reached for the door handle to let herself out.

He called her back. 'Wait, Liza. I'm sorry I can't help you with this Fletch business, but I just haven't got that kind of money.'

'Jesus, Jo, it's fine . . . but I appreciate you saying. We're all in the same boat. I was actually building up the courage to ask Nora, but the other day I saw one of her bank statements and she's hardly got anything either.'

'Are things really that bad?'

Liza sighed. 'You have no fucking idea.'

'So what are you going to do?'

Liza shrugged. 'I dunno.' She did, but there was no way she was going to tell Joseph. She liked and respected him. Maybe it was stupid, but she couldn't stand the thought of him thinking less of her. 'I'll sort something though.' She tried to sound casual, but it was all she could do not to be sick.

Nora appeared at her front door. She must have seen Jo's van pull up.

'I'd better say, hello.' Joseph grinned. He'd thought about Liza a lot recently. Not the thoughts he usually had; these thoughts seemed different somehow, not as loud, not as fierce as the ones that kept him awake at night when he pictured all the others.

Liza was different to them. She hadn't been contaminated.

'She'll never forgive you otherwise, Jo.'

Joseph snapped himself away from what he was thinking. He wound down his window as Liza got out. 'How you doing, Nora?'

Nora hobbled across to her garden gate. 'I was hoping to do

a bit of weeding, make the most of the sunshine, but it looks like it's going to rain again.'

'You want to mind how you go, Nora. I don't want you tripping on that crazy paving. I'll sort out the garden for you.'

'You do enough,' Nora called back.

Liza grinned up at him. 'Saint Joseph.'

Unlike Nancy, she wasn't jeering when she called him a saint. He turned the engine back on. 'I'll see you ladies later.'

'You won't come in, Joseph?' Nora sounded disappointed.

'Not today, I've got a few errands to run. But I'll be around tomorrow to bring you the delights of Medway meals on wheels.'

Nora's false teeth, which were slightly too big for her, moved forward in her mouth as she laughed.

As Joseph set off in the van, his mind wandered to the Scottish whore who'd jeeringly called him 'Saint Joseph' that time he refused her offer of a blow job. She'd been another of the refuge regulars. She used to go in there and whine to Steph about how she wanted to get away from Artie, leave the life behind. What a joke! As if a whore could become a decent woman simply by moving from one place to another.

He turned left into Jeffery Street. He'd been just north of here, driving around in the small hours, when he'd spotted her tottering along in her high heels. He didn't have his hammer with him, so he'd parked up near a skip, filled his sock with broken bricks, and used that to smash her over the head. The sound when it cracked her skull had been so loud he'd almost come there and then. He burst out laughing, remembering the fun he'd had with Bridget when he'd taken her home.

The laughter turned to anger when he saw Steph up ahead. Beeping his horn, he pulled over and wound down his window.

Forcing a smile to his face, he watched her saunter over, breasts wobbling and hips gyrating. Gagging for it.

'Hiya, you all right?' she screeched in that awful voice of hers. 'I popped round to yours earlier.'

'To mine? I didn't know you knew where I lived . . . Is everything all right?' He didn't say he'd seen her sticking her dirty nose into his business. 'What a shame I missed you.'

'I was passing' – Steph, who didn't usually lie, found herself doing just that – 'and on the spur of the moment I thought maybe Zack and Bel might want to pop over and see Stace. She's getting a bit bored with the holidays. She'll be pleased when she gets back to school, if you ask me.'

'You were passing? Where were you coming from?'

The lying bitch hadn't been expecting that. It took her a minute to come up with an answer.

'I, er . . . I . . . was visiting a friend. She doesn't live far from you.'

There was an uncomfortable silence.

'How are you, anyway?' Steph eventually said. 'You know, if there's anything I can ever do for you, you only need to ask.'

'I appreciate that.' His fingernails were digging into his palm as he said it.

She nodded. 'Anyway, I better get on. I'm heading off to see Rob. He hasn't been well and I'm shitting myself a bit. It's one thing us getting a chest infection, it's another thing for him. It can be really dangerous in his condition.'

Steph turned and started to hurry away.

'Oh, Steph . . .' Joseph called after her. 'I wanted to thank you for the present you gave Bel.'

Steph whirled round. 'Present?'

'The chocolate.' Joseph held her gaze. 'The chocolate you gave her.'

She frowned. 'You must have got it mixed up. I didn't give her anything, hun.'

'Yeah, right, I must have got mixed up.' Joseph nodded. 'Anyway, I better shoot off.'

Steph began to walk away again, but, suddenly uneasy, she turned round. 'Joseph, wait! I do remember now. My head's a bit of a mess, what with Rob an' all. Of course I got her the chocolate . . . Sorry, slipped right out of my mind.'

He could feel his erection growing as he thought of the many ways he'd make her suffer before putting her out of her misery.

'What chocolate was it?' he asked innocently. 'The kids seemed to enjoy it so much, I thought I'd buy them some more. They've been so good lately.' His stare didn't waver.

'Er . . . er, God, now you're asking . . . Yorkie bar, I think.' Steph clocked his expression. 'Actually, no. No, I don't think it was.' She scrambled for an answer. 'Er . . . let me think.' Why would Bel tell him she'd bought her chocolate? It was a strange thing to do. 'You know, it was actually from Stacey, Jo. She chose it . . . I'll ask her, if you like.'

For the first time, Steph noticed how dark Joseph's eyes were when he looked at her.

'Yeah, you do that, Steph.'

And with those words, Joseph drove off.

As Steph watched Joseph go, she recalled what Danny had said: *there's something not right . . . I'm telling you, darlin', that Joseph Potter isn't what he seems.*

Chapter Fifty-Eight

Over in the Potter house, Zack was pushing his eye against the keyhole. It was no use though – he couldn't see anything. It was too dark. He'd taken the key down from the top of the door frame where his dad had left it, but his hands were trembling so much he found it hard to put it in the lock.

Taking a deep breath, he tried again. This time he managed to do it. He turned the key and the sound of the padlock popping off the door seemed to echo around the whole house, causing Zack to freeze.

His legs shook and the tiniest yelp left his lips. He was terrified his dad would come back. Breathing in and out deeply, as his mum had taught him to when he'd get upset after watching the things Dad did to her, he managed to calm himself down.

Feeling slightly braver now, Zack opened the basement door . . .

He knew the risk he was taking, but he needed to do this. His bedroom was directly above the basement; night after night he'd lain awake listening to the noises. He needed to see for himself . . .

The thought of how much he hated his father made Zack's breath catch in his throat. Even having that thought, petrified him. At times it seemed his dad was able to tell what he'd been thinking.

Carefully, Zack descended the stairs into the darkness, taking care not to trip. He trailed his fingers along the damp wall. On reaching the bottom step, his hand hovered over the light switch. He was scared to turn it on. He remembered the blood the last time he'd been down here. Zack squeezed his eyes, trying to erase the image of the lifeless body from his mind.

He heard a noise, a shuffling sound in the darkness. To Zack it sounded like a monster, like his dad. Everything about his dad was evil. His dark, lifeless eyes, the things he used to do to him at night that made it difficult to walk the next day, and the things he now did to Bel.

Shaking, Zack wiped his tears in the crook of his arm, and turned on the light . . .

Nancy had been expecting Joseph, but instead a tall, painfully thin boy – fourteen or fifteen at most – stood staring at her from beneath his straggly auburn fringe.

Instinctively, she shrank as far back as she could against the cold wall.

The woman's eyes were wide open, and Zack recognised her fear. He'd seen the same look in Bel's eyes . . . and in his mum's. Her mouth and wrists were bound with the grey gaffer tape that his dad kept in his van. Her ankles were tied with rope.

Zack felt uncomfortable, seeing her naked. It made him feel strange.

Slowly, he moved towards her, keeping his eyes locked on hers the whole time. His ears were on the alert for sounds from upstairs, and he was crouched, ready to run or hide if he heard someone coming.

He reached out to peel the gaffer tape off her mouth, hesitating until she nodded for him to go ahead.

As soon as he tore it off, Nancy gasped for air. Her words tumbled out:

'My name's Nancy, and I need you to help me . . . Please, help me . . . You've got to help me get out of here. Quickly, please . . . *Hurry up . . . Hurry up.*'

'I . . . I . . .' Zack froze.

'Please, Joseph's going to kill me . . . Do you understand? *He's going to kill me.*' Her eyes were wide with terror.

Zack's heart leapt into his mouth at the sound of a vehicle pulling up on the gravel. His father was back! Terrified, he stuck the tape back on Nancy's face and raced from the basement, switching off the light as he went. He turned the key in the lock, put it back on the ledge of the door frame.

He made it back to his bedroom in the nick of time. No sooner had he thrown himself on his bed than he heard the front door open.

As he listening to his dad moving around downstairs, Zack stared up at the ceiling . . .

Nancy, her name was Nancy . . .

Chapter Fifty-Nine

'I know you're in there!' Fletch was hammering on the door of Liza and Jack's house. 'Open up *now*. You can't hide from me, you understand? I want my money, and if I don't fucking get it in my hand soon, you can pick which one of your girls you want to say goodbye to.'

With the rumour mill in overdrive with shit about Danny coming back to reclaim his turf, Fletch and Artie had decided to show their faces in each estate in the area so everyone would know they were still very much in charge.

'Shall I boot it down?' Fletch gestured to the door.

'Nah.' The place was in darkness, and Artie doubted anyone was in. Besides, he wanted to get to the hospital, see how Rob was doing.

'Leave it until Thursday. That will give them the full week. You don't want people to think we're not true to our word.' Artie laughed and glanced around at all the flats overlooking them. 'And there are enough twitching nets around here for word to get back to Jack that we were here to pay him a visit.'

'Shame,' said Fletch, disappointed. 'I was looking forward to having a bit of fun.'

*

Inside the flat, Liza cowered in the hallway as their voices faded away. She waited a few more minutes before running through to the front room where Jack lay drunk on the couch.

'Jack . . . *Jack*, wake up . . . Jack, come on, wake up.' She shook him by the shoulders. He groaned and turned over. 'Jack, you've got to wake up . . . Fletch has just been. Fletch and Artie. Jack, for fuck's sake!'

Getting no response from her husband, Liza rushed for the phone. She needed to talk to Steph, but after a few rings she heard Steph's new answer machine kick in.

There were some crackling noises, followed by Steph's voice: *Steph here . . . not in, so leave me a message won't you.*

'Steph, it's Liza. I need to talk to you. Fletch and Artie have been round. I heard every word they said. I'm scared, and I dunno what to do . . . but they're going to be back on Thursday . . . Call me.'

Liza put the phone down. Not only did she need to get the money, she had to get the girls out of the house before Fletch came back. Maybe Steph would take them to keep them safe. It was a lot to ask, but she was desperate, and there was no one else. Nora was too old, and her friend Amy, who usually babysat for her, lived right next door, so that was no use. Then again, there was always Joseph. He had kids and he also knew how desperate she was. Maybe she could ask him to help if Steph couldn't. At least they'd be safe there.

In the meantime, her priority was getting her hands on some cash. She grabbed Jack's half-empty bottle of whisky, which was lying on the floor, and rushed upstairs. Throwing off her blue tracksuit, she put on a black dress and slipped on the white stilettos she'd worn for her wedding. Then she wriggled out of her knickers; after all, there was no point wearing them. With that thought, she dropped the whisky and Valium into her handbag, picked up her coat and ran back downstairs and out of the door into the rainy night.

Chapter Sixty

It was pitch-dark by the time Liza got to the lane. She couldn't walk that fast in the stilettos, so it had taken her ages and her feet were killing her by the time she got there. Thankfully, she hadn't seen anyone she knew. In fact, the town seemed practically deserted tonight; there was hardly any traffic and most of the houses were in darkness. Even the pub on the corner, which was usually heaving, was quiet.

'All right, hun? I didn't think you'd be back again, darlin'.' Mary sauntered up to her, and Liza wondered how she wasn't freezing. She was only wearing a pink boob tube and a leather miniskirt with red patent boots.

'I didn't want to, but I need to pay Fletch.' Liza heard the bitterness in her own voice.

'None of us want to, hun. It's just what we have to do though. How's your old man? He giving you agg about being on the lane?'

Liza wasn't sure how Mary knew about Jack; she doubted Steph would've said anything – it was more likely Janey. But the mention of him stirred a deep resentment in her. She couldn't help feeling she'd be better off without Jack – something she never would have imagined just a month or two ago.

'He's burying his head in the bloody sand, Mary. Spends all

his time drinking himself into oblivion and pretending none of it is happening, leaving me to sort it out.'

'Fucking typical. Blokes are more trouble than they're worth.' Mary rolled her eyes. 'You need to leave him. He sounds a right selfish bastard.'

'I love him though.'

Mary cackled. 'You see, that's the problem. It ain't money that's the root of all evil, it's love. What we fucking do for it, eh? But I'm telling you, if he can't be there in the bad times, he doesn't deserve to be there for the good times.' Mary had a thought. 'Tell you what, you should have a word with Danny.'

'Danny?'

'He's one of Steph's mates. Easy on the eye as well.' She laughed. 'He used to run the area before he was banged up. He's always hated Artie and Fletch and, now he's out, he wants to put those cunts in their place. Between you and me, I was talking to him, and he's looking to put some of the women up in a house, so they can work out of it . . . Nothing's sorted yet, but it's worth thinking about. Keep your mouth shut though, yeah? He doesn't want word of it getting to Artie.'

Liza nodded.

'Anyway, it'll be better than working on the lane. Safer . . . I'd usually steer well clear of pimps – too much fucking grief, plus they take all your money. Danny's different though. But you want to get in there quick – it won't take him long to get all the toms he needs.'

A car pulled up by the side of them. The driver was a small Indian man with a bald head and a messy beard. He gestured with his head to Mary.

She turned to Liza. 'He's one of my regulars. Likes me to

humiliate him.' She grinned. 'Believe me, hun, that's easy.' She giggled and tottered to the car, which immediately drove off.

With Mary gone, the lane was deserted, and Liza decided to stay near the street light, however dim it was. She hoped some of the other women would show up soon, although with the weather being so shitty, Liza wouldn't blame them for not bothering.

She reached into her bag and pulled out the bottle of Bell's and the Valium. Popping a couple of pills into her mouth, she washed them down with the whisky, wincing at the way it burned the back of her throat. Then she glugged down two more large mouthfuls, knowing she'd need it if she was going to do this. Then she began to pace up and down to keep warm. She blew on her hands. They were bloody freezing.

Liza's heart suddenly jumped as she caught sight of the sil-houette of a man on the grassy verge overlooking the lane. He didn't move, and she had the sense he was standing there, watching her. Maybe he was a punter. But then she noticed the way he held his arm by his side. She tried to work out what he was holding . . .

Liza felt her bladder loosen.

He was holding a hammer.

Oh fuck . . . *Fuck.* She started to back away, but she didn't want him to know she'd seen him. What the hell had she been thinking, hanging around here on her own?

The wind had caught up with the rain, making it harder to see, but she kept her eyes on him. As she watched, he began to walk down the verge towards her. *Fuck!*

She kicked off her shoes and started to run.

She'd never been a fast runner, but in her panic she took the concrete stairs two at a time. Her heart was pounding as she ran along the deserted street. Though she daren't look back, she could sense him behind her. Her mouth was dry, and bile rose in her throat. Struggling to catch her breath, she rushed across the road, heading for a row of shops.

Hearing the screeching of brakes, Liza spun round and found her hands on the hot metal of a car bonnet.

'You've got to help me.' She rushed round to the driver's side and banged on the window. 'Let me in . . . *open the door.*'

DS Walker rolled down his window. He looked her up and down. 'You looking for business, love?'

Liza glanced to the side of her. She shook her head. 'No . . . no, there's someone following me. Please, I need a lift.' Her words tumbled out and she rattled the door handle.

'Step away from the car, love.' Fred frowned. He could smell the booze coming off her.

'But you don't understand – there's someone following me.'

Fred glanced in the wing mirror. Drunken cow. Without another word, he put his foot on the accelerator and sped off.

'No! *No!*' Liza screamed. 'Wait . . .' She chased after the car, waving and shouting, but it disappeared into the night.

Sobbing, she turned round, her eyes darting about. The only thing she could see now was darkness . . . but that didn't stop Liza running to the nearest house and pounding on the door.

Chapter Sixty-One

Joseph paced around the basement, his mouth set in a grim line. He felt a rage that he hadn't felt since his mother had died. At first he hadn't realised it was Liza on the lane – he'd been too busy watching the slut in the tight skirt and boob tube. Then he'd recognised her, and disbelief had given way to a sense of betrayal that cut through him like a knife.

He'd wanted to go and speak to her, but when he'd set off down the grassy verge towards her she'd run away. He'd followed, keeping to the shadows as she flagged down a car. He'd watched her, flapping her arms as the car sped off, looking like she was going to be sick, then she'd run to the house on the corner and disappeared inside.

Bitch. BITCH. BITCH.

He kicked the workbench, swiping his arm across the top of it and sending his tools clattering to the floor. 'BITCH!'

They were all the same. Only his mother, Mildred, was different. She'd warned him that sex was sinful, that women were infected with sin. She'd told him they were whores and not to go near them or he'd end up in hell. She'd been right. Liza was walking proof of how right his mother had been.

He'd worshipped the ground Mildred walked on, devoting himself to pleasing her and caring for her. In return, she'd protected him when he'd been bullied for his shyness at school, comforting him when he'd been beaten up. And after his father had left the family house, for some filthy whore he'd met in Clacton, his mother had taken Joseph into her bed and held him close night after night.

Sometimes, it had made Joseph feel strange, especially when his mother had asked him to touch her in places he wasn't sure he should, but he'd adored his mother and trusted her, so he'd done what she'd told him to.

When she was dying, his mother had made him promise that he would stay away from the evil of sex.

He'd kept his promise until that day on Danbury Common. He could still picture her, looking for punters in her short leather mac and high heels. She'd flirted with him, letting him know that she liked him. That's when he'd suggested they go to the pub. He'd waited until the path entered the woods before slipping his hammer from his coat pocket and aimed it at her head, but he tripped on a root and only landed a glancing blow.

The bitch had screamed and tried to crawl away, begging him not to hurt her. He'd dragged her behind the bushes, but she'd continued to make a noise and he'd been worried that someone might hear them. Fly-tippers had dumped a load of household rubbish back there, including an old torn chair, so he'd grabbed a handful of stuffing from it, forcing it down her throat to shut her up. Still she kicked and writhed, scrabbling to get free, making gurgling sounds as she choked. So he'd clamped his hand over her nose, watching the life drain out of her.

'BITCH!'

As he neared his climax, the memory of Liza touting for

business on the lane in her short skirt and white stilettos intruded. The pain of her betrayal turned ecstasy to rage.

Nancy stared at him, terrified.

His face was twisted, his eyes were dark and focused on her, but to Nancy it was like he wasn't actually seeing her. She watched him rock back and forth on the balls on his feet, kicking and throwing things, oblivious to the blood dripping from his hand as he clenched the end of the claw hammer.

She closed her eyes and forced herself not to cry, knowing it only made it harder to breathe.

Then he suddenly fell still. A moment later, she heard him climb the stairs and the light went off . . .

Chapter Sixty-Two

It was Tuesday lunchtime and Liza had just come off the phone with Steph. She'd wanted to meet up, so she could tell her what had happened last night, but Steph was heading out to take her daughter to the dentist. She promised she'd catch up with Liza later.

When she went back into the front room, Jack was still on the couch. His face was strained, and his voice matched it, but Liza kept thinking of what Mary had said: *if he can't be there in the bad times, he doesn't deserve to be there for the good times.*

'It was her who put you up to it, wasn't it,' he said, pointing at the phone. 'Steph.'

'No, of course not. The only person who's put me up to it is you. You and Fletch.'

He shook his head and took a swig of whisky. 'You can't make me feel any more guilty than I am already.'

She sank into the armchair, weary of the conversation that had been going on all morning. 'Fletch is coming tomorrow, and we've got fuck-all money to pay him. Are you listening to me, Jack? Stop playing the fucking victim.'

'I can't do what you're asking me to do. It's fucked up.'

Liza was furious. 'Yeah it is, but do you know what's really

312

fucked up? *Do you?* It's that you expect me to sort all this out on my own while you bury your head in the fucking sand.' She was crying now, which wasn't helping.

'You're asking too much of me.'

'Of you? I'm asking too much of YOU!'

'Just leave me alone,' Jack muttered, reaching for the bottle.

Liza swiped it from his hand. 'Oh no you don't. You don't get to drown your sorrows when I can't. I'd love to forget all about this and lie in a drunken fucking heap, but I can't because if we don't come up with the money by tomorrow, Fletch will make good on his threat.'

'He only said that to scare you.'

'And you know that, do you? You know that for sure? You can promise me he's not going to hurt Mandy or Jess or Bonnie?'

Jack turned his head away, but Liza moved round to get in his face.

'We need to do this. I need you to help me do this, Jack.'

'Not that!' Jack slammed his fist on the arm of the couch. 'I can't deal with it.'

He began to weep, but Liza had no pity for him. He had plenty of his own – he didn't need pity from her as well.

'You think that I can deal with it?' She swiped away her tears.

'I'm not saying that. I just can't get my head around it . . . What the fuck will people think? What will my mates think? What will Ricky think?'

'*Ricky?* You're bothered about fucking Ricky? That's the least of our worries.' She shook her head. 'Look, we don't have to tell anyone, do we? All families have their secrets, but I can't do this on my own. I *can't*, Jack. I need you. *Please*, just ask Ricky if you can borrow his old van. He never uses it. Tell him . . . Tell him you want to get out and about more. He won't mind.'

'But I mind – *I* fucking mind, Liza. Don't you get it?' Jack stared back at her. Then he crumbled. 'Fine . . . fucking fine . . . I'll do it.'

Chapter Sixty-Three

A few hours later, Liza and Jack were sitting in Ricky's old Transit van. As soon as Jack had asked, Ricky had brought the van over, telling them they could use it any time.

Liza tried to turn up the heat. 'I'll leave the engine on, shall I?' Jack shook his head. 'No, it's fine. Turn it off.'

'You'll be cold though,' Liza fussed.

He scowled at her. 'You think I fucking care about that?'

'Jack, stop doing this to me. Stop making me feel like shit, like I'm doing something wrong.'

Sitting in the passenger seat, Jack looked out of the window. His back was in agony, but that was nothing compared to how fucked his head was right now. 'Just *go*.' He wouldn't look at her.

Liza turned off the engine. She was about to say something else, but there were really no words for the way he was behaving towards her.

She got out and glanced over her shoulder in case Jack looked her way. He didn't.

'All right? How's it going?' Claudette grinned at Liza as she tottered down the lane towards her. 'Look at you! That's better – you could pass for a whore now.'

Liza had taken the scissors to one of her skirts and turned it into a mini. She wore black tights and high heels. She was also wearing a red top that she'd cast aside as too small for her, but it was perfect for this.

'I'm all right.' Liza shrugged.

'You sure? The other girls told me you had a bit of a rough time the other night. First time on the lane is always difficult. It'll get easier, and before you know it you won't even think about it. Besides, we'll look out for you.' She nodded towards the van. 'Is that yours?'

'Yeah.' Liza was just about able to see Jack in the van from where she was standing. She knew it'd been a lot to ask . . . *a hell of a lot*, beyond any marriage vow, she was sure. Obviously, she knew that if it came down to it Jack couldn't fight anyone off in his condition. But having him would put off any weirdos. And after the scare she'd had last night, she'd been too terrified to come down here on her own.

'I don't blame you – that hut is fucking minging.' Claudette made a gagging sound.

'It ain't only that. Last night, there was some weirdo here. He was over there –' Liza nodded towards the grass verge – 'and he was watching me. It looked like he was holding a hammer or something.'

Claudette's jaw dropped. 'Are you sure?'

'Yeah, I mean . . . it was dark, but that's what it looked like.' Liza started to doubt herself. 'I don't know for sure . . . I didn't stick around to see.'

'Try not to look so worried. It was probably nothing. You do get a lot of nutcases about, but most of them are harmless. It pays to be careful though. I used to get a battering from one punter or another every other week – that's why I stick to my regulars now.' She smiled. 'You'll be all right. And, like I say, we'll all keep an eye on you.'

Guilty

'Thanks, love. I appreciate that.' Liza glanced round. The lane didn't look very busy. 'Is Jean not working tonight?'

Claudette shook her head. 'I haven't seen her since the last time I saw you.' She shrugged. 'She's probably off on a mad one somewhere . . . Here you go, look.' Claudette nodded her head towards a bloke who was walking towards them. 'Why don't you go for it?'

'What about the other girls?' Liza pointed to a couple of women standing on the other side of the lane.

'They won't mind if you jump the queue this time. They know you're new. Get it over and done with. The less time you have to think about it, the better. Go on . . . and good luck. You'll be fine, love.'

Liza turned and walked towards the bloke.

She took a deep breath.

'You working, darlin'?' He slurred his words as he came up to her. He was on the small side, average build and bad teeth.

'Yeah.'

He looked her up and down. 'How much for the full works?'

Liza swallowed. It took a beat for her to answer.

'Twenty quid.'

'Fine. Where?'

Liza nodded over to the van. They wandered across to it, and she opened the double doors. She clambered in, and switched on the battery torch that was in there. The punter followed her in, shutting the doors behind him.

Breathing hard, Liza tried to calm her nerves and tell herself it was no different from when she'd messed about with lads when she was a teenager at a school.

Shaking, she lay back and hitched up her skirt. Once again, she hadn't bothered wearing knickers.

317

She turned her head as the punter unzipped his trousers, pulling out his erect penis.

Oh God. Liza felt his weight on her.

She tried not to tense as his body pressed down and he buried his face into her neck, making groaning sounds. She felt sick. He grabbed her breast through her thin top. Then Liza felt his penis begin to enter her. She bit down on her lip. Tears pricked in her eyes. It would be over soon. *It would be over soon.* That's what she had to keep telling herself. Then he drove in deeper, thrusting away harder on top of her.

Liza closed her eyes. Knowing that Jack was on the other side of the metal partition messed with her head, but it was the only way she could go through with this. She desperately needed to feel like she wasn't on her own. That they were in this together. She needed to feel he'd look out for her when the punters touched her, fucked her, paid her and wanted her to do things to them she didn't want to do. She needed Jack to be there to pick up the pieces.

As the van rocked, Jack leaned forward and vomited in the footwell. He clenched his fist and smashed it on the dashboard until his knuckles began to bleed. Then he took a gulp from the whisky bottle he'd brought with him. It didn't help. His head was spinning, and even when he covered his ears it didn't block out the sound of his wife being fucked by another man.

In the back of the van, Liza sat up.

It was over. She'd done it. She pulled down her top. She was part way to paying Fletch off. 'That'll be twenty quid, mate.'

'Fuck you . . . Oh I have!' Pete laughed hard and backed away, opening the door to jump out.

'Oi, hold up, where are you going? *Oi, what about my money?*' Liza scrambled out of the van after him and watched him sprint down the lane.

She didn't even bother running after him, it was a waste of time.

'Is that a runner?' Claudette strolled up to her.

'Yeah. I can't believe it.'

'What a bastard. You get the occasional one. It happens to us all, but there's nothing you can do apart from get back on the horse.' She laughed. 'You did it though, Liza, and the night is still young.'

Pete kept running until he reached the end of the lane. Only then did he glance over his shoulder to see if she was following him. She wasn't. *Result.* Panting, he slowed down to a stroll.

As he drew level with the trees, he saw a bloke with a beard sitting in his van. The dome light came on, and Pete got a good view of his face as he turned to reach for something in the driver's door pocket. He frowned, trying to work out where he knew him from . . .

Oh yeah, that was it: he'd seen him at Stacey's school on parents' evening with his two kids. Pete laughed. He'd known the bloke was a perve soon as he looked at him.

The bath was running and in the safety of the bathroom Liza stared at herself in the mirror. She hated what she saw. She made herself feel sick.

Unable to stand the sight of herself any longer, she grabbed the bottle of bleach and poured it into the hot bath.

She stepped in and winced. It was scorching. Then she lowered herself into the water and, using the stiff brush which she usually used only for the kitchen floor, Liza began to scrub her skin as hard as she could, flinching at the pain of it scratching her flesh.

As steam filled the bathroom, Liza began to cry silent tears as she scrubbed harder and harder, causing herself to bleed and the water to turn red. She hoped that somehow the bleach and hot water would wash away how dirty she felt inside.

Chapter Sixty-Four

Steph was running late. Carol had called to ask if there was any news on Hennie. It was obvious she was struggling to cope and had no one to turn to in London, so Steph had listened and tried to be supportive while she poured her heart out. By the time she finally ended the call, opening time at the refuge was just five minutes away. Even if the traffic was light, she wasn't going to make it.

She ran out of the house – and stopped dead.

'*Bastard.*'

Someone had placed a large wreath on her car's windscreen. She glanced around, looking for DS Walker's car. There was no one about, apart from a group of kids over near the bus stop.

She snatched up the wreath and chucked it in her wheelie bin. If she weren't so late, she'd have gone round to the station and given him what for. But then she remembered the look of genuine puzzlement on Walker's face when she'd pulled him up about it.

Dismissing the thought, she got in the car, turned on the radio and headed for the refuge. She had been thinking of putting on a little do today to celebrate New Year's Eve, but with Rob's chest infection showing no signs of improvement, and Artie and Fletch on the rampage, she was in no mood for partying. Truth was, she couldn't wait to see the back of this year.

It took Steph around fifteen minutes to get there. As she parked the car, she saw Joseph and Liza nattering away outside. Liza looked terrible. Poor cow was under so much pressure from Fletch, and Jack seemed to be no bloody use whatsoever.

And then she noticed that Liza had her three daughters with her.

'Everything all right?' She smiled at Liza and nodded to Joseph, while Mandy and her sisters ran across to greet her. Steph gave them each a hug.

Leaving Joseph by the door, Liza hurried over to Steph.

'Are you okay?' Steph frowned.

'I worked last night,' Liza blurted it out, keeping her voice low. She glanced over her shoulder. 'Joseph doesn't know anything about it. I don't want him to know what I'm doing.'

'Don't worry, I won't say anything . . . Was it all right? I would've come down and supported you if I'd known.'

'It was fine . . . I took Jack.'

Steph didn't quite know what to say. '*Jack?*'

'Yeah, we borrowed a van from his mate, Ricky, so I could use that instead of going in the hut. I know it sounds weird, but then everything about this is messed up. Not that Jack was much help . . .' She trailed off.

'Do you want me to have a word with him? Make him cop on to himself a bit?'

Liza shook her head. 'No, it'll only make everything worse . . . He's pissed out of his head at home right now.'

'I'm sorry you're having to deal with this, hun.'

'The thing is, I took Jack along because the other night –' Liza continued, glancing over her shoulder to make sure Joseph couldn't hear – 'I was bloody terrified.'

'When you were in the hut, you mean?'

'No, I went back to the lane the following night on my own, and there was this bloke – he was just watching me. What really freaked me out was it looked as though he was holding a hammer.'

Steph's stomach tightened. 'Are you sure?'

'That's what Claudette asked me last night, and, no, I'm not sure. I didn't see it close up. I only saw his silhouette – he was up on the verge and I was in the lane. But I was bloody scared. Course, I probably wound myself up a bit, being there on my own and all.'

Steph nodded. The lane was certainly a scary place at night. But alarm bells were ringing in her head. She stayed quiet as Liza went on:

'Claudette was lovely though, and Mary, she was all right as well. She introduced me to another couple of girls, and they were all looking out for me. Main thing is, I managed to get Fletch's money, well almost. I borrowed twenty quid from Nora this morning.'

Steph was delighted for her. She'd been so worried. 'That's brilliant. It must be a relief.'

'It is.'

'And how was Jean?' Steph always smiled when she thought about her.

'I dunno, she wasn't there. Claudette said she hadn't seen her since Sunday, when she got into a car with some punter and didn't come back.'

Steph frowned. 'Really? Did she say why?'

'No. Claudette reckons she must've got a better offer else-where.'

Steph felt sick. So Jean was missing as well. It was pointless going back to the police station; they wouldn't take it seriously.

And it was no good asking the girls not to work – that wasn't even a possibility.

She could warn them to be extra careful and keep an eye out, and hopefully they'd listen to her, like they had when that Sutcliffe was on the prowl a few years back. Or she could try having a word with Artie, or Danny. Perhaps when it came down to it, she was wrong not to get the girls to work for Danny in this knocking shop he was talking about setting up, especially the girls that worked on the lane. At least the ones who worked for Artie had a bit of protection. The others had none.

'. . . I got a runner as well.'

'What?' Steph had been too distracted by her own thoughts to pay attention to what Liza was saying.

'A runner,' Liza repeated. 'He had the full works and then ran off without paying the twenty quid— Oh my God.' Liza stared across the road.

'What is it?'

'That fella, the runner, he's over there by the bench.'

'Fuck!' Steph's heart sank. She rolled her eyes. 'That's my ex-partner. Believe me, it doesn't surprise me that he dipped out on you.'

'Oh shit, I'm so sorry.' Liza was mortified.

'There's nothing to be sorry about . . . Hold on a minute.' Steph stormed across the road. 'Pete! *Oi!*' She waved to him. 'Pete, come here *now*. I want a word with you.'

Pete saw Steph hurrying towards him. He'd actually been on his way to see her at the refuge. His neighbour had told him that the Old Bill had showed up looking for him yesterday, so he was hoping he might be able to change her mind about the alibi.

'Where's the money, Pete?' Steph stopped in front of him.

Guilty

'What money?' He had a hangover, and he didn't need her starting any shit with him. He wanted an alibi not a grilling.

'The money, Pete. The money that you owe to the woman you ran off on last night. Twenty quid, I think it was.' She was so angry with him. Fucking typical of Pete. She grabbed him by the coat and tried to put her hand in his pocket.

'Get off me, you crazy bitch. *Get off me!*'

'I want the money, Pete. Give me the bloody money.' She tussled with him.

'I haven't got it. I don't even know what you're talking about. I never did anything.'

'*You're lying.* Now come on, hand it over.' Steph was losing her rag. She'd reached her fucking limit with him.

'You're off your head. I don't know how Stacey puts up with you, you mad fucking witch.'

Just then, a siren made both Pete and Steph look towards the road. The next minute, a police car pulled over, the doors flew open and the Old Bill charged towards them.

'Oh fuck.' Pete began to run, but he hadn't got more than a few hundred feet when they caught up with him. They rugby-tackled him and when Pete toppled to the floor, they piled in. Pete shrieked as he got a boot in the ribs.

'Peter Brown, we are arresting you on suspicion of theft. You do not . . .'

Pete, who was well known to the Old Bill, didn't bother listening to the rest. He knew how it went. Instead, he yelled at Steph, 'Are you happy now?' Then he sniggered nastily. 'But don't complain I never give you anything.'

325

Chapter Sixty-Five

Steph was surprised that Pete didn't put up more of a fight. Whenever she'd seen him arrested in the past, he'd resist for all he was worth. And she wasn't quite sure what he'd meant about not giving her anything. Still, Pete would always be a mystery to her. The main thing was she'd have a bit of peace for a while with him behind bars.

'See you later, Steph. I better go in case Fletch comes round today. I don't want Jack to have to deal with him. The way he is right now, he'll try to cause murders.' Liza hurried past her. 'I'll speak to you later . . . and thanks for everything.'

'Sure— Hold up, what about the kids?' Steph saw Liza's three girls skipping around Joseph.

'I don't want them to be there when Fletch comes round, and Jo said he'd look after them. I know how busy you are, and he said Bel would love to play with them.' She glanced towards the bus stop. 'Sorry, Steph, but I have to dash.' Liza turned and jogged away.

'Liza, *wait*.' Steph called after her. '*Liza!*'

But she was already boarding the bus.

Steph turned and watched Joseph take Mandy's hand as he led the girls up the street.

Guilty

Steph had the keys to the refuge in her hand, ready to open the door, but for some reason she found herself glancing in Jo's direction. He was dressed in a dark blue anorak and polyester brown trousers.

She couldn't stop thinking about what Danny had said: *that geezer is a wrong 'un. His daughter is terrified of him . . .*

She shook her head, put the key in the door and unlocked it, then started gathering the morning's post from the doormat.

Slightly distracted, she flicked through the bills and leaflets, but she suddenly dropped them back on the floor and rushed out.

'Jo . . . *Joseph!*'

She tottered down the street, struggling to run in her tight skirt. 'Jo . . . *Joseph!*' He was almost at the corner. '*Joseph!*' When he didn't respond, Steph shouted as loud as she could. 'JOSEPH!'

This time he did turn round.

He waited for her to catch up as, red-faced and feeling like her lungs were about to burst, Steph hurried towards him.

'Is everything all right?' he asked.

Steph thought she was going to be sick. God she was so unfit. It took a moment before she managed to speak. She rubbed her chest and smiled. 'I'll take the girls, Jo.'

A frown appeared on Joseph's face. 'Liza asked me.'

'Oh, that was only because she thought I couldn't have them.' Steph held her smile.

'As I say, it's fine.' Joseph clutched Mandy's hand firmly and smiled down at her while her two sisters stood on the other side of her. 'We're going to have fun, aren't we, Mandy?'

Shyly, she nodded.

'I can take them, Jo. I've got loads of Stacey's old toys that they can play with.'

Joseph looked as if he was struggling to control his temper. 'Bel's got lots too,' he snapped, and started to move away.

'Jo, *no*. I *said* I'll take them.' Steph used her firmest tone.

'Is there a problem, Steph?'

Once again, she noticed how dark his eyes were. 'Not that I know of.'

'Then have I done something?' He tilted his head. 'I don't understand.'

'No, of course you haven't done anything, and there's nothing to understand, Jo.' Steph wasn't sure why she was so determined not to let him have the kids. He'd never shown her any reason to doubt him. Not really, but she couldn't shake off Danny's warning or that day he'd asked all those questions about what chocolate she'd given Bel.

She reached for Mandy's other hand. 'I'm sure Liza would be pleased if I took them . . .' She looked at him, but he didn't budge. 'Give me them, Jo.'

She gently pulled on Mandy's hand. Joseph tugged the girl's other hand.

They held each other's stare.

'Jo?'

After a beat, Joseph dropped his hold on Mandy's hand.

A large smile spread across his face. 'Well, I'm sure they'll have a great time with you. Better than with me. Another time, maybe . . . Have fun, girls.'

He appeared calm enough, but there was something off about his behaviour and Steph felt sure she'd done the right thing in insisting he hand over the girls.

'Okay, well, I'll see you later then, Jo . . . Come on, you lot, let's go.' Steph walked backwards as she called after Joseph: 'I'll let Liza know I've got them . . . Will I see you later?'

'No, I don't think so.' Joseph's voice was tight.

'Okay. Happy New Year!' She sauntered off with the girls, who were giggling away.

Joseph gripped the nail in his pocket, driving it into his skin. He felt the warm blood trickling over his palm . . . He smiled then as a thought came to him.

By the time he got to Nora's house, the noise in his head was deafening. He parked the van and marched down the path.

Opening the door, he stomped in, slamming it behind him. He marched through to the front lounge to find Nora dusting her ornaments.

'Oh, Jo, you're a sight for sore eyes.' Her face lit up and she hobbled across to greet him.

Joseph was so angry he couldn't speak. He began to pace up and down. He could almost taste the hatred swirling in him. It was like Steph and Liza were mocking him, like those kids at school used to, until his mother had put a stop to it.

The worst of the bullies, a kid called Barry, would follow him all the way home, taunting and mocking him. Until the day he'd followed Joseph right into the garden where Mildred was hanging out the washing. She'd taken a stone and smashed down it on Barry's head.

Even at twelve years old, watching Barry take his last breaths had aroused Joseph. He'd picked up the stone and dropped it again on Barry's broken head. His mother had smiled at him, and stroked his hair. *That's my boy* . . . Barry's body was never found. And the police, useless as usual, had assumed he had run away from his dysfunctional family.

'How are Bel and Zack?'

Joseph continued pacing the lounge. The noise in his head was so loud he didn't hear her.

Stinking sluts. Steph and Liza were two of a kind, but he expected more from Liza. He'd expected her to be sweet and clean like his mother was. Instead, she was dirt. Just like his wife, she'd tricked him into believing she wasn't a whore.

'Is everything all right?' Nora was looking up at him, worried. 'Joseph?'

Joseph blinked rapidly. He stared at her, realising where he was.

'You don't look very well, dear. Are you okay?'

Joseph gritted his teeth and shook his head. He brought his voice down to a whisper and frowned at her from under his bushy eyebrows. 'No, Nora.' His breathing was getting heavier.

'Joseph?'

'Shut up . . . shut up. SHUT UP. SHUT UP!' The noise was hurting his head, pounding behind his eye. He was tired of mouthy bitches chattering away.

A sound behind him made Joseph whip around. 'What are you doing?' He stared at Nora.

She had the telephone receiver in one hand and was dialling with the other. The colour drained from her lined face. 'I'm calling Liza,' she said, her voice strained.

'Liza? You're calling Liza. She's probably too busy sucking cocks.' He sneered at her and laughed nastily.

She started to dial faster.

'I don't think so, Nora. I don't think we'll be doing that, will we?' He snatched the phone from her.

Nora stepped back. Her eyes widened. She stared at Joseph's hand, which was covered in dried blood. Frailty made it difficult for her to get away, and she stumbled. Images of Liza whoring herself on the lane flooded Joseph's head and he struck Nora hard, causing her to fall backwards and smash her skull on the stone hearth.

Joseph tilted his head. 'Whoops, Nora.' He smirked. 'You should've looked where you were going, I always warned you to be careful in case you tripped.' He knelt down next to her, stroked her hair and turned his ear towards her. She was still breathing. He reached across to the cushion on Nora's favourite chair. Then he hovered it over her face. 'Blame Liza, Nora. This is all her fault.' Then he lowered the cushion, covering her nose and mouth making sure it didn't come into contact with the blood which was trickling out of her ear.

Nora's body writhed and he watched her feet spasming as the life drained out of her. After a few minutes, Joseph stood and placed the pillow back on to the chair. He walked over to the sideboard, opened it and grabbed Nora's bottles of painkillers and sleeping tablets.

Stuffing them in his anorak pocket, he wandered over to the phone, cleared his throat and dialled a number.

It was picked up.

'Liza . . . Liza, it's me, Joseph.' He spoke quickly and urgently. 'There's been an accident. It's Nora . . . I came to see her, and I found her on the floor. She must have tripped and banged her head . . . I'm so sorry, Liza. She's gone.'

Having comforted a distraught Liza, Joseph put the phone down. He laughed. Betrayal came in many disguises. Then he let his stare wander over Nora. He looked down at her, another smirk spreading across his face. 'Sweet dreams . . .'

Chapter Sixty-Six

It was six thirty and Steph was locking up the day centre. She wanted to get home and put her feet up, but she was going to swing by the chippie first and pick up some fish and chips for her and Stacey and the girls – assuming they could stay awake. Rachel, who had volunteered to babysit, said they'd had a lovely day, playing non-stop.

Outside, the New Year's fireworks were starting already. She paused by the window to watch the cascading colours, then turned to go. As she did, one of the photographs on the wall caught her eye. It had been taken a couple of years ago at the refuge Christmas party. The women were all wearing their party hats and having a right laugh. Steph smiled, but her smile faded as she looked at the faces of Hennie, Cheryl, Jean, Nancy and Bridget. All gone, all vanished. 'Where are you? What happened?' she asked softly. Then she switched off the light and walked out.

Chapter Sixty-Seven

Zack crept down the basement stairs. He'd left the door open so he could listen out for the sound of his dad returning.

At the bottom, he switched on the light.

'*Nancy.*'

He said her name out loud, which made him feel strange. It also made him feel scared. He hadn't been able to stop thinking about her though. He'd wanted to tell someone what his dad had in the basement, but he didn't know who, and he was too frightened of his dad to actually go through with it. He hated himself for that, but then he really didn't want Nancy to end up like the other ones . . . Like his mum.

Once again, Zack squeezed his eyes shut, not wanting the images the basement conjured to come into his mind. As before, he approached cautiously then carefully tore away her gag. His hands were shaking, and he looked at her shyly. He thought how beautiful she was. 'I brought you some food.' He broke the biscuit that he'd saved for her. 'I brought you this too, but I'll have to take it away with me when I go.' He placed the blanket from his bed over her naked body. 'It'll keep you warm for now.'

Nancy stared at him. Maybe there was some hope for her after all . . .

Book Five

1987
February

Something wicked this way comes.

William Shakespeare, *Macbeth*

Chapter Sixty-Eight

Steph was making a cup of tea for herself. She dropped in a large spoonful of sugar and grabbed her cigarettes from the side. 'Close the window, will you?' she called across to Rachel, who was sitting chatting to Mary. 'It's bloody freezing.'

'I heard on the radio we're going to get some more snow soon. Apparently this is one of the coldest winters in years.'

Steph, dressed in a thigh-length red tartan skirt and a red belt tied round the waist, with matching fishnets, grinned as she blew on her tea. 'Is that supposed to cheer me up?'

The door opened.

'All right, Jo?' Steph automatically started to make a coffee for him.

He hadn't expected her to be here. Wednesdays were her day off. 'Busy as usual. But I thought I'd pop in and pick up the towels for the laundrette.' He wandered casually over and opened the cupboard, grabbing a large armful of laundry. 'Anyway, I best get off.'

'Yeah, cheers, Jo,' Rachel called over. 'No one wants to dry their face on a towel that someone's dried their minge with.' She and the others roared with laughter.

Joseph turned to walk away. They made him sick.

'Have your coffee first, Jo.' Steph walked across to him.

337

'I haven't seen you for a couple of weeks or so. How have you been?' Steph smiled at him.

'I'm good, but work is keeping me busy. We're short-staffed, so I've got extra rounds to do, plus it's not really fair to give the old dears only a few minutes each, especially as I might be the only person they see all day. So it takes a lot of time, and when I am finished it's late, so I go straight home.'

'You're a good bloke, Jo.' Rachel came up to him. 'I don't know many fellas who would care about old people.'

'I cared for my mother a lot when I was younger, and when she was dying I was there until the end, so it comes naturally to me.'

Steph looked at him. This was the first time Joseph had ever mentioned his childhood. 'That must've been tough.' Without thinking, she touched his hand, and although it was only for a split second Steph felt him almost recoil from contact.

'You deal with what life dishes out to you, don't you?'

'I guess you do.' Steph stared into his steely eyes. He looked agitated.

'I really have to go.'

'Not until you have your coffee . . . What's so urgent you can't have a Mellow Bird's?' She laughed, but there was something different about Jo recently, though she couldn't put it into words. 'Anyway, how are you all? Stacey says Bel and Zack haven't been in school much.'

'Oh, they've had the flu bug.' His tone was flat once again.

'Yeah, it's doing the rounds.'

'I was sneezing my tits off last week,' Rachel butted in.

Joseph gave a tight smile and watched Steph over the rim of his mug.

'Eh, are you working tonight—Sorry, Jo, give me a minute.' Steph broke off to hurry over to the two women who were leaving. They were new to the area, although not new to the game.

'Yeah, probably.' Trixie, a tall bleach-blonde whose arms were covered in self-harm scars, nodded.

'Okay, so don't forget what I said, you stay in pairs, all right? Use the hut if they aren't your regulars? Even if it means losing a punter, it's better than anything happening to you.'

Penny, the small black girl with her, pulled a face. 'That's a right fucking pain though. The other girls on the lane aren't happy about it either – we're losing money. Mary reckons it's all bullshit. She says those women just fucked off by themselves.'

Steph wasn't going to start arguing with them. She knew what she believed, and she also knew that once a week she had a phone call from Carol, who was still desperate for answers.

Trixie nodded. 'It's true. Everyone thinks it's safe – well, as safe as it can be.'

Steph tried to keep the irritation from her voice. 'Only because me and Rachel and the others are patrolling at night. Believe me, sweetheart, I'd rather be tucked up in my bed than sitting in a car on the lane babysitting you lot.' She smiled warmly then, and they grinned back at her. She and a couple of other volunteers took it in turns to park up in the lane at night, making sure that the women were safe.

So far it seemed to have worked, but as the weeks had passed, the girls had started taking risks. Take Mary. Twice she'd gone off with some random bloke in a car. The second time, she'd come back bruised and battered, with a couple of broken fingers as well as a tooth knocked out. Women on the game were used to that level of violence – it was nothing out of the ordinary. But there was no telling whether the next time they got into a car, they'd vanish of the face of the earth like Jean.

That was why she kept going down the lane, even though nothing had happened so far this year. Steph was terrified that the day she didn't go would be the day one of them got hurt, and she would never forgive herself. Every time she thought of Hennie, Cheryl, Jean, Nancy and Bridget, she felt like crying. The sadness she held in her heart overwhelmed her at times, but she was determined to find answers, no matter how long it took.

'All I'm saying is be careful, okay?'

While Steph was talking upstairs, Janey was wandering along the street towards the refuge. It had just started drizzling again and her greasy hair was stuck to her forehead. She'd wanted to get away from the flat and Bill, as well as the kids. They were all doing her head in.

Since New Year's, she'd been pleading with Artie to let her go back and live in the house on Maidstone Road, but he had insisted that she stay at Bill's and keep her ear to the ground.

Danny hadn't been around for a while. She didn't know where he was, so she had nothing to report to Artie, which meant he wouldn't give her any free gear. So here she was, having to turn tricks so she could buy herself a fix. And all Bill was doing was moaning about it.

Janey was almost at the door of the refuge when she spotted Joseph's van parked up outside with the window partly open.

She glanced around to see if he was about, then up at the refuge windows. Seeing no one in sight, she ran to the van, slipped her hand through the gap and reached for the door handle. Before she pulled it open, she looked up at the window again to make doubly certain no one was watching.

Once inside, she rummaged in the glove compartment hoping to find cash. *Shit.* Nothing there apart from some gaffer tape and old tools: a hammer and other bits and pieces. She wouldn't even be able to sell them, no one would give her fuck-all for crap like that.

Next, she shoved her hand down the back of the seat – not so much as a coin. She'd always had Potter down as a tight bastard. She flipped down the sun visor; a lot of people tucked a fiver or two there for emergencies. *Fuck*. Nothing. She glanced in the footwell, then she got down to look under the seat.

A broad smile lit up her face.

She could see something.

Pushing her hand under as far as it would go, she grabbed the plastic bag and pulled it out. It held three plastic medicine bottles. She looked at the labels and grinned. Two of the bottles contained Valium and the other one was full of sleeping tablets. She could get a few quid for these. Today was turning out better than she'd thought. Shoving the bottles in her pocket, Janey turned away from the refuge and set off down the road.

Chapter Sixty-Nine

'Steph! *Steph!*' Danny beeped on the horn and waved, pulling over. He watched in the driver's mirror as she sauntered up to the car. She looked good, but then Steph always did.

Steph bent to look at him through the open window, a smile on her face. He hadn't been around for over a month, and during that time she'd tried to put him out of her mind. She couldn't let her mind go there when Rob's condition was steadily deteriorating. Yet she couldn't help being pleased to see Danny, which made her feel guilty all over again. 'All right?'

'Yeah, I am actually.' Danny beamed at her. 'It's good to see you. Hop in.'

Steph did just that. She wasn't dressed for this weather and a lift sounded perfect.

'How's it all going then?' she asked.

Danny pulled away from the kerb and glanced across at her. 'It's been a right fucking pain, to tell you the truth. I managed to get rid of all the gear and, like I said before, I tapped some old mates of mine to get onboard a few jobs.'

Steph knew when Danny said *a few jobs* he didn't mean some shifts behind the counter of a Wimpy bar, he was talking about armed robbery.

'To tell you the truth, my heart wasn't in it, babe. I must be losing my bottle. I was shitting it.' He looked at her again as they waited at the traffic lights. 'All I could think of was having to go back to Maidstone Prison. Fuck that.'

Steph nodded. She knew that Danny hated prison, as most people did, and he certainly hated the idea of going back there, especially as he'd be looking serving significant time: the four years remaining on his sentence, plus extra for whatever other jobs they could pin on him. Whereas petty criminals like Pete were always in and out for short stretches.

She'd got a message from Pete the other day. He'd actually had the cheek to ask her to put him up for a while so he could use her home as his bail address. Sometimes Steph wondered if Pete actually lived on the same planet as everyone else.

'. . . But at least I've got the money I need for everything,' Danny added. 'And I've sorted out the house. The place has got a bit of land, and it needs a bit of work still, but once it's done up the girls will be able to work out of there, or stay there if they want. Don't worry, I promise I'm not going to ask you to get involved. I was out of order last time. I've spoken to a few of them already and they're up for it.'

'Actually, Dan, I don't mind mentioning it to some of them. I won't push it or anything like that, but I want them to be safe. After all the shit recently, I'd rather them be working out of your house than on the lane . . . as long as you mean what you say about not taking all their money.'

Turning right, he shook his head. 'This isn't about me being a pimp, Steph – it's about bringing down those two cunts.'

Steph nodded again. She too wanted Artie and Fletch brought down. According to the women who worked for them, the beatings were more frequent – if that was even possible – and they were off their heads on drugs most of the time, which made them unpredictable. 'Where's the house?'

'It's a bit out of the way – that's why I'm recruiting Bill to drive them there and back if they're not up for staying there. It's over in Boxted Lane on the other side of Rainham.' He paused. 'I wondered if you fancied coming over to see it?'

'When?'

He shrugged. What was it about being with Steph that made him feel so at ease? He'd been shagging about in London for the past few weeks – he was only human, after all – but they were faceless one-night stands. Being with Steph made him feel like a fucking kid. 'There's no time like the present . . . What do you say?'

Steph glanced at her watch. 'Okay, but I have to pop in at Liza's first – she's over on the Queen's Estate, so if you don't mind taking me there. I'll only be a few minutes, but yeah, I'll be up for it.' She smiled at him again, but looked away quickly. She'd missed him, not that she liked to admit that to herself. With all the shit happening around her, he gave her a sense of normality.

'Pull over, will you?' Steph shook her head. 'For fuck's sake, she never changes.'

He parked up quickly by the bus stop. 'What is it?'

'Janey. I'll be back in a minute, yeah.'

Steph jumped out of the car without waiting for Danny to answer. She marched across to the small patch of grass where Janey was talking to a group of teenagers. 'Janey! Janey!' she shouted, and from the expression on Janey's face, Steph could see she knew she'd been caught red-handed.

'What are you doing?' Steph shouted at her again.

The teenagers scampered, leaving Janey standing on her own.

'What's it fucking got to do with you?' Janey was aware that Steph and Artie had fallen out, but that didn't mean that she was entirely comfortable standing up to Steph.

'You're dealing.' Steph was furious.

'So, it's a free world.' Janey shrugged and pulled a face.

'Not when it comes to kids, it ain't.' Steph drew the line there. She wasn't going to stand by and say nothing. 'Some of them can't have been older than Stacey's age, and you're serving them gear?'

'It ain't gear.' Janey crossed her arms, which had fresh track marks up them.

Steph shook her head. 'I don't fucking care what it is, *you don't do it* . . . Hand it over.'

Janey scowled. 'You're not the Old Bill, you know. You may think you are, but you ain't. You're no different to me.'

'That's where you're wrong, love. I might have sold my arse, but what I never did was sell my fucking soul. Now give it me.'

Danny, who'd been watching from the car, suddenly made an appearance. It was difficult for him to sit back and do nothing when it came to Steph.

'Oh, so you're back?' Janey looked at him, making a mental note to tell Artie. Who knows, it might even be worth a bag.

Steph directed her words at Danny. 'She was dealing to them kids.'

Danny stared at Janey in disgust.

'So come on, hand it over,' Steph repeated.

'Why should I?'

'Because I'm not having you walk round the corner and start selling to them kids again.'

Danny grabbed Janey's arm and went into her pocket.

'Fuck off!' Janey whined, and tried to wiggle out of his grip. 'Fuck off . . . They belong to me.'

Danny let her go and handed the three medicine bottles to Steph. She glanced at them, reading the names on the labels. 'I see you've been thieving again then?'

'No.' Janey pouted, which emphasised the scabs around her mouth.

'Yes you fucking have . . . Mrs Smith?' Steph read the names out loud. 'Mr Adams . . . Mrs Patel.' She shook her head, noticing the date of birth on each label. Janey should be ashamed of herself. 'And don't even bother trying to tell me that they're your relatives . . . You make me sick, Janey. Is that what you're doing now, going round breaking into old people's houses?' Steph had no time for addicts who stole from people's homes.

Janey shrugged. 'I'm telling you, I fucking didn't. I found them.'

'Oh, do me a favour – stop the bullshit, Janey.'

'I'm telling you, I found them.'

'You're a liar, Janey, you always have been,' said Danny. 'We all know you've been thieving.'

Janey didn't take kindly to Danny having a go at her as well. 'That's where you're fucking wrong.' Her eyes flashed with anger, and she raised her voice. 'I found them in Joseph's van.'

'What?' Steph frowned.

'See, you think you know everything and you fucking don't!' Janey shouted over her shoulder as she marched off.

As Danny and Steph walked back to his car, Steph stopped. 'There must be an explanation why Jo's got these, right?'

Danny unlocked the car. 'Yeah, an explanation, but not a good one . . .'

Chapter Seventy

Steph was smoking a cigarette in Liza's front room as Danny waited for her in the car. The bottles of medicine were playing on her mind. She needed to decide what to do but first she'd wanted to pop in to see Liza. 'Are you working later, babe?'

'Yes, she fucking is.' This from Jack who sat in the corner of the room, moodily drinking a glass of whisky. Although his injury had got a lot better, his recovery had been much slower than both Liza and Jack had hoped for. He still wasn't able to do any labouring, and the few driving jobs he'd had applied for, he hadn't even got an interview. The same had gone for Liza; she'd tried to get a few shifts in the pub as well as the cafe on the high street, but there just wasn't anything available.

Steph couldn't help herself. She was sick of him. 'Maybe instead of sitting there feeling sorry for yourself, mate, you could try supporting her for once.'

'Fuck off.' He threw his empty packet of cigarettes at her, but it missed. Steph turned her back on him.

'Sorry, perhaps I shouldn't have said that.' Steph brought down her voice.

'Someone has to tell him. He's a joke.' Liza gave Steph an apologetic smile.

'You all right though, hun?' Steph liked to check up on Liza. She'd noticed how much Valium Liza had been popping. Since Nora had died, Liza had slumped into a bit of a depression. She'd loved her aunt and had taken the accident very badly.

'Yeah, not too bad. It's been quiet lately on the lane though. A lot of the punters hate going in the hut, so we're losing business.'

Jack slammed down his glass and poured himself another one.

Since Steph and a few other volunteers had been keeping an eye on the lane, Jack hadn't bothered to come down in Ricky's van. In truth, she was relieved; all she ever got from him was grief these days.

'How long have you got until you pay Fletch off? It can't be long now.'

Liza looked upset. 'That's the thing, because we've been late twice with the payments, Fletch fined us.'

'He did what?'

'Yeah, so we owe almost as much as we did at Christmas.'

Steph glanced across to Jack, who was muttering to himself. 'I'm so sorry, Liza – they're complete bastards.' She had a thought. 'Listen, I have this friend called Danny Denton—'

'Yeah, Mary and Claudette mentioned him a while ago, but he's gone a way, hasn't he?'

'Between you and me, he's back, and he's looking to put some of the girls up in a house to work out of. He's not a pimp – not like Artie anyway. If he were, I wouldn't suggest this, but I think you should have a chat with him, babe. You might prefer to work at his place rather than the lane. It would be safer and perhaps you'd get more business. And that way you'd be able to pay Fletch off quicker.' Steph chewed on her lip, hoping she was doing the right thing. 'Anyway, the option's there if you want, hun. But for God's sake don't mention it to Artie or Fletch, will you.'

Liza shook her head.

'I'm sure they'll find out sooner or later, but I think Danny would prefer to get it off the ground before word reaches them.'

'Well, look who it fucking is?' Fletch's voice boomed out behind them. He walked into Liza's lounge followed closely by Artie. 'Stephanie.' He laughed nastily. 'How are you doing, girl?'

Steph stared at them. She'd seen Artie once since January, and that had been from a distance, in the hospital car park when she was visiting Rob. At the beginning of February, Artie had tried to get her banned from the hospital, but as they were both listed as Rob's next of kin, he hadn't succeeded.

Ignoring them, she turned to Liza. 'I'll pop back this afternoon, babe, all right . . . We'll talk some more later . . . Bye, Jack.'

Artie glared at Steph. As she made to pass him, he grabbed her arm. 'You know it's fucking rude to ignore people.'

Steph held his stare. 'I'd rather be rude than be a bullying bastard like you.'

Artie slapped her, hard.

The impact knocked her head to the side. She breathed deeply, forcing herself to stay calm. She touched her mouth, which was bleeding, then she stood straight and looked at Liza. 'Kiss the girls for me, won't you.' And without saying another word, she walked away with dignity.

Infuriated, Artie wiped his mouth, and glared at Liza. 'I hope you've got our fucking money?'

Liza nodded, and opened the jar where she'd kept the weekly instalment. Artie counted the money slowly and nodded to Fletch, stuffing it into his pocket.

'So, I hear you've stopped watching your missus fuck other

men.' Fletch winked at Jack. Janey had told them that Liza took Jack down the lane with her, which had given Fletch no end of amusement, but Jack apparently hadn't been around lately.

Liza glanced at her husband nervously. Each time Artie and Fletch came for their money, they would say something to provoke him, and each week Liza was scared that something terrible was going to happen.

'What was it, you got bored? It didn't do it for you any more?' Fletch chuckled.

'Go to hell.'

'Jack!' Liza panicked. 'No!'

'What the fuck did you say to me, mate?'

Fletch began to walk towards him, but Liza rushed in front of Fletch, trying to block him. 'He's drunk, Fletch. Leave it, please . . . He always mouths off when he's pissed.'

'Shut the fuck up.' Fletch grabbed her by the hair and threw her across the room. She crashed into the table, cutting the side of her head on the corner.

'I said, *what the fuck* did you say?'

Jack stared up at Fletch. 'I said, *go to hell.*'

Fletch raised his foot and did a flying kick into Jack's head. The chair he was sitting on toppled over, along with Jack.

'Come on, let's go.' Fletch nodded to Artie. They headed off, but Fletch paused at the door and stared at Jack, who was groaning on the floor. 'If you ever give me any of your fucking lip again, I'll double what you owe me, and your missus will be getting her arse fucked for the next twenty years to pay me off.'

Chapter Seventy-One

Danny was still talking about it. 'I can't fucking believe he smacked you one. Why didn't you come and get me?'

'Leave it, Dan – it's no big deal.'

He pulled over sharply on the country lane. They were off to see the place over in Boxted Lane. '*No big deal*, are you fucking kidding me, Steph?'

'And how would that have worked, eh? Me coming to get you . . . I thought you didn't want a lot of agg until everything was sorted.'

Danny gripped the steering wheel. 'I don't, but that doesn't mean I'm going to let him give you a clump.'

'I've told you *it's fine*.' Steph dangled her cigarette out of the open window. 'I've had worse.'

'And that's supposed to make me feel better, is it?' Danny grumbled.

'No, it's supposed to reassure you that I'll survive.' She smiled then. She was so at ease with Danny that she didn't feel like she was always on guard. 'Dan, come on, put your knight-in-shining-armour costume back in your suitcase.' She winked. 'Right now, I'm more worried about Liza. She's in a right mess, what with Jack being a complete arsehole, then owing Artie and

351

Fletch all that money. And, on top of that, she lost her aunt at New Year's.' Steph frowned. 'Did I tell you about that?'

Danny shook his head.

'Yeah, it was just before you went up to London. She fell and smashed her head on the hearth. She was dead when they found her, poor cow. Apparently, she'd got a bit wobbly on her feet this past year, but you know what old people are like – they want to keep their independence. It's thrown Liza into a bit of a dark place.'

'Yeah, it can't have been nice, finding her aunt like that.'

Steph shook her head. 'Oh, Liza never found her, Joseph did.'

'Wait, what?' Danny swivelled round in his seat. 'That cunt found him? As in Joseph Potter?'

'Yeah, why?'

Danny rubbed his eyes. He pinched the bridge of his nose. 'I told you he wasn't right!' His voice was low and filled with rage. 'You do realise he was the one who found my mum. She had a "fall" as well – that's how she died.'

Steph stared at him. 'You think Jo's responsible?' It sounded hard to believe. Old people had falls all the time and someone like Joseph who was in and out of their houses would naturally be the first on the scene on a lot of those occasions. The old dears loved him. A lot of people did. So why was her gut telling her something else?

Danny nodded. 'I fucking am saying that – I know it – and I'm going to nail him on it somehow.' He began to think, but he caught another glance at Steph's mouth, which wound him up all over again. 'Let's have a proper look at it.' He put his hand on her chin, turning her face gently towards him. 'It'll be sore in the morning.'

Steph smiled. 'It's sore now.'

'I'll kill him.'

They held each other's stares. Steph's gaze searched Danny's face.

'I missed you.' Danny's voice was husky.

'Dan, I . . .'

'Shhhh . . .' His finger outlined her lips. Then he leaned forward and kissed her mouth lightly. It was like an electric shock had rushed through Steph. She knew she shouldn't be doing this, but she couldn't quite pull herself away, though within moments the guilt washed over her again. 'I'm sorry, Danny . . . I shouldn't.' She shook her head, angry with herself.

He nodded. He wasn't going to push it. He smiled at her and started the car.

They drove in silence for a while as Steph watched the Kent countryside go by. She glanced at him. 'Do you fancy a detour?'

Danny kept his eyes on the road. 'A detour?'

She stared down at the medicine bottles she'd dropped in the car's door pocket. 'Yeah . . . how about we pay Joseph a visit – we're not too far, and I've got time. I told Liza I'd catch up with her again this afternoon, so we can go and have a word with Jo about this medicine . . . What do you reckon?'

Danny slammed his foot on the brakes and spun the car round to face the other way. He grinned, enjoying being with Steph. 'There's your answer. So let's go and see what this cunt has to say.'

Chapter Seventy-Two

While Danny and Steph were driving towards the Potters, Zack was kneeling down in the basement next to Nancy. She was propped up against the wall naked. She was in agony from last night. Joseph was a sadistic bastard and in all the time she'd been on the game, Nancy had never experienced anyone so brutal. She had cuts all over her and she was sore inside from the home-made devices he used on her.

'Zack, you've got to do something . . . *Zack* . . .' Nancy was breathless. Her matted hair was stuck to her forehead. Her ankles were tied tightly so she could only move her legs at her knees. It was impossible to get a position that was anywhere near comfortable, and she was so cold. Last night she'd begged Jospeh for a blanket, but all he'd done was leave her to freeze.

'You've got to do something, Zack, *please*. I'm not well . . . it feels like the baby isn't moving any more.'

'What can I do?' Zack placed his hand on Nancy's large stomach, but she slapped it away.

'Don't fucking touch me . . .' She breathed deeply and looked at him. 'Sorry . . . sorry, I don't meant it. I'm just scared . . . I'm think I'm dying, Zack.' Her eyes filled with tears.

She'd hoped that Zack would be her ticket out of here, but he was too scared to say anything, no matter how much she begged him. It was hardly surprising when Joseph had been terrorising his children since they were toddlers. Zack had told her some of the things Joseph had done to his mum, and how he'd made him watch. He was traumatised to the point where it was impossible for him to even think about asking for help . . . Zack was as much a prisoner as she was.

But his little acts of kindness – bringing her small snacks, talking to her, keeping her company – had kept her from going crazy. And for that she was grateful, because she got how risky it was for Zack and how scared he was each time he came to the basement to visit her. And although he was so careful not to leave any evidence he'd been down here, Nancy thought it was only a matter of time before Joseph find out.

Zack was afraid Nancy was going to end up like his mum, but he didn't know what he could do to prevent that happening. Bel might know. He'd wanted to talk to her about it, but his sister had such a fear of the basement that she would shut him down if he tried to mention it. Just like she shut out the noises. She would withdraw into herself, trying to block out the knowledge of what her father did down here.

His heart thumped hard in his chest, and he leaned over to wipe Nancy's fringe away from her forehead.

She began to sob.

'Zack, listen to me. I know you're scared of your dad – I get that.' Nancy's words were staggered, and her voice was so quiet. Her lips were dry and sticking together. Joseph only allowed her a few sips of water when he came to see her. 'And I don't blame you. I'm not angry . . . I think what you've done for me is so brave; I don't know if I could've done what you have . . . but . . . but you need to stop him.' She stared into Zack's eyes. 'I don't want anything to happen to this baby, Zack . . . and if I die, so will the baby . . . You don't want your sibling to die, do you?'

Zack blinked. 'My sibling?'

Nancy nodded. 'Yeah, Zack, your sibling.' Her wrists were tied, but she was able to use her hands to take Zack's and place them on her stomach. She was so exhausted, and in so much pain. She closed her eyes for a moment, before opening them again to look at Zack.

'You've got to stop him. You've got to stop your dad.'

Zack stared back at Nancy. He'd had no idea Nancy was carrying his sibling in her belly. He hadn't thought it possible to hate his father more, but—

He whipped his head around, listening, then jumped to his feet. 'Dad's back . . . I have to go . . . I'm sorry, I have to go.' He was trembling and it was all he could do not to wet himself.

'You can't leave me . . . *Zack*, Zack, you can't leave me like this, please . . . please, Zack. Get me out of here, please.'

'I'm sorry.' Trying not to cry, Zack placed the gag back over her mouth. He didn't want to leave her, but he couldn't be found down here . . . He *couldn't*. Feeling ashamed, he rushed up the stairs, turning the light off on the way, his head full of what Nancy had said. Somehow he needed to stop his dad.

Joseph slammed the front door closed and strode down the corridor, opening the basement door. He flicked the light on and marched down the stairs. His face was stern and flushed. He stormed over to Nancy, ripping off her gag.

Breathless, Nancy looked up at him. 'Have you got them? HAVE YOU GOT THEM?' She found the strength to yell at him.

'No.'

'What . . .?' She blinked the sweat away from her eyes. Even though she was so cold, she was sweating. She felt ill. 'You said you'd get them. You promised. You said you'd *fucking* get them.'

Joseph stared at her angrily. 'I did get them, but now they're gone.'

'How can they be gone?' She never trusted anything he said. Joseph liked to play mind games.

'I don't KNOW!' Joseph had put the Valium along with the sleeping pills and painkillers under the seat of the car, but what he'd forgotten to do was close the window properly. Clearly some junkie had broken in. It was all because of Steph, who'd insisted on keeping him talking, making him coffee and asking questions. If it wasn't for her, he'd have been in and out within seconds.

'I need something . . . *Joseph*, you need to fucking give me something. I'm in so much pain. JO!'

'Shut up, SHUT UP, SHUT UP . . . Stop screaming.' He grabbed a clump of her hair and shook her by it. Then he bent down, his face inches from hers. 'Keep that dirty mouth of yours shut, understand?'

Joseph slapped the gag on again.

She couldn't breathe; she needed more air. Her chest felt like it was going to explode. She snorted up through her nose frantically trying to get more breath in her body, the lack of oxygen was making her dizzy.

Panicking, Nancy shook her head furiously and shuffled her bum towards him, kicking her legs at Joseph. Joseph raised his foot and stomped down hard on her ankle. There was a sickening snap of breaking bones. Her ankle flopped sideways, and she screamed in pain, but it only came out as a muffled sound from behind her gag.

Then they heard a loud knock on the front door.

Chapter Seventy-Three

Danny and Steph were standing together outside Joseph's front door. 'He must be in . . . Look, his van's over there, as well as his car.' Steph knocked again, feeling the cold get right into her bones.

'I've got a good fucking mind to walk in – it is my house.'

Steph elbowed him gently in the side. 'It *used* to be your house . . . It's Jo's now.'

Danny turned his head and glanced round. 'It's a fucking liberty, that's what it is.' He lowered his voice then. 'He's going to pay for what he did.'

Steph was just as quiet. 'Yeah, but let's stick to asking him about the meds right now, and see what he has to say. We can't just go accusing him – on paper, Jo's as clean as a whistle.'

'Yeah,' Danny agreed. 'He's made sure of that. Mr fucking Helpful.'

'Everyone thinks he's an angel.'

Danny shook his head. 'What's that old saying . . . the devil was once an angel too.'

The door opened, but not wide, and Zack stood staring at them. Steph noticed how smart he looked, always clean and well dressed, but always with that look of a startled rabbit in his eyes.

'All right, babe? Is your dad in? We'd like a word with him, if that's all right.'

Zack's gaze moved from Steph to Danny. He nodded, but he didn't move away from the door to get him. Thoughts of Nancy whirled through his mind. He needed to help her. He had to do something to stop his dad.

She smiled at him and tried again. 'Stace says you haven't been at school much. Everything all right, babe?'

For a second time, Zack nodded. He tried to build up the courage to tell them. If he said it, if he told them Nancy was in the basement, she'd be free. They all would. But, as hard as he tried, Zack couldn't find the words. All he could do was taste the fear.

'I bet you're pleased its half-term. I know Stacey is – she's got a whole heap of plans sorted. Most of them involve me driving her somewhere. You and Bel should come along sometime. We're going to Margate. It'll be bloody freezing, but it'll be a laugh. It would be nice if you came.'

Zack stared at her. He held on to the door for support to stop himself trembling. '*Help Nancy.*' He silently mouthed the words.

'What was that, hun?' Steph asked. She'd always found Zack to be chronically shy and awkward. On the rare occasions he did speak to her, it was almost inaudible, like now.

Terrified, Zack mouthed again. Why couldn't Steph understand what he was trying to tell her? If they came in now, they'd see, and they'd believe him. Unlike in his other school when he'd tried to tell the teacher about what was happening at home, what his dad was doing to his mum. They didn't believe him; the school had called his dad and spoken to him about it. Even now, Zack tried to block out the things that had happened to him when his dad had taken him home that afternoon.

'I can't hear you, babe. I must be getting old.' Steph bent towards him.

The door suddenly opened wide.

Joseph stood there. 'Zack, why don't you go back in the kitchen and finish off the dishes . . . There's a good lad.'

Zack glanced at Steph. Why couldn't he do it? Why couldn't he just say? He opened his mouth again, but he saw his dad looking at him and the terror clutched him. He lowered his head and hurried away.

Joseph ruffled Zack's hair as he walked past. 'He's getting nearly as tall as me.' Joseph smiled at them both. The whore had come here again, though this time she'd brought along that goon with him. 'This is a nice surprise. Would you like to come in?' He gestured to the hallway.

'No, it's fine, thanks,' Steph said firmly. 'We were just passing—'

'You're making quite a habit of that, Steph,' Joseph interrupted, and laughed sarcastically. 'Sorry, go on.'

'I wanted to have a quick word with you, Jo.' Steph was distracted by a swarm of flies buzzing around the drain at the side of the house.

'Fire away.'

'Apparently, these were found in your van.' She showed him the medicine bottles.

Joseph stared at them. 'My van?' He raised his eyebrows. 'No, not in my van. Why would they be in my van? Who told you that?'

'Someone who found them.' Steph stared at Joseph. If he was lying, he was clearly very good at it.

'Sorry, I don't understand. *Who* found them?' He frowned.

Danny was watching Joseph as well. He was too calm. Too slick with his answers. He was bullshitting. Janey could've said a lot of names, so why choose Joseph's if it wasn't true? No. Potter was lying.

Steph continued to question him. 'We caught someone trying to sell them, and they said they'd taken them from you.'

'I'm not sure why they'd say that, and I'm not sure why you would think I'd have them in my van either.' There was a definite note of irritation in his voice. 'Can I see them?' He took the bottles from Steph's hands, and then his hand trembled and he let out a groan.

'Jo, are you all right?' Steph was taken by surprise.

'Sorry, my back . . . it's giving me jip. I've been gardening, doing a lot of digging, and this cold weather makes it worse.' He looked back down at the medicine bottle, studying the labels. 'Well, these names are some of the people on my rounds, and I've heard there's been a spate of break-ins. But that's all I know, I'm afraid.' He shrugged and gave Steph and Danny a steady look. 'Sorry . . . Is there anything else, because I wanted to take the kids out later. I'm looking forward to it, actually. It's been a while since we went on a day trip.'

'No, there's nothing else. Thanks for clearing that up, Jo . . . And have a good time, won't you.' Steph nodded to Danny. 'Come on, let's get out of here.'

Steph got back in the car, wondering what Zack had been trying to say to her. She glanced at Danny. 'So, what do you think?'

Danny turned on the engine. 'I think he's a lying cunt.'

Steph glanced out of the window. She nodded. 'Me too.'

Joseph watched them leave. Every time he saw Steph it was the same: the white noise rose in volume until it was more than he could stand.

When she'd handed him the bottles and her skin had come in contact with his, he had an urge to inflict on her the same agonies that Bridget, Hennie, Jean and the rest had undergone. The vision of Steph, gagged and bloody and screaming in pain, was so vivid that he'd let out an audible groan of ecstasy at the thought of it.

For now she was the queen bee, protected by her goon and her sluts, but he would keep watching and waiting . . .

Chapter Seventy-Four

After Danny had dropped her off, Steph returned to the Queen's Estate, where she found Liza, medicated to the eyeballs with Valium.

'I'm so sorry Fletch did that to you,' said Steph, eyeing the nasty cut on the side of Liza's head. 'Have you got time for a coffee?' She wanted to tell Liza more about Danny's place in Boxted Lane. From what she'd seen of it, it would be great for the women. Safer for sure. And with the amount of punters he was looking to bring in, there was a good chance Liza and the others would earn much more money than they were now.

Liza glanced at Jack, who looked awful. 'Yeah, but not here, eh? How about we go to the cafe on the corner?'

'Take your time,' Jack piped up. 'Ricky's coming round in a bit. He's bringing a couple of beers.'

'I've got the car. We could nip down the Pentagon, get something to eat?' Steph suggested, thinking it would do Liza good.

'Sounds good. The girls are having a sleepover at their mate's house, so I don't have to worry about picking them up from school,' said Liza. 'You sure you'll be okay, Jack?'

He nodded and reached for the whisky glass. So she followed Steph out into the cold of the late afternoon, leaving him on his own.

*

Jack waited to make sure they'd gone. Then he limped through to the kitchen, grabbed one the chairs and dragged it over to the cupboard. He had to stand on tiptoe and reach his hand as far back as he could before his fingers touched the bag he'd hidden there. He pulled it towards him, climbed down and put the chair back.

Wincing with each step, he returned to the lounge and poured himself a large drink. Full of self-pity, he stared at the wedding photo of him and Liza. He couldn't think of his wife now without imagining all those men groping her.

He took a swig of whisky and reached into his pocket for the speed he'd bought from one of his mates. He opened the wrap and lay it out on the small coffee table, then used Liza's Post Office card to chop it up. He tore off a strip of the *Radio Times*, rolled it up and leaned over the speed, snorting it up desperately.

He held his nostrils. Fuck, that burned! The bitter taste hit the back of his throat. With the speed running through his veins, Jack took a deep breath and finished off the glass of whisky.

Wiping his mouth, he picked up the telephone and dialled a number.

It was answered after a short while.

'It's Jack from Queen's Estate . . . I need to see you. *Now.*'

He listened to the person on the other end of the phone, then spoke again.

'Yeah, that's right . . . It'll be worth your while, I promise.'

Then he put the phone down. Now all he had to do was wait . . .

Fifty minutes passed before he heard the front door opening and closing.

'All right, mate?' Fletch bowled in, rubbing his hands together gleefully.

'Haven't you heard of knocking?' Jack sounded slurred. He hadn't stopped drinking or snorting since he'd made the phone call to Fletch.

'I'll stop knocking, mate, when I've got all my money back. Until then what's yours is mine.' He shrugged and laughed. 'So come on then, you've got some more for me, I take it?'

Sitting in his chair, Jack stared at Fletch with hatred. 'Yeah, I have.'

'I don't know why you didn't fucking give it me this morning then.'

'I didn't want Liza to know that I had more cash kept back for you, she'd only worry that we'd be short.'

Fletch roared with laughter. 'I hope you haven't been a stupid cunt again and borrowed more money than you can pay back?'

Jack was completely wired. 'Something like that, mate.'

'Come on then, where is it? I ain't got all day – some of us aren't fucking losers who sit around doing nothing but watch their missus suck dicks.'

'Keep talking, mate.' The bitterness poured out of Jack. He glared at Fletch. 'Keep talking.'

'What the fuck are you on about?'

Jack continued to stare. 'Because if you keep saying that shit to me, it makes it easier to do what I have to.'

'Stop being a cunt and give me the fucking notes.'

'Here it is . . .' Jack slipped his hand down the side of his chair. 'Here you go.' In his hand was the gun he'd got from Ricky's mate, that until this afternoon had been stashed in the back of a kitchen cupboard. He pointed it at Fletch.

Fletch's face drained of colour.

Jack's finger hovered over the trigger, then he pulled it . . .

Chapter Seventy-Five

Liza and Steph heard the bang before they got to the front door. They ran in and Liza screamed when she saw Fletch lying in a pool of blood, a gaping hole in his chest.

'What have you done?' she yelled at Jack, who was sitting with a blank expression on his face. 'What have you fucking done?'

Steph hurried in and dropped to her knees next to Fletch, who was bleeding out. She ripped off her jacket and pressed it on to the gaping wound.

'Call the ambulance . . . Call the fucking ambulance,' Steph yelled at Liza. 'Fletch, Fletch, can you hear me?' She stared at him. He was white as a sheet. 'It's me, Steph . . . *Fletch.*'

Fletch slowly opened his eyes.

'That's it . . . that's it – no, don't shut your eyes, babe. You hear me? You've got to talk to me. You've got to stay awake. The ambulance is going to be here very soon. You're going to be all right.' She couldn't let him die. Not because she gave a fuck about him – she hated the bastard – but she couldn't let Jack go down for murder – it would destroy Liza.

'I'm dying, ain't I?' There was real fear in Fletch's eyes.

'No, no that's not going to happen.'

'I'm so cold.'

'I know, but try to stay focused on me . . .' She glanced back up at Liza. 'How long did the ambulance say they're going to be?'

'Ten minutes. I'm going upstairs to keep an eye out for them – I'll be able to see them coming from the girls' bedroom window.'

Fletch was getting weaker. His face was deathly white. Blood was pouring from the gunshot wound, staining the carpet and Steph's jacket.

'Fletch, talk to me. Try to talk to me. Come on, Fletch, come on . . . Think of Artie.'

'Artie.' Fletch repeated the name as he struggled to talk. His eyes began to roll, and Steph could see he was having difficulty breathing.

'That's right, he won't want to lose you, will he . . . Fletch? Fletch?'

Exhausted Fletch closed his eyes.

'Fletch . . . Fletch . . . Fletch . . . *No!*' Steph watched his chest stop moving. She slapped his face hard. 'Come on, Fletch, don't die on me. You can't die . . . Fletch, no, *no.*'

He was gone.

Steph looked down and saw that she was covered in Fletch's blood. She felt sick for Liza, having to fend for herself and the girls while Jack served a life sentence. Unsteadily, she got to her feet.

Jack was sitting in his chair shaking, the gun in his hand.

'Why don't you put the gun down, hun?'

Jack didn't reply. He kept staring at the wall, but Steph was worried about what he might do with the gun if she left him alone.

'Jack, Jack, give it to me.'

He moved his gaze to stare at her, and then, drunkenly, he pointed the gun to his head.

'No! Jack, no . . . Don't do that . . . Oh my God, Fletch ain't worth it, darlin'. Do you hear me, Jack? Don't do this, please don't do this to Liza.'

He blinked then moved the gun away from his head and pointed it at Steph. 'This is your fault.'

'Jack . . . please, don't do this.' Her heart was banging in her chest. 'Don't make this any worse.'

'It can't get any worse.'

'Jack, listen to me. I've got a kid, Stacey, and she needs me – just like your kids need you.'

She watched him pull back the trigger.

'*Jack.*' Steph's voice was a whisper. She knew that one wrong word from her, and it would be over.

She stared down the barrel of the gun. 'Please, please, I'm begging you, Jack, don't do this.'

Snot and tears were running down Jack's face. He was trembling so much the gun was shaking violently in his hand.

'Think of your girls . . . If you kill me, then you'll never get out. You'll be banged up for a while for killing Fletch, but it might not be for as long as you think – you were under strain; they'll take that into consideration. One day you'll get out and you'll be able to pick up the pieces, but not if you do this. Don't let Fletch and Artie destroy you and your family any more than they have already.'

Jack blinked again.

Steph was shaking now.

'Please, Jack, give me the gun.

Jack continued to stare, but then he suddenly dropped the gun and covered his face with his hands. Steph rushed over and picked up the gun. She felt sick, and she gulped down air to steady herself. Jesus Christ, she'd thought that was it.

'I'm sorry.' Jack glanced at her. 'I'm so sorry.'

Overwhelmed with emotion she shook her head and wiped away her tears, snarling at him. 'You fucking selfish arsehole! I should shoot you my fucking self, but I think I'll leave the Old Bill to deal with you.' Then she ran upstairs to where Liza was looking out of the window for the ambulance, oblivious to what had just happened.

'They should be here soon,' said Liza, looking frantic.

Steph tried to steady her voice. 'It's too late . . . Fletch is dead.'

Liza screamed and collapsed on the nearby chair. 'Oh my God . . . Oh my God, no. Oh Jesus, what are we going to do, Steph? Jack will be looking at a murder charge.' She rocked back and forth in her chair, wrapping her arms round her waist. 'Oh my God.'

'I'm so sorry, doll.' Steph placed the gun on the side. The Old Bill would be here soon, and she didn't want to be holding a gun when they stormed in.

As if on cue, Steph heard the sound of sirens.

'Will you stay with me?' Liza clutched Steph's hand.

'Of course I will, whatever you need.'

And as Steph squeezed Liza's hand, she thought about the money Liza and Jack owed. The debt certainly wouldn't die with Fletch. Artie would want cash now more than ever before, but what Steph didn't know was what he would do to Liza to get it.

369

Chapter Seventy-Six

Later that night, after Jack had been taken away by the Old Bill and Liza had sedated herself with Valium and gin, Steph curled up on her sofa next to Danny. She was still in shock from having a gun pointed at her – not that she'd told Danny about that part – but she felt better for having him beside her.

'I can't fucking believe it. That bloke has done me a favour.'

Steph frowned. 'Don't sound so pleased, Dan. A family's life has been destroyed.'

When the police had let Steph leave Liza's flat, she'd gone to the nearest phone box and called Danny. He was the only person she could think of calling. He came and picked her up straight away and brought her home.

'He'll be looking at fifteen years, I reckon. It's going to be hard on Liza, but she's stronger than she gives herself credit for. My biggest fear is that Artie might have a go at her. He'll be in shock, that's for sure.'

'Then this is the time to do something about him,' said Danny.

'I wouldn't be so sure about that.' Steph felt frightened. 'If I know Artie, he'll be more dangerous than before. He loved Fletch, and he'll go off on one like he did when the hit-and-run happened with Rob. He literally prowled the streets like a man

370

possessed, trying to find who was responsible. He battered more than his fair share of blokes.'

Danny remembered – if he hadn't been in Spain when it had happened, they'd have come after him. Even Artie's Old Bill contacts hadn't been able to find whoever had done it. In fact, he couldn't recall them even pulling in a single suspect.

'Yeah, but if his head's all over the place over Fletch,' Danny continued, 'Artie won't be thinking straight – and that's when he'll make mistakes.'

She took a sip from the iced glass of Coke next to her. 'You need to be careful.'

Danny got up from the couch and kissed her on the top of her head. 'Listen, will you be all right for a little bit? I have to go and do something.'

She stood up to walk him to the door. 'Yeah. Listen, you don't have to bother coming back. I'm all right now. Thank you for today though . . . I'll see you tomorrow.'

He gazed at her. Even under these circumstances, he'd enjoyed being with her. 'What if I want to come back?'

'Danny . . .'

He held up his hands and grinned, something he often did. 'All right, I get it . . . It would've been nice though.'

Steph nodded. She wasn't going to deny it. Right now she could do with being close to him. 'Yeah, but my head's all over the place.'

'I hear you.' He kissed her again, but this time on her lips. Then he pulled away, and winked. 'You know how to kill a man, don't you . . . Oh, and make sure you lock the doors, cos, like you say, Artie won't be happy right now.'

'I don't think a front door will stop him, do you?'

Danny frowned. He wasn't comfortable with her saying that.

When Artie was pushed, he was capable of anything, and he didn't care who he hurt. 'Are you sure you don't want me to come back later? And I'm not saying that so I can have another shot at you.'

She rolled her eyes and laughed. He made her feel good, and she'd missed that the last four years. Of course she didn't want Artie finding out – it would only give him another reason to step up his anger towards her – but she was sick of worrying about what he'd think. Just for one day, she wanted to be selfish and only think about herself. Was that so wrong? She wasn't sure. 'Who said romance was dead, eh?'

Danny laughed too, then he leaned in and kissed her again, only this time for longer. It was a long, slow kiss, and Steph allowed herself to get caught up in it. She could feel Danny getting hard as he pressed against her.

He moved away from her lips, holding the back of her head and kissing her neck sensually. She was breathless, the waves of excitement washing over her.

'Are you okay? I don't want you to regret it tomorrow, babe,' Danny mumbled. He wanted her so badly, but he wanted her to be absolutely sure.

'I won't,' Steph whispered back. She felt his hands running over her breasts and she gasped. Danny kissed her neck again, then effortlessly scooped her up, placing her back down on the couch. She looked up at him and he began to undress her, undoing the buttons on her top and the zip on her skirt.

Steph caught her breath, letting him slip her out of her lacy white underwear. He took off his own top and jeans then, revealing his taut, heavily muscular chest. He lay on top of her, pressing his hard, naked body against hers. He slowly moved down her, circling her erect nipples with his tongue.

Guilty

Steph closed her eyes in ecstasy.

Every touch of him felt charged. She arched her back as he wrapped his arms underneath her, bringing her even closer to him. Steph felt him enter her slowly, and she bit down on her lip, letting out a soft groan. He thrust harder and deeper, and she responded to him, kissing him passionately and letting herself push any other thoughts away, letting herself think of nothing but Danny.

Standing by the row of garages, Joseph Potter watched them through the window. He smirked to himself as he enjoyed watching, the goon and the whore.

Chapter Seventy-Seven

Zack was sitting on the end of Bel's bed in her small bedroom, something he didn't usually do. His dad had told him he wasn't allowed to go into Bel's room in case he had bad thoughts about her, but he wasn't like his dad. He loved his sister the way his mum had loved them: kind and gentle. He'd never felt unsafe with her, and she'd never asked him to do any of the things his dad asked him to do . . . *made* him do.

But his dad was out somewhere and usually when he went out at night he didn't come back until the early hours of the morning. This time he hadn't bothered locking them in. He didn't always, but their dad knew that usually they'd be too terrified to break the rules and leave their room like Zack was doing now.

'Please, Bel, let me show you something.'

Bel touched Zack's hand. This was the most her brother had spoken to her for a long time, but she was terrified of the basement. The last time she'd been down there . . . Bel didn't even want to think about it, and she focused instead on the threadbare rug on the floor, hoping to rid her mind of the memories. 'I can't, Zack.' She was shaking. She didn't want to let him down, but she couldn't do it. 'I'm sorry.' She was starting to get upset.

'I'll be there with you. I won't let anything happen to you, I promise. I won't make you stay down there.' Zack stared at her from under his fringe.

'Tell me what it is now.' Bel looked at him. Whatever it was down there, it was beginning to frighten her. 'I don't understand why you won't.'

'I can't,' Zack whispered. Like Bel, living with his dad, he was frightened of things. He needed Bel to see it herself. He daren't tell her in case she didn't believe him, and if she told their dad he'd been talking about the basement, Zack was terrified he'd be chained to the bed again . . . along with all those other things he'd done to him. *Please, Bel,* for me.' He needed Bel to help him stop their dad. He didn't feel brave enough to do it on his own. And if she saw Nancy, she might know what to do.

'Why, Zack, what's this about?'

He clenched his hands. 'I've got to stop Dad. I've got to stop Dad doing all these things.'

Bel slammed her hands over her ears and began to rock back and forth. She didn't want to hear that. 'Zack, you can't,' she whispered. Her voice shook. 'Don't say that . . . He'll hurt you.' Her eyes welled with tears. 'Please, Zack, don't ever say that again.'

'Then come with me . . . You'll know what to do.'

Bel could see how important it was for him. She loved her brother so much and wanted to do anything she could for him, but she didn't know if she could do this. 'I can't.'

'Bel, please. Just try.'

Trembling, she gave the tiniest nods. 'Okay . . . okay, I'll try . . . When?'

'*Now*, before Dad gets home.' Zack was filled with fear too.

Bel stood up, shaking so much she could feel her knees

banging together. Zack wrapped his hand over hers and gave her a gentle smile before leading her out of the room. 'It's all right, I promise.'

They walked down the stairs together and along the hallway.

Bel glanced towards the front door, thinking about her dad coming back, and then she turned her gaze to the basement door. It was in the basement that she'd last seen her mum. Her dad had made Bel watch as he took the hammer and hit Mum over and over and over again. Bel could still hear her screams, and the way the blood had gurgled out of her mouth, the way her eyes had bulged out of her head as her face collapsed into a bloody pulp.

She pulled back, wriggling her hand out of her brother's grip. 'I can't . . . Zack, I can't.'

'*Bel.*'

'No . . . No.' She shook her head and stepped away, running back upstairs to her room.

Zack heard her door slam. He heard her sobbing.

He didn't blame Bel for being scared after what had happened. He blamed his dad. This was all his dad and Nancy was right, he needed to be stopped.

Zack opened the door and headed down the creaking wooden stairs to the basement. He switched on the light.

'Nancy?' Seeing her, he panicked and ran over to her. She was lying on her side, shivering. Her ankle was huge and misshapen. Her foot was pointing the other way and dried blood covered the inside of her legs.

He pulled off her gag gently. 'Nancy?' He leaned down to her. 'Nancy . . . Nancy, can you hear me? It's Zack . . . Nancy, please wake up.'

She struggled to open her eyes. '. . . Zack.' Her voice was so weak. '. . . Zack . . . Zack . . .' A tear rolled down her cheek and she closed her eyes.

Zack felt a deep, burning rage inside him. He *hated* his dad. He hated him.

Standing up again, Zack walked across to his dad's work-bench. Shaking, he grabbed a box of matches, and one of the small red jerry cans of petrol from under the bench. He blew off the dust. He didn't think his dad would miss it – or at least he hoped he wouldn't.

He glanced at Nancy and her large stomach. There was no way he was going to let his dad hurt her unborn child. He real-ised he was the only one who'd be able to stop his dad. And, with that thought, Zack gently placed the gag back on Nancy and walked out of the basement as he began to think of a plan.

Chapter Seventy-Eight

Steph was hard at work, scrubbing casserole remains off her Pyrex dish, when the phone rang. It was Liza and she sounded in a right state. It was all Steph could do to make sense of her drunken babble. Thankfully, she'd had the sense to get her mate next door to look after the girls for a couple of hours, but Steph knew if she didn't get herself sober by the time they were due back, she was going to risk losing them to social services. She told Liza to get herself in the shower and get a few coffees down her, then ended the call with a promise she'd look in on her.

Steph hung up the phone with a sigh. As if she didn't have enough grief in her life already.

After Danny had gone, she'd spent most of the night worrying about how Artie would react to losing Fletch, and when she did finally drop off to sleep she'd had a nightmare where she was trying to get to Andy, lying on the ground in his Babygro, bleeding to death, but Jack was pointing a gun at her and refused to let her pass. She'd woken up in a cold sweat.

And then Rob's doctor had phoned to say they were putting him on a ventilator to help him breathe. If she hadn't been feeling guilty enough already, seeing Rob in that state had left her in bits.

As soon as she'd got home from the hospital, she'd got stuck in, peeling vegetables and chopping potatoes, browning the meat and making dumplings for a casserole. Not that she was in the mood for eating; she just needed to stay busy. Anything to take her mind off Rob – and to stop beating herself up over what had happened last night with Danny. What had she been thinking? God, she'd acted like a teenager on heat.

'Stace, are you ready, babe?' she called up to her daughter. She'd promised she'd take Stace to the cinema soon as they'd had dinner, but now she needed to drop in at Liza's on the way.

Stacey ran down the stairs, wearing the new denim jacket she'd bought with her pocket money. 'You look lovely, but you're going to freeze to death. Have you seen the weather? It's like Siberia out there.'

Stacey smiled and slipped on her matching denim wedge sandals. 'Mum, you sound so old. I'll be fine.' She grabbed her scarf off the peg and wrapped it round her neck. 'See, I'll be warm now, so you don't have to worry.'

Steph laughed as she locked up behind them and they set off towards where her car was parked.

'You're kidding me!' Steph stared at her car. It was drenched in thick red paint. She didn't bloody need this now. Christ almighty.

'Who's done that, Mum?' Stacey sounded worried. She'd seen her mum's car smashed up in the past when some fella hadn't liked Steph helping his girlfriend; she'd also witnessed blokes threaten and shout at her mum outside the refuge.

Steph rolled her eyes. She'd thought all this shit had stopped. It had been a good six weeks since the last incident.

'Oh, it's just some bloody idiot who thinks it's funny to do shit like this,' she said, playing it down for Stacey's sake. 'Don't worry, babe, we can still go to the cinema. I'll go and get some water and wash it off.'

'I'll help you, Mum.'

'Thanks, sweetheart.' Steph smiled at her. She was such a good kid.

For the next twenty minutes, Steph and Stacey threw buckets of hot water over the car, trying to get it off the windscreen and the bonnet.

Finishing off, Steph smiled. 'That's not bad. I reckon we've done a good job, don't you? It needed a clean anyway. It looks better than it did before.' She dragged on her cigarette. 'Come on, babe, let's go. I have to pop in and see Liza first, but we'll still make the eight o'clock screening.'

Liza had sobered up a bit, thanks to the shower. She was drying herself with one of the fluffy cream towels Nora had given her last year. She wrapped it round her and stared at herself in the mirror. Her wet hair was scraped back and dripped down her shoulders. It was like she was staring at a stranger. She reached for the bottle of Valium, then remembered what Steph had said and poured herself a glass of water instead.

If it weren't for Steph, she'd swallow every pill in the house, but the reminder of what would happen to her girls had brought her to her senses.

'*You fucking bitch. You fucking, fucking bitch.*'

The door banged open on its hinges and Artie stormed in. He lunged at Liza, grabbing her by her throat and shoving her hard against the wall. He raised his fist and smashed it into her head.

Liza screamed. She slid down the wall, but Artie wasn't finished with her yet. He picked her up and threw her against the sink. She yelled in agony and tried to scramble away, but he booted her in the side. A rattle of air escaped her. 'Please, Artie . . . no.'

Artie's eyes were wild. After Fred Walker had taken him to the morgue to see Fletch, he'd gone home and tried to numb the pain with coke and the whisky, but nothing could dull that unbearable loss. It was a repeat of what had happened when Rob got hurt, only this time he knew who was to fucking blame.

'Stand up. STAND FUCKING UP!' he panted.

Liza couldn't move, so Artie took a running kick, his foot landing in her belly. Winded, she began to cough, spitting up blood. He grabbed her by the hair. Her towel fell off, leaving her naked as he dragged her out of the bathroom and down the stairs to the front door.

'Artie, please . . . no . . . I'm so sorry about Fletch.' She was in excruciating pain. Each time she took a breath, it felt like someone was stabbing a hot poker in her ribs.

He turned and slapped her, then slapped her again, harder. 'Don't say his fucking name! I never want to hear you say his fucking name again – if you do, I swear I'll cut your fucking tongue out.'

Terrified, Liza nodded.

'From now on, you work for me. You're going to pay off that fucking money you owe me, and then you're going to spend the rest of your life paying for what your bastard husband did to Fletch. You ain't never going to be free of me.'

Sobbing and humiliated, Liza tried to scratch at his hand, but it only made Artie clamp her hair harder.

'*Artie.*'

'Shut the fuck up.' He booted her in the arse, sending her

sprawling into the street. A crowd of kids began to point and laugh at the sight of Liza naked.

'Go on, get moving . . . I said, *MOVE*.' He kicked her again and she crawled towards his car, where two of his goons were waiting.

From the corner of his eye, Artie saw a police car heading towards him. Some nosy fucker must have called the Old Bill.

The police car slowed to a crawl.

Artie raised his hand in acknowledgement. He recognised the two coppers in the car, both regular punters. 'All right, lads, there's nothing to see here. It's a domestic, that's all. She's pissed.' He shrugged and winked at them.

The officer in the passenger seat glanced down at Liza with a sneer of disgust. 'I'll leave you to it then . . . Hope to see you soon.'

The police car reversed and drove away, leaving Artie with Liza. 'Come on, I ain't got all day,' Artie snarled.

A crowd had gathered to watch the naked woman crawl across the estate.

Steph, wondering what the commotion was, had told Stacey to wait in the car, then she'd made her way through the throng of onlookers.

As soon as she saw Liza, with Artie standing over her, she broke into a run.

'What the fuck is wrong with you?' she screamed at Artie, reaching out for Liza, who was crying hysterically.

'Leave her a-fucking-lone. She's coming with me.' He grabbed Steph and pulled her back.

Steph was shocked at the state Liza was in. 'No, mate, you

don't do this. I don't care how much you're hurting, you don't fucking do this.'

Again she reached out to help Liza, but Artie had other plans. He dragged Steph back by her blouse.

'I said, LEAVE HER ALONE!' Artie bellowed in her face.

'No, Artie, I'm not letting you do this to her, you understand?'

'And how the fuck are you going to stop me, eh?' he snarled, shoving his finger into her forehead.

She tried to step around him, but he blocked her. 'You don't fucking learn, do you, Steph?' He jabbed his finger in her chest. 'What my brother saw in a whore like you, I'll never know.'

Steph wasn't going to rise to it. All she cared about was helping Liza. 'Move out of my way, Artie.'

He laughed. 'Come on, make me, bitch.'

She shoved him then, and Artie clenched his fist and threw a quick straight jab that caught her in the mouth. Her lip split and she stumbled back, but Artie held her up with one hand while he gave her a slap with the other.

'*Mum!* Get off her! Don't touch her!' Stacey suddenly appeared and launched herself at Artie.

Steph screamed, terrified he was going to clump her, but instead he dropped his fist and stared off into the distance.

Steph turned to follow Artie's gaze. The winter sun was low in the sky, and she had to squint to see.

It was Danny, coming out of the corner shop, oblivious to what was going on.

That's when she shouted. 'Danny! Run! *Run!*'

Hearing someone call his name, Danny glanced over just in time to see Artie hurtling towards him.

Steph turned to her daughter. 'Stace, you need to get out of here. There's going to be trouble. Get the bus home, babe – I'm sorry about the cinema – we can go another day.'

'Are you sure you'll be all right, Mum?'

'I'll be fine, but I can't leave here until I've got Liza sorted. So please, run.'

'Okay, I'll go to Tammy's – you can pick me up when you're done, yeah?'

'Fine. Now go.' Steph gave her daughter a quick kiss then rushed to Liza.

Stacey ran through the estate and out on to the main road. She was crossing over to get to the bus stop when a van pulled up alongside her.

Joseph wound down his window. He smiled. 'Are you all right, Stacey? Bit far from home, aren't you?'

Stacey smiled back at him. 'Yeah, there's a bit of agg that Mum's sorting out, so I'm off to stay at my mate's till she's finished.'

'Are you getting the bus?'

She nodded.

'Well how about I give you a lift, save you waiting. It's a cold night to be standing around in sandals.'

Stacey's face lit up. She'd been wishing she'd put on a winter coat and boots instead of the denim outfit – she was bloody freezing already and didn't fancy hanging around at a bus stop. Delighted, she skipped round to the passenger side and opened the door.

'You look as if you could do with something to warm you up.' Joseph nodded to the flask in the cup holder. 'Help yourself to some of that.'

'What is it?'

'It's sweet tea.' He laughed. 'Lots of milk and lots of sugar. Bel loves it.'

He put the van in gear and pulled away from the kerb, glancing down at her bare legs.

'You're a lot like your mother, aren't you,' he said.

Chapter Seventy-Nine

Danny was running. He was furious with himself. He knew he should've been more careful, but nipped out to get a couple of cans of Coke and next thing he knew Artie was pounding down the road after him.

He was unfamiliar with this part of the estate; he'd been lying low at Bill's place, not swanning around exploring. He'd managed to lose Artie and his goons by ducking into a block of flats and slipping out through a rear entrance, but if he wasn't careful he'd run into them again. Somehow he needed to get back to where his car was parked, opposite the block where Bill lived.

Breathing hard, Danny raced across the estate, hoping he'd recognise some familiar landmark, but all these fucking blocks of flats looked the same.

His pounding footsteps echoed off walls as he charged through the narrow alleyways. *Shit, shit, shit.* He had no clue where he was going. This fucking estate hadn't even existed when he got sent down; while he was in prison, the whole area had changed beyond recognition.

He paused to draw breath, but immediately started running again when he heard footsteps behind him.

He darted round the next corner, nearly slipping on a pool

of vomit. Heart thumping against his ribs, he charged towards a row of wheelie bins. Suddenly, he realised Bill's flat was just ahead of him.

'Danny, Danny! Where the fuck are you? You can't run, mate.' Artie's voice sliced through the air.

Danny couldn't tell where the sound was coming from, didn't know which way to run. He leapt over a low wall, deciding his only hope was to make a run for Bill's flat.

He sprinted through the main entrance and up the concrete stairs to the third floor, then along the communal corridor to Bill's door.

He pounded on the door until Janey opened it.

'What's all the fucking racket? You'll wake up the kids.'

He ignored her, knowing she didn't give a shit about the kids. He rushed into the front room to find Bill skinning up in the same chair he'd left him in, only twenty minutes before.

'Fucking hell, what's happened?'

Danny tried to get his breath. He grabbed his car keys off the table. 'Artie saw me.'

'Oh fuck.'

'I need to get out of here,' Danny panted. 'I'll go to Boxted Lane, lie low there for a while.'

'I'll come with you,' said Bill. 'Then we can put our heads together and sort out when to start bringing the women there. Sounds like it'd better be sooner rather than later.'

'Yeah, I agree. Come on, I don't fancy hanging around here much longer.'

'Hold up.' Janey looked at Bill. 'You can't go. What about the kids? Who's going to look after them?'

'For once, sweetheart, look after your fucking kids yourself, all right? Try to be a fucking mother,' Danny yelled in her face.

'Are you going to let him speak to me like this?' Janey whined to Bill.

Bill stared at her. All she'd been doing lately was complaining. 'You know what, babe? Yeah, I fucking am.' And with those words Bill and Danny charged out of the flat.

Janey was seething. First Steph and Danny had nicked her pills yesterday, leaving her with nothing, and now she was being spoken to like a piece of shit in her own flat. Well, she wasn't having it. It was about fucking time she put herself first for once.

Stomping into the kids' bedroom, Janey saw they were still fast asleep. Holly in her cot and Cory in his toddler bed, which was getting too small for him now. Not wanting to wake them and have to deal with their noise, she placed Cory's beaker by his side, crept out of their room and slipped out of the flat. She had someone she needed to see.

Ten minutes later, Janey caught sight of the man she was looking for. He was standing by his car, which was parked just up the road from the corner shop.

'Artie! Artie!' She ran over to him. 'Artie?'

Artie scowled.

'What the fuck do you want?'

'A bag.' Janey forced a grin. She'd lost another tooth recently, and her gums were sore and red.

'Have you lost your fucking mind? You want me to give you some gear? If you don't get out of my face within two seconds, you'll end up in A & E.'

Janey had heard Danny and Bill talking about how Artie was gonna lose his head over Fletch getting shot. Far as she was concerned, the biggest surprise was that it had taken this long for someone to kill the bastard. But it looked as though they'd been right about Artie losing it.

'I've got some info you might be interested in,' she said.

Artie narrowed his eyes. 'Go on.'

She held her hand out. 'For some brown.'

'You're bargaining with me?' His eyes darkened.

Janey didn't like the way he was looking at her. She stepped back, not wanting to be in range of a clump. 'No, Artie, it's just . . . you told me that if I found out some info, you'd sort me out.'

Artie opened and closed his fists. Still keeping an eye out for Danny, his gaze darted around the estate. 'Go on, what have you got to say?'

'It's about Danny.'

He looked at her then.

'I know where he is.'

'You what?' Artie did a double take. 'This better not be a wind-up.'

Janey shook her head. 'It isn't.' She was delighted with herself. She could see that Artie was interested, which meant he might give her some extra gear. 'So will you give me some then?'

'Yeah.' His stare was cold.

'Danny's gone to this new place that him and Bill have.' Janey didn't see any reason to keep Bill's name out of it. The way he'd let Danny treat her, and then left her to babysit, was bang out of order.

'What place?' This was the first Artie had heard about it.

'That's why Danny hasn't been around. He went off to earn some dough so he could sort a place for the girls to work out of.'

'And why haven't you fucking told me before?' Artie grabbed her arm, squeezing it hard.

Janey didn't like the way this was going. 'I didn't know . . . I didn't know until now, I swear.'

'Where is it?'

Janey hesitated.

'I said, WHERE IS IT?'

'Boxted Lane, Newington Cemetery end.' Janey hurried out her words. 'It's a big white house, set back from the road.'

Artie let her go. Fucking Danny. He walked away towards his car.

'Artie, wait! Artie.' Janey raced up to him. 'The gear.'

'Fuck off.' He elbowed her away.

'Artie, please, you promised.'

'How many times have we been through this?' He started to get into the car.

'Artie, you can't do this to me . . . *please.*' Janey scrambled up to him.

The coke and pills he'd taken had left Artie so wired he had no time for anything but catching up with Danny fucking Denton. Pausing only to headbutt Janey in the face, he got behind the wheel, gunned the engine and took off for Boxted Lane.

Janey was still sitting on the kerb, sobbing, when Steph showed up half an hour later. She'd stayed at the hospital while Liza was admitted, then driven back to tell Amy, the neighbour who was looking after the girls, that they'd be keeping Liza in overnight.

'Janey?' Steph crouched next to her, trying to ignore the smell of piss. 'Janey what's going on . . . Jesus Christ, who did this to your face?'

'Artie, fucking Artie.' Janey's nose was so swollen where Artie had headbutted her that it sounded as if she had a cold.

'You need to stay away from him right now – he's completely gone off on one.'

Janey wiped her nose with the back of her hand. 'He's a fucking liar.'

'And you're just finding that out now?' Steph's voice was warm, and she smiled.

'It's not fucking funny. You're as bad as he is.'

'Me? What have I done?'

Janey was furious. Life wasn't fair. She'd given Artie prime information, and all he'd given her was a bust nose. 'You took those pills from me.' She was winding herself up. 'And if you hadn't, I wouldn't have had to ask Artie for gear, and then I wouldn't have had to tell him about—'

Steph frowned. 'Tell him about what, Janey?'

She shook her head. 'Nothing.'

'Janey, what have you done? What have you fucking done?'

'Why do you always think I've done something?' Janey whined.

Steph grabbed her shoulders as if she was tempted to shake it out of her. But then she let her go and reached into her pocket, pulling out a couple of fivers. 'You can have these – but first you're going to tell me what you told Artie. And don't lie to me, babe, because I'll know if you do.'

Janey's eyes lit up. She snatched at the money, but Steph pulled the notes away from her, holding them up in the air. 'Not unless you tell me.'

Janey kept her stare on the money, thinking about the fix she could buy. 'It wasn't my fault.'

Steph shifted her position slightly. 'What wasn't?'

'What I did.'

'Janey, what did you do?' Steph was sounding worried now.

The temptation of being able to score was too much for Janey. 'I told Artie where Danny was going.'

'You did what?' Steph's voice was a whisper. The colour drained out of her face.

Like she always did, Janey pulled a face. 'I told you, it wasn't my fault.'

'Then *whose fault* was it?'

Janey whined. 'What was I supposed to do?'

Steph stepped away from her. 'Not that, babe. You weren't supposed to do that.'

'What about the money? *Steph!* Steph, you fucking bitch, what about my money?'

Steph didn't bother answering as she ran to her car.

Chapter Eighty

Bill was standing in the front room of Danny's place when an excruciating pain suddenly exploded in his leg. He fell forward, dropping to the floor.

'I've been shot! I've been fucking shot! *Dan!*' He clamped a hand to his torn thigh, trying to staunch the blood oozing from the bullet hole.

Danny, who'd been in the kitchen fixing sandwiches for them, came rushing through, but he leapt back immediately when he glanced out of the window and saw Artie and another bloke walking towards the house.

Fuck.

He rushed back into the kitchen and reached under the sink for the shotguns he kept there.

While Bill groaned in agony, Danny burst out of the kitchen and fired a couple of shots through the window. The goon went down, but Artie dived for cover. Danny seized the opportunity to grab Bill and drag him into the kitchen. He was bleeding, but not gushing blood like he would be if the bullet had hit an artery. While it must be fucking agony for Bill, Danny could see it wasn't going to be fatal. Thank fuck.

'Here, mate.' He gave Bill one of the guns, then left him in the kitchen while he ran into the hallway. From the corner of his eye, he saw Artie creeping towards the dining room. Danny pivoted on his heel and fired. The bullet missed and Danny jumped back through the doorway. Keeping low, he stuck his head out.

Where the fuck had Artie gone?

Thinking he'd heard something behind him, Danny spun round and fired off a shot. Too late, he realised he'd only succeeded in obliterating the hall mirror. Trying not to panic, he turned towards the door and ran up the stairs. His hand was slick with sweat, making it hard to grip the gun as he moved along the landing. *Fuck, where was he?*

'Looking for me by any chance?'

Danny's stomach dropped as he felt the nozzle of a gun at the back of his head.

'Drop it.' Artie pushed the gun harder into Danny's head. 'I said, fucking drop it.'

Danny let go of his gun and closed his eyes, preparing himself for the end.

'Get down on your knees.'

'If you're going to shoot me, mate, just do it, because I ain't getting on my knees for you.'

Artie let out a manic laugh. 'Then get ready to say your good—'

There was a loud bang and Artie suddenly fell forward.

Danny looked down and saw a gaping hole in the back of Artie's head. When he looked up again, he saw Bill. Somehow he'd managed to drag himself to the top of the stairs and fire off a shot.

He dropped the gun and slumped against the wall, holding his wounded leg.

Danny shook his head and closed his eyes again. Jesus, he'd

thought he was a goner. He opened his eyes and winked at Bill. 'Fucking hell, was I glad to see you . . . I owe you one, mate.'

'Too fucking right you do,' Bill hissed through gritted teeth.

'Danny! *Danny!* Bill? Dan?'

Danny heard Steph's voice. He glanced at Bill. 'I'll be back in a minute, mate, and we'll get your leg sorted.'

He didn't want Steph to see this. He rushed down the stairs, along the hallway and out of the front door, closing it behind him. Steph was standing in the driveway. From where she was, she couldn't see the dead goon lying in the shrubbery.

'Danny! Thank God you're all right.' She started to run towards him. 'When I heard Artie was coming after you, I thought—' She stopped.

Danny touched her face. He was glad to see her, and he had to admit to himself he felt properly shaken up. 'I'm okay . . . Bill's been shot though.'

'Oh Jesus, is he all right?' The colour drained from her face.

'He'll live. It's messy in there. You better go. I don't want you involved in this.'

'Are you sure?'

'Yeah, I'll clear up, make a couple of phone calls, then I'll take Bill to a mate of mine who'll be able to fix his leg. If I take him to hospital, the Old Bill will be crawling all over it.'

'And Artie?'

Danny paused. He wasn't sure how she'd take it. 'I'm sorry, babe.'

Steph shook her head. She shouldn't feel shocked – she'd known something like this was going to happen. 'No, no . . . it's fine.' It would take time for it to sink in, but she knew the sadness washing over her wasn't for the bastard that Artie had been these past few years. She was mourning the Artie she used to know: Rob's younger brother, a bit of a tearaway. 'I better go, Dan.' She felt overwhelmed. It was all too much.

'How did you know we were here?' Danny frowned.

'Janey. She told Artie where to find you both.'

He rubbed his head. 'Fuck! If Bill won't see fucking sense about Janey after this . . . What a bitch.' He shook his head and looked directly at Steph. 'Can I come and see you tomorrow?'

Steph hesitated. She didn't know if it was a good idea, but she found herself nodding. 'Okay, yeah.'

'I should go and check on Bill.'

'Yeah, yeah, you do that . . . take care, Danny.' She watched him walk away, then went back to her car. When she turned the key in the ignition, it spluttered, but the engine didn't start. Oh, great. She pulled out the choke and tried again. This time it started and revved loudly. Almost in a trance, Steph drove to the hospital to tell Liza the news.

Chapter Eighty-One

'I'll be really quick. It's about her kids,' Steph lied, knowing the nurse wouldn't let her in otherwise. 'Please.'

'Five minutes, that's all.' The nurse, who had a Northern accent and looked ready to retire, pointed to the far bed. 'She's over there.'

'Thank you.' Steph hurried over. The curtains were pulled round. 'Only me, babe. Is it all right if I pop my head in?'

'Yeah. What was that about the kids?' Liza must have heard what she'd said to the nurse. 'They let me phone Amy earlier and she said she'd look after them while I'm in here.'

Steph dropped her voice to a whisper. 'I was only using the girls as an excuse to get me in here. The real reason I came by was to let you know that it's over.'

Liza frowned. She wasn't sure what Steph was talking about. 'What?'

Steph lowered her voice. 'I'll tell you everything in the morning, but Danny's sorted it. You won't have to worry about Artie any more . . . He's gone.'

Liza burst into tears. She couldn't believe it. She'd been living a nightmare ever since Fletch had showed up at the house. She couldn't remember what it felt like to be safe. Then it hit her: 'So Jack is going to serve a life sentence for nothing?'

Steph shook her head. Her heart went out to her. 'He did what he thought he needed to do. And maybe, if he hadn't, Artie and Fletch would still be around.' She gave Liza a smile. 'Try not to be angry with him any more.' Then she grabbed a tissue and wiped Liza's tears for her, making a mental note to call Sharon in the morning. She'd been so terrified when she was finally released from hospital she'd gone down to stay with her mum in Broadstairs.

'I'm not angry,' said Liza. 'One of the girls down the lane said something that opened my eyes: "If he can't be there in the bad times, he doesn't deserve to be there in the good." I decided a while back that me and the girls would be better off without Jack. Does that make me sound like a cow?'

Steph tried to reassure Liza. 'No, not at all.'

'I'm not going to tell him though, not while he's serving his sentence. That can wait. I don't want to hurt him. I just don't want to be with him any more.'

Steph smiled. It seemed to her that was the best decision Liza could make. 'You and the girls will be just fine. You'll get on with your life and I'll be around and there's always the refuge to pop into if you need some support. You got through it, hun, and that's the main thing. I'm so proud of you.'

'Can you leave, please?' The nurse didn't mince her words.

She stared at Steph, who bent down and kissed Liza on the cheek. 'I'll come back tomorrow if you're still in here. If not, I'll swing by the flat.'

'That's great.'

'Wait, Steph!' Liza called after her as she moved away from the bed. 'Thank you, thank you for everything . . . If there's any good to come out of this whole bloody thing, it's meeting you.'

Steph grinned and gave her a wave.

*

By the time she got to the car park, the wind was starting to pick up. She hurried to the car, got in and put the key in the ignition.

'You're kidding me.' This day couldn't get any better. The bloody engine was completely dead. 'She threw her head back against the head rest, closing her eyes for a moment. Then she took several deep breaths – there was no point getting upset about it.

Steph sighed, and got out. With no buses in sight, her best option would be to walk to the primary school, then cut through to the main road where she could pick up a taxi and swing by Tammy's to pick up Stacey before heading home.

Once she got going, she found that being out in the fresh air was just what she'd needed. The walk was helping to clear her head.

She was almost at the school when she spotted a battered old car parked up under an oak tree. The dome light was on, and the man inside looked familiar.

'Pete?' She was sure that was him. She knocked on the window. 'Pete.'

Pete, who'd been busy looking at porn magazines, jumped and sat up straight. He scowled at her. 'Fucking hell, do you usually go round trying to give people a heart attack.' He leaned over and wound down the window.

'What are you doing in the car?'

'I haven't escaped from prison, if that's what you think. I'm on bail. I had to use my mate's address, but his missus won't let me stay there.' Pete looked as if he hadn't shaved in days and he stank.

'I can't say I blame her.'

'That's typical of you, isn't it. Here I am, having to kip in my mate's car, and all you can do is crack jokes?'

Steph sighed. She'd enjoyed these past six weeks or so without him. Every time Pete went away and came back, it felt like groundhog day. 'What do you want me to say, Pete? Did you really think I was going to bring out the welcome-home banner for you?'

'Seeing as it was your fault I was banged up in the first place, that would've been nice.'

He was still going on about that alibi she hadn't given him. Nothing changed. Steph doubted it ever would.

Steph looked inside. Apart from a footwell of porn mags and cans of cider, she could see Pete had a sleeping bag and pillow in the back. For once, he wasn't lying.

She shook her head. 'Fine.' It was against her better judgement, but it was cold, he was clearly at rock bottom, and she never liked to see anyone in that position, not even Pete.

'One night. You can stay at my house for one night. That's all, and then you're gone in the morning. I mean it – no longer than that. And you sleep on the couch, understand?'

A large grin spread across Pete's face. 'You're a diamond.'

'No, I'm an idiot.'

'Does the couch come with a nice cooked breakfast?' He rubbed his hands in delight.

'No, it bloody well doesn't.' She opened the passenger door. 'You might as well give me a lift.' She got in and curled her nose at the smell. 'Jesus, Pete, you need to have a shower.'

'I can have a bath when I'm at yours then.'

'That's not going to happen.' She tutted, already starting to regret her offer.

As Pete started the car, she glanced down at the cider cans and remembered the many times he'd been picked up for drink driving. He was probably over the limit now. Instead of picking

Stacey up on the way, she would have to wait till they got home, then call Tammy's mum and ask if it was all right for Stacey to stay the night.

'What's wrong with your boat race?' Driving through a set of red traffic lights, Pete glanced at her.

'I'm tired, Pete. It's been a long day. You have no idea.'

They spent the rest of the journey in silence, and it was another fifteen minutes or so before they arrived at her house. He parked up badly by the wheelie bins.

Steph looked at him. 'I mean it, Pete: one night.'

'Okay, fucking hell, anyone would think you didn't want me staying.'

She shook her head. At least him irritating her would be a distraction from her thoughts. 'You'll need these,' she said, reaching over into the back seat for his pillow and sleeping bag. 'I'm not having you sleeping—'

She froze and caught her breath. 'What is that?' She pointed at the large tin of red paint on the back seat.

Pete's face went white.

Chapter Eighty-Two

Steph was staring at him. 'Pete, I asked you a fucking question, why the hell have you got a can of red paint in your car?'

Ignoring her, he got out and stomped down her garden path towards the house, hunching his shoulders against the rain.

Steph ran after him. 'Don't walk away from me.' Shivering, she unlocked the back door, and stepped into the kitchen. 'Pete, I'm talking to you. Why have you got the paint?'

He shrugged. 'I was helping my mate with some decorating.'

'Coming from anyone else, I might believe them, but you've never done a bit of fucking work in your life . . . It was you, wasn't it? You poured the paint on my car this morning, didn't you?'

'No.'

Steph hissed at him. 'You're lying. Why, Pete? Why would you do that to me? Do you hate me that much?' She suddenly blinked and stared at him. A cold chill ran through her. 'The wreath, the grave . . . Oh my God, the Babygro.' She stared at the floor; she couldn't even bear to look at him. 'That was all you, wasn't it?' Her voice was a whisper as she struggled to get her breath. 'You did it . . . That's why nothing has happened these past six weeks while you were banged up. It was you.'

She looked him in the eye. 'Why? Why, Pete?'

'Do you fucking blame me?' Pete was on the defensive.

402

Steph was trembling. 'You destroyed my son's grave – what sort of sick bastard are you to do that? I thought it was Fred Walker, but it was you all along.' She could hardly get the words out through her tears, but they were tears of rage. 'Isn't it enough I lost my son?'

'But you had everything else, didn't you, when I had fuck all.' He sneered at her. 'You and your new life, thinking you're better than everyone else. You couldn't even give me a fucking alibi when I asked.'

She tilted her head to stare at him. 'Is that what this is about, a fucking alibi? You did all this to me because I wouldn't lie for you?'

'No, it's about *you* not thinking about how other people might feel. How *I* might feel about the way you've treated me.'

Steph wasn't listening. Her mind was working overtime. 'How did you know?'

'Know what?' Pete snapped.

'How did you know what Andy was wearing that day?' Steph looked at him then. 'The Babygro you splattered in red paint, how did you know it was almost identical?'

Pete shrugged again.

'*I said*, how did you know, Pete?' Steph's whole body was shaking.

'I guessed.'

She shook her heard furiously. 'No . . . no, no, you don't just guess that. You don't just guess that and get it right . . . How did you know, Pete?' She grabbed the knife from the draining board and pointed it at him. 'I said, how did you *fucking* know?'

Pete stared at Steph. 'You're crazy, you know that? Fucking mad bitch.'

She jabbed the knife in the air. 'Don't push me, Pete . . . Tell me how you knew what Andy was wearing that day.'

His stare moved from Steph to the knife. 'I already told you – I . . . I guessed.'

It was like someone had punched her in the stomach.

It all made sense now. Steph could hardly speak. 'Oh my God, oh my God, it was you . . . it was you. IT WAS YOU!' She screamed at him and dropped the knife as she wrapped her arms round her stomach, trying to stop the pain inside her. She let out a deep cry, like a howl. 'You killed my son . . . You killed him.' Steph held on to the sink, but her legs wouldn't hold her up and she collapsed to the floor. 'My baby, my beautiful, beautiful baby, you killed him . . . Oh God, oh God.' She rocked back and forth on her knees, clutching her waist tighter.

'It wasn't like that . . . It was an accident.'

Steph wiped the tears and snot from her face. She looked up at him, and once again she felt her anger take over. 'What?'

'I'd wound myself up, hadn't I? You know, when I saw you with Rob. You'd upped and left me, and the next thing I find out you're shacked up with someone else and he's playing fucking daddy to Stace . . .'

Steph had to cover her mouth to stop herself being sick.

'. . . I followed you that day.' He shrugged. He'd actually been following her and Rob a lot. It had pissed him off and he'd been jealous, but the way Steph was acting now, Pete decided it wasn't the best time to tell her that. 'I saw you come home from the pub. And then I was just leaving when he came out again with the pram. I'd had a few beers—'

'You were drunk?' Steph's words were almost inaudible.

'I dunno.' Pete did know – he'd been absolutely hammered. 'I only wanted to talk to Rob. You know, ask him what the fuck he was playing at, but when I drove up it was icy, and I lost control of the car.' He trailed off. Pete decided it sounded worse than it actually was. He really hadn't meant to plough into them, but the weather had been shit. 'It was an accident.'

Steph was trying to make sense of it all. 'But Andy was in his pram. How did you know what he was wearing?'

He shrugged again. 'I got out, didn't I?'

'And you never thought to call a fucking ambulance?' Steph blinked. 'You . . . you just left them to die? YOU LEFT THEM THERE!' Her scream filled the room, anger rushed through her.

'I didn't know they were still alive. Andy's head was all mashed up, and Rob—'

'Stop it . . . stop it!' She didn't want to hear it. 'You're going to pay for this.'

Pete was irritated that Steph was acting like the accident had happened yesterday. She should've got over it by now. 'What are you doing?' He watched her hurry through to the front room.

'I'm calling the Old Bill.'

Pete panicked. He picked up the knife from the floor and chased after her. 'No you ain't.'

'I told you, you need to fucking pay for what you did.' Normally she'd never dream of calling the police, but this was different.

As she picked up the phone, Pete lunged for it, knocking it out of her hand. 'There's no way I'm serving life for your bastard kid!' he yelled.

Steph tried to grab the phone from the floor, but he charged at her again, and this time he caught her face with the tip of the knife he was still holding.

Pete saw her looking at the door. Guessing she was going to make a run for it, he grabbed her arm, tussling with her. He pushed her then, whacked her across the face, but she pushed him back harder, causing him to drop the knife.

He rushed to pick it up, then turned back to face her. But as he moved forward, he tripped and fell.

The knife plunged into Pete's chest.

He let out a rasping sound and stared down at the knife sticking out of him, then he looked up at Steph, his eyes rolled backwards, and he collapsed to the floor.

'Oh my God.' Steph dropped to her knees. 'Pete.' She touched him, getting her hands covered in blood.

Horrified, she stood up, looking at the blood running between her fingers. She leaned against the wall, smearing her handprints all over it, then she staggered out of the room.

Chapter Eighty-Three

There had been a moment when she'd thought about calling the Old Bill. Telling them what had happened, that it had been an accident, that Pete had fallen on the knife. But she couldn't imagine Fred and his mates believing that. After the grief she'd caused them, they'd do everything in their power to see to it that she went down for a long time.

And there was no way she was going to serve one day in prison for Pete, not after what he'd done. No fucking way.

She took a deep breath to calm herself, wrapped her hands round the handle of the knife and, squeezing her eyes shut, began to pull. As she did, a noise came from behind her.

Startled, Steph let go of the knife and spun round, her heart dropping as the front room door began to open.

She waited for whoever it was to walk in, but no one did.

Her heart pounding, Steph ran to the kitchen. The back door was still open and, in the distance, she saw someone running by the garages. Steph rushed out herself. She needed to know who it was and who'd seen her . . . *what* they'd seen.

'Wait, hold up!' Steph ran across the road towards the bus stop. '*Wait!*' She still couldn't work out who it was. 'Wait, please!'

Then he turned round to face her.

'Zack.'

Joseph's son was the last person she would have expected to see. He looked terrified.

'Zack, what's the matter?' She hoped to God he hadn't seen Pete lying on the floor, but the way he was acting, he must have done.

The boy began to back away.

'Sweetheart, what's going on? Please tell me.' Steph was worried, but more for him than herself.

She reached out her hand. 'Whatever is going on, you can tell me.'

He stared at her for a moment. Then he muttered something that Steph couldn't hear.

'Zack, you need to speak louder.'

'Stacey.'

'Stacey? What about her?' Steph's head was all over the place, why was he talking about Stacey?

He stared back at Steph from underneath his fringe.

'Zack, what are you saying? What's going on? I don't understand. You're shaking, please tell me what's happened.'

'Stacey . . . my . . . my . . .'

She could see he was trying, but just couldn't get the words out.

'Your what, honey?' She tried to hold his hand, but he shied away from her. 'It's okay – you can tell me anything.'

'. . . my dad . . . she's with my dad. I was going to stop him but then . . . then I saw Stacey.'

Steph shook her head, stunned. 'Stace? No, babe, she's at her mate's house.' In all the commotion, Steph had forgotten to call Tammy's mum to ask if it was all right for her to stay the night.

'Why would she be with your dad?' A shiver crept down Steph's spine.

Zack shook his head and, seeing a bus coming, he ran to catch it, banging on the doors for the driver to let him on.

'Zack, wait! Zack!' Steph wasn't fast enough to stop the bus, so instead she raced back across the road to the house.

She dialled Tammy's number. Her mum picked up – she didn't know what Steph was talking about. Tammy had spent the evening watching telly with the rest of the family. Stacey hadn't called or dropped by.

Steph hung up and dialled again.

'Dan, Dan, it's me, Steph.' She was on the verge of hysteria. 'I need you to listen to me. I think Stace is in trouble.'

'What's happened?'

She didn't have time to go into details. 'It's Jo – Zack says Jo has her. I don't know what's going on, I don't understand why he would . . . but I have to go over there.'

'Steph, wait, we'll go over together, yeah?'

'I can't wait. And anyway, I need you to do something for me first. I need you to come to the house right away – you'll under-stand when you get here. I'll leave the back door unlocked. I have to go now.'

'Steph, don't do anything stupid. Wait for me, please. You can't go over there. He's—'

Steph didn't listen to the rest. She put down the phone and ran to Pete's car.

The drive over to the Joseph's house seemed to take an eter-nity. She parked in the road and hurried up the drive, still trying to work out what was going on.

As she passed Joseph's van, Steph did a double take.

'Stace?'

Her daughter was asleep in the passenger seat. What the fuck!

'Stace?'

Panicked, Steph banged on the driver's window, but her daughter didn't stir. Oh my God. She raced round to the passenger side and opened the door.

Stacey slumped towards her.

'Stace, Stacey, can you hear me?' She could see her daughter breathing, but she wasn't conscious. It was then Steph noticed the buttons down the front of Stacey's skirt were wide open.

Steph covered her mouth.

Oh Jesus Christ, no. 'Stacey what's he done to you?'

Feeling sick, and praying it wasn't what she thought it was, Steph leaned into the van and scooped her arms under Stacey to lift her.

Stacey was heavier than she looked, but somehow she managed to stagger over to Pete's car without dropping her. Then she opened the door and heaved her daughter on to the back seat. Shrugging out of her coat, she laid it over Stacey, then she locked her in the car and rushed over to the house.

She hammered on the door. A voice in her head was screaming at her to get back in the car and drive Stacey to A & E, but she couldn't stop worrying about Zack. She needed to see that he and Bel were all right. Plus she wanted to know what the hell Jo had done to Stacey. Her stomach twisted at the thought, and she banged on the door again.

'Joseph? Joseph?'

There was no answer. She kicked it this time. 'Joseph, open the fucking door. It's Steph.' Not getting any answer, she tried the door handle.

It was unlocked.

She glanced behind her, wondering if Danny would show up here, or do as she'd asked and go to her place.

It was then she smelled something burning.

Steph threw open the front door and smoke came billowing down the hallway at her. She wasn't sure where it was coming from, but she needed to be quick.

'Zack? Zack? Bel? Where are you?'

Covering her mouth, Steph hurried down the hallway, calling their names and looking into each room. There was no one in sight. She paused at the end of the hall and listened.

She heard someone groan. It was a faint sound, but there was no mistaking it. She listened, trying to work out where it had come from.

There was one room she hadn't checked because it had a padlock on it. She'd noticed that all the doors had bolts with padlocks hanging from them, but none of them had been secured. She looked up at the top of the doorframe, and sure enough there was a key sitting there. She unfastened the padlock and opened the door.

The basement light was on but she couldn't see whether anyone was down there.

When she got to the bottom of the stairs, her mouth dropped open.

'Nancy! Nancy!'

Steph ran over to her. She was tied up, her whole body bloody and bruised. It was like the house of horrors. Petrified, Steph ran to her. 'Nance, it's me, love – Steph. It's all right, hun. I'm here now.'

Steph's head was swimming. What the fuck! She had to get Nancy out, but her ankle was obviously broken and she was barely conscious.

Trying not to panic, Steph looked towards the stairwell. Smoke was billowing into the basement from the fire upstairs. As she watched, a figure emerged from the smoke.

It was Joseph.

She backed towards Nancy.

'Jo.' Her heart pounded.

The expression on his face was blank, and his eyes were dark and cold. He was carrying a hammer.

'Jo, listen to me . . . the Old Bill are on their way.'

'You've always been a stupid whore, haven't you. A filthy, stupid tart.' He smirked at her. 'Don't you see, Steph, as long as the police aren't here yet, that means I've got time.' He took another step towards her.

'Jo, you don't want to do this . . . They'll lock you up. They'll throw away the key.'

'I don't mind.' He pointed to his head. 'I've got all the memories in here. They can lock me up, but I'll always remember what it was like . . .' He brought his voice down to a whisper. 'What it tasted like, what it sounded like when I heard you scream.' She saw the bulge in his trousers grow. 'They won't be able to take that away from me.'

'Jo.'

'*Jo.*' He mimicked her voice. 'You sound like Hennie, but then she was a slut like you. That's what she said: "*Jo*," that's what she screamed, that's what they all screamed in the end – all of them had my name on their lips when they died.' He groaned at the memory of the look of fear on their faces. 'That's what I'll remember you by, Steph: you calling my name as you die.'

He stepped towards her again and began to raise his hand.

'You stupid slut, all this time and you never knew. I was right there, Steph. I was right under your nose the whole time, laughing at you, but you were too busy stinking of filth to realise it was me.'

'Jo, no . . . no.' She cowered from the hammer, but he reached out with his other hand and grabbed her round the throat.

Steph tried to scratch at his hands, but his grip was so tight she couldn't prise them off. She could feel her windpipe closing as he squeezed harder and harder, and her chest felt like it was going to explode.

She heard herself gasping for air, and the room began to spin. Her legs were giving way and her body felt heavy.

But when she looked up at the hammer, Steph suddenly saw Zack standing behind his father. And as she watched, he swung back his arm and smashed Jo over the head with an old iron kettle.

Jo immediately released his grip on her and collapsed to the floor.

Zack stared at Steph. 'You came. You believed me.'

Steph choked and spluttered, struggling to breathe.

'I didn't think you'd come.' He stood frozen in place, trembling.

'You were brave.' It was painful to speak, and the smoke filling the basement wasn't helping. 'We need to get out of here, Zack. Where's Bel?'

'She's outside. I told her to wait by the trees.'

'Good. We need to get Nancy out, but I'll need you to help me – can you do that?'

He nodded.

'It's okay, Zack, you don't have to be scared any more . . . It's over now. It's all over.'

They stepped round Joseph, carrying Nancy between them, and made their way up the stairs.

*

As the fire took hold of the house, Joseph began to stir. Blood pouring from his head, he staggered towards the stairs, but the flames drove him back. He could feel his chest getting tight and he covered his mouth as the black smoke filled the basement. His mind raced in panic. He was trapped.

The heat intensified as the fire roared towards him. He could smell the stench of his burning hair. His clothes melted on to his body, his skin blistered and began to peel off.

A scream tore from his throat as he fell to floor. While the flames danced round him, he clawed at the ground, trying to crawl away. A white-hot agony engulfed him, torture beyond anything he could imagine.

Joseph Potter's reign of terror had finally come to an end.

Epilogue

Ten Weeks Later

Chapter Eighty-Four

The contractions had been coming hard and fast every few minutes for the past hour. Nancy leaned forward and gritted her teeth, bending her head down as she lay in the labour room. She gulped as shooting pains clenched her stomach and wrapped round her back.

'That's it, love, keep blowing those candles out.' Steph held her hand, encouraging her at the same time as discreetly glancing at the clock on the wall.

Covered in sweat, Nancy looked at Steph. 'What the fuck are you on about?' she panted.

'You're breathing: pretend you're blowing out a whole load of candles.'

'Oh piss off.' Nancy grimaced and laughed at the same time, which made Steph roar with laughter.

'You're doing great, darlin'. I'm proud of you. It won't be long now.'

Nancy grabbed her hand. 'Fancy swapping places?' Another contraction ripped through her. 'Fuck . . . *oh God*.' Her face twisted in pain as her pregnant stomach contracted, pulling the skin on her belly tight with the purple, silvery streaks looking like huge scratches across her stomach.

Nancy's foot was still in a cast from where Joseph had shattered her bones, but she'd been told the baby would be healthy despite the torture she'd endured during her pregnancy.

The midwife, a small blonde Irishwoman, smiled at Nancy. 'You're doing grand. One more push and it should all be over . . . that's it, my love.'

'*Jesus* . . . OH GOD . . .' Nancy threw her head back, and gave one final push.

Steph beamed. 'You've done it . . . You've done it, darlin'!'

She couldn't be prouder of Nancy, what she'd been through was unimaginable and she was still clearly traumatised. She'd been placed in a convalescent hospital, and she would go back there after giving birth, to continue receiving treatment until she was fully recovered.

The baby would be going home with Steph as soon as the doctors gave the all-clear. It would be a squeeze. Zack and Bel had been living at Steph's ever since the fire. Social services had agreed to let the kids stay for the time being, and Steph was determined to put up a fight to make the arrangement permanent. Stacey now shared her room with Bel, while Zack had the spare room to himself.

'Is it a boy or a girl?' Nancy stared at the midwife as she wrapped the baby in cotton blankets.

'It's a girl . . . Congratulations!'

The midwife handed her to Nancy before busying herself with changing the sheets.

Steph watched Nancy cradle her baby in her arms. 'You're a natural.'

Nancy grinned. She was suddenly overwhelmed with love for her daughter. She was so tiny with soft curls of auburn hair and green eyes. She'd already gone through so much, but it was clear her daughter was a fighter. 'I'm going to call her Katie.'

'That's beautiful.' Steph walked to the door then and opened it, popping her head out. 'Do you two want to come in now?'

She smiled at Zack and Bel, who'd been waiting outside in the corridor. Zack was starting to come out of his shell, and Stacey had taken Bel under her wing. They both had a long way to go, but there was no rush. It would take time, but Steph was confident they would get there.

Zack and Bel nodded and shuffled in.

'Come and meet your sister . . . You can hold her, if you like.'

Steph watched their faces light up. 'Listen, I'll leave you to it . . . Have you still got your taxi money to get home?'

Zack nodded. 'Yes, thanks.'

'Okay, I'll see you later . . . I'll come by tomorrow, Nance – there's somewhere I need to be right now.'

Steph walked out of the room, her stomach twisted in knots for what she was about to do.

Chapter Eighty-Five

Steph stood by Rob's bed. She'd asked Rob's nurses to let her know if there was a sudden change in his condition, and the call had come just as Nancy was giving birth. Steph couldn't abandon her until the baby was safely delivered, but she'd come as soon as possible.

Rob's face was pale, and he'd lost so much weight he was just skin and bones. His chest rose and fell as the ventilator breathed for him. He'd been in a bad way for some time. Steph had hoped he'd turn the corner, but he hadn't.

When Artie had died, she'd panicked about finding the money to pay Rob's hospital fees. Danny had offered to do what he could, but it turned out Artie had left money for his brother's care, as well as leaving Rob his house. So money wasn't a problem, but even with the best medical support, Rob hadn't been responding to treatment.

Steph glanced at the male nurse who was quietly sitting in the corner. She kept her voice to a whisper: 'How long have I got?'

'Not long. We've done everything we can, but as you know his organs are failing rapidly. We were about to call you to come straight over, so it's really good that you're here . . . I think he was hanging on for you.'

Steph turned back to the bed where Rob was hooked up to a

monitor and multiple machines. His eyes were closed, which made him look like he was asleep rather than in a coma. She smiled at him, then gently opened his hand and placed her engagement ring in it, wrapping his fingers round it.

She bent forward and kissed him gently on the lips. Then she stroked his face. This was the moment she'd been dreading. 'I'm here now. I'm here. Thank you for waiting for me.'

She switched on the cassette player and smiled as the song they were going to play at their wedding came on. Memories of their time together flooded her thoughts.

She touched his face again. 'Rob, I love you so much. I always have – you hear me? If you need to go, you can go now. I'll be okay, I promise.'

She clung on to his hand and within minutes the monitor started beeping. The nurse stood up and walked over to it and silenced the alarm.

He turned to Steph. 'I'm so sorry. He's gone.'

Steph nodded. She kissed Rob one last time. 'Goodbye, darlin' . . . Look after Andy, won't you? Give him a cuddle from me.'

And, with those words, Steph got up and walked out.

Chapter Eighty-Six

It was a couple of hours later when Steph arrived at the riverside. She smiled as she saw the women waiting for her.

'Are you all right? I didn't think you'd make it, hun.' Claudette smiled at her. Danny had told them the news about Rob; their hearts had gone out to her, knowing how much she'd loved him. 'It's great about Nancy having the baby, ain't it?'

Steph nodded. 'Yeah, she did brilliantly.'

'We're all planning to go and see her later. Can you imagine!' Mary laughed, but then she fell serious. 'I'm so pleased you're here, Steph.'

'Thank you . . . I wanted to come. I didn't want to miss it.'

Steph waved to Carol, who was standing by the river's edge.

'Hi, Mum, are you all right?' Stacey walked up to Steph, and gave her a hug.

'Yeah, I will be.' She squeezed her daughter hard. Stacey had been so strong. The doctors had checked her over, but couldn't find any injuries, so Steph liked to pretend nothing had happened during the time she lay drugged in his van. Joseph had robbed too many lives, and she wasn't going to let him ruin Stacey's or hers.

Taking a deep breath, she glanced around again. All the women from the shelter were here, everyone apart from Janey, who'd been kicked out by Bill. He was chatting to Danny over by the sandwiches the women had made.

Danny had been her rock. Since Pete's death, he'd looked after her without trying to put her under any pressure. She hadn't been able to face asking him what he'd done with Pete's body. She didn't want to know: some things were best left unsaid. She was determined to look forward rather than back. There was a lot of healing to be done by everyone, but Steph had no doubt they'd get there.

'Steph! Now you're here, darlin', do you want to do the honours?' Rachel called across to her.

'Okay, if you're sure?'

She walked to the edge of the River Medway and the women crowded around her. She smiled at them all. 'For Hennie, for Jean, for Bridget, for Cheryl, for all the forgotten women who lost their lives through violence.'

Then everyone threw the yellow flowers that they'd brought with them into the river, watching them float away.

Steph didn't know what tomorrow would bring, but tomorrow was another day.